"You take _____
She glared at him defiantly, her
lips still puffy from his kiss.

"No matter what you've decided about me, I am
a square deal player, Serena," Nathan replied
impassively. "I play by the rules. When I win a
lady's favors, I win them fair and square."

"So this was just a game to you," she accused.

"Isn't that what it was to you?" he drawled,
narrowing the distance between them in one step.
"You didn't have to come out into the moonlight
with me. You didn't have to look so . . . inviting. But
you did. You can't blame me for claiming the prize."

"You disreputable son of Beelzebub, I ought to
ventilate your mangy hide with my grandfather's
shotgun."

"That will hardly be necessary," he assured her, his
face stony. "I won't kiss you again. Save your
shotgun for the next poor fool who tries!"

Dear Reader,

April brings us another great batch of titles!

Readers of contemporary romance will surely recognize Judith McWilliams. In her first historical, *Suspicion*, she pens a tale of intrigue and danger in which young Lucy Langford must team up with Colonel Robert Standen in order to find a would-be killer.

Popular historical author Elizabeth Lane brings us *MacKenna's Promise*. Meg MacKenna travels to East Africa to get a divorce from her estranged husband, Cameron. But when tragedy strikes, they must band together to save their family and their love.

When ruthless businessman Oliver Keane inherits part of a Barbados plantation, he learns how to love from Alexa Fairfield—a woman he's been raised to despise. *Island Star* is by Kit Gardner, one of the 1992 March Madness authors.

In *The River Sprite* by Kate Kingsley, Serena Caswell is determined to take over as pilot of her father's steamboat. But handsome riverboat gambler—and half owner of the boat—Nathan Trent has other plans.

We hope you enjoy these titles. Next month look for four brand-new releases from your favorite Harlequin Historical authors!

Sincerely,

Tracy Farrell
Senior Editor

Please address questions and book requests to:
Reader Service
U.S.: P.O. Box 1325, Buffalo, NY 14269
Canadian: P.O. Box 1050, Niagara Falls, Ont. L2E 7G7

KATE KINGSLEY

THE RIVER SPRITE

Harlequin Books

TORONTO • NEW YORK • LONDON
AMSTERDAM • PARIS • SYDNEY • HAMBURG
STOCKHOLM • ATHENS • TOKYO • MILAN
MADRID • WARSAW • BUDAPEST • AUCKLAND

ISBN 0-373-28818-2

THE RIVER SPRITE

Copyright © 1994 by Karen Delk.

Books by Kate Kingsley

Harlequin Historicals

Ransom of the Heart #72
Season of Storms #100
The River Sprite #218

KATE KINGSLEY

loves to write historical romance. Brought up in South Louisiana, she certainly has the background to bring history to life. Kate, who now lives in Northern California, is vice president and partner of a broadcasting-consulting firm. She also volunteers at a local hospital and enjoys reading, taking long walks and traveling—when she can find the time. The mother of a recent college graduate, she plans to write more novels while enjoying life with her husband, an actor and announcer whose voice is inescapable on both cable and network television.

To my sister, Gayla,
a River Sprite from way back

Chapter One

"Sometimes I do not know what to make of you, Nathan."
Antoine La Branche frowned at the young man who sat across
from him. Iced drinks in their hands, they lounged in the
courtyard of Antoine's house, relishing a breeze from the river.
"How can you speak of going to California when you only just
returned to New Orleans from who knows where—"

"Texas." Stretching his long legs in front of him, Nathan
Trent observed his uncle lazily in the dusk. "Before that, I was
in the Indian Territories."

"You have a restless spirit like your father." The Creole
shook his head. "When your mother, my only sister, chose to
marry a Kaintock—an outlander—so many years ago, I
thought I would die of shame, but I have come to admire your
father. Micah is a good man, though *les Américains* seem always to yearn for what they do not have. A store...a warehouse...then a cotton plantation to fill both the store and the
warehouse." Antoine regarded his nephew shrewdly. "Do you
know what you want, Nate?"

"For now—" Nathan grinned and sipped his lemonade
"—a visit and perhaps some supper. Later I'd like to return to
my card game. It was just getting warmed up and I was winning."

"Warmed up, indeed, you roué," Antoine sniffed. "I know
you have been at Madame de Tournay's ... er ... establish-
ment for nearly a week."

Nathan's deep laugh boomed up past the wrought iron gallery to the red-streaked sky. "I'll bet you are the most straitlaced Creole the Crescent City has ever produced, Uncle. Why, I'd even be willing to bet you've never seen the inside of a bordello."

"How would it look, a banker in a house of assignations?" Antoine demanded indignantly. "My depositors would never understand. Besides, I am a gentleman."

"Even gentlemen play cards," the other man drawled, fanning away a venturesome insect, "which is what I was doing at Madame de Tournay's. How did you know I was there?"

"I...er...hear things," the Creole muttered uncomfortably.

"You hear a lot...for a gentleman," Nathan teased, rising to pace beneath the huge magnolia tree that sheltered the courtyard. "Why did you want to see me, 'Toine? Surely not to lecture me about gambling? I can hear that from my father if I choose to go up to Baton Rouge."

"Have you been there yet?" Though he had business to discuss, Antoine could not resist the question. "Have you seen your family since your return from the West?"

"No."

"Four years is a long time to stay away, Nathan," Antoine said gently, "and all because of a woman. She was not worth it."

"I know that." The gambler's expression was bland as he set his drink on the table. "If there's nothing else, Uncle..."

For a moment, the only sounds in the courtyard were the tinkling of the fountain and the rustle of wind among the leaves of the banana trees. From inside came the muted clatter of china and crystal as the table was set for evening meal.

Antoine studied his nephew closely in the dwindling light. Nathan had changed. As a boy, he had been amiable and easygoing, but now he wore his affability as an armor and allowed nothing to touch his emotions.

"Sit down, *s'il vous plaît*," he requested at last. "I have a business proposition for you."

"Another investment?" Nathan asked as he complied.

"Perhaps." His uncle would not be rushed. "Nathan, you've been at loose ends since . . . since the war in Mexico, I think. That's a long time. Aren't you interested in doing something besides scouting for the army or becoming a professional gambler?"

"I am thinking of going to California."

"Ah, yes, California." Antoine sighed. "Well, before you run off to another faraway place, hear me. A steamboat captain is coming to see me this evening about a loan in addition to the one he already has from my bank. I cannot give it to him, though I like him very much. He needs money, *oui*, but just as much he needs a good manager to make his business pay."

"Are you asking me to lend him the money," the young man asked idly, "or to become his manager?"

"I'm asking you to invest in his steamboat, to become his partner."

"And you call *me* a gambler!" Nathan barked with laughter. "You want me to go into business with a man you consider a poor risk? I thought you liked having my money in your bank."

"I do, but I also like to see money put to good use. You have a great deal of it which is doing nothing."

"Given my current profession, I thought that just as well."

"Just listen," Antoine urged. "This man, Capitaine Caswell, is an experienced river man and quite a favorite with his passengers. And you've always had a head for business. A partnership between you could work."

"Non, merci," Nathan replied firmly, but his uncle was not listening.

"The biggest difficulty, as I see it," Antoine mused, "is that Henry Caswell is quite proud. He probably would not like the fact that I have discussed him with you."

"Then he needn't know. I see a lot more gamblers than steamboat captains these days."

"Won't you even consider the possibility?" the banker beseeched. "All we have to do is to convince Henry Caswell he needs a partner."

"Uncle," Nathan explained with exaggerated patience, "I plan to head west very soon. I'd be a damn fool to take on an unwilling partner and half of a steamboat now."

"He's coming to supper. You will stay and meet him?"

"I'll stay, but I won't change my mind."

"He's bringing his daughter," Antoine threw in. "I met her once on the boat. She is rather pretty, as I recall, and I'm sure she'll be a charming dinner partner. You have always had a weakness for the ladies, *hein?* And they, for you."

"I told you I would stay," Nathan said with a fond, exasperated smile.

"Très bon." Antoine beamed. "I know you will like *le capitaine.* And who knows? You must go to St. Louis, anyway. Perhaps you will decide to take a trip on the *River Sprite.* You can look things over. Perhaps you will work out a deal."

"I don't want to work out a deal." Nathan's smile rearranged itself into a warning frown.

"You are probably right," the banker conceded with a dramatic sigh. "Such an arrangement would be risky. I was going to wager you could make the boat profitable within one year, but now I see..."

"Do you think you can trick me so easily, Uncle?" Nathan chuckled. "Besides, I thought you disapproved of gambling."

"Even bankers take a chance now and again," Antoine defended himself.

"This is one chance I'm not taking."

"As you say, nephew." The Creole shrugged indifferently and fought back a smile.

"Jehoshaphat, Papa! Don't you think I know how I look?" Serena Caswell exploded in a loud whisper. Standing beside her father on the banquette, the broad wooden sidewalk outside Antoine La Branche's town house, she adjusted the bulky shawl she wore over her gray dress and added testily, "How many times do I have to explain? The plainer I look when doing business, the more comfortable it seems to make the men."

"And how many times do I have to explain?" Frowning irritably, Henry Caswell rang the bell on the ornate iron gate.

"Creoles are never comfortable discussing business with a woman. Even when she's done up—"

"Like your maiden aunt, Hermione," Serena finished flatly for him. "I know. You've told me a hundred times."

"Furthermore," he went on, ignoring the interruption, "Antoine La Branche did not invite you here to talk business."

"And what did he invite me for?"

"For dinner," Henry snapped. "If you'll hold your temper and your tongue and conduct yourself like a lady this evening, Rena, we'll be fine. Though we'd probably have a better chance to get this loan if you'd gussied yourself up a little," he added glumly.

With an unladylike snort, the girl glared at her father through the dusk. "You may find this hard to believe of your own kin, Cap'n, but if you're depending on my beauty to bring in some money, we're liable to starve."

"Serena Elizabeth—"

"Don't worry, Papa," she soothed him hastily. "I'll keep quiet."

"I'll hold you to that," Henry whispered as the butler approached to lead them into the leafy, magnolia-scented courtyard.

"Yes, sir." Mutinously she added under her breath, "Unless I have something to say."

The La Branche house was elegant, built in the West Indian style so well suited to Louisiana. Common rooms, built along an ell on the lower floor, opened onto the courtyard. Faint light, from a window above, where the bedrooms were ranged along a gallery, gilded the glossy leaves of the sheltering magnolia tree. Under the tree, two men waited near the door to the dining room.

"*Capitaine,* welcome to my home." Their host stepped forward to greet them.

"Good evening, Antoine. Sorry to be late. We had a slight problem. The boilers, you know...."

"No need for apologies, *mon ami*. Mademoiselle Caswell..." Antoine faltered when he turned to Serena and finished lamely, "How nice to see you again."

"Thank you, Monsieur La Branche." Unruffled by his surprise at her changed appearance, she allowed the butler to take her wrap and bonnet. Smoothing her tightly bound hair over her ears, she added, "It's good to see you, as well."

"May I present my other guest?" Gesturing toward Nathan, Antoine tried to ignore the ominous gleam in the other man's eyes.

From where she stood, Serena could not see the newcomer's face, but his lean, broad-shouldered figure, silhouetted by the light from within the house, nearly took her breath away. As lithe and graceful as a big cat, he walked toward them.

"*Capitaine*, Mademoiselle Caswell, this is Nathan Trent, my nephew," Antoine performed the introductions graciously. "Nathan, these are the Caswells of the *River Sprite*."

"Good evening, Miss Caswell. It's a pleasure to meet you." With practiced ease, Nathan bowed and brushed a polite kiss onto the back of Serena's hand.

She reclaimed it with unseemly haste, tucking it among the gathers of her skirt. Her skin felt as though it were afire. Feeling Nathan's curious gaze upon her, Serena ducked her head and cursed for the thousandth time her tendency to blush. When Antoine pulled out a chair for her, she sat down, busying herself with arranging her hooped skirt, glad she did not have to meet his nephew's dark eyes.

"Sherry, *mam'selle?*" The butler appeared at her side.

"Thank you." As she took the delicate glass he offered, she glanced at her hand, almost expecting to see the mark of Nathan Trent's lips on it. She sipped the sherry, watching through her lashes as the young man engaged in animated conversation with Henry.

Clad in silks and brocades, the man was unmistakably a gambler. She had seen his kind up and down the Mississippi, but suddenly, illogically, she wished she were not "all done up like Aunt Hermione."

Nathan's olive skin, inherited from his Creole forebears, was bronzed from the sun and his curly brown hair was streaked with gold. His face was handsome enough, Serena decided in grudging admiration, but it was a study in contrasts. His mouth quirked up at one corner above a dimple in his chin, but his eyes were hooded, guarded somehow. Their wary expression did not match the laugh lines at the corners of his eyes.

But he was not at all amused when he escorted Serena to dinner. Behind a carefully neutral facade, Nathan fumed. Antoine had lied to get him to stay for dinner. The girl was rather pretty, he had said. Damnation! She was a skinny little mouse in a dowdy dress. Her nose was freckled and her auburn hair, probably her most promising feature, was pulled back in a tight, unattractive knot. Serena Caswell was about as far from pretty as New Orleans was from Paris, France.

And as for being a charming dinner partner, he had his doubts. She had accepted the arm he offered, but she flushed crimson and would not meet his eyes again as they went into the house.

By the time they reached the dining room, Nathan remembered himself. He had been brought up to be a gentleman and a gentleman he would be. He resolved to do his best to put Miss Serena Caswell at ease and through the first few courses, he tried diligently.

In the face of his indisputable charm, Serena began to wish he would turn his attention elsewhere. Her drab masquerade had always worked for her before. Male business associates had treated her considerately, as if they were sorry for her plain appearance. They had explained minute points of business kindly and thoroughly, seemingly relieved to offer any attention to the captain's daughter that could not be misconstrued as interest.

Nathan Trent did not behave in the accustomed manner. He was courteous, even solicitous. But as he smiled at her over the centerpiece, Serena realized with a flash of irritation that his gallantry was no more than habit. He apparently expected the captain's homely daughter to be charmed and grateful for his kindness; she suddenly wished she were anywhere but at Antoine La Branche's table.

"I understand you are from Vicksburg, Captain Caswell," Nathan was saying when she returned her attention to the conversation.

"Yes." Henry nodded. "Grace, my wife, is at our home, River's Rest, with our younger children, Pandora and Henry, Jr."

"How old are your other children?" he inquired politely.

"Dory is sixteen and Hank will be ten in a few days. We'll be home just in time for his birthday."

"I suppose you'll be glad to be home, Miss Caswell," Nathan addressed Serena.

"I'm always glad to stop in Vicksburg, but the *River Sprite* is home to me."

"Rena's been running the river with me much of her life," Henry explained. "She's becoming a fine pilot."

"A river pilot?" Antoine choked on his wine.

"Is there something wrong?" the girl asked haughtily, receiving a warning glance from her father.

"Nothing, I suppose," Nathan replied smoothly, though he, too, was taken aback. "Are you all right, Uncle?"

"I am fine," Antoine answered between fits of coughing. "I have just never met a female pilot before."

"Not many people have." Henry beamed with pride despite their obvious disapproval. "Serena is Caswell through and through. She can do most anything she sets her mind to. My brother has been teaching her to read the river."

"I couldn't ask for a better teacher than Uncle Will," she added staunchly. "Anybody on the river will tell you, he's a lightning pilot. He learned from my grandfather, who piloted one of the first steamboats forty years ago."

"And you intend to carry on the family tradition?" Nathan asked.

"I don't see why not," she answered, shrugging carelessly.

"Do you not really?" Antoine was genuinely curious.

"What my uncle means," Nathan clarified as she scowled at the man, "is that Creoles live in a society where women have no place in commerce . . . or in the pilothouse of a steamboat."

"And, as a Creole, you believe that?" Serena regarded him challengingly, two bright spots of color staining her cheeks.

So the little mouse had spirit. Nathan smiled inwardly before answering, "Being only half Creole, I have never bothered to think about the subject of women in business one way or the other. But now that I do, I must say, my mother and all of my sisters seem quite happy at home with their needlework."

Before the irate girl could respond, he turned to her father. "Won't you tell me about your boat, Captain? Antoine says there is not a more dependable paddle wheeler on the Mississippi."

A glow in his eyes, Henry began to expound on his favorite subject. Though he listened with interest, Nathan was acutely aware of the volcano of feminine ire across the table from him. Serena's eyes, which he suddenly noticed were blue, rested on him with unmistakable dislike and, for a moment, he felt an inexplicable twinge of regret.

When the dinner party ended and the four had congregated in the courtyard, Henry drew the banker to one side and asked quietly, "Have you thought about my request, Antoine?"

"*Oui, mon ami,* but the bank can lend you no more money. All is not necessarily lost, however," he quickly reassured the captain. "If you can find an investor, perhaps we can arrange a favorable refinancing of your loan."

"I don't think so," Henry demurred sadly. "The *Sprite* is a Caswell boat. Always has been and always will be."

"But you might sell only a small percentage, Henry. Think on it," the Creole urged as they joined the young people near the fountain.

"Good evening, Mr. Trent." Serena smiled insincerely as she donned her bulky shawl. "If you ever decide to travel on the *River Sprite,* please visit me in the pilothouse. I enjoy company while I do my needlework."

"It would be my pleasure, Miss Caswell," Nathan replied coolly.

You conceited, superior son of a rattlesnake, she thought, departing with a polite nod.

It'll be sooner than you think, he mused, bowing in farewell. *You can bet on it.*

Nathan halted on the levee at the Canal Street dock to scan the busiest harbor in the world. For nearly a mile in either direction, immense steamboats, each one more elaborate than the next, lined the piers, their gangplanks lowered to allow sweating Negroes to load and unload cargo. The stevedores' songs and the shouts of the boats' mates drifted up to the spring sky with the black smoke billowing from a forest of towering stacks.

Along the open wharves, laborers, passengers and vendors swirled and eddied around crates and kegs and cotton bales stacked precariously high. The atmosphere was a potent, intriguing potpourri, the essence of New Orleans: muddy river smells; the aroma of spices, molasses and rum; and the faint perfume of flowers wafting from somewhere upriver.

How had Antoine talked him into this? Nathan wondered as he picked his way through the crowd. Stopping before the *River Sprite,* he inspected the steamboat. A stern-wheeler, she was not the largest or the newest, but she was solid and well kept.

Though he could not say why, Nathan liked her looks, from her shallow hull to the fanciful domed pilothouse that topped her three decks. His dark eyes took in every detail, resting at length on the paddle box at the stern, adorned by a painted water sprite with flowing red hair and magnificent blue eyes before rising to the uppermost deck.

The texas, or hurricane deck, took up only about three-quarters of the boat's length, leaving a portion of the deck below visible. Though windy when the boat was in transit, it was a favorite spot for passengers to watch the passing scenery. The cabins on that deck were used as offices and living quarters for the officers.

The forward section of the second deck, the boiler deck, was open and airy, offering space for a pleasant promenade. The salon, which also served as the dining room, was lined with windows and doors to provide travelers with cool breezes and magnificent views of the river. Ranging along the deck on both sides of the boat to the stern were the staterooms.

The lowest tier, the main deck, was dark and shadowed; it was given over to furnaces, boilers and machinery. At the bow, a graceful staircase led up to the boiler deck. The forecastle, the crew's quarters, was tucked under the stairs. Steerage passengers slept here and there among the cargo.

"The loading is just about done, sir," a burly, round-faced man wearing the ratchet on his belt that marked him as first mate bellowed from the bow.

Captain Caswell appeared at the rail of the boiler deck. "Did you load Mr. Jagger's black devil of a stallion?"

"We're about to, sir. We made a stall just forward of the boiler room, across from Gustave's chickens. The beast ought to be cozy enough there."

"Very good, Mr. Douglas. Secure the horse and stand by to cast off." Catching sight of Nathan on the dock, Henry's amiable face broke into a smile. "Trent, what are you doing here?"

"I'm going upriver, if you have room for another passenger."

"More than enough," the captain shouted as his crew hastened to their posts. "Come aboard."

Nathan walked up gangplank just ahead of a nervous deckhand who was leading the skittish horse aboard. When the stallion stepped on deck and felt the boat bob beneath him, he whinnied shrilly and reared.

Nathan dodged back from his flailing hooves, giving the crewmen more room to work. Murmuring softly and dancing nimbly out of the way, they settled the excited animal into its stall amid the dismayed squawks of the caged chickens nearby.

As he stood at the door to the engine room, waiting to pass, Nathan heard a voice inside, speaking with a broad Scots brogue, "Tell yer father we're nae likely to leave by five o'clock as the harbor master has decreed, bairn. The *Sprite* maun ha'e a wee bit longer to build steam."

"I'll tell him, Jamie," a youthful voice promised.

Barefoot and wearing a straw hat, the lad who emerged from the engine room looked as if he should be fishing. But his trousers and red cotton shirt were grease stained and his thin face was streaked with black. Looking back over his shoulder, he nearly collided with the man on deck.

"Watch where you're going, you little scamp," Nathan ordered, dropping his bag to catch the boy by skinny shoulders. "You could have ruined my shirt." Holding him at arm's length, he inspected the front of his snowy shirt for signs of oil and did not even bother to look at the grimy form struggling in his grasp.

"I came nowhere near your precious shirt, you cross-eyed, lop-eared son of a monkey. And who do you think you're calling a scamp?" the boy blustered, lifting narrowed blue eyes to Nathan's for the first time. The eyes widened and the lad gasped.

"Settle down, son," Nathan advised.

"Oooh!" The boy tried to wrench free, but only succeeded in dislodging his own hat. Abundant auburn curls tumbled from beneath it to settle sinuously around Nathan's hands. Suddenly the man was acutely aware that the shoulders he grasped were not skinny after all, but soft and round and feminine under the baggy cotton shirt, which was tied around a slender middle.

"Miss Caswell, I didn't recognize you." Staring down at the girl in feigned horror, Nathan made no move to release her. She was softer than he had imagined.

"Let me go," she demanded in a tight, breathless voice, her cheeks as red as her unbecoming shirt.

So he did have some effect on her. Nathan allowed himself a satisfied smile. He had begun to wonder last night if he had finally met a female immune to his charm. Releasing her, he bowed deeply. "I do apologize, ma'am. I don't usually mistake a lady of quality and breeding for a young boy, but…" His voice trailed off meaningfully as his eyes roved down her petite frame, lingering on shapely hips, then stopping at her bare feet.

"What do you want here, Mr. Trent?" she asked, scowling at him as she straightened her clothes.

Even dressed as a boy, she was more attractive than she had been last night. She might not be a beauty, but she did have her good points. Her auburn hair glistened in the sun, and today the light dusting of freckles across her nose gave her face a sauciness that was refreshing. Her mouth was wide and mobile, but the corners were turned down in a frown that was directed at him.

"I'm pleased to see you again." Nathan chuckled, admiring the outline of her rounded derriere she unthinkingly presented as she bent to scoop up her hat.

Remembering she wore trousers, Serena shot erect and threw a hostile look over her shoulder at him as she strode toward the bow.

Falling into step beside her, Nathan said with ill-concealed amusement, "I thought you were the pilot aboard the *River Sprite*. Whatever were you doing in the dirty, old engine room?"

"Working on the dirty, old engine."

"Are you also the striker? That is what they call the engineer's assistant, isn't it?"

Halting to face him, she explained coldly, "I'm a Caswell and this is a Caswell boat. I do whatever is needed. Now why don't you state your business and let me get about mine?"

"Such manners," he chided. "Shouldn't you show more cordiality toward a prospective passenger?"

"We don't have room for any passengers this trip, especially not underhanded, conniving, mendacious riverboat gamblers." She glared up at him, hoping she insulted him as thoroughly as he had insulted her. She was disappointed.

"You cut me to the quick, ma'am," the man reproached mockingly. "I haven't given you any reason to distrust me."

Her narrowed eyes raked him from the expensive Panama on his head to the tip of his well-polished boots. His dark blue jacket was well tailored, his ruffled shirt made of fine white linen and his immaculate silk cravat adorned with an enormous diamond. "You deny that you're a gambler, my fine-feathered friend?"

"I don't deny I've carried a few dollars from the gaming tables now and again," he answered mildly. "But appearances can be deceiving. Yours was last night . . . and still is."

She felt her color rising, but she refused to take his bait. "I'm not deceived by you, Mr. Trent. I think you're exactly what you seem."

"And what is that?" His voice was silky.

"A peacock, a rascal and a gambler . . . maybe even a sure-thing player. I wouldn't trust you any further than I could throw you."

"And I wouldn't rely on the judgment of a girl who dresses up in a boy's clothes." He found himself suddenly out of patience. "It doesn't show an abundance of good sense or good taste."

"Why, you low-down, despicable, pernicious—"

"Nathan, welcome aboard!" Henry's greeting drowned out her tirade as he joined them. "I see you've found Serena . . . though, at the moment, she looks more like her brother."

"If you're finished insulting me, Cap'n," she said balefully, "we've found the problem with the engine, but Jamie said to tell you we won't be able to leave for a while. Maybe until evening," she exaggerated shamelessly without realizing Nathan had overheard the engineer's instructions.

"Another delay?" The captain sighed. "Tell Will for me, would you, sugar?"

"Yes, sir." Poised at the foot of the stairs, she suggested, "Due to the lengthy delay, I'm sure Mr. Trent would prefer to make other arrangements for passage upriver."

"I wouldn't think of it," Nathan murmured, watching as she climbed up. Serena Caswell might not be a beauty, he decided, but she had her appeal.

"I really should insist she keep to her dresses," Henry said more to himself than to Nathan, "but I keep putting it off. Serena's temper matches that red hair of hers, not her name, I fear."

"I just saw it," the gambler acknowledged with a rueful smile.

"And heard it, if I know my daughter. I suppose I should do something about her vocabulary, too," the captain muttered. "She definitely has a colorful turn of phrase."

"I never would have guessed it last night," Nathan said dryly.

"No, not when she's done up all prim for business," Henry concurred. Putting aside the thought of a confrontation with his daughter, he smiled. "Come and I'll show you to your stateroom."

Serena was still fuming as she marched along the boiler deck in search of her Uncle Will. Absorbed in her ire, she passed Roger Blake, the *Sprite*'s clerk and one of her oldest friends, without even seeing him. The young man watched her in puzzlement, but, recognizing the signs of temper all too well, made no attempt to stop her.

Nathan Trent *was* low-down, despicable and pernicious, Serena seethed. She hadn't known it was possible to hate someone so much, so quickly. And remembering the glint of amusement in his dark eyes moments before, she did hate him. She had actually been attracted to him last night, in spite of herself, feeling unsure and fluttery in his presence. But today she was certain. He might be the handsomest man she had ever seen, but he was, without a doubt, the rudest.

Muttering under her breath, the girl found Will Caswell in the deserted men's lounge where he often went when his leg was giving him pain. A glass of whiskey on the table in front of him, the old man sat with the stiff limb propped on a chair and his huge calico cat, Catastrophe, asleep in his lap. Both doors, on opposite sides of the boat, stood open to the breeze.

"Jamie says we'll be late getting away," Serena announced as she entered the dim room.

"Fine with me. You're takin' the boat out." Will squinted up at his niece. "Tarnation, Rena, under all that grease, you look fit to be tied. What's got your dander up?"

"Nothing."

"Nothin'?" The elderly pilot fixed her with a skeptical stare.

"Just a no-account popinjay of a gambler."

"The big, good-lookin' feller I saw comin' aboard while ago?"

"That's the one," she admitted reluctantly, "Nathan Trent. Papa and I met him at Antoine La Branche's last night. The cap'n likes him," she added gloomily, perching on the edge of the table.

"What'd he do to get under your skin so quick?" Will asked, stroking the cat's fur idly.

"Last night or today?"

"Today'll do."

"He thought I was a boy," she answered with a sullen frown.

Her uncle looked her over consideringly. "Well, Serena Elizabeth, I'd have to say it was probably an honest error."

"Well, it's an error he won't make again," she snapped, irked by his candor, "so help me Hannah."

Shooing Catastrophe gently from his lap, Will rose and limped toward the door. "See you in the wheelhouse directly."

Alone except for the cat that had already usurped Will's seat, Serena rounded the counter and leaned near the mirrored back bar. Pulling off her hat, she inspected her reflection. She would never be a belle, she told herself honestly, but she didn't like being mistaken for a boy.

There was nothing masculine about her face. Her eyes were wide and blue and fringed with long dark lashes. Her features were delicate, though, even she would admit, the streak of oil across her nose did not exactly add to her femininity. Scrubbing at the stain with a handkerchief, she managed to lighten it, but in the process, made her nose quite red.

Scooping the sleepy Catastrophe into her arms, she sat down in Will's chair to brood. Maybe Uncle Will was right. Maybe Nathan Trent had made an honest mistake. And maybe she should give him the benefit of the doubt.

Out on deck, people came and went, chatting among themselves as the cabin boys settled them in their staterooms. From the dim interior of the lounge, Serena caught glimpses of them as they passed. It was nearly time to go to the wheelhouse when she saw Nathan position himself at the railing outside the door.

Framed by the doorway, he watched the activity on the dock, one broad shoulder braced against the brightly painted post. When a familiar voice hailed him, he turned. "Uncle! What are you doing here?"

"I came to see if you had decided to catch the boat this afternoon." Dapper and elegant, Antoine stepped into view.

"Since I have to get to St. Louis," the gambler countered, "it might as well be aboard the *River Sprite.*"

"Did I not tell you, you would change your mind?" Antoine asked smugly. Unaware anyone was near, he and his nephew lingered at the rail.

"You told me a lot of things last night," Nathan snorted. "You also told me Captain Caswell's daughter was rather pretty."

"But Nathan," the Creole protested, "all women are beautiful."

"So far Serena Caswell has exhibited a hot temper, an arresting vocabulary and an independent nature," the other man retorted, "but I have yet to see beauty."

"Still, here you are."

"Here I am," Nathan acknowledged drolly, "but not for the company of the captain's charming daughter."

Serena did not wait to hear more. Her face aflame, she fled the lounge through the opposite door and climbed up to the refuge of the pilothouse.

Chapter Two

Serena halted on the dark deck, her skirt swirling around her, and gauged the river with a practiced eye. The *Sprite* was steaming along the stretch of river the natives called "The Coast," past gracious plantations, their lights barely visible on the dark shore. A full moon shimmered on the water and there were no clouds in the sky. Smooth running tonight. For almost everyone, she amended as the horse kicked in his stall below.

From the salon came soft music and the murmur of conversation. Smoothing her skirt nervously, the girl stepped inside. Across the room, at the big, round captain's table, the places were nearly filled by honored passengers. Polished and elegant, Nathan sat beside Henry and engaged in a discussion with Mademoiselle Prados across the lamplit table.

Serena had met the thin, pleasant-looking Creole woman once before. Her youth nearly past, Mademoiselle Prados would soon have to don a spinster's cap, but for now she basked in Nathan's courteous attention.

Serena hesitated in the doorway, considering retreat. She sometimes dined with the passengers in the salon, but she seldom took pains with her appearance. Even wearing the apricot satin gown she had selected to complement her fair complexion and auburn hair, she felt ill prepared to join the sophisticated company at the captain's table.

But it was too late to go back. She knew her father had seen her when his eyebrows shot up in amazement. Taking a deep breath, she sailed forth to meet him.

"Serena, my dear!" Beaming, Henry met his daughter and led her to the table. "You look so pretty."

If the captain had been surprised when he saw Serena, Nathan was utterly stunned. This was not the gamine he had met on deck this afternoon, nor the mouse of last night.

Serena seemed to glow in a fashionable apricot gown that nipped in at her slender waist before belling gracefully over wide hoops to the floor. Her lustrous hair was swept up in a simple chignon, leaving her shoulders bare. In the lamplight, her skin had the look of milky porcelain.

"I believe you all know my daughter, Serena," Henry said.

"Good evening, Miss Caswell." With a charming smile, Nathan rose and pulled out the empty chair beside him for her.

"Good evening, everyone." With more composure than she felt, Serena joined the party. She was relieved when the pleasantries were past and the first course, a thick, savory gumbo, was served. Three or four different conversations resumed around the table.

"Nathan was just saying he's headed for California," Captain Caswell informed his daughter.

"By way of the Mississippi?" Serena turned to Nathan curiously.

"I'm meeting an old friend in St. Louis.... if I can locate him. Amos and I have been talking for some time about traveling the California Trail."

"But overland travel is dangerous, *oui*, M'sieur Trent?" Mademoiselle Prados asked, eager to be a part of the exchange.

"*Oui, mam'selle*, but all of us face peril when we stray beyond our own front doors," the gambler replied lightly.

"Usually those perils do not include Indians or wild animals," Serena countered. "Wouldn't it have been easier and safer to have caught a clipper in New Orleans and sailed around the Horn?"

"I hope to hire on with a wagon train in Missouri."

"Nate's got the experience to be a guide," Henry contributed enthusiastically. "He's roamed all over the West."

"And still managed to be in time for dinner," a teasing voice interjected from behind them. "Good evening, everyone."

"Ah, Roger, I was beginning to think you were going to miss dinner completely," Henry greeted his clerk congenially.

"I had some last-minute work to finish up," the young man answered, sitting down beside Mademoiselle Prados. Instantly a waiter set a bowl of gumbo before him, but, staring at Serena, Roger did not notice. His admiring smile was, Nathan decided privately, rather silly and besotted.

Throughout the elegant meal, Serena was scarcely aware of Roger's adoring gazes or the conversation around her. She hardly knew what she ate. She was not a vain person. Usually she told herself that it did not matter how she looked. But tonight, it mattered very much and she was pleased that Nathan seemed affected by her presence, his eyes constantly straying in her direction.

While they lingered over coffee and dessert, Nathan leaned near to speak to her. Across the table, both Roger and Mademoiselle Prados frowned to see their heads so close. Their frowns deepened when, at Serena's nod, the big gambler led her onto the dance floor and drew her into his arms.

Joining the circling dancers, they waltzed for a moment without speaking, their movements perfectly synchronized. Though powerfully built, Nathan was a graceful dancer and Serena felt as though she were floating as they swept around the cramped floor.

"I'm glad you agreed to dance with me," he said softly. "I wanted to speak to you alone, to apologize."

"To apologize?" Serena lifted her gaze and found him smiling down at her. The corners of his dark eyes crinkled appealingly and his expression was warm. Her heart skipping a beat, she blushed and looked away.

"I'm sorry for the things I said this afternoon," he murmured.

Serena managed a breezy laugh. "Oh, you mean when you thought I was a boy? I thought it an innocent enough mistake, Mr. Trent."

"Yes, but looking at you now, I can't see how I made it." His arm tightened at her waist.

She tried not to smile in triumph. Tonight was going just as she wanted. Nathan was seeing her as a woman. Before the evening was over, she would make him eat the words she had heard him speak to Antoine La Branche that afternoon.

Drawing back slightly within his embrace, she railed flirtatiously, "Such kind words. Your gallantry may cause other ladies to forget themselves, Mr. Trent, but I have the presence of mind to notice that you are holding me too close."

"Surely it is not decorum that leads you to that conclusion," Nathan demurred, but he loosened his hold obligingly. "A girl who wears trousers must care little for propriety. Are you afraid then?"

"Afraid? Of you?" Serena asked challengingly, the question catching in her throat when he smiled wickedly at her. Tossing her head, she concluded carelessly, "I do not recall that I have heard you are particularly dangerous."

"No?" His smile widened and he spun her around the floor.

At the captain's table, Henry turned in his chair to watch the couple. His daughter and Nathan Trent made a handsome pair, he reflected. They seemed a good match, too: Rena, so small and peppery; the gambler, big and easy and likable. Henry wished Serena would settle down. He wanted the same joy for her that he had found with her mother.

It was not as if Serena did not have prospects . . . the young men who traveled on the *Sprite* or bachelor planters up- and downriver, Henry thought, turning back to his guests. Even Roger, who watched the dancing couple so grimly. He was in love with Serena and she didn't even know it.

The captain sighed as Nathan returned the girl to her seat. As much as he loved having her with him, life aboard a steamboat offered no future to a young woman. To insist she leave the river would be the beginning of a long battle. He would not have an easy time overruling his strong-willed daughter. Nor could he condemn her love of the river, a passion she had inherited from him.

"What time is it, Papa?" Serena asked at once.

Henry dug his watch from his pocket and consulted it. "Half past ten. You still have some time before after-watch."

"What is this . . . after-watch?" Mademoiselle Prados asked in her French-accented English.

"It's the duty between midnight and four in the morning," Henry answered. When the Creole woman's brow furrowed in confusion, he attempted to elucidate. "Serena is one of the *River Sprite*'s pilots."

"And tonight I have the after-watch," the girl added.

Mademoiselle Prados stared at her in sudden, horrified understanding. "You will drive this big steamboat tonight? In the dark? A woman? *Non!*"

Roger leapt to Serena's defense. "It may be unusual for a woman to become a pilot, Miss Prados, but Rena's an unusual girl."

"And she's an excellent pilot," Henry reassured the woman. "Have no fear, *mam'selle*, you will be in good hands tonight."

"What does it take to become a good pilot?" Nathan asked Serena.

"Common sense, a cool head, a prodigious memory," she answered promptly. "A pilot not only needs to know how to read the river, he—"

"Or she," the gambler interjected with a grin.

"Or she," Serena revised, returning his smile, "must remember every curve and reef, every island and chute along the way."

"But doesn't the Mississippi change course every so often?" one of the planters asked, diverted from his own conversation.

"The river changes with each season," she replied, her eyes sparkling.

"And you remember all that?" The man regarded Serena with grudging admiration, then he added as if remembering himself, "But you probably get plenty of information from the Pilots' Benevolent Association."

"No." Her smile faded. "They don't accept women as members."

"Don't get her started," Henry said with a sigh, "or we'll be here all night."

"Not if she will consent to get a breath of fresh air with me before she goes back to work," Nathan cut in smoothly. "May I accompany you on a promenade around the deck, Miss Caswell? That is, if it's all right with you, sir," he deferred respectfully to the captain.

"I'd say that's up to Serena," Henry responded politely, knowing his daughter never promenaded with anyone.

"I would be delighted, Mr. Trent," she agreed. Fighting the urge to laugh at her father's dumbfounded expression, she allowed the gambler to lead her out onto the dark deck. No one seemed to notice the hurt that flickered in Roger's hazel eyes.

As Nathan and Serena strolled along the boiler deck to the moonlit bow, soft music drifted up from steerage. Even the horse was quiet in his stall for the moment. Nathan looked down at the delicate profile of the girl at his side and wondered what she was thinking.

She was playing a game she hadn't realized she knew, Serena exulted, and she was enjoying it. Nathan found her attractive. He might even try to kiss her. Roger had kissed her once and she had not found it unpleasant.

Leading Serena to stand at the forward railing, Nathan turned his back to the view and lounged against the rail, braced on stiff arms. She was suddenly aware of his size and masculinity. Kissing Nathan Trent might be a very different experience from kissing Roger, she realized with a flash of trepidation.

"Thank you for the walk, Mr. Trent," she said nervously, "but I really should go and change clothes now."

"You have plenty of time," he argued softly.

Casting a sidelong glance at him, she saw an intensity in his gaze that made her shiver.

"Are you cold?" Taking her arm, he drew her to stand in front of him so his big body blocked the wind of their transit.

"N-no." She could have sworn she felt his warmth.

"Let me see," he murmured, "you are not cold and you've already told me you are not afraid. Can it be anticipation that makes you shiver?" Pushing himself erect, he stood very near. "Is it because you know I've been waiting all evening to do this?"

The end of his question was lost against her lips. The kiss was like the man . . . easy and confident. Serena stood very still, savoring the feel of his mouth, warm and inviting, against hers.

Drawing her up against his hard chest so that her feet barely touched the deck, Nathan deepened the kiss. Hungrily his lips slanted across hers, hot and demanding, turning her knees to water. She gasped in shock as his tongue teased the corners of her mouth, enticing her, inciting a storm of unfamiliar sensations.

She had lied, she thought hazily, she was afraid. Surely only fear could make her heart pound so. Perhaps someone should have warned her about Nathan Trent. There was indeed something dangerous about him.

In an attempt to marshal her roiling thoughts, she tried to pull away. But he held her, his mouth claiming hers in a relentless demand for surrender. When, in spite of herself, Serena's lips warmed and parted under his, Nathan gentled his kiss and loosed his grasp even as he molded her trim body to his muscular length. Slowly, as if she had no will of her own, her hands ran up his arms, over his shoulders, and locked around his neck.

The feel of Serena, soft and yielding in his arms, threw Nathan off balance. Rocked by longing, he found himself thinking the most foolish thoughts. How refreshing, how different she was from the women he had known in the past. He wanted to know her, to spend time with her, to hear her laugh, to laugh with her. What he did not want was for this interlude to end too quickly.

His mouth left hers to trail kisses across the line of her jaw, and he nuzzled the sensitive place below her ear before moving down to her neck to kiss the hollow of her throat. He felt intoxicated by the feel, the scent, the taste of her.

Serena stirred in his arms when his lips skimmed her bare shoulder. When his head dipped toward the soft mounds visible at her décolletage, she stiffened. This was not what she had intended. Enthralled by his kisses, she had allowed him to go too far. She wanted him to know she was a woman; she was not prepared to prove it to him. Summoning all her strength, she tore from his embrace.

Baffled by her sudden change of mood, he scowled down at her.

"You—you low-down snake in the grass," she panted, wrapping her arms around her waist as if protecting herself, "how dare you take liberties with me?"

"How dare you enjoy those liberties so much?" Nathan's eyes hardened to become glistening onyx.

"You take unfair advantage." She glared at him defiantly, her lips still puffy from his kiss.

"No matter what you've decided about me, I am a square deal player, Serena," he replied impassively. "I play by the rules. When I win a lady's favors, I win them fair and square."

"So this was just a game to you," she accused, stung by his words.

"Isn't that what it was to you?" he drawled, narrowing the distance between them in one step. "You didn't have to come out into the moonlight with me. You didn't have to look so...inviting. But you did. You can't blame me for claiming the prize."

"You disreputable son of Beelzebub, I ought to ventilate your mangy hide with my grandfather's shotgun."

"That will hardly be necessary," he assured her, his face stony. "I won't kiss you again. Save your shotgun for the next poor fool who tries."

"How dare you—"

"I don't know how I dare," he muttered, suddenly weary. "I just know if you belonged to me, you'd spend less time being a river pilot and more time being a woman."

"Well, I don't belong to you."

"Thank God." He smiled crookedly. "I don't have the time or the patience." The familiar mocking expression returned and he said formally, "It's late. May I walk you to your cabin, Miss Caswell?"

"You may go to the devil for all I care, Mr. Trent," Serena retorted unsteadily. Then she wheeled and marched away.

Clad in a plain brown dress, one long braid slapping against her back, Serena went down to breakfast just after dawn. Before she entered the galley on the main deck, she stepped around the corner to take a look at the stallion, bumping and thrashing in its stall. It turned malevolent eyes on her, its yellowed teeth snapping in the air near her shoulder.

"Please, *mam'selle,* do not go near that monster and do not expect one of my magnificent breakfasts this morning," the cook warned her from the doorway. "*C'est impossible.* There are no fresh eggs, *non.*"

"And good morning to you, Gustave," she greeted him airily.

"That horse out there, he writhes like a demon in holy water, him," the temperamental cook grumbled, his waxed curled mustaches bobbing up and down as he spoke. Vexation made his Cajun accent thicker than usual. "He scares *mes poules* so they will not lay. Even *le coq* does not crow on time."

"Chanticleer never crows on time," Serena reminded him, but Gustave's attention had been diverted.

"Simon, *imbécile,* do not spill *le café* all over my clean napkins."

Unnoticed by the cook, Roger took the seat across the officer's table from Serena. Slight and not much taller than the girl, he was a pleasant-looking young man. But this morning, his expression was sulky.

"The passengers, they will want my famous omelets, *oui?*" the cook complained, his back to the table while he located a delectable croissant for Serena. "But I used the last of the eggs for the pastries. What is Gustave to do?"

"Gustave is to have patience," Roger advised dourly. "The captain says we'll stop at the first farm we come to and buy them out of eggs."

"M'sieur Roger, you startle me!" the Cajun gasped, whirling so fast that the pastry flew off the plate and skidded under the table.

Snatching up the biggin from the stove, he filled two cups and instructed, "Me, I will bring you both fresh brioche and big, juicy strawberries, *oui?*"

Regarding Serena accusingly over his cup, the clerk said nothing.

"How are you this morning, Roger?" she inquired at last.

"Fine."

"Are you feeling all right?" she asked, mystified by his behavior. She had eaten breakfast with him most mornings for almost three years and had never even seen him in a bad mood.

"I'm fine," he mumbled, staring at a point somewhere over Serena's left shoulder. After a moment, he shifted his gaze to her and asked morosely, "Did you have a good time last night?"

"Good enough," she answered, a spreading blush belying her nonchalance.

"I don't think you should have gone walking with that Trent fellow," he blurted. "He's a gambler... or worse. Aren't you worried about damaging your reputation?"

"When or if I do anything to damage my reputation, I'll be the one to worry about it, Roger. And I'm not worried," she added pointedly.

Seemingly relieved by her words, the young man quickly changed the subject. "That animal is more trouble than he is worth," he griped when the horse set up a new round of banging on deck. "I don't see why your father agreed to take him as cargo. Jagger already owes us five hundred twelve dollars and thirty-seven cents. I imagine he'll be as reluctant to pay us as always. And I've stretched the profit for our last run as far as I can stretch it."

"I know, and you do a good job, Roger," Serena sympathized. "The problem is that Papa is too tenderhearted. People like Mr. Jagger take advantage of him. And I'm sure 'Out-of-the-goodness-of-my-heart' will be waiting for us in Vicksburg."

"Out-of-the-goodness..." The clerk looked puzzled for a moment, then he laughed. "Oh, Mr. Hart. He lends money—

"At usurer's rates," Serena interjected, "out of the goodness of his heart."

Gustave served their breakfasts and the couple shared a few minutes of quiet conversation. As the sun began to climb in the sky, Chanticleer crowed halfheartedly to remind Serena that she had only a few hours to sleep before her next watch.

High in the wheelhouse, Serena steered the *River Sprite*. The midmorning sun was warm, but the wood-framed windows were open on every side and a breeze caressed her face and lifted her spirits. How she loved the pilothouse with its great wheel almost as wide as she was tall, the high chairs, the single low bench and Will's spittoon filled with sawdust. Here she could see up and down the river. Here she was on a level with the treetops. Here she did what she felt she was born to do.

Though Serena had not seen Nathan all morning, she could not fail to know he was aboard, talking to the crew, poking his nose into the cargo hold, even inspecting the engine.

When she called down the tube to the engineer, Jamie McPherson did not answer. His striker, Charlie Flowers, an amiable young man from Arkansas, said Jamie was showing Mr. Trent the boiler room.

Below, Nathan and Jamie returned to the engine room just in time to hear an angry tirade pour down the speaking tube.

"You tell that fancy sharper to keep out of the engine room," she shouted, causing Charlie to glance at Nathan in chagrin. "Tell him he has no business there."

Motioning the striker aside, the gambler spoke calmly into the tube. "I was just leaving, Miss Caswell. If my presence in the engine room was a nuisance to you, I humbly apologize. Perhaps I could make it up to you later if I were to come up and keep you company while you knit?"

At a renewed eruption from above, he withdrew, chuckling, leaving Jamie and Charlie to frown at each other in puzzlement.

As he climbed the stairs to the boiler deck, Nathan's mood was light. He did not know when he had enjoyed crossing swords with anyone as much as Serena Caswell. Pausing at the railing, he looked out at the river, recognizing the landmarks, then strode to his cabin. He had business to tend to before they reached Baton Rouge.

In his stateroom, the man located paper, pen and ink and sat down to write.

My dear Uncle,

I have inspected the *River Sprite* and believe, as you say, she can be made profitable. If I can convince Captain Caswell to allow me to invest in the boat, I will take you up on the wager you proposed before I left New Orleans. I imagine one thousand dollars should be sufficient to make it interesting.

Lest you think I regard this bet as easy money, you should know Serena Caswell will be a certain obstacle to my success. But do not delude yourself either that you will be the victor. You know I enjoy a challenge and on the *River Sprite* I confront two: the captain and his daughter. I remain

your damn fool nephew

Outside the post office in Baton Rouge, Nathan paused on the sunny street to set his hat on his head.

"Nathan!" A female voice cried and he was nearly bowled over by a flurry of skirt and ribbon and lace.

"Diane!" Nathan smiled with delight and hugged his little sister, who had turned into a young lady since he had seen her last. "You've grown, little bit."

"And so have you, I think." She craned her neck to look up at him. "When did you get home, *mon frère?* How long are you staying?"

Laughingly he answered, "I arrived less than a half hour ago and I'm not staying. This trip," he added hastily, seeing her crestfallen expression.

"But it's been so long, Nathan."

"I know, *ma petite,* but I'm a passenger on a steamboat which has made only a brief stop. I must get back to the dock."

"If you must go, I'll take you in my carriage. We can visit on the way," Diane insisted.

When they were settled in her open rig and headed toward the waterfront, she asked, "When will you come home, Nathan? Even to visit? *Maman* and Father miss you very much. So do I."

"And I miss you," he said gravely, remembering the jolt of familial longing he had felt at seeing his sister. "But since I cannot stay today, you must tell me all the news as quickly as you can," he instructed with a grin.

"You know there is no news." Diane pouted playfully. "Nothing ever happens in Baton Rouge, but I will try to think of a tidbit or two to interest you." To her brother's amused amazement, she launched into a brisk monologue, filling him in on an impressive number of relatives and friends during the short trip to the dock.

"Is that your boat?" she asked dubiously when they stopped in front of the *River Sprite.* "It's certainly not very fancy."

"No," he agreed with a smile, "but it's dependable enough to have brought me all the way from New Orleans."

At the boiler deck railing, Serena gazed down at the pair, the handsome gambler and the lovely young woman who stood beside him on the dock.

"He is handsome, is he not?" Mademoiselle Prados joined her at the rail.

"Handsome is as handsome does," Serena answered carelessly.

"In this case, handsome breaks hearts...everywhere he goes," the Creole woman said sadly. "He was only in New Orleans for two weeks, but I heard he broke a heart a day...on both sides of Canal Street."

"Don't Creole mamas object to such ladies' men?"

"*Mais oui,* but M'sieur Trent would be quite a catch as a husband. He is rich, you know, even without what he is sure to inherit from his father. His wealth makes it possible for even *les bonnes familles* to forgive him for being half *Américain.* I forgot it myself for a few moments last night."

Opening her parasol, she regarded Serena with a watery smile. "Mark my words, *mam'selle,* in the end, he will marry *la crème de la crème.* I suspect he is a proud man and nothing less will do." With that prediction, Mademoiselle Prados strolled away.

With one last look at Nathan and his lovely companion, Serena turned on her heel and marched to the wheelhouse.

Halted at the foot of the gangplank, Nathan asked through gritted teeth, "Are you telling me Adele is a widow?"

Diane stared up at her brother, aghast. "I thought you would have heard by now...or even seen her. You said you just came from New Orleans. Since her husband died, she spends much of her time there."

"No doubt we move in different social circles," he answered hoarsely.

"You don't still love her, do you, Nate?" Diane surveyed him with concern, tears glazing her dark eyes.

"I don't love anyone... anymore," he answered shortly.

"I didn't mean to bring back bad memories, *chéri.*" Diane's tears were dangerously close to overflowing.

His hands on her shoulders, Nathan kissed his sister's forehead lightly. "Don't look so stricken," he said gently. "It's not your fault Addie jilted me."

Realizing the deckhands were standing by to take in the stageplank, he hugged Diane quickly. "Give my love to the family and tell them I will try to stop the next time I pass through."

Her pretty face lit with a smile, she tiptoed to kiss his cheek.

Their farewells were lost in a long blast of the *Sprite*'s whistle. Leaping onto the boat just as the gangplank was being drawn aboard, Nathan waved to his sister as the distance between them increased. Up in the pilothouse, Serena straight-

ened the boat to make a "good ready," then with a lurch of the
paddle wheel, the *River Sprite* was on its way upriver.

Slowly Nathan trudged up the stairs to his cabin. So beautiful, deceitful Adele was a widow, he brooded; in spite of himself, he tried to conjure up the image of her face, but he could not. All that remained was the memory of betrayal, a dull ache in his chest.

The sun was dipping toward the western horizon when Nathan went out on deck again. At a landing where a flag hung limply in the breeze to signal the first passing steamboat, Serena ordered the engines cut. The wheel was stopped, steam was released from the stack and the *River Sprite* edged toward the dock.

Because such stops were short, slaves from the plantation and deckhands alike helped load the cargo and baggage. Henry and Nathan went ashore where Henry greeted the new passengers, Kermit Howard, a planter, and his daughter Viola, a confection of blond hair and pink ruffles.

Viola simpered predictably, twirling her lace parasol, when she was introduced to Nathan. He bowed, then after a moment, offered an arm to escort her aboard as Henry and her father followed.

Watching from the pilothouse, Serena rolled her eyes in exasperation. If Nathan Trent wanted to spend his time with that scatterbrain, maybe he'd stop poking around the *Sprite.* And if he was busy with a new conquest, there wouldn't be a repeat of last night's scene between them. She ought to thank Viola personally, she thought sourly as she guided the boat upriver again.

Serena returned to her stuffy cabin between shifts, her mood dreary. Her disposition was not helped by the apricot dress hanging on the back of the door. Running a finger over the rich fabric, she remembered how Nathan's eyes had lit when she entered the salon. She had felt beautiful for one of the first times in her life.

Then, recalling his kiss, she scowled and went out on the shady deck where the air was cooled by the mist sifting through the slats of the paddle box. Unwilling to sacrifice one of the better staterooms, she had taken a cramped cabin on the stern. It suited her and had its benefits. Passengers seldom strayed aft, preferring to promenade forward or up on the texas.

Dropping onto a dilapidated chair confiscated from the galley, she leaned her head against the bulkhead and closed her eyes. But Nathan Trent still occupied her thoughts. *He has been all over the Sprite from waterline to wheelhouse*, she mused. *He's been charming to everyone and everyone likes him. Everyone, but me. But then, everyone was not on the dark deck with him last night. He's a womanizing cad*, she told herself drowsily. But her last waking thought was of dark eyes, their corners crinkled in a smile.

A few hours later, as Serena went to relieve Will, she found herself looking for Nathan, though she had not intended to. He was nowhere to be seen, but Viola Howard moped alone on the boiler deck. Serena climbed to the wheelhouse, somehow cheered by the sight.

But her mood plummeted when Nathan leaned from the open doorway and offered a hand. Having hauled herself into the pilothouse at all hours in all kinds of weather, she was tempted to refuse his assistance, but she did not. Gingerly she placed her hand in his and allowed him to draw her inside.

"Your relief is here, Will," he called.

"Howdy, Rena." Will did not even look back from the wheel as he crossed over toward the other bank. "See what I'm tellin' you, Nate? Easy water is always found closer to shore when you're headed upriver."

"Are you taking a new cub, Uncle Will?" Serena asked, glad for Will's presence.

"Not a chance. Trainin' you plumb wore me out," the old pilot kidded.

"It looks as if we've been making good time," she commented. Positioning herself behind Will, she studied the river with exaggerated interest.

"Yep. I reckon you'll be able to hit Chute 82 before nightfall if we're not hailed between here and there."

"I hope so," she answered with feeling.

"Eighty-two is surrounded by woods," Will explained to Nathan. "Black as pitch at night and a trial to navigate. Rena can do it, though. She's done it before."

Lounging in the doorway, his shoulder against the frame, the man watched Serena, who scrupulously avoided his gaze. The afternoon sun washed over her, igniting a hidden fire in her auburn hair. Her face was still puffy with sleep and as his eyes rested on her lips, he was surprised to feel a stir at the memory of her kiss.

The night before was the last thing he should be thinking about, he chided himself. He shouldn't have kissed her. He had regretted it at once, even before she called him a snake in the grass.

She had actually made him lose his temper, he mused with something akin to wonder. He hadn't lost his temper in years. When he had deadened himself to pain four years ago, it was as if he lost the ability to care about anything. First desire, then irritation had overcome the numbness for a time last night. Even now, in the clear light of day, he was still uncertain what to make of the experience.

Though she kept her face averted, Serena was aware of his scrutiny. He would not mistake her for a boy today, she thought ruefully, but the dress she wore was old and outmoded. She had discarded her hoops to allow for freer movement, choosing cotton petticoats because they were cooler than crinolines.

Suddenly disgusted with herself, she wondered why she should care what Nathan Trent thought of her appearance. Last night should have taught her something. The less she had to do with him, the better.

So absorbed was she in her thoughts that she started when he spoke. "How are you today, Miss Caswell?"

"Very well, thank you." Caught off guard, she looked at him for the first time since she had entered the pilothouse.

With a nod, Nathan indicated the ancient double-barreled shotgun hanging beside the door and inquired innocently, "Is this the gun you mentioned last night?"

"It is and, I assure you, Mr. Trent, I know how to use it."

"'Miss Caswell,' 'Mr. Trent.'" Will cackled, oblivious to the tension between them. "Aren't we formal? Hope y'all don't expect me to be as highfalutin as you."

"This weapon is quite old, Serena." Nathan pronounced her name deliberately before turning to inspect the decrepit fowling piece. "Aren't you afraid it will blow up in your hand and ventilate more than my mangy hide?"

Returning her attention to the river ahead, she refused to answer, but she could have sworn Will's bony shoulders were shaking with contained laughter.

The silence lengthened until the old pilot could stand it no longer. "You shoulda been here earlier, Rena," he ventured, stepping back to allow her to take the massive wheel. "We've been tellin' tales. Nate's got a supply almost big as mine."

"And just as tall, I expect," she muttered as Will settled on the bench. She was uncomfortably aware that Nathan continued to lounge in the doorway.

"You gonna be playin' cards down in the salon again tonight, Nathan?" Will asked idly.

"I was thinking about it."

"Might come down and test my luck when I get off at midnight. You'll still be playing then, won't you?"

"Last night's game didn't get started till midnight."

"I thought I told you how we feel about gamblers on this boat," Serena interrupted waspishly.

"You told me how you feel about underhanded, conniving, mendacious riverboat gamblers." Nathan ticked off the words on his fingers. "Did I leave anything out? Since I'm none of those things, I can't see why I should pass up a friendly game of poker."

"Must you repeat everything I've said to you?" she complained.

"I, too, have a prodigious memory, Mademoiselle Pilot. I remember every name you've called me. I just keep waiting for you to forget yourself and say something kind to me."

Her cheeks flaming, she informed him, "The kindest thing I can say or do is to offer you some advice, Mr. Trent—"

"Call me Nathan."

"Consider yourself warned, Mr. Trent. On the *River Sprite,* we've been known to throw sure-thing players overboard."

"I told you last night I play fair and square." Pushing himself off the door frame, he stepped forward so Serena could see him without turning her head. "I don't cheat, I don't take unfair advantage . . . and I don't change the rules as I go along."

Serena's blush deepened, if that were possible. Only Will seemed to find any amusement in the situation. His green eyes were bright as he looked back and forth between the pair.

"Why don't the two of you go somewhere else for your yammering?" she demanded hotly. "How am I supposed to concentrate with a pair of magpies behind me?"

Will's jaw dropped. Many times he had sat up here with Serena and visiting pilots and there had never been a problem. The picture of wounded dignity, he rose. "Come on, Nate. Let's go."

"All right. I'll see you at dinner, Serena."

"I won't be there," she answered sharply. "But you'll have Viola Howard to keep you occupied."

"Yes, a charming girl, so feminine," Nathan drawled as he descended the ladder after Will.

He could not see Serena's reaction, but he could hear the ire in her voice as she called down to him, "From now on, stay out of the wheelhouse when I'm on duty, Nathan Trent."

Chapter Three

Nathan stood on the texas, overlooking the dock in front of Conrad Jagger's opulent plantation house. On the boiler deck below him, passengers gathered at the rail to watch the vicious stallion being unloaded. A familiar lace parasol identified one of the spectators as Viola Howard. Taking to the texas to preserve his sanity, Nathan had evaded Viola and her infernal giggling and had found the best position to observe the events of the morning.

He had watched as Jagger, stout, red faced and richly clad, had come aboard, striding up the gangplank as if he owned the steamboat. Henry had met him, taking him to the captain's cabin where they could discuss their business in privacy.

The gambler watched distractedly as the stallion bucked and kicked its way ashore. In a friendly if somewhat probing chat with the clerk, Blake, he had learned Jagger owed the captain a substantial sum. Nathan was interested to see how much Henry would collect today.

The answer came when Jagger stormed out of the captain's cabin, pausing in the doorway to shout, "I'll pay when I have the money, damn it! I have other bills to pay besides yours, you know. Don't I always get around to paying you?"

From within, Henry's response was placating. "Please, Mr. Jagger—don't be offended . . . it is only that—"

Suddenly aware of the presence of passengers on the texas, Jagger stepped back inside and closed the door. For a time, nothing could be heard from within but the indistinct rise and fall of voices.

"There you have it . . . fifty dollars and no more! That's all I can give you." The door opened again and Jagger's voice rang out over the sound of the idling engines. "I swear, Caswell, I've never been treated in so shabby a manner . . . and after doing business with you all these years."

His face angry and resigned, Henry emerged to watch the planter depart. Catching sight of Nathan nearby, he grimaced ruefully. "I was about ready to pay him to take that damned horse off our hands."

"You might've come out ahead." The gambler grinned at him from across the deck. "I never saw such a cantankerous piece of horseflesh."

"I guess you heard everything," Henry said sheepishly, joining him at the railing.

"Only part of it."

"I suppose it doesn't really matter, seeing why you're aboard the *River Sprite.*"

"To get to St. Louis?" Nathan queried blandly.

The captain fixed him with a baleful stare. "You could have taken any steamboat. I figure your uncle asked you to look the *Sprite* over and see if she's worth sinking any more money into."

"Not exactly. He suggested I might consider investing."

"I knew it," Henry fumed. "La Branche means to saddle me with a partner whether I want it or not."

Unprovoked by the other man's words, Nathan shrugged. "Antoine is trying to find a way to keep the *River Sprite* on the river."

"Well, it won't be with a partner. I don't need one."

"But you do need the money a partner would bring," the younger man ruminated. "And my uncle thought I might have some suggestions to make the *River Sprite* solvent."

"What kinds of suggestions?" the captain asked suspiciously.

"Just some recommendations regarding the *Sprite*'s everyday operation. She's a sound vessel, but she's getting old. Still, with some added maintenance, she'd make quite an investment for the right man."

"And what makes you think you're that man?"

Nathan considered the question before he answered. How could he tell the captain that he was unexpectedly intrigued by the idea of keeping the *River Sprite* afloat and the Caswells from failing? How could he explain that he hadn't felt this kind of excitement in years and it felt good? At last he simply said, "I like a challenge. And I suspect, if I examine your books, a challenge is what I will find."

Henry smiled wanly. "You're probably right about that, son. I warn you, I couldn't sell a full partnership in my boat, but I'd be willing to talk."

In the captain's cabin, lamps had been lit against the dusk as Henry and Nathan signed the paper on the desk between them. Outside, the wind was rising and the scent of rain was in the air.

"I'll admit I don't know the first thing about the river," Nathan said, standing erect, "but I do know business and I believe we've just entered into a promising partnership."

"Judging from the suggestions you've already made and your down payment of one thousand dollars, I'd have to agree," the captain granted with a weary smile.

"You'll get used to having a partner, Henry," Nathan reassured him. "And I'm the best kind for you, an absentee partner. Once the *River Sprite* is profitable, I'll make myself scarce. I'm headed for California, you know."

"I don't think I'm going to mind so much, now that the deed is done," Henry confessed grudgingly. "Shall we toast our success, Nate?" Picking up a bottle of whiskey and two glasses from a tray on a nearby table, he paused, frowning. "Or do you drink spirits? I've never seen you drink anything but a little wine with dinner."

"That's about it. I don't care for what alcohol does to me. Besides, in my previous line of work, I found it paid to keep my wits about me," Nathan said lightly. Taking one of the glasses from Henry's hand, he poured some water into it from a nearby pitcher and lifted it high. "But we can still toast."

While they drank, the captain sank glumly onto the chair behind the big desk. "I dread telling Serena about this."

"I could tell her," Nathan suggested.

"No, it's my place as her father and as captain of this boat," Henry insisted staunchly. "Besides I wouldn't do that to you. I'm not blind to my daughter's temper. It's her greatest fault."

"Why don't we cut the cards, partner?" Nathan pulled a deck from his pocket and began to shuffle. "Low card has to tell her."

Suddenly the door flew open and Serena stormed into the cabin as if carried by the wind.

"Has to tell me what?" she demanded, her skirt whipping around her ankles as she stopped to regard them accusingly. "That you're playing poker? I knew you were gambling when I heard you two had holed up here all afternoon." Her auburn hair tumbled to her shoulders in riotous disarray and spots of color in her cheeks denoted temper. Her gaze resting grimly on the cards in Nathan's skillful hands, she was scarcely aware when her father closed the door behind her.

"How did you leap to the conclusion that we were gambling?" Nathan asked mildly.

She sent him a withering stare. "Because my father has a weakness for cards. You're just the man to take advantage of it, aren't you, Mr. Trent? And shame on you, Cap'n, gambling when the *Sprite* is just waiting to blow a gasket."

"That's enough, daughter," Henry commanded sternly. "Though I don't owe you a explanation, I assure you we are not gambling."

"Then what are you doing?" she demanded, glaring back and forth at the men.

"We were about to cut the cards to see who was going to tell you that Nathan has invested in the *River Sprite*."

"What?" The girl's jaw sagged in dismay.

"I took a partner, Serena."

"But this is a Caswell boat!"

"I suppose I could marry into the family, if it would make you feel better," Nathan suggested drolly.

"You damn fool, grinning jackanapes," she sputtered, her face flooding with color. "I wouldn't have you on a silver platter!"

"Such insults—and to your new partner, no less." He grinned shamelessly at her as she glared at him.

Serena turned urgently to her father. "What can you be thinking, Papa? Nathan Trent is a gambler, not a river man. Besides, we have enough trouble just feeding the boilers without having to feed a conniving polecat like him."

"Precisely the reason you need an investor," Nathan responded, suddenly serious.

"This boat is our livelihood and our family's future. We don't need help from you... or anyone." Squaring her slender shoulders, she addressed her father, "Do we, Cap'n?"

"Glad you're willing to consider my opinion, Serena Elizabeth," Henry answered tartly. "As head of the Caswell family and captain of this boat, I try to do what I think best. This time I think it's best to take a partner. Nathan has agreed to purchase a one quarter share of the *Sprite* and we've signed this letter of agreement."

"But we could change our minds, couldn't we?" she argued desperately. "It's not official yet, is it?"

"It will be as soon as we meet with the lawyers in Vicksburg. Now, I want you to apologize to Nathan, Rena. We're going to be seeing a great deal of him for some time."

"All I want to see of Mr. Trent is his back when he gets off the boat in St. Louis," she announced, slamming the door behind her.

Henry dropped into his chair again with a sigh. "Sometimes I wonder if I was wrong all these years to keep Rena with me on the boat. She should have been doing the things a young girl does instead of becoming attached to an old stern-wheeler."

"Don't worry," Nathan found himself reassuring the older man. "Serena wants what's best for the *Sprite*, too. She'll come around."

"Of course," Henry muttered, "she'll come around."

Most of the passengers had sought their beds when Nathan stood on the boiler deck, watching the shadowy shoreline of

northern Mississippi slip silently by, its thick forests dense and
murky against the moonlit sky. Here and there ashore, lantern
light dotted the darkness. The only sound was the gentle slap
of paddles against the water.

He was waiting for Serena. After the scene in her father's
office, she had taken refuge with Will in the pilothouse. Surely,
by now, her anger had cooled. He hoped so, for he needed to
talk to her, to see if he could set things right between them.
They had gotten off to such a bad start. Ambling a little far-
ther down the deck, he positioned himself to catch her if she
returned to her cabin before the after-watch.

Behind him, a door opened softly and Viola Howard stole
out on deck. Unaware he had been loitering in front of her
stateroom, Nathan looked around dumbly when she joined
him. "Miss Howard, what are you doing out here?"

"Well you might ask, Mr. Trent, after you neglected me all
day." She pouted coyly. "But why didn't you knock? I didn't
even know you were here until I happened to look out the window."

"You shouldn't be here." He peered toward the companionway Serena would descend at any moment.

"Don't worry," Viola murmured reassuringly, mistaking his
glance for apprehension. "My daddy would sleep through Ga-
briel's horn."

"Not everyone on the boat is abed, Miss Viola," he maintained, "and you should not be seen alone with a man on a
dark deck."

"I don't think anyone can see us," she objected, looking
around as he herded her toward her door.

"Still you must think of your reputation."

"You are so gallant, Mr. Trent," she twittered, balking on
the threshold. "I don't think I've ever known such a gentleman."

"Nor I such a lady," he answered through gritted teeth.

Without warning, the girl whirled, threw her arms around
him and kissed him squarely on the mouth. "Why, Nathan,
you say the sweetest things."

Viola's giggly voice reached Serena on the night breeze just as she stepped down to the boiler deck. Glancing forward, she froze momentarily when she saw the couple in the pool of faint light outside the open door of a stateroom. Nathan Trent and Viola Howard! Pivoting, she hurried toward the stern.

Glimpsing Serena over the top of Viola's head, Nathan groaned aloud. She would never listen to him now. Wordlessly he peeled the clinging girl's arms from around his neck, bowed slightly and set out after the slight figure disappearing into the darkness.

Oblivious to Serena's presence and the man's predicament, Viola flounced inside indignantly. Nathan hadn't even kissed her back.

He overtook Serena as she rounded the cabin section onto the stern. Catching her wrist, he spun her to face him. "Wait, I want to talk to you."

"No, thank you," she spat, jerking from his grip. "You'll pardon my saying so, but it's not safe for a girl to be alone with you."

"You didn't see what you thought you saw."

"I didn't see you kissing Viola Howard just now?" Even in the murky dimness, he could see her eyes flashing.

"You saw Viola kissing me," he explained reasonably.

Serena hooted with laughter. "You are modest, Mr. Trent, not to take credit for your conquests."

"Just listen—"

"No, you listen. I don't care who you kiss, Mr. Trent. You can kiss my Aunt Kate's cow or an old jenny mule. And you don't have to explain anything to me. All you have to do is leave me alone. Good night."

"Serena—" Nathan stepped around to her block her way.

"You can call me Miss Caswell," she interrupted, refusing to retreat.

"You stopped being Miss Caswell to me when you kissed me."

"I kissed you," she erupted incredulously. "Viola kissed you. Don't you ever kiss anyone?"

"I do, indeed," he growled dangerously, wrapping one arm around her waist and hauling her against him.

Serena's eyes were wide with alarm, but her chin rose defiantly. "If you're considering trying it again, I'd think twice. I told you what would happen if you did."

"So you did." Bending so his face was very close to hers, he reminded her ruthlessly, "But I'm a gambler. I'll take a chance."

He claimed her lips for a perfunctory, dispassionate kiss, refusing to allow it to deepen, refusing to admit, even to himself, that it aroused him. He released her so abruptly she staggered.

Serena felt as though she had been slapped. Her face pale and taut with anger, she glared up at him and rubbed her lips with the back of her hand as if she could erase the memory of his touch.

"As I said before, I'm a gambler... and I think I just won that hand." Nathan smiled down at her smugly, hating himself.

"Damn you and your games," she choked. "Why don't you go back to Viola Howard? At least she's a willing player."

So angry that even epithets were driven from her mind, she went into her cabin and slammed the door. Disturbed by his own behavior, the man stalked forward toward his stateroom.

Chapter Four

In dry-eyed misery, Serena hunched on the edge of the bed and stared at the wall of her room at River's Rest. Muted voices reached her from downstairs where black-clad strangers came and went.

Dispiritedly she went to the window to stare at the green lawn below. The warmth of the spring sunshine, the breeze from the river did nothing to lift her spirits. She felt as though she would never be happy again.

The *Sprite*'s homecoming last week had certainly been joyous. Even now Serena nearly smiled at the memory. Out-of-the-goodness-of-his-heart had arrived promptly at the boat, so pompous and official, and had departed moments later, crestfallen, with the payment he had sought but not expected. He had been so certain he would be able to foreclose on the *Sprite*.

During the evening, the entire family had been reunited for Hank's birthday. Grace, Dory and Hank had met the travelers at the door and everyone had talked at once as they trooped into the parlor where Bonnie and Orren Ralston, Grace's sister and brother-in-law, waited. The birthday party had been noisy, jolly and a complete success. But what Serena remembered most clearly now was the love her parents had shared and their joy at being together again.

The next morning, the joy had ended abruptly. While a cargo was being loaded, a cable on the winch broke and the load fell, pinning Henry to the deck not five feet from where Serena stood. His body crushed and mangled, he had died within hours.

She and her mother had been at his side at the end, each holding one of his hands, silently. All the words had been spoken and the promises made. The lace curtains had rustled softly on the spring breeze, and outside the window, the call of a mockingbird could be heard. Then, suddenly, her father was gone.

This morning had been the hardest. Serena closed her eyes wearily against the flood of memories: her mother's pale face behind her veil, red eyed from weeping; the captain's brief, dignified funeral; the faces, both black and white, of the boat's crew gathered under a tree in front of Christ's Church; the respectful silence as Henry was carried to the cemetery.

She could still envision the family standing in a circle around the grave. Uncle Will, his green eyes watery and dull, supported Grace. Beside Uncle Orren, who was staid and solid in his mourning clothes, Aunt Bonnie stood with her arms comfortingly around Dory and Hank. Serena had clung to Roger's arm as if it were a lifeline. Surrounded by townspeople she hardly knew, she had found their sympathy difficult to bear.

Now she lingered, though she knew her place was downstairs with her mother, greeting the callers. Dreading the press of people, she forced herself to leave her quiet room and descend the back stairs to the kitchen. She hesitated when she realized two women stood at the counter, talking, as one of them washed the luncheon dishes and the other dried.

"That poor girl," one of them said. "When I saw her at the funeral, I thought I would weep. She looked as if she lost a piece of her heart when they buried her father."

"Poor Grace, I'd say," the other sniffed. "Henry allowed Serena an appalling amount of freedom. I hear she's learning to be a river pilot. I cannot imagine how Grace will find a husband for her. I've always thought her a rather plain little thing."

"I don't think she's plain. I think she's practical. Some men appreciate that in a woman," the sympathetic matron defended her.

"Whatever she is...plain or practical...she has a wild streak."

"Perhaps the right man will come along to take her in hand."

"He'd better come along soon, else she'll be an old maid."

Drained of emotion, Serena could not even summon up anger at the women. Finishing her descent, she passed silently through the kitchen and out the door. The women stared after her, chagrined to think she might have overhead their conversation.

"Come on, Nate, I reckon we'll find Grace and the children in the parlor," Will said, climbing down from Nathan's hired rig.

As they walked up the driveway, crowded with the carriages of callers, Nathan surveyed River's Rest. The Caswells' home had the same kind of unassuming grace as their steamboat. The frame house, surrounded by a low rail fence, was large, though not grand. A shady veranda wrapped around three sides of the house, and flowers bloomed in boxes at the second-floor windows. Huge oak trees dotted the lawn. On the branches of three of them, rope swings hung in various stages of aging. A swing for each child, he thought as Will led him into the house.

The widow and her younger children were indeed in the the parlor. Grace Caswell was a small woman, but her poised, elegant manner made her an impressive presence. Her carefully coiffured hair was so blond it was almost white. Her blue eyes, the same dazzling shade as her elder daughter's, were evenly set in a surprisingly youthful face.

"Mr. Trent, is it not?" Her voice was well modulated as she greeted the newcomer.

"Yes, ma'am," he said with a bow. "My condolences, Mrs. Caswell. Your husband was a fine man."

"Thank you. I understand you were a friend of Henry's. I have appreciated your kindness over the past few days, especially the offer of your hired rig. It was very thoughtful of you."

"You're more than welcome, ma'am."

"You must know my daughter Serena." Grace looked around distractedly. "She's not here at the moment. I expect she's found a place where she can be alone for a few minutes."

Serena was indeed alone when Nathan found her. She stood on the bluff overlooking the Mississippi, her back against the rough trunk of a big oak tree, as she stared at the broad river. He faltered, uncertain he should disturb her solitude, then remembering her grief-stricken face at the grave side that morning, he went to stand beside her.

He said nothing when he joined her. Crossing his arms on his broad chest, he too looked out at the river, seemingly unconcerned when she did not speak.

Silently Serena willed him to leave. She had not seen Nathan Trent since the night he had kissed her on the *Sprite*'s stern and she did not feel up to facing him now. She did not want him to see her cry.

Her eyes on a passing steamboat that seemed to shimmer through unshed tears, she asked in a tight voice, "What do you want, Mr. Trent?"

"I came to offer my condolences," he answered quietly.

"Thank you very much. Good day," she choked, refusing to look at him. Her head ached and the sun was growing warm against her black bombazine dress.

"Serena..." Nathan laid a comforting hand on her shoulder and squeezed gently. "I'm truly sorry. I liked your father very much."

Turning a bleak face to him, she whispered, "I still can't believe he's dead." With a strangled sob, she covered her face with her hands and began to cry for the first time.

Tenderly Nathan pulled her into his arms. "I'm sorry," he whispered against her hair. "I'm sorry for everything."

Serena did not hear. "I n-never cry," she sobbed against his cravat.

"It's all right. It's just us right now. Go ahead and cry," he murmured, musing as he held her. The last time they had met, Serena had fought his embrace. But today she needed his strength and he was glad to give it to her.

"Here," he said softly, offering a snowy handkerchief when the wrenching sobs subsided and she was nearly limp in his arms.

"Thank you," she murmured, her voice husky from crying. Suddenly realizing she was cradled against Nathan's chest, she withdrew. "I haven't thanked you for your kindness toward all of us during this time."

"I was glad to do whatever I could for your family. I've been thinking, Serena. I could stay in Vicksburg a while longer," he added seriously. "You may need a man around more than ever—"

She stiffened abruptly. "I have no need . . . no use . . . for a partner, if that's what you're getting at."

"That wasn't what I was getting at," he replied, irked by her reaction, "but since you bring it up, a quick look at the *River Sprite*'s books will show you need a partner very much. Your father and I agreed—"

"I don't care what you agreed," she broke in, shoving his damp handkerchief into his hand. "You never signed a real contract. Whatever you and my father agreed does not signify."

"I gave him a down payment, a thousand dollars." Nathan was unwilling to let Serena have the last word. "What about that?"

"I'll pay you back," she spat, her temper high.

"With what?"

"I'll get my hands on the money somehow and it'll be worth every penny to be rid of you."

"I doubt any decision regarding the *River Sprite* will be yours alone. I understand your mother owns it now."

Still pitiful and red eyed from weeping, she faced him defiantly. "You odious, low-down scalawag—"

"I think it's rather soon to be talking business, Miss Caswell," Nathan cut her off with a disgusted frown. "You and I will talk later."

Fuming, he strode away. He didn't care if he ever got the money back. He had not mentioned the partnership to anyone, feeling it was inappropriate. And he had no intention of

speaking to Mrs. Caswell about either subject, but Serena
somehow made him lose his temper and say things he did not
mean.

Unable to sleep that night, Serena paced restlessly in her
room. Through the wall, she could hear her mother crying.
Resolutely she threw on a dress and a shawl and set out for the
River Sprite. If she was to take care of her family, she might as
well start now.

Near dawn, she closed the books and sat back wearily in her
father's chair. Caswell & Company was in worse trouble than
she had thought. People up and down the Mississippi had owed
Henry money, but even worse, he had been in debt to others.
For the first time, she understood why he had planned to take
a partner; nevertheless, she was determined to operate the
Sprite alone . . . without Nathan Trent.

"Serena Caswell, bring that boat back here!" Nathan
shouted from the end of the dock. "You can't take her out until we talk."

"Talk to yourself, you puffed-up son of a bullfrog. I've got
a cargo to get to St. Louis!" Serena yelled, standing on the
River Sprite's bow. Her voice was faint over the sound of the
engine as the big boat backed away and straightened, its bow
pointed north. Will waved from the wheelhouse, unaware of
what was going on.

"You have a passenger, too," Nathan bellowed in exasperation. "I paid my fare to St. Louis."

"A refund is waiting for you at the harbor master's office,"
drifted back to him.

"I should have turned you over my knee the first day I met
you, you little hoyden."

"You missed your chance, you—" The rest of her taunt was
lost in a blast of the boat's steam whistle.

"Come back here," he roared, though he knew she could not
hear him. Cursing under his breath, he watched the boat steam
away. When he turned, Hank stood behind him.

"You don't cuss nearly as good as Rena," the boy observed.

"I don't get nearly as much practice," Nathan growled.

"Mr. Trent, sir, I'm Henry Caswell, Jr." Hank remembered his errand. "The man at the hotel said I would find you at the dock. Can you please come to our house so my mother can talk to you?"

Nathan was still struggling with his anger when he climbed the steps to the broad veranda at River's Rest.

"Mr. Trent, how good of you to come," Grace Caswell greeted him at the front door. "I hope I haven't inconvenienced you."

"No, ma'am."

When they were settled in the parlor with their coffee, the woman pulled a folded paper from the pocket of her apron. "In going through my husband's belongings, I came across this paper. It seems to be a letter of agreement between the two of you to undertake a partnership in the *River Sprite*."

"It was never formalized," Nathan reassured her. "I certainly wouldn't hold you to it, Mrs. Caswell, especially knowing you have other plans for the *Sprite*."

"What do you mean?"

"I had a brief . . . er . . . run-in with Serena this morning."

"Exactly what did she say about my plans?"

"Exactly what she said won't bear repeating in front of a lady," he said directly, feeling guilty when Grace blushed.

"Now I understand why she didn't want me to see her off at the dock," the woman mused. "Mr. Trent, I did not know about this agreement when I allowed Serena and Will to take the cargo to St. Louis. And I allowed it only because we needed immediate income.

"I have considered what to do in the long run to meet our obligations," she continued. "Taking in boarders or opening a school for young ladies does not seem feasible. I considered selling the steamboat and the house and finding a governess's position . . ." She paused, her shoulders sagging as she remembered her daughter's reaction to that idea. "But I still have not made a definite decision about what to do when the *Sprite* returns."

"I am sorry," Nathan murmured sympathetically. "If there's anything I can do to help...."

"You've already been very kind...even beyond the requirements of a partner." Consulting the letter she held, she asked, "You were Henry's partner, were you not? It appears you invested one thousand dollars in Caswell & Company."

"Let's say I gave it to the captain to pay a pressing debt."

"Gave it?" she repeated skeptically.

"Yes, ma'am." He nodded with a bland smile.

"That is kind of you, but we cannot accept charity."

"It's not charity."

"Then what is it, Mr. Trent?"

"A loan and I'm in no hurry to be repaid. In fact, I won't even be here. I'm on my way to St. Louis...as soon as I can get there," he muttered with a forbidding frown.

Grace consulted the letter again. "This does not say it was a loan. Henry did not discuss business with me, but he did mention that he had finally found a way to make the *River Sprite* pay off. I did not remember until I found this paper. Taking you as a partner was the way he had found, wasn't it, Mr. Trent?"

"We did write the letter, ma'am, but no contract was ever signed."

"You do think the *River Sprite* can be made profitable?"

"If it's managed properly."

"Can you manage it?"

He stared at her in astonishment. "That was never the understanding. When I supplied new working capital, I also made some recommendations your husband was going to initiate."

"Will you tell me about them?"

Grace listened attentively as Nathan recounted the discussion he had had with her husband. While he talked, her mind worked. She could see why Henry had been willing to listen to the young man and she knew he would be a better manager than the captain had been. Henry, bless him, had buried them so deeply in debt they might never see light.

When Nathan finished his summary, Grace was silent. Then, summoning her courage, she looked him in the eye and asked,

"Are you willing to honor your commitment to my late husband, Mr. Trent? I know Caswell & Company is currently a rather shaky venture, but if you agree, I'll make you an equal partner in the *River Sprite*."

"Equal? That's hardly necessary, Mrs. Caswell."

"It is," she answered positively. "Despite what Serena thinks, we cannot operate the steamboat alone. If we are to have a partner, I would like him to be you. I offer an equal split or nothing."

"But you don't even know me," he sputtered. "I make my living at the gaming tables."

"So William told me." She smiled at him. "My brother-in-law also said you are a 'fine feller.' And Henry must have liked . . . and trusted . . . you to draw up this letter."

"But, ma'am—"

Grace's chin rose stubbornly. "Can you raise the rest of the money, the amount you discussed with Henry?"

"I already have it, but—"

"Then if you concur, I will have the lawyer draw up the papers. If you do not, we will repay you somehow."

Though he had resolved to help the Caswells when Henry was alive, he had never intended to be an active partner, Nathan thought helplessly. He was on his way to California, after all. But without the *Sprite* to support them, the family faced nearly overwhelming debt and now there were medical bills, as well.

"Can't I have a little time to think about it?" he asked feebly at last.

"Of course." Grace nodded. "But while you are thinking, perhaps you would be so kind as to offer me some advice. I think the first thing to be done when the *River Sprite* returns is to allow Mr. McPherson to overhaul the engines. Do you agree?"

"I think the first thing to do is to hire a reliable captain."

"I supposed you would be captain, Mr. Trent."

"Me?" Nathan nearly choked on his coffee. "I know precious little about boats and nothing about being a captain."

"Serena will help you," Grace countered.

"Serena? Begging your pardon, ma'am, but she would just as soon tell me to jump off the boat than how to run it."

"Surely not." Grace frowned. "She must realize that though she knows the river and the cargo and our shippers, she doesn't know the business. You see, Mr. Trent, we need you . . . as the captain."

"I'm not so sure, Mrs. Caswell."

"I believe you can deal with the passengers and the problems which arise, Mr. Trent. And Serena can attend to piloting."

"She's not going to take this well . . . if I agree."

"If you agree, she will become accustomed to the idea," Grace responded firmly. "She is a practical girl. She will see this is the best way . . . perhaps the only way.

"Never fear, sir." She overrode any protest he might have made. "All will be well. Of course, you must forswear gambling. But I should think the *River Sprite* is quite enough risk for anyone."

Nearly speechless in the face of such determination, Nathan floundered, "Have you thought what people will say as your daughter and I bob merrily up and down the river with only Will as a chaperon? No offense, ma'am, but when your brother-in-law isn't steering, he's napping."

"You will be quite well chaperoned, I assure you, by the entire Caswell family."

"The entire . . ." He trailed off weakly when she nodded.

"Dory, Hank and I shall move onto the *River Sprite* as soon as she returns to Vicksburg."

"Does Serena know this?"

"Not yet." Grace smiled confidently. "I know my daughter is somewhat headstrong at times, but she will do as I ask. Henry and I tried to bring her up to be polite and respectful and obedient."

Nathan sat back in his chair, thinking that both mother and daughter were about to receive the surprises of their lives. After a moment, he said, "You're determined to go through with this?"

"I'm willing to take a chance if you are, Mr. Trent. And I believe you will find—how do you put it?—that the odds are in your favor. We are Caswells. And, as Serena reminded me just last night, we can do anything we set our minds to."

Sluggishly the *River Sprite* moved against the current, her engines wheezing and rattling. Every report from below poured through the speaking tube on a vivid streak of broad Scots-accented cursing. Alone in the pilothouse, Serena wearily looked around from the wheel when Roger entered.

"How are you doing?" he asked encouragingly.

"We should make Vicksburg by late afternoon if the engine doesn't give up the ghost. How's Uncle Will?"

"About the same. You must be tired," Roger sympathized, "trying to care for him when you're not piloting."

"I'll be glad to get home. We all will. I know we can't afford it, but I wish we could give the crew a week off."

"We may have to, if Jamie can't repair the engine right away."

"He will," she answered confidently. "He has to."

If Roger disagreed, he kept it to himself. But, after a moment, he said reluctantly, "You should know that three of the men won't be staying on, Rena. I tried to change Vernon's mind, but he's set on going."

"Too bad," she responded curtly. "Good stewards are hard to find. Did they say why they're leaving?" Nearly eye to eye with the slight clerk, she fixed him with a level gaze, as if daring him to prevaricate.

Roger squirmed, anxious to depart. "I know you talked to the crew before we left and they agreed to serve under you, but after the last month, they...er...they think having a woman as captain is bad luck."

"Most of them think fog comes from a giant alligator who smokes the cigars they throw over the side for him, too," she said dryly as the clerk let himself down the ladder.

Glad they were navigating a familiar stretch of river, Serena allowed her thoughts to turn to the past month. Her maiden voyage in command had started well enough, but it had been fraught with mishaps. The *Sprite* had delivered its cargo to St. Louis and been contracted to transport a load of furs to New Orleans. Pressed for time, they had bypassed Vicksburg on their way downriver.

As the boat passed through Kentucky, Will had become ill. A doctor in Hickman had said the elderly pilot had a weak heart and must have bed rest. For two days, they had remained docked while Serena nursed her uncle. Then, despite his weakened condition, he had insisted the *Sprite* continue downriver while he lay in his cabin, recuperating little by little.

In Memphis, Serena had hired a visiting pilot who was working his way downriver. Though his salary cut into the profit of the trip, she had felt lucky to have Mr. Forbes. Unwilling at first to partner with a female, he gave in at last, working in uneasy tandem with Serena all the way to New Orleans.

There a new round of difficulties had begun. The consignment was less than originally stated and Serena could not find a visiting pilot for the return to Vicksburg. The trip upriver had taken twice as long as usual, for she was not foolish enough to run when she was overtired. Finally, just fifteen miles south of their destination, the *Sprite*'s coaxed and coddled engine had broken down. They had spent the night tied up at the bank while Jamie banged and toiled and swore.

As the *River Sprite* approached Vicksburg, Serena gave her full attention to mooring the big boat. When the lines were secure, she sent a note to her mother, explaining the *Sprite*'s long absence and describing Will's illness.

Grace came at once. As she stood on the deck outside her ailing brother-in-law's cabin and watched her daughter hurry away to supervise the unloading, she decided it was just as well that Serena was busy. She dreaded telling her of the partnership with Nathan Trent.

In the past weeks, Grace had made her arrangements, overcoming objections on every side. Nathan's initial doubts about her plan had been only the beginning. She had heard arguments from Orren and Bonnie and from her own children, but their most vehement protests would pale beside Serena's. Even as she busied herself caring for Will, Grace mentally rehearsed how to break the news. Serena was going to be furious.

"A profit?" Serena repeated delightedly. Perched on a trunk, she squinted up at Roger in the bright sunlight. "Even after hiring Forbes?"

"It's only a small profit," the clerk responded cautiously, "but there's enough to pay the crew with a little left over."

"We did it! We made money on our first trip in spite of everything." The girl's smile was jubilant. "This should convince Mother we can't sell the *Sprite*."

Roger returned her smile, but his hazel eyes were concerned. "Don't you think you should have consulted her before agreeing to take on another cargo tomorrow?"

"There wasn't time," she responded breezily. "Lowell would have found another boat for his goods."

He did not bother to remind her that Grace was as near as Will's cabin. "What about the engine?" he asked instead.

"Jamie McPherson can fix anything but an act of God," she declared, picking her way among piles of crates and barrels. "Speaking of the engine, I should see how the repairs are going."

When she emerged from the engine room a few minutes later, Serena's elation was gone. Jamie had listed the parts he needed to get the *Sprite* running again, ticking them off until he ran out of fingers. Their profit would go for nothing but parts. If there were passengers, there might be funds to wood up for the trip upriver. But they needed more money just to cover expenses.

Serena walked to the other side of the boat, away from the bustle of the dock. It seemed they were always at the brink of ruin, she brooded, looking out over the muddy river. Though she hated to ask, maybe Uncle Orren would make them a small loan. Only a loan, she resolved, setting out to convince Grace of her plan.

When Serena peeped into Will's cabin, the old man was sleeping peacefully. Certain her mother was in the captain's cabin engaged in tearful reminiscence, the girl steeled herself and climbed to the texas. But as she reached for the door handle, it was yanked from her grasp and Nathan Trent stood before her. He did not see her right away. His hat in his hand, he looked over his shoulder into the room.

"What are you doing here?" Serena demanded in surprise. She had not seen him come aboard.

"Well, good afternoon." He smiled when he saw her. Stepping back to admit her, he reached over her head to place his hat on the rack beside the door. "Won't you come in?"

"Yes, Serena, come in," Grace called from inside.

The girl entered warily. What did Nathan Trent want on the *Sprite?* With inappropriate glee, she thought he would be disappointed if he had come for the return of his one thousand dollars.

He must not have asked Grace for the money, however, for she showed no sign of distress as she sat behind Henry's big desk. Gesturing to an empty chair, the woman invited, "Sit down, dear."

Serena obeyed, apprehensive when Nathan closed the door and moved to sit on the other vacant chair in front of the desk. He lounged, his long legs crossed at the ankle, and observed her. Her mother seemed to be watching, as well.

"We have some matters to discuss," Grace began with characteristic composure.

"We?"

"Yes, we. Though you may first explain to me, Serena Elizabeth, why you did not mention the agreement your father had made with Mr. Trent."

"I didn't tell her," Nathan was quick to absolve himself from blame when Serena turned an accusing gaze on him.

"A formal contract was never drawn up," she explained stiffly. "Mr. Trent was not really a partner."

"A letter of intent was written and he gave your father one thousand dollars," her mother pointed out.

"I told him we'd pay him back."

"And I told you," he retorted mildly, "I'd like to know where you expect to get the money."

"From hauling a cargo to St. Louis. I already told Lowell we'd do it."

"Even I know that will not enable us to repay the entire thousand dollars," Grace interjected. "Fortunately it is not necessary."

"We must pay him back. Surely you don't intend to accept charity from Mr. Trent." Serena's tone dripped venom.

"Not at all. Nor do I intend to be responsible for breach of contract. I've made him an equal partner in the *River Sprite*."

"What?" The girl jumped to her feet, quivering with indignation. "You made this jackass an equal partner in our boat?"

"Serena!"

"A jackass or worse." She rounded on the man furiously. "What kind of man threatens a widow with a lawsuit?"

"That is quite enough," Grace cut in. "Mr. Trent made no threats. In fact, I asked him to become my partner."

"How could you ask him?" Serena yelled. "You don't know him. Just look at him. He's a gambler—"

"He is, indeed, to invest in Caswell & Company," the woman concurred. "However, he has agreed to abandon professional gambling in favor of our partnership."

"Mother, please, why can't we go on alone?" Serena argued desperately. "We can manage."

"I fear that is not so," Grace disagreed softly. "We need Mr. Trent and we need each other. We must support ourselves and we must stay together as a family. Therefore, Dory, Hank and I will move onto the *River Sprite* tomorrow."

"Tomorrow?" Serena seemed numbed by the additional news.

"I am sorry to tell you so precipitously, dear," Grace said with a sigh, "but we're already packed and ready."

"What about River's Rest?"

"Orren has convinced me to rent it out for a while."

Their blue eyes locked, both women seemed to have forgotten Nathan was present.

"What about Dory and Hank? They must go to school."

"They will be fine. I will teach them once summer is over. I'm quite qualified to do so," Grace interjected, overcoming her daughter's objections. "I believe we will manage quite nicely."

"Oh, yes, quite nicely." Serena laughed mirthlessly. Going to the window, she stood looking out, her back to Grace and Nathan.

"Can't you see, dear?" her mother entreated. "I want what is best for all of us."

"I see," the girl answered bitterly, "that I have nothing to say in what becomes of the *Sprite*."

"That's not true," Nathan dissented, his deep voice gentle. "What you have to say is important, Serena. No one knows the *River Sprite* better than you, but I know business. Together we can make her profitable. Isn't that what you want?"

"I want to take care of my family," she said coldly. "It's what the cap'n asked and what I promised." Poised in the doorway, she looked back at the pair in the room. "And I can do it without any help from an interfering sharper."

"Damnation!" Expelling his breath in a puff, the man stared at the door that slammed behind her. "What have I gotten myself into?"

"Oh, Nathan, I am sorry," Grace murmured. "I truly thought she would be more accepting of my decision."

"Maybe she'll get used to the idea, as you say, Grace. I'll give it the six months we agreed upon, but if it doesn't work, I say we hire a real captain and I head for California."

"Are you sure you won't need more time?"

"What I'll need is determination and a thick hide—" Nathan ran his fingers through his hair in a harassed gesture "—because I think the battles have only just begun."

Out on deck, Serena was hailed by the first mate. "Miss Rena, there's a man below, looking for a berth as a deckhand. I thought you might like to see him—"

"Where is he?" She pulled herself from her stupor. They did need a hand or two and she would hire them. The *Sprite* was still a Caswell boat.

Levi pointed toward the dock. Muscular and good-looking, the fellow flashed a blinding smile as she joined him.

"Afternoon, ma'am," he greeted her, "My name is Fiske Patterson. Is the captain about?"

"I'm Serena Caswell."

"Surely you're not the captain," he protested playfully, "not a lady as lovely and delicate as you."

"Are you looking for a berth or not?"

Assured that he was, she questioned him about his experience and asked if he would be willing to serve under a female captain. When he answered in the affirmative, she hired him on the spot, because he was immediately available and the *Sprite* was scheduled to leave the next morning.

"Do you have any questions?" she asked as he hoisted his bag onto his shoulder.

"Well, miss, having never worked for a lady captain before, I wonder if there is any special service you require of your able-bodied crew members?"

"What exactly do you mean?" she asked icily.

Fiske's leering smile faded. "Nothing exactly, ma'am."

"Then report to Mr. Douglas, Mr. Patterson." Dismissing him, she turned and walked away toward town.

A resentful glower on his handsome face, the *Sprite*'s newest deckhand watched his employer disappear between the warehouses.

Serena found River's Rest empty, but Dory, too, had come to pay a sentimental call. Sitting in the swing that had been hers, she greeted her older sister forlornly, "What are you doing here, Rena?"

"I just came to look around," Serena mumbled, already wishing she had not.

"Mother told you then?" Dory asked glumly.

"She told me." Serena leaned back against the tree trunk and sighed gustily. "I still can't believe it."

"I know," Dory sniffled. "Papa built this house for Mother." Leaning her head against the rope, she began to cry. "I'm so unhappy. I don't want to go. Vicksburg is my home, but Mother won't let me stay, not even with Aunt Bonnie and Uncle Orren. She says the family must stay together . . . on that dirty old steamboat. What kind of home is that?"

Ordinarily Serena would have defended the boat, but today she simply said, "The *Sprite*'s been my home for a long time, Dory. It's not so bad."

"That's fine for you," the younger girl muttered sullenly. "You're getting what you want."

Serena shoved herself away from the tree and said sarcastically over her shoulder, "Yes ... my entire family underfoot while I try to work and a low-down, duplicitous gambler as a business partner."

"You mean you don't want us on the boat?" Dory dashed the tears from her eyes and followed.

"I just don't think it's ..."

"Seemly?"

"If you like."

"It's really not like Mother," the younger girl said when they walked toward the street. "She's always been so proper. Uncle Orren and Aunt Bonnie were horrified when they found out what she was planning. Everyone in town was. The only one who is happy is Hank. He wants to live on the boat."

"Where is Hank?"

"At Aunt Bonnie's. We've been staying there for the past week while we waited for you." Halting at the foot of the driveway, she asked, "Are you coming?"

Serena shook her head. "I'm headed back to the *Sprite*. I have to help Jamie and Charlie."

"With the engine?" Dory asked distastefully. "You'll never find a husband that way."

"I'm not looking for one."

"It's probably just as well. You won't meet anybody on a steamboat but river rats and scoundrels." Suddenly the girl looked as if she would cry again. "That's the worst part, Rena. We'll probably both end up being old maids."

Patting her sister's shoulder, Serena comforted her dubiously, "Don't cry, Pandora. Everything will be fine."

" 'Twas the crack of dawn when the dray brought them." Jamie gestured excitedly toward the boxes of parts stacked outside the engine room. "Trent must ha'e ordered them right after he left yesterday. One thing aboot yer mother's new partner, lass, when he says he'll do a thing, he does it."

Serena examined the unexpected bounty with mixed feelings. "Then we'll be ready to leave this afternoon?"

"More like tomorrow afternoon, unless ye'd like to lend a hand..." He trailed off, smiling when she hurried away to change her clothes.

When the girl returned, clad in stained trousers, she discovered Jamie and Charlie had taken the engine apart. The temperature in the sweltering engine room was not helped by the lantern, which burned to provide more light but, absorbed as she was in the intricacies of machinery, Serena scarcely noticed. She worked through the afternoon, unaware when the roustabouts moved the Caswells' possessions, including two rosebushes from River Rest's front yard, onto the boat.

Late that afternoon, Grace, crisp and immaculate, stood on deck outside the engine room, peering inside. A movement caught her eye and she made out two faces, dim blurs in the dark interior. "Good afternoon, Mr. McPherson, Mr. Flowers," she called. "Is my daughter in there?"

"Here I am." Crawling out from behind the crankshaft, Serena stepped into the light.

"Serena Elizabeth!" her mother gasped. "What are you wearing?"

"A pair of Roger's old trousers," the girl answered unconcernedly. Moving to the doorway, she turned her face appreciatively to the breeze. "I wear them when I work down here."

"Don't you have an old dress that would be more... suitable?"

"'Twould be dangerous, Mrs. Caswell." Mopping his face with an oily rag, Jamie also emerged into the fresh air. "A skirt would likely get tangled in the machinery, taking your bairn with it."

"I see," Grace muttered. "Is it really necessary for you to be here, Serena?"

"I help wherever I'm needed, Mother."

"Of course." The woman sighed in resignation. "Well, I wanted you to know we are here and settling in.

"Do you know when we'll be leaving, Mr. McPherson?" she asked the grizzled Scotsman.

"Weel, thanks to Rena here, we should be ready by morning."

Serena flashed Jamie a fond look. "Then I must tell Levi to post our rates on the dock with an eight-o'clock departure."

"I'll do it," Grace volunteered. "We all assist where we can." As she swept away, she called over her shoulder, "Dinner is at seven-thirty in the salon, dear. Please don't be late."

"Yes, Mother," Serena muttered, throwing a dire glare at Charlie as he rolled his eyes skyward in silent amusement.

At dusk a cabin boy appeared reluctantly to announce, "Miss Rena, your mother sent me to tell you there's hot water waiting in your cabin."

"Thank you, Simon. I'll be up as soon as I tie the striker to the stroke rod," she answered when Charlie sniggered behind her.

A few minutes later Serena stepped out on deck, as smudged and rumpled as she had been the first time she met Nathan on the ship. She groaned aloud to see him arriving, lock, stock and steamer trunk.

"I see McPherson got the parts," the elegant gambler called when he saw her sauntering toward him.

"Yes, thanks." Nodding toward his baggage, she asked, "Isn't that a lot to take on the trail? I thought you were joining a wagon train."

"I'm going to be a working partner aboard the *Sprite*. I guess we didn't get around to mentioning it this afternoon."

"I guess you didn't," she answered through tight lips.

"Where does a partner sleep around here?" he asked casually.

Serena smiled nastily. "I don't know, since the captain's cabin is taken."

"Most any place I can stow my gear will do. How about the forecastle?"

"That would hardly be fitting for an owner and you know it."

"Well, since we want to save the staterooms for the paying guests, why don't I room with Hank?"

"Hank doubles up with Uncle Will."

"What about the clerk? What's his name . . . Blake?"

"He shares a cabin with Jamie."

"Let's see, the clerk and the engineer share quarters. Hank's with Will, your mother with your sister. Who doubles up with you?"

Serena glared at him a long moment before beckoning a deckhand. "Luke, take Mr. Trent's trunk to the cabin next to mine. He should enjoy all the benefits of ownership . . . on the stern."

"Sure you don't want to share a cabin?" Nathan goaded as he followed her along the boiler deck. "We could flip a coin to see who has to take the top bunk."

"Despite the promise you made my mother, I suppose you'll always be a gambler, won't you, Mr. Trent?"

"I suppose." His grin was wickedly unabashed. "Would you like to bet on what would happen if you started being nice to me? I'd lay even money we'd both be happier."

"Oh, I hope you are happy, Mr. Trent," she cooed with an insincere smile, throwing open the door of the tiny cabin next to hers. "You'll love being right next door to the paddle wheel."

"Your gracious hospitality is matched only by your beauty and refinement, Miss Caswell," he murmured, tracing the dark smudges on her cheek with his fingers.

Drawing back as if burned, she darted into her own cabin. While he unpacked in his cramped cabin, Nathan could hear the sounds of her bath next door, innocently suggestive.

"I think a toast is in order," Grace proposed brightly when they had gathered around the captain's table. "Nathan, would you do the honors?"

Lifting his glass, the man surveyed his companions: Grace, slightly nervous despite her calm facade; Serena, her face scrubbed and wary; Dory, a pretty, younger version of her mother with sad, red-rimmed eyes; Hank, squirming with excitement; Roger, regarding him with guarded interest. Only Will was absent.

In a ringing voice, he pronounced, "Good fortune to Caswell & Trent and smooth sailing for the *River Sprite*."

"Smooth sailing for the *Sprite*," his partner echoed softly, her worried blue eyes resting on her elder daughter.

No business was discussed during dinner, but when they had finished, Grace announced, "Because we leave in the morning, we must discuss the running of the boat tonight. With the new partnership come new responsibilities and new ways of doing things. We hope to make the changes as easy as possible for everyone.

"First, since we no longer have a head steward, I shall oversee housekeeping and help Roger with the accounts when he needs me. I doubt that will be often." She smiled at the young man who beamed at her praise. "You are a great asset to the *Sprite*.

"Pandora, for the summer, you will assist with the domestic chores, especially when we have passengers aboard."

"I'm not a maid," Dory protested, tears springing to her eyes.

"We must all help," her mother admonished. "Hank, you will serve as cabin boy. Simon will train you."

"Hooray!" The boy bounced in his chair, the only happy Caswell sibling.

"Now, Serena." Grace regarded her anxiously. "It will be appreciated if you would continue as head pilot."

"But Uncle Will is head pilot."

"William and I have talked," Grace replied carefully. "His recovery will take time. He says you're doing a fine job in his absence. In fact, he says you are a...er..."

"A lightning pilot," Nathan supplied the term.

"Then who is to be captain?" Serena asked with dread.

"There will be two captains," Nathan answered before Grace could. Disregarding his partner's forbidding glance, he smiled at Serena. "What would the *River Sprite* be without a Captain

Caswell? But we thought, since you will be busy piloting the *Sprite,* I could deal with passengers and cargo. Together, we can keep the *Sprite* running smoothly. Don't you agree?"

Serena knew that what Nathan offered was an honorary title, that he would truly be the captain. But he was right. The past month had shown her she could not be both pilot and captain. As the assembled company waited breathlessly to see what her reaction would be, she took a deep breath and answered, "I think we can."

"Well, that's all for now," Grace blurted, obviously relieved that Serena had held her temper. "Let me remind you what your father would have said. We Caswells can do anything we set our minds to and we are going to make a success of the *River Sprite.*"

"Everything will work out all right, Serena. You'll see," Roger reassured her as they walked to their cabins after dinner. "Your mother is right. You need a man to represent Caswell & Trent...though I wish she had trusted me to do it," he added regretfully. "I could have learned to be a captain."

"I'm sure you could have, but what is done is done," Serena said woodenly. "Nathan Trent is the captain of the *River Sprite.*"

"Well, there is one good thing to come out of tonight." Roger halted suddenly. "If you're not really the captain, it's easier for me to do this." Leaning toward her, he brushed her lips tentatively with his.

Blinking in surprise, Serena backed away. She had known for some time how Roger felt about her, but she had not encouraged him. He was her friend. She should tell him she did not share his feelings, she realized, but as he gazed at her tenderly, she could not bear to hurt him.

"Good night," she whispered, and kissed his cheek. A dazed expression on his pleasant face, he watched her disappear into the darkness near the stern. Then, slowly, he went to his own cabin.

Stopping at the railing, Serena stared at the moon over the roofs of the waterfront warehouses and listened to the crickets

along the riverbank. With a start, she realized Nathan stood in
the shadows near the paddle box, one broad shoulder braced
against a strut as he looked out, as well. Uncomfortably, she
wondered how long he had been there and whether he had seen
her kiss Roger.

Though his eyes were shadowed, she knew he watched her
now and she was glad he could not see her blush in the moonlight. Her head high, she strolled past him. "Good night, Mr.
Trent."

Long after she had gone inside, Nathan remained on deck,
pondering what he had seen. Serena and Blake . . . he should
have expected it, but he had not. And he had not expected the
disappointment he felt so acutely.

Chapter Five

Though the sky was overcast and ominous, Serena was hopeful when she headed down to the main deck the next morning. Nathan Trent would soon change his mind about staying aboard, she told herself. After all, he was a rich man, a gambler, and unaccustomed to the hard work it took to be the captain of a steamboat.

"Morning, Miss Serena, don't you look fetching today." The new man she had hired paused in his duties to smile at her as she rounded the main deck, her braid swinging as she passed.

"Thank you, Mr. Patterson," she responded without slowing her pace. But outside the door of the galley, she faltered. From inside came laughter and a deep voice speaking French. Her optimism waned when she stepped inside.

Nathan sat at the table, chatting with Gustave and sipping coffee. Gone were the extravagantly ruffled shirt, the dandified frock coat and the resplendent brocade vest. Though impeccably tailored, his black broadcloth suit was discreet and serviceable. Under a striped waistcoat, his white linen shirt was plain. His dark green silk cravat was adorned by a simple golden stud rather than the gaudy diamond stickpin worn by gamblers. But he still looked unreasonably handsome, Serena thought in spite of herself.

Smiling when he saw her, he rose and pulled out a chair. "Good morning, slugabed."

"Aren't you cheerful for a man who opened the wrong trunk this morning?" she sniped as Gustave set her breakfast before her. "Whose clothes are those?"

"Don't you like them?" He made a show of inspecting his attire critically. "I thought they were more fitting for my new position of respectability."

"You wouldn't know respectability if it jumped out and bit you."

Unperturbed, he sat down and grinned at her. "A gentleman would ignore that remark and so will I."

Staring at him with ill-concealed impatience, she did not reply.

"You know, *ma petite*," he commented mockingly, "if a man is going to sit across the table from the same woman every morning, he likes for her to be pleasant as well as pretty."

She glared at him in earnest. She had no doubt how she looked...plain and practical Serena, wearing plain, practical clothes. She had always known she was no beauty, but it had never mattered before. Why did he have such an unsettling effect on her? Was it because one moonlit night he had made her feel beautiful?

"Just because I have to work with you, doesn't mean I have to like you," she retorted after a moment.

"First you drive me from my cabin, bellowing songs next door," he grumbled good-naturedly, "then you insult me."

She blushed predictably when she realized he must have heard her singing through the wall while she was dressing. She would know no peace...or privacy with him aboard the *River Sprite*.

"Come on," Nathan cajoled with an expectant grin, "give me a smile and start my day right."

Leaving her breakfast half-eaten, Serena got to her feet. "Save your charm for our poor, unsuspecting passengers. I already know about you."

"What do you know?"

"That you're a terrible ladies' man."

"Oh." His eyes, glinting in amusement, held hers as he rose.

"That's what people say," she said nervously. "Besides I've seen you in action—"

"Yes?" he smirked.

"With Viola Howard." Gustave was listening avidly and Serena wished she had never begun this conversation. "I have work to do," she blurted, and bolted from the galley.

Watching from the boiler deck later as Nathan greeted the arriving passengers, even Serena had to admit he had a way with people. The crew had taken to him from the moment Grace had introduced him, addressing him as Cap'n Trent while calling her Miss Rena as they always had.

But her eyes brightened impishly when the Bransons, a family with six children, five of them boys, poured from two carriages and surrounded the new captain, all talking at once. Nathan's maiden voyage might not be as disastrous as hers, she mused with perverse pleasure, but it would not be quiet.

"See here, young lady," an angry voice bellowed on the texas.

"What on earth?" In her cabin, Grace frowned toward the noise. Everything had been running smoothly when she had come up to fetch a needle and thread for a bachelor passenger.

Stepping out on deck, she saw Serena striding across the texas with a short, round officious-looking man on her heels.

"Maybe you didn't hear what I said," he shouted. "I told you I lent your father a good deal of money."

"And I told you, he paid back most of it, Mr. Hart," Serena tossed over her shoulder.

"I am still owed five hundred dollars, which I expect you to pay immediate—" His demand ended in a yelp when she whirled, nearly causing him to collide with her.

"I have a copy of the note," she retorted, her blue eyes snapping. "It says the next installment of the loan is due on the first of July and that is when I expect to pay it." Pivoting, she headed toward the pilothouse with Mr. Hart on her heels.

Standing at the foot of the ladder as she clambered up it, he blustered, "Since that note was signed by your deceased father, Miss Caswell, I should have received payment from his estate. I did not, so I am calling the loan. Now."

"I warn you, Hart," Serena yelled down at him, "you're in danger of being deceased yourself, if you don't get off the *Sprite!*" She appeared in the doorway, carrying a shotgun as long as she was tall and it was trained on him.

The man moved as if he would scale the ladder, halting when she pulled the hammer back. "You can't get away with killing me," he ranted up at her, his face reddening apoplectically.

"Maybe I can get away with wounding you." She seemed to be enjoying herself.

"How dare you threaten me, you little witch!"

"You threatened me first." Smiling sweetly, she motioned with the barrel of her gun. "Go on, get, you ring-tailed baboon. I don't really want to shoot you. Buckshot leaves such a messy corpse."

Hart retreated a step. "I'll have the sheriff on you."

"Then you'll both be picking shot out of your hides. Now get off before your next of kin has to claim your body."

Serena watched from the pilothouse as the protesting creditor disembarked. When she descended, she found Nathan waiting at the bottom of the ladder to assist her. Around him, the Branson brothers capered, thrilled by the scene they had just witnessed.

"Don't get in the lady's way, boys," the man ordered jokingly. "The way to certain ruin lies there."

With peals of boyish laughter, the lads retreated a safe distance away, watching as he lifted her easily from the ladder and set her down, his hands lingering at her waist.

"Thank you," she said, stepping back, "but I'm perfectly capable of coming and going from the pilothouse without your help, Mr. Trent."

"Captain Trent," he corrected softly, "and I just want you to know how glad I am that we're on the same side now."

With a scowl for his grin, she snapped, "I wouldn't be so sure of it, Captain." As she stalked to Will's cabin, she did not see her mother, staring after her, aghast.

Serena found her uncle propped up in bed, Catastrophe curled in his lap, as he enjoyed Hank's vivid and voluble description of the clash between his sister and Mr. Hart. Noting her chagrin with amusement, Will sent the boy on an errand.

"What's the problem, partner?" he asked when Hank had gone.

"Everything," she confessed glumly. "I'm so nervous, having the whole family aboard. I'll probably plow the *Sprite* right through the harbor master's office."

"Naw. You're the pilot. They're only the passengers."

"And Nathan Trent is the captain. Did you know that?"

"Grace told me and she told me her reasons."

"You mean she has a reason besides being taken in by that—"

"Listen to me, Serena," the elderly pilot commanded, taking her hands in his. "This boat needs a pilot *and* a captain. Much as you'd like to, you can't do everything. You've got to consider what's best for the *Sprite*."

"And you think Nathan Trent is best?"

"I think the two of you together can be the best."

"Uncle Will." She frowned at him in exasperation. "Of all the addlepated ideas—"

"Glad to see you're feelin' better, gal." Grinning, he released her hands and pulled the cover up over his skinny chest. "Now take the *Sprite* out and let an old man rest."

Her mood improved, Serena paused on deck to observe the sky. Though it had been dark to the south all morning and dark-bottomed clouds loomed on the horizon, she could see no reason to postpone departure. Whistling in a most unladylike manner, she went down to tell Jamie to start building steam.

"Yoo-hoo, Serena!" Viola Howard minced up the gangplank, the curls around her face bobbing on the rising wind. Clad in pink with ruching and flounces, she was a spot of color against the gray sky.

"Welcome aboard, Viola," she greeted her without enthusiasm.

"How are you, sugar? I was so sorry to hear about your father. You do look nice, wearin' a dress and all, instead of those horrible trousers," Viola flitted from subject to subject. "You know my aunt, Miss Sophie Duffy, don't you? We're just on our way to visit my sister in Memphis."

All the way to Memphis... Serena nearly groaned aloud. The girl seemed to spend her life visiting relatives up and down the Mississippi. Collecting herself, she turned to Viola's pale, pinch-faced kinswoman. "Welcome to the *River Sprite*, Miss Duffy."

"Thank you." Sophie eyed Serena's unfashionable black gown and the single braid looped over her shoulder disapprovingly.

"Serena, you're just the one who can tell me what I want to know," Viola gushed. "I thought I'd ask that handsome Nathan Trent myself, but he doesn't seem to be here."

"He was up on the texas the last time I saw him."

"Is it true then . . . that he owns this big old boat now?"

"He's a partner," Serena answered curtly.

"Just a partner." Viola sighed. "That is what he told my daddy when he stayed with us for a week last month, but I had hoped . . ."

"Please pardon me, ladies." Serena attempted to be about her business, but the other girl gripped her arm.

"We saw you with that Mr. Hart from the dock," Viola confided. "Weren't you afraid that old gun would go off and hurt somebody?"

"No." Serena disengaged herself. "I know how to shoot it."

"Is there anything you can't do, Serena Caswell? Shootin' guns, workin' on steamboats. I fancy you'll be smokin' cigars or chewin' tobacco next." Laughing merrily as she and her aunt ascended the stairs to the boiler deck, Viola paused to warn, "You best be careful, sugar. Men don't like girls who are too smart or too . . . unrestrained, you know."

Mildly annoyed, Serena went to the engine room. When she emerged, she spied Nathan lurking in steerage near the stern.

"Is it safe to come out?" he asked, looking around.

"Who'd believe it?" Serena laughed when he drew her behind a stack of cotton bales. "The lady-killer hiding from a lady?"

"That particular lady is looking for a husband," Nathan retorted.

"She's looking for you. I sent her up to the texas. I didn't think you'd mind. After all, didn't you visit her last month?"

"I visited Viola's father last month," he corrected. "He's one of the biggest planters in the Delta and I convinced him to ship his cotton on the *Sprite*."

"And it took you a whole week?" she asked before she thought.

"Serena Caswell, I believe you're jealous." Nathan grinned roguishly. "It's all right," he assured her before she could deny it. "I don't mind. In fact, I'm rather pleased."

"I am not jealous," she insisted, wishing she could wipe the smug expression from his face.

"Not even a little?" he coaxed, taking her chin in his big hand and turning her face so she was forced to look at him. "Tell the truth now, Serena, don't you care at all for me?"

"N-no." Her breath caught in her throat as his dark eyes held hers.

"The truth," he demanded softly, his curving lips close to hers.

All at once, Serena felt a flash of anger at his playful confidence. She had told him to save his charm for the passengers, but the riverboat Romeo thought every female should swoon in his presence. Not this female!

"The truth is," she informed him coldly, yanking her chin from his hand, "I'd prefer the company of some billy goats to yours."

As she fled toward the bow, Nathan wondered ruefully if she knew how close he had come to kissing her again.

In the short time that he had known her, he had enjoyed their lively clashes and verbal sparring. He delighted in her blushes, which told more than her stinging retorts, and found her spirit refreshing and alluring. But one thing was plain if he was to work in tandem with Serena Caswell, he was going to have exercise a good deal of self-control.

* * *

Despite her earlier fears, Serena did not run the *Sprite* into the harbor master's office. Her family lined the railings with the passengers as she backed the great steamboat from the dock with the whistle blowing and the flag fluttering on the jack staff.

The rumbling vibration of the idling engines could be felt on every deck when the boat straightened, its bow pointed upriver. Then, with a groan and a jolt, the wheel began to rotate, the paddles cutting into the water.

The crew, assembled at the capstan, sang and waved to the crowd on the levee. At an order from the chief fireman, pine pitch was tossed into the furnaces and black smoke billowed into the gray sky from the smokestacks. On the boiler deck, the Branson children leaned far over the railings and cheered to be underway.

By late afternoon, a squall hit with fierce gusts whipping up whitecaps in the river. When the first huge raindrops peppered the decks, the *Sprite* was already nosed up against the bank and the deckhands were securing the lines. Because it was not safe to hold their steam, Serena ordered it released, knowing an hour or more would be lost building it again.

The downpour turned into a torrent and she hurried to close the windows around her. While the wind lashed the saplings ashore, she wondered what to do about Nathan. How was she to work with the man when she didn't like him...or the way he made her feel?

Though clouds still roiled overhead, the rain stopped as suddenly as it had started. Deciding to heed her rumbling stomach before the next shower began, Serena went down to the salon in search of a pastry and a cup of coffee.

Opening the door to a clap of thunder that seemed to rock the boat, she was borne into the salon on a gust of wind. Nathan sat at a table in the center of the room with three other men while all five Branson boys, aligned like stair steps, jockeyed for position at his elbows. In his deft, graceful hands, the *Sprite's* new captain held a deck of cards, shuffling rapidly, effortlessly performing sleights of hand. Looking up as the girl passed, he smiled and winked, seemingly unconcerned by her disapproving frown.

When she had gotten her coffee from the urn in the corner, she paused at Nathan's table to request, "May I have a word with you, please, before the next hand?"

Excusing himself politely, he shoved the cards into his pocket and followed her to a table near the rain-washed windows.

"What in the name of blue-eyed Lucifer are you doing?" she whispered hotly before he was even seated. She hoped no one could overhear their confrontation, but she need not have worried. The Branson boys had instituted a game of tag that took them, pounding, from one end of the long, narrow salon to the other.

"You mean this?" A challenging glint in his eyes, he pulled the cards from his pocket and fanned them expertly in one hand.

"Did you or did you not promise my mother you would stop gambling?"

"I did."

"Then why, on the very first day out, do I find you at the gaming table?"

"Is that what that is?" He glanced with contrived amazement at the place he had vacated. "I thought it was a table like any other in the salon."

When he turned back to Serena, Nathan's expression was neither incredulous nor amused. "Now that you have set me straight on my responsibilities, Miss Caswell, let me set you straight on a couple of things. First, what I was doing, was showing the boys a few card tricks to keep them occupied . . . and quiet." He grimaced when his words were accented by a thud and a wail. "Their being cooped up because of the rain has been hard on everybody.

"Second," he went on, "I would appreciate it in the future, if you did not call me away from the passengers in such a high-handed fashion. It's bad for morale. Mine," he concluded, getting to his feet.

"I'll attempt to keep our differences private, Captain Trent,"
Serena replied acidly, unwilling to allow him the last word.
"But be assured, I will be watching you very closely."

"And I, you, Miss Caswell," he said with a wry smile, "with
great pleasure. Now if you will excuse me, I'll go see to my responsibilities."

Serena glared at his broad back as he left the salon. The rain
had stopped and Mrs. Branson was herding her brood out onto
the wet deck where raindrops dripped from the *Sprite*'s gin-
gerbread trim. The afternoon seemed to glisten as the sun broke
through the clouds and, on the deck below, Chanticleer crowed
lustily.

"Judas Priest," Serena muttered at the sound of another
loud thump. "I told you to stop that," she yelled through the
window, scowling as giggles drifted up to the pilothouse. On the
texas, the Branson brothers huddled, daring one another to
climb the ladder and bang on the wheelhouse door before skit-
tering away.

Muttering darkly, she maneuvered the *River Sprite* through
a crossover, careful to steer clear of a keelboat approaching
from upriver. Without warning, the broadhorn veered directly
into the steamboat's path.

"What the devil?" Yanking the bell to the engine room, she
shouted, "Slow engines."

Just as it had earlier that afternoon, steam billowed from the
smokestacks. The *River Sprite* seemed to dance sideways along
the water in its efforts not to crush the lesser vessel, the paddle
wheel turning slowly, biting into the current so the boat would
not be carried downstream. On the river below, the raftsmen
hauled at their oars, edging the keelboat to fit snugly against
the *Sprite*'s larboard bow.

"What do you think you're doing, you slack-jawed spawn of
a mule?" Down on the main deck, Nathan could hear Serena
yelling. "We nearly steamed over you."

Apparently unconcerned about his craft's close call, the
keelboat captain scratched his balding pate and called to his

men, "They's a gal up in the wheelhouse. Ain't that some-thin'?"

He hollered up to the steamboat, "We been five weeks comin' from Indiana, cut off from the world. Ain't spoke to a soul. Throw us a paper, boys, so's we know what's goin' on."

"Throw them a paper, Roger," Serena called, never taking her glowering stare from the bobbing vessel below. "Then you get that soggy bundle of logs out of the way before our wheel breaks you into kindling wood," she yelled at the keelboat captain.

From the engine room door, Jamie remarked to Nathan, "Our lass is turning into a lightning pilot. 'Twas a fine stop she made."

"Sure was," Nathan agreed, turning to look at the engi-neer.

A streak of oil ran across the Scotsman's forehead and dis-appeared under the grimy tam he wore, but his smile was proud. "Those rascals down there dinna know how lucky they are."

As Jamie joined Nathan at the rail, a newspaper, tightly bound, plummeted past them and hit the keelboat's deck with a solid thud. Leaning out over the rail, Nathan could see Roger on the deck above, outlined against the crimson, mottled sky. Will stood beside him, shaky and out of bed without his sister-in-law's knowledge.

"Consarn it, this paper's a week old," the keelboat captain yelled up at Serena.

"Is that all you can say, you plug-ugly, ungrateful stepchild of calamity?" Will bawled before he was swooped up by Grace and returned to his cabin.

On the deck below, Nathan laughed and shook his head. "What a family the Caswells are."

"Aye, but after a time, ye get used to them. Then mayhap ye should worra," the engineer warned with a chuckle, disap-pearing into his domain.

Down at the waterline, the raftsmen braced their oars against the *River Sprite*'s hull and shoved away from the steamboat. As the current carried the broadhorn beyond the paddle wheel, the *River Sprite* slowly resumed its trip upriver.

No sooner were they underway again than Serena heard her mother's voice below. "No, you may not go up to the wheelhouse. Run along now to your mother," Grace dismissed the Branson lads firmly, before climbing cautiously to the wheelhouse.

"May I come in?" she asked, poised in the doorway.

"Of course." Serena smiled, watching her compress her voluminous skirt enough to pass through the narrow doorway.

"Now I see why you do not wear hoops," the woman admitted. "I never understood before."

"Thank you for getting rid of the five horsemen of the apocalypse for me, Mother."

"There are only four horsemen, dear."

"Not anymore." The girl grinned.

Standing beside her daughter at the wheel, Grace breathed in delight, "Look at that sunset."

"Red sky at night, sailor's delight. It is beautiful, isn't it? Sometimes I get so busy I forget to notice."

As she sat down on the bench, her mother was silent, then she said, "Serena, you are probably wondering why I hazarded the climb to the pilothouse."

"Yes?" Serena responded politely though she continued to watch the river.

"I really must speak to you about your language."

"My language?" Serena whipped her head around to stare at her in disbelief. "Hell's bells, Mother, that keelboat swerved right into my path. We could have killed everyone on it and sunk the *Sprite* to boot. And you're worried about my language?"

Grace winced. "Having just dealt with William, I have no doubt where you get your vocabulary, but I have attempted to bring you up to be a lady, Serena—"

"Being in the wheelhouse has nothing to do with being a lady." Keeping her face turned toward the river, the girl attempted to control her temper. "I'm the pilot, Mother, responsible for the lives of everyone on this boat. And that son of a—"

"It's not just this afternoon's occurrence which concerns me," Grace cut her off. "It is also your exchange this morning with Mr. Hart."

"The black-hearted, chicken-livered—"

"That is quite enough name-calling, my girl," her mother enjoined. "I realize you perform a man's job, Serena Elizabeth, but you are a well-bred young lady and I expect you to behave as one. Will you try...especially when Dory or Hank are present?"

"I'll try," Serena choked, swallowing her anger.

"Then all will be well." As she prepared to depart, Grace patted her daughter's rigid shoulder. "I'll see you at dinner."

"I won't be there."

"Why ever not?"

"Because if we are to keep to any kind of schedule, we won't be able to tie up for the night until late," Serena explained. "Without Uncle Will to relieve me, I have to get the boat as far as I can before I tire out."

"Surely we can stop long enough for you to eat dinner."

"That's not the way a steamboat operates, Mother. I thought we were going to run the *Sprite* as a business."

For a moment, the woman looked as if she would argue, then she sighed. "I suppose you are right. I will send a tray up, but I do hope you'll soon be able to eat dinner with the family."

Watching her leave, Serena did not know whether to laugh or cry. Her mother had much to learn about the operation of steamboat. There would be no regular meals and very little rest for Serena until Will improved enough to resume his duties.

She hoped it would be soon. Her legs were tired from long hours of standing, her shoulders ached from guiding the big boat. But worse was the weariness she felt when she thought of the changes in her life.

"Here I am, with a midnight supper," Roger announced, climbing up to the wheelhouse. Secured for the night, the *Sprite* bobbed gently against the bank.

"It's just as I thought." Frowning, he lifted the napkin from a tray on the bench. "You didn't touch the food your mother sent up. And now it's stone cold."

"I don't have much experience steering and devouring a four-course meal at the same time," Serena retorted. Examining the congealed food dubiously, she muttered, "Though it seems I'd better learn. By the time I get off these days, the galley is closed."

"Not to the resourceful." With a flourish, Roger produced a cold turkey leg and a dinner roll. "And—" he held out a badly misshapen fried pie "—peach, your favorite, I believe."

"Oh, thank you, Roger!" Sinking down onto one end of the bench, the girl attacked the drumstick gratefully. "I was starving."

When she had finished eating, he suggested kindly, "Come on, I'll walk you to your cabin."

Most of the passengers were in bed or lingering in the salon and the night was quiet as the couple walked to the stern. Washed by moonlight, they halted near the still paddle wheel and listened to the crickets and the croaker frogs along the riverbank.

Serena leaned against one of the tall railing posts and closed her eyes. It had been a very long, eventful day.

"You must be tired," Roger murmured beside her.

"I am," she replied without opening her eyes.

"You should get some rest. I worry about you, Rena."

"Clerks worry about everything." She smiled, her eyes still closed. "That's their job."

"You wouldn't tease me, if you knew how I feel about you," he said earnestly, leaning close.

Her eyes flew open and she found herself looking directly into his hopeful hazel eyes. "Roger, you mustn't—" she began gently.

"I mustn't keep you out here on deck when you're so tired," he said in a rush as if he did not want to hear what she would say. "That's certainly no way to show you I love you."

"Roger—" she tried again, but was thwarted when he kissed her cheek tenderly.

"Get some sleep," he whispered. "I'll see you in the morning."

Serena remained on deck after he had gone, trying to sort out her thoughts. Too much had happened today and she was very tired. Shaking her head as if to clear it, she turned to go to her cabin.

"A penny for your thoughts."

Startled, she whirled and sought the source of the deep voice. It took a moment to make out Nathan sitting in her chair, tilted on its back legs against the shadowy wall.

"What are you doing there?" she demanded indignantly. "Are you spying on me?"

"I wasn't spying." He set the chair down on all four legs and rose, his big bulk black against the night. "I was waiting for you and dozed off. When I awoke, Blake was in the middle of his impassioned declaration of love. I could hardly interrupt."

"Don't make fun of him," Serena snapped, irked by his sarcasm.

"I'm sorry. I wanted to talk to you. That's why I waited. Will you sit down for a moment?" Without waiting for an answer, he moved the chair out of the shadows and directed her to it, one big hand resting lightly against the small of her back.

"What did you want to talk about?" she asked when she was seated, the moonlight silvering her hair. She looked up at the man who had positioned himself against the rail, but, with the full moon behind him, she could not see his face.

"About this afternoon."

With a groan, she started to rise. "Did you want to chastise me some more for what I said in the salon or did you wish to lecture me about the treatment of keelboat captains?"

A hand on her shoulder, he pressed her gently back onto her chair. "I'm willing to forget our little disagreement in the salon, if you are."

"I'm willing," she conceded, unexpectedly relieved.

"Good." Nathan slouched against a strut, watching her. "I wanted to tell you I was pretty impressed by the way you handled the *Sprite* when that broadhorn cut into your path."

"Thank you." She relaxed somewhat.

"Why would I lecture you?" he asked in puzzlement.

"I thought you might've taken exception to what I said, too."

"Not me." He smiled, his teeth white in his shadowy face. "I'm amazed by your command of the language. Not every woman calls me a cross-eyed, lop-eared son of a monkey so soon after our first meeting. She usually waits a week or two."

Serena laughed in spite of herself. "You're doing it again."

"Doing what?"

"Repeating the terrible things I've said to you."

"As I told you that day in the wheelhouse," Nathan murmured. "I keep waiting for you to say kind things."

"I haven't been very nice to you," she acknowledged in a low voice, staring down at her hands clasped in her lap.

He squatted on the deck next to her, steadying himself with a hand on the back of her chair. Nearly at eye level with her, he was so close that she could smell the scent of bay rum on his skin and feel his warmth, but he made no attempt to touch her.

"I think I understand some of what you've been going through, Serena. I know the past month has been difficult for you...your father's death, trying to keep the *River Sprite* running, having your family aboard. You've been very strong, but you must feel like I'm the last straw."

"It's not just you," she murmured, still unwilling to lift her gaze to his. "It's the idea of having a partner at all. I grew up on the *River Sprite*, feeling that she was almost as much mine as she was Papa's. She's my home. She's my family's hope. If we lose her, I can't take care of the others."

"You mean your mother and your sister and brother?"

"And Uncle Will."

"That's a pretty tall order all by yourself," he said softly, wishing he dared take her in his arms to comfort her, knowing what her reaction would be if he tried.

"I promised the cap'n."

"Serena, look at me," the man commanded gently. When she complied, he told her sincerely, "No matter what you think of me...as a partner or a man...I want you to know that I don't want to take the *Sprite* from you. I never wanted to take her."

"Then why are you here, Nathan?" She did not seem to realize she had just used his given name for the first time. "Why did you decide to become my father's partner in the first place?"

Frowning thoughtfully, he rose and began to pace the tiny space. "I undertook the partnership as an investment and a challenge, at first," he answered at last. "Then I realized I had found a place to settle, if only for a while.

"I've been on the move for four years without much purpose. When I saw the *Sprite* in New Orleans . . . I can't explain it." He gestured helplessly. "It was as if I were coming home and that was a good feeling. You see, I hadn't felt good . . . I hadn't felt much of anything for a long time."

He stopped pacing. "Maybe emotions are not the best reasons for making decisions," he muttered, as if he had revealed too much, "but this time, they were all I had."

"I think I understand, too," Serena said quietly. "But having a partner aboard is going to take some getting used to."

"I'm getting used to it already. And I suspect I could come to like it." Taking her hand, he pulled her to her feet and led her to her cabin door. "Can we declare a truce between us?"

"We must." She smiled wryly. "I'm too tired to fight with you and pilot this boat, too."

"Good night then, partner," he murmured, shaking the hand he held. "Sleep well."

Tossing and turning on her narrow bunk that night, Serena wondered why Nathan had not tried to kiss her again . . . and why she should care that he had not.

Chapter Six

Steering with practiced proficiency, Serena played tag with the afternoon sun as the river switched back and forth. She was glad to be traversing an easy stretch of the river, for she was tired. Stop and start, build steam only to release it. It was what the *River Sprite* had done all day. It seemed they were barely underway before they were hailed again from shore.

Looking out over the texas, she saw Nathan emerging from the clerk's office. Since they had left Vicksburg, her days had been filled with glimpses of him as he supervised the crew or roamed the boat, greeting passengers with a smile and a tip of the planter's hat he wore.

He was working hard, harder than she had thought possible, performing unfamiliar tasks willingly, if not expertly. He was unfailingly amiable and got along well with his newfound colleagues. Grace relied heavily upon him, Roger respected him somewhat grudgingly, and the crew obeyed him without question.

Everyone loved the new captain but her, Serena brooded. She no longer believed she hated him, but, despite the truce they had declared three nights before, she still was not at ease with him. For his part, Nathan seemed satisfied with their tentative alliance, but she noticed he avoided being alone with her. Perhaps he thought it was the only way to keep the peace.

Out on the texas, Hank hurried to join Nathan. He idolized the big man and Serena had to admit his loyalty was not misplaced. Nathan had been very kind to the boy who had just lost his father.

Their friendship had begun in earnest two days before when the *Sprite* stopped in response to a farmer's signal. While the boat was stationary, Hank had found a deserted section of deck and played with his top. He set it spinning a score of times, improving his aim and his reach every throw. Just as he placed it quite skillfully on the bow, the *Sprite* had swayed on the wake of a passing boat. The top had hovered for an instant on the very edge of the deck, then disappeared overboard into the murky water.

Giving a cry, the boy had scrambled to the bow, looking as if he would jump in after his treasure. Suddenly a big hand had gripped his shoulder and Nathan advised, "Don't do it, son. The currents are deadly."

"But my father gave me that top for my birthday." Hank had been near tears.

"I'm sorry about that, but if you jump in after it, we'll lose you too. I wouldn't want that to happen to one of my best men."

"Me?" the lad sniffled.

"Yes, you." Nathan had smiled. "Don't ever jump in the river after anything. And that's an order."

"Yes, sir," Hank mumbled, trudging away.

"Hank," the captain called after him, "take some lemonade up to the wheelhouse, will you?"

"You want me to be the texas tender?"

"Just for this afternoon," Nathan had answered cautiously. "Your mother assigns duties. She'll tell you when she wants you to tend it again."

"Aye-aye, Cap'n."

A short time later, Hank had come to the pilothouse, his attention focused on scaling the ladder without spilling the pitcher he balanced on a tray. While Serena sipped lemonade, he had told her about his new friend and hopped around. When he became too rambunctious for the small space, she had put him out.

And probably taught him one or two choice phrases, she thought guiltily as she watched the man and boy on the texas. They sat on a bench, hunched over whatever Nathan held in his hand. Earnestly explaining, he hefted it in his hand, then swung it.

"Just what we need," Serena muttered crossly, "a sling."

"You won't get a real chance to test it till we're stopped, but I brought a couple of rocks to show you the principle," Nathan was saying as he led the boy to the rail. Overlooking the wide expanse of the Mississippi, he placed a rock in the sling and began to spin it, raising it above his head. When he released one of the straps, the rock flew far out into the river and Hank cheered.

"Now you try it," he coached the boy. "Spin it . . . nice and smooth. Don't let go until you're in a forward swing."

Hank followed his instructions clumsily. When he released the strap, a crash and the tinkling of broken glass came from behind them.

"Damnation." Nathan flinched. "We're in trouble now."

"You rude, rambunctious fugitives from Hades, Satan won't have you!" Serena leaned from the wheelhouse to shout at them.

"I'm sorry, Rena." Her brother gazed back at her, stricken.

"You might have broken the skylight over the salon. Then where would we be?" she scolded. "We certainly can't afford a new one."

"The rock just got away," Hank defended himself.

"I know it got away. It passed within inches of my head. You could have killed me deader than a doornail."

"I don't think you would have been killed," Nathan called up, grinning, "though you might have been knocked unconscious. Either way, it would be quieter now."

Serena's jaw dropped, but amusement flickered in her eyes. "Nathan Trent," she yelled, "you're a hazard to our paying customers and anyone else who happens by."

"Stop," he cautioned, laughing. "If Hank and I didn't brain anyone with a rock, don't you deafen them with your caterwauling."

To her brother's utter amazement, Serena began to laugh. "Come on," he urged, tugging Nathan toward the wheelhouse. "Let's go say we're sorry while she's in a good mood."

At the top of the ladder, the boy poised, the picture of contrition. "We're sorry, Rena. Nate was just showing me how to use the sling he gave me. Can I come in and show you?"

"May I," Serena corrected, smiling. "Do you promise not to bounce around?"

"I do, on my honor," Hank vowed solemnly.

"I do, too." Nathan winked at her over the lad's shoulder. "On my honor... such as it is."

She laughed and shook her head. "Come in."

"Look, Nate says it's the next best thing to a shiny red top. Isn't it a beauty?" Hank proudly presented his new treasure.

"Pretty as a summer sunrise." Serena examined the sling before throwing a quizzical look at the man who had taken his favorite place, lounging in the open doorway, his shoulder against the jamb.

"I have to go show Uncle Will," the boy said eagerly. "Did you know he walked all the way to the salon for breakfast and is sitting on deck right now?"

"No, but you can tell him I'm glad he finally moved his lazy bones from his bed," Serena teased as Nathan shifted to let him exit. When her brother had gone, she said seriously, "It was very kind of you to give Hank a gift."

"I wanted to do it."

Her eyes on the river, Serena was aware that he watched her. "Looks like a sawyer ahead," she said, glad for a diversion. Signaling the engine room to reduce speed, she maneuvered around the obstacle. The submerged tree bobbed below the surface, barely visible. Buffeted by the Mississippi's tumultuous current, it endured to tear the bottom out of a passing steamboat.

"You make steering look easy," the man complimented her when they were past it. "I know it's not."

"It's not hard if you learn to read the water." She shrugged self-consciously. "I'm glad you came up when you did."

"So am I," he murmured lazily, crossing his arms on his chest.

"I need to talk to you."

"My pleasure, I'm sure."

"Our truce does not give you the right to try to charm me."

"Then I won't," he acquiesced with a charming grin. "What do you want to talk about?"

"We need to wood up. All the starting and stopping we've been doing has eaten up our fuel."

"Is there a wood yard along this stretch?" he asked, pushing himself erect.

"Peter Shadwell gave us permission to chop trees in a section he's hoping to clear, anytime we want. We should reach his place in the next twenty minutes or so."

"Just tell me when," the new captain requested, scuttling down the ladder to organize the deckhands and the male passengers who exchanged labor for transport in steerage.

On Serena's signal, Nathan rang the big brass bell on the texas three times, giving the signal to land. At once, the paddle wheeler slowed, steam was released through the gauge cocks and the *River Sprite* crept toward shore.

Wooding up was hard work, but the air was festive as the crew and the steerage passengers set to work in a small clearing. The first-class passengers watched from the boiler deck as Nathan divided the men into crews. While some felled trees, others stripped the branches from the trunk and sawed the timber into manageable lengths. Still others kept up a steady parade, hauling the wood to huge bins outside the *Sprite*'s boiler room.

On the bench outside the galley, Serena could hear Grace and the kitchen staff as they prepared a picnic supper. When she saw Nathan and a couple of crewmen return to the boat, she joined the captain on the bow.

"We need some illumination," he explained when he saw her. "It'll be dark soon."

"How is the work progressing?"

"It's taking longer than I anticipated, but I think we've hit our stride," he answered, watching the hands prepare a cresset for lighting. "Levi is as good a logger as he is a first mate."

Her attention drawn by a youthful, frustrated scream at the top of the stairs, Serena looked up to see Mrs. Branson gathering up her smallest son. "I think that poor woman may be the hardest working person here tonight," she said with a chuckle. "She has her hands full, keeping those boys on the boat."

"She looks exhausted." Nathan grinned before adding seriously, "But so do you. The circles under your eyes are almost as dark as your dress."

"Thank you, I'm sure," the girl retorted, stung by his unexpected and accurate observation.

With a sideways glance at her, he commented casually, "I think we'll stay here for the night."

"I think not," she dissented. "As pilot, I'm responsible for getting the *Sprite* to port, as close to schedule as possible."

"You're also responsible for the safety of the passengers."

"What does that have to do with whether we spend the night tied to the bank?"

"When was the last time you got more than five or six hours of sleep?" Nathan met her question with a question. "I've been worried about you since before we left Vicksburg and tonight you're going to get some rest."

"The captain cannot give orders to the pilot."

"The owner can. Both owners can," he appended rapidly when she opened her mouth to object. "Should we bring your mother into this dispute?"

Before the irate girl could respond, a man on horseback emerged from the woods and hailed the boat, "Hello, *River Sprite!*"

Turning her back on Nathan deliberately, Serena waved and shouted, "Hello, Pete."

"Who is that?" Nathan asked behind her.

"Our benefactor," she answered coldly, walking down the gangplank to meet the new arrival.

"My overseer just told me y'all were here," Peter Shadwell called as he dismounted, "or I would have ridden over earlier." Taking Serena's hand in his, he added solicitously, "Captain of a steamboat through here last week told me about your father, Rena. I was mighty sorry to hear."

"Thank you, Pete." Conscious that Nathan had followed and now stood at her side, the girl made perfunctory introductions. Then she dragged Pete up the gangplank to visit the rest of the Caswell clan.

As Nathan supervised the wooding up, Hank was at his side, steadfast and helpful, but mindful not to interrupt the captain's concentration. But Nathan could not keep his mind on the labor. His eyes strayed all too frequently to the boiler deck where Serena and the young planter stood in the lamplight, visiting with Will.

And he had felt sorry for her because she looked tired, the captain brooded. She certainly seemed lively enough now. Caught unaware, he winced when a familiar feminine voice rang out from the head of the gangplank.

"Have I the captain's permission to come ashore? You know you have to give it," Viola called coyly, oblivious to the string of roustabouts behind her who nearly collided in their efforts to sidestep her. "Dinner is to be served down there."

"Do come down." Nathan plastered a smile onto his face.

When she joined him on the bank, Viola received a look of pure dislike from Hank, who refused to be chased away from his hero. Flirtatiously she laid a hand on Nathan's arm and giggled. "You don't mind if I hold on? I've been on that boat so long, I could swear the ground was rockin'."

"Perhaps it would be better if you sat down." Freeing his arm, he spread his handkerchief over a tree stump and gestured grandly. "Your chair, my lady."

With a dubious glance, Viola sat down and spread her skirt becomingly. The young men admiring her from the steamboat seemed to enjoy the effect, but Nathan was too busy even to notice. Opening her fan, she plied it industriously. "It is not even cool in the evenin'," she complained. "It's uncommonly hot this summer, don't you agree, Captain?"

"Indeed," he answered distractedly, his eyes on the *Sprite.*

Following the direction of his gaze, she asked, "Who is that good-lookin' man? I don't remember seein' him before."

"That's Peter Shadwell, the owner of this plantation."

"Why on earth is he wastin' time with Serena Caswell?" she asked peevishly. "She's as plain as a mud fence."

"You take that back," Hank choked, his small hands clenched into fists.

Viola blinked in surprise. She had forgotten the boy was there.

"We think my sister is beautiful, don't we, Nate?" Hank insisted.

"We do," the man agreed obligingly.

She had the grace to blush. "I didn't really mean anything by it. It's just that she's not the kind of girl men usually like."

"Mr. Shadwell likes her," Hank contended.

"He seems to," Nathan murmured, turning his gaze back to the *Sprite*. A movement on the texas caught his eye and he saw Roger at the rail, watching resentfully as Serena and Peter returned to shore.

Dinner was served to passengers and crew alike around a bonfire Peter built with some assistance from the Branson boys. As the first-class passengers took their places on blankets on the ground, Nathan and Grace moved among them, making sure everyone was comfortable and well fed. Serena, her back against a tree, sat with Roger in the flickering firelight and ignored the big captain.

He had never known such a girl, Nathan seethed, sitting across the fire from her. Upset just because he had expressed concern for her. She was undoubtedly the most difficult female who ever lived.

But the hard expression in his eyes softened when he saw her head beginning to nod. When her fork slipped unnoticed from her hand, he went to kneel beside her, disregarding Roger's look of surprise.

"Serena," Nathan said softly, taking the precariously tilting plate from her lap, "the main reason for spending the night here was so you could rest. Don't you think you should go to bed now?"

Drawing a startled breath, she opened her eyes and frowned at him sleepily. "You can't order me around. Do you think you're the captain of everything now?"

"Nope, just of the *Sprite* and I'm going to see you to your cabin." Taking her hand, he rose, drawing her with him.

"I'll do it." Scrambling to his feet, Roger wrapped a possessive arm around Serena's waist. "I mean," he amended when the big man swung around truculently, "your place is with the passengers. I'll take her, Captain."

"I don't need anyone to take me," Serena erupted.

"A lady should be walked to her door," Nathan insisted with a strained smile. Stepping back, he let the couple pass.

As Roger walked her along the boiler deck, Serena glanced down at the company clustered on the riverbank and stiffened. In the firelight, Viola moved to Nathan's side, her smile inviting as she looped her arm through his.

Long after the fire had been doused and the passengers were abed, Nathan lay on his bunk, one arm cocked behind his head, and watched the reflection of the moonlit river on the ceiling. What was wrong with him? he asked himself savagely. Even though he had vowed he would not come between Serena and the clerk, he had nearly challenged Roger this evening on the riverbank.

He knew that he was not ready to settle down, that he had no room in his life for a stubborn, red-haired vixen who was angry at him as often as not. But something about Serena drew him.

With a strangled curse, the captain turned over and punched his pillow decisively. He couldn't let down his guard for a moment. He and Serena Caswell were business associates, nothing more, and he would do well to remember that.

The *River Sprite* arrived in Memphis the next afternoon. Built on Chickasaw Bluff, high above the Mississippi, the town was pretty and tidy with warehouses lining the road from the orderly docks.

After the boat was moored, Serena tarried in the pilothouse, savoring the end of the journey. Down on the dock, the

Branson family spilled off the boat and eddied around an unfortunate cabdriver. Viola and her relatives stood by as her luggage was loaded atop a coach. Soon the passengers would be gone and no one would be left aboard the *Sprite* but Caswells and crew . . . and Nathan.

He had come to breakfast before dawn in an ill humor, scowling darkly when he found Serena and Roger already together in the galley. With little to say to either of them, he had taken his coffee and departed, leaving them baffled and annoyed.

It would be just as well to steer clear of him this afternoon, Serena told herself as she disembarked onto the dock, cluttered with crates from the *Sprite*'s hold. But as she made her way through lengthening shadows, another large shadow loomed over her.

"Where are you going?" Nathan demanded.

She shot him a hostile glance. "To the harbor master's, if it's any of your business."

"You shouldn't go alone."

"I've gone a hundred times before. Alone."

"A young lady should not walk around unescorted, especially on the waterfront . . . especially in a strange town."

"I have one mother, Nathan," Serena replied scathingly.

"I have one pilot," he retorted, his voice just as cutting, "and I wouldn't want anything to happen to her.

"Roger," he bellowed over his shoulder, "come and see Miss Caswell to and from the harbor master's in safety."

By the time, the couple returned to the *Sprite*, Nathan seemed to have put aside his displeasure. Engaged in conversation with a prosperous-looking man on the dock, he beckoned Roger and nodded to Serena as she boarded the boat.

Looking over her shoulder, Serena nearly ran into her sister and Gustave as they rounded the main deck from the bow.

"I think this dinner is going to be wonderful," Dory was saying excitedly.

"I know it will be wonderful," the cook responded positively, twirling his mustache.

"Oh, Rena, you'll never guess," Dory cried. "Mother says we may have dinner on the hurricane deck tonight and she let me plan it since there's only family aboard, except for Roger... and Nathan, of course."

"Of course." Serena's voice was heavy with irony.

"And, me, I promised to cook my specialties," Gustave contributed, scowling when Chanticleer crowed for no apparent reason. "Perhaps I will add chicken to the menu," he muttered. "*Le coq*, he can do nothing right. He needs only keep the hens happy, but he does not even do that."

"What brings this on?" Serena asked as the Cajun returned to the galley, mumbling.

"What?" Dory asked gaily.

"This dinner party... your good mood."

"I guess I have been behaving like a sulky baby," the younger girl admitted, "but it's going to be different now that Nathan explained everything to me."

Nathan again. Serena sighed exasperatedly. "What exactly did he explain?"

"How the *River Sprite* is a big machine and all the parts must work. He says the housekeeping on this boat just wouldn't be the same without me assisting Mother. And we really should help Mother, you know, Serena. The past two months have probably been harder for her than for anyone else."

"Did you think of that yourself or is this part of our fearless captain's lecture?"

"I don't care what you say," Dory said adamantly as she headed for the galley. "Nothing can spoil our good time tonight."

On the boiler deck, Serena found Will and Hank hunched over a game of checkers. "Who's winning?"

"It's a draw so far," Will answered just as the boy jumped two of his men. Frowning in mock exasperation, he grumbled, "Consarn it, you remorseless young pup, you would take advantage of an old man's weakened condition."

"I don't think it has anything to do with your being sick, Uncle Will," Hank countered innocently. "I jump you all the time."

"Remorseless and impertinent," Will griped good-naturedly.

"Mother said to tell you she's dressing for dinner." Hank remembered his instructions. "She'll be down in a moment."

"She's already here." Grace stepped from the companion-way, elegant in her black gown. "My dear, just look at you," she murmured when she saw Serena's rolled sleeves and open collar.

"It gets very hot in the pilothouse," Serena defended her appearance.

"Come." Grace led her daughter to the stern. "I have a sur-prise for you." Flinging open the door to Serena's cabin, the woman moved aside to admit her.

"You must be a mind reader," the girl breathed in delight when she saw the tub of steaming water awaiting her.

"No, just a mother," Grace answered with a smile, "a proud mother. I had no idea how much was involved in navigating a steamboat, Serena. I still do not know much about it, but I think you've performed superbly."

"Thank you." Serena's eyes glazed with tears at the unex-pected praise.

"There is one other thing before I leave you to your bath," Grace mentioned from the doorway. "Don't you think you would be cooler in that lovely dark blue gown I made for you last fall?"

"But . . ." With a dubious expression, Serena plucked at the skirt of the stiff black bombazine dress she had come to de-spise.

"I know it is proper to wear black for a full year," Grace said softly, "but I believe Henry would have preferred that you children honor him by living your lives."

With a tender smile, she closed the door. There were too many burdens in Serena's life. How long had it been since she was able to be the carefree girl she should be? Grace asked herself. Now she was sure she had done the right thing when she took Nathan as a partner and asked him to be the captain. He would be good for Serena . . . if they could ever work out their differences.

In her cabin, the girl slipped contentedly into her bath. Though she was well accustomed to washing from the basin every day, she missed long, steamy soaks when she was on the river. Allowing the water to lap up around her neck, she delighted in its warmth.

Slowly Serena relaxed, feeling the tension ebb away, half-listening to the sounds of the waterfront, which diminished as night began to fall. Down on the dock, Nathan was probably still completing the day's business, but the cargo was his job. She had done hers, she thought, feeling lazy and satisfied.

In danger of falling asleep, she finished her bath, washing her hair until it squeaked cleanly under her fingers. Stepping from the tub, she wiped steam from the mirror over the washstand and combed the tangles from her hair.

As she drew on her frilly undergarments, she realized her weariness would not pass. There was time before dinner, so she lay down, spreading her hair on the pillow to dry. She did not know how long she had dozed when she was roused by insistent pounding.

"Serena," Nathan's voice bellowed through the door, "are you in there?"

Disoriented and startled, she threw on a flimsy wrapper and flung the door open, emitting a rush of warm, moist, perfumed air. "What is it? What's wrong?"

Nathan's hand, poised to knock again, dropped to his side and he stared at her, openmouthed.

Clad in the dressing gown with her hair flowing down her back in a heavy auburn riot of curls, Serena looked utterly feminine and utterly desirable. She was obviously fresh from her bath, for tendrils had dried and curled around her flushed face. Her robe, hastily belted, plunged in a deep vee between her breasts to reveal a bit of lace. Without her shoes, she seemed smaller than ever. As she looked up at the man towering over her, the pulse pounded in her throat and her blue eyes were wide with alarm.

"Nothing is wrong. I didn't mean to alarm you," he managed at last, his voice husky.

The heat of his gaze was nearly her undoing. "Wh-what did you want to see me about?"

Smiling bemusedly, he murmured, "I came to tell you we made a profit on this load and I already signed another for New Orleans. We don't have to go on to St. Louis this trip." Involuntarily he reached out and picked up a lock of hair from her shoulder.

Certain the heat of his touch had burned through her wrapper, Serena nervously retreated a step. The long auburn lock stretched between them, a fragile bond. "Is it a good cargo?" she forced herself to ask.

"Cotton headed for England ... for Trevarian, Limited." Nathan rubbed the lush strands between his fingers.

"Cotton brokers?" The question was not much more than a whisper.

"Biggest in the world," he affirmed dreamily.

"That's wonderful." Fighting the urge to sway against him, she tried to withdraw, lengthening the silken span between them. "That means we'll be able to pay some of our bills."

Nathan's mind was no longer on business. His dark eyes caught and held hers. "I've never seen you this way. So..." His voice trailed off when her face flooded with color.

When she had been awakened, she had not thought how skimpily she was clad. Now, clutching her wrapper closed at the neck, she tugged gently on her hair and commanded with more composure than she felt, "Let me go, Nathan. I must dress for dinner."

"Not unless you promise..." he teased, closing his hand gently on the tress sliding sinuously through his fingers.

"What?" Breathlessly she lifted her questioning eyes to his.

As Serena stood before him, still, almost expectant, Nathan knew he should go. But he could not. At last, unwilling to reveal how her nearness affected him, he released the lock of hair he held and said lightly, "Promise you'll allow me to escort you to dinner. Dory tells me it's to be quite elegant. I wouldn't think of appearing without a comely companion. Shall I call for you at seven-thirty?"

"Very well." Serena agreed with a sigh, uncertain whether she felt relief or disappointment when he departed.

When Nathan had not come for her at seven forty-five, Serena started to the texas in high dudgeon. Just as she was about to mount the companionway, Simon burst from Will's cabin and called, "Oh, there you are, Miss Rena. The cap'n told me to tell you he's going to be a little late."

"What a surprise," she proclaimed sarcastically.

"He's helping Mr. Will dress," the cabin boy revealed. "Mr. Will says he missed the picnic last night and he'll be hornswoggled if he'll miss Miss Dory's dinner tonight."

"Uncle Will is going up to the texas?" Thrilled by the news, Serena forgot her pique.

"Yes, ma'am, though he'll need some help getting up there." His eyes shining, Simon changed the subject, "Did you know Cap'n Trent fought in Mexico? He even got a watch in appreciation from his commander. Can you beat that?"

"No, but I'll bet Uncle Will can." Serena grinned. "Has he shown off his watch fob yet?"

"Yes, ma'am. Did he really get that ball at the Battle of New Orleans?"

"Right in his leg. That's why he limps to this day."

"Holy Moses," Simon mumbled as he hurried back to the galley. "Two war heroes on the same boat."

"Looky here, Rena," Will groused, limping out on deck. "Here I am feelin' pert near good as new and Nate's hoverin' over me like a mother hen."

"Just staying close to keep you out of trouble," Nathan retorted as he emerged from the cabin behind the old man. His eyes lit with approval when he saw the girl, and he offered his arm. "Sorry to keep you waiting, Serena. You look lovely."

Serena glowed. She felt lovely. She had actually liked what she had seen in her mirror. The dark blue of the gown made her ivory skin look like alabaster and brought out the blue of her eyes. She had brushed her hair to a sheen and wore it down, trying to tell herself it wasn't just because Nathan had liked it that way.

Dory's dinner was great success. Each of Gustave's offerings was better than the last. And once Roger got over his vexation at seeing Serena arrive with Nathan, the conversation around the table was lively and companionable.

"I can't wait any longer," Will complained when dessert was served. "Did you tell everyone your news, Nate?"

"Not the ladies." Rising, Nathan announced, "Tomorrow we will be taking on our first load of cotton for Trevarian, Limited. If they are pleased with us and continue to use our service, Roger and I figure we could be solvent in three months."

When the buzz of excited conversation around the table diminished, he lifted his coffee cup. "To our first successful run together and to many more.

"To celebrate, I have small gifts for each of you. Except for you, Roger," he amended. "I'm afraid you'll have to make do with congratulations for a job well-done."

The clerk basked in the captain's commendation while the others opened their gifts. For Grace, Serena and Dory, there were small satin sachets. For Uncle Will, a plug of chewing tobacco and a licorice whip for Hank.

Everyone was pleased by Nathan's thoughtfulness, but Dory was giddy with delight. "Oh, thank you," she bubbled. "I've never had a gift from a man before...besides my father, I mean. It's just beautiful." Putting the sachet to her nose, she inhaled deeply.

"You're gonna sniff up all the smell-um," Will warned, getting to his feet slowly. "Sorry, but I've got to get to bed. I've had more excitement today than I've had in a month of Sundays."

"I'll go with you, Uncle Will." Hank followed, unwilling to allow the old man to descend the companionway alone. "I have to get up early so I can help Nathan."

"Not too early, Hank," the captain requested. "It'll be eight or nine o'clock before the cargo arrives."

"I think I'd better turn in, too," Roger said. "May I escort you to your cabin, Serena?"

"I'll walk with you," Nathan interjected before she had time to answer. Roger looked displeased, but he did not protest.

At the foot of the companionway, the trio stopped. The clerk's cabin was forward while Nathan's and Serena's were at the stern. Roger hesitated for a moment, then he veered determinedly aft.

As they passed along the shadowy deck, Nathan had to admit to himself what he was doing. He had decided not to interfere in the relationship between Serena and Roger, but now he found he did not want the other man to be alone with her...to touch her. It was unfair of him, because he had no claim on her. And he wanted no claim on her, he reminded himself.

But when they reached the stern, he could not bring himself to leave them. Roger showed the same reluctance. Awkwardly both men crowded into the tiny space, as Serena looked back and forth between them helplessly.

She had seldom had the attention of one man, not to mention two, she agonized. With no idea what else to do, she bade them both good-night and went inside. Poised on the other side of the door, she listened as Roger's footsteps faded away.

She knew Nathan lingered on deck. She could see his shadow against the closed louvers of her window, smell the smoke from his cheroot. She considered going out again. But for what reason? she asked herself. Then determinedly, she began to prepare for bed.

At the railing, Nathan stared at the deserted waterfront and contemplated knocking on Serena's door, but he could think of no excuse. Irritably he pitched his half-smoked cigar into the water and stalked into his own cabin, closing the door firmly behind him.

Chapter Seven

What a wonderful day it had been, Serena exulted. The sun, now a crimson ball, set behind the dark outline of forest on the western shore. Below her on the dock, stevedores hauled cotton bales aboard the *River Sprite*.

The cargo was huge, for Trevarian had apparently been holding its cotton in order to drive the prices up on the world market. Though the brokers had wanted the *Sprite* to leave as soon as possible, their wagons had not begun to arrive until late morning. Throughout the afternoon, they had come and gone, moving their loads from nearby warehouses to the waiting steamboat.

The morning had been the best part of the day for Serena. Her spirits soared to remember it. After the *Sprite* had been unloaded and the men paid, Nathan had taken her aside and thrust a small stack of twenty-dollar gold pieces into her hand.

"What is this?" she had asked.

"Your wages for the trip from Vicksburg."

She had shaken her head wonderingly. "I can't take this."

"Why not? You worked for it."

"I'm also a part of the family."

"But without you as the *Sprite*'s pilot, we couldn't have brought our cargo and passengers to Memphis."

"I...I've never been paid for it before," she had whispered, gazing down at the coins in her cupped hand. "I couldn't be paid when I was Uncle Will's cub and when I became a pilot, the cap'n never had the money..."

"All the more reason to take it," he had insisted softly, closing her fingers over the money. "You deserve every cent."

Nathan's voice was not soft now as it drifted to her in the dusk. Lowering it with effort, he concluded his discussion with Trevarian's lead driver. His face impassive, the driver climbed up on the seat of his empty wagon and drove away.

Serena joined the captain on the dock. "What's wrong?"

"They can't finish loading this evening." Pushing his hat back on his head, he sighed in frustration.

"But we're supposed to leave in the morning."

"He says they can't bring the last of the cotton till then." Surveying the nearby steamboats, he grumbled, "There go our passengers. Everybody else is ready to take off at the crack of dawn."

"At least we've got a full load."

His eyebrows lifted in surprise at her encouragement, and he nodded toward the *Sprite*. "A full load and then some."

A dark shape against the gathering night, the boat rode low in the water, her graceful silhouette made blocky by cotton bales filling every nook and cranny of the main deck and a good portion of the upper ones. No lanterns would be lit on deck tonight for fear of fire.

Offering his arm, Nathan escorted Serena aboard, their laughter mingling when Chanticleer, seemingly inspired by his position atop a bale, crowed at nothing in particular.

Wearing the visor and cuffs of his profession, Roger looked up from his high accountant's desk and blinked owlishly.

"Gustave says if M'sieur Roger cannot come to dinner, someone must take dinner to him." Serena breezed in with a tray.

"I'm glad that someone is you." Stepping down from his tall stool, the clerk relieved her of her burden.

Looking beyond the circle of light given off by his lamp, Serena surveyed the wadded paper littering the office floor. "What are you doing?"

"Correspondence," he replied with a scant glance at the mess. "I've never been very good at it."

"It's getting late, Roger. Can't it wait until morning?"

The look he turned upon her was tender. "Don't worry about me, Rena. This is one of most gratifying duties I've ever had aboard the *Sprite*. Nathan asked me to write to each of our creditors. We earned enough this trip to pay everyone a little." He gestured toward the bank drafts stacked tidily on his desk. "It looks as if this old boat can be profitable, after all."

"That's wonderful." Serena beamed. Then, remembering she was interrupting his work, she started for the door.

"Are you going so soon?"

"With the number of creditors Caswell & Trent has, you'll be writing all night if I don't," she teased.

"Caswell & Trent," Roger repeated. "Funny, I still think of it as Caswell & Company. Do you like Nathan Trent, Serena?"

His unexpected question halted her at the door. "I suppose I'm getting used to him."

"Don't get too accustomed to having him around."

"Why?" She fixed him with a level stare.

"I—I just think he's not the type to stay around for long," the clerk stammered.

"At least, I hope he is not," he mumbled to himself, watching through his window as Serena crossed the texas. Out on deck, Nathan called to her from the railing and Roger wondered if he had been waiting for her all along. His face was bleak as the couple disappeared down the companionway.

"I would offer my arm," Nathan joked when they stepped onto the boiler deck, "but there's too much cotton aboard to leave room for gallantry. After you..." He gestured politely.

They walked aft, single file, between the bulkhead and the bales ranged along the outside railing. Progress was slow as Serena's skirt caught on the hemp-wrapped bundles. No breeze penetrated the stacked cotton and the heat was oppressive.

"What is it?" Nathan nearly collided with her as she halted abruptly on the stern. Peering over her shoulder, he roared, "What the hell . . . ?"

In the shadow of the paddle wheel, a couple sat in Serena's chair, intertwined in a lascivious embrace. When she saw Nathan and Serena, the woman, one of the maids, jumped from the man's lap. Her hair atumble and her bodice gaping, she gave a dismayed cry and fled. Fiske Patterson, his shirt hanging open, rose more slowly.

"Evening, Captain, Miss Serena." He nodded coolly."

"In the future, Patterson," Nathan said, his voice as cutting as a whiplash, "I'd appreciate it if you would not do your courting outside our cabin doors." ·

Gazing back and forth between the adjacent doors, then at Serena's red-stained cheeks, the man smirked. "Aye-aye, Captain."

When the deckhand had gone, Nathan turned to the embarrassed girl. "I'm sorry, Serena."

"It's not your fault," she answered awkwardly. "Usually you don't have to worry about anyone coming back here. I mean . . ." She trailed off, afraid her words sounded like an invitation. Suddenly aware of their relative isolation and Nathan's unsettling nearness, she whirled and went into her cabin.

Nathan made no mention of her flight the next morning. In fact, he said very little at all as he alternately watched the empty road from town and the boats steaming out of the harbor.

"Three wagons!" he exploded when the cargo train finally appeared. "That scoundrel told me they couldn't finish loading last night and now I find out we waited for three wagons." Jamming his hat onto his head, he bolted down the staircase to the main deck.

"Nathan." Serena followed him anxiously. "Trevarian could be a good client. Try to control your temper."

"Control my temper?" From the foot of the stairs, the big man looked up at her, his face reflecting disbelief and irritation. "I'll do that, if you'll be so kind to tell Jamie to finish building steam."

He did not see her ominous scowl as he bellowed, "Prepare to cast off as soon as the last of the cargo is aboard."

A few minutes later when Roger clattered down to the main deck, an angry Serena passed him on the stairs, her head held high.

The moment the cotton was loaded, Nathan ordered the gangplank to be drawn aboard. But before the boat could ease away from the dock, a buckboard rolled down the pier toward the boat, its driver shouting and gesturing and a mighty din rising from the rear of the rig.

"Now what?" Nathan muttered.

"It's Cyrus, Mrs. Winslow's man," Roger answered. "He and his mistress have traveled on the *River Sprite* many times."

"Let's see what he wants." Nathan jumped to the dock as the rig rolled to a halt. The aged black driver descended unsteadily from the seat.

"Hello, Cyrus," Roger greeted him. "You almost missed us."

"Glad I kotch you. I gotta talk to the cap'n."

"This is Captain Trent." He gestured to the man at his side.

"How do, suh," the servant said when Nathan nodded amiably. "I need to ax you . . . Miz Winslow was all set to visit her nephew. He jes' married and got him a new farm north of Helena. We was to go an' visit him, but the mistress started feelin' poorly and the doctor say she gots to keep to her bed. Cain't go nowheres.

"But she still wanna send this prize shoat an' that little sow to he'p him get his farm started off right." He indicated a ramshackle, slatted crate on the back of the buckboard. "She'd be much obliged if you take 'em. She give me the money to pay you."

Nathan examined the pigs, who had settled to a nap in the sun once their riotous ride was finished. Hauling animals could be a pain, he deliberated, but it wasn't far downriver to Helena. And Mrs. Winslow was an old customer of the *Sprite*'s.

"We'll be happy to take them," he told Cyrus. "Mr. Blake will settle on a price with you." Heading back to the boat, he ordered, "Levi, find a place on top of a cotton bale and secure this crate."

As he climbed to the pilothouse, Serena blocked the way. "What's the holdup? Why haven't you given the order to cast off? We've got steam and we're ready to go."

Nathan continue to climb. He did not stop or even slow his progress toward her. When he reached the top, she was forced to step aside and let him enter. "We're taking on a couple of passengers," he said, leading her to the window. Down at the dock, a crate was being brought aboard.

"What in blue blazes?"

"Two of Mrs. Winslow's prize pigs."

"Pigs are our passengers?" She glared at him scornfully.

"In a manner of speaking. They're the only ones we've got for this portion of the run."

"That's a first, even for the *Sprite*." Shaking her head, she sighed in resignation. "I guess we should take our fares where we can get them."

Stepping in front of her when she turned away from the window, Nathan said quietly, "I'm sorry if I snapped at you this morning."

Serena's smile was rueful. "I guess my telling you to mind your temper was like the pot calling the kettle black."

"Maybe a little," he acknowledged easily. "But this time, the kettle lost his temper first."

"Shall we be off, me lass?" Distant and tinny, Jamie's voice floated up the speaking tube. "Young Blake says to tell ye yon beasties are aboard."

"Aye, Jamie," she called. "Levi can give the order to cast off as soon as the captain gets down there."

Serena was happier than she had been for some time when she guided the *Sprite* out of the dock and felt the current catch her. This was going to be a good run. The river was not yet at its summer low. She and the captain were at peace . . . at the moment. And they should have plain sailing all the way to New Orleans.

The boat had been underway for more than an hour when suddenly, in a narrow bend of the river, Serena made out a black mass bobbing in the water ahead. Yanking the cord beside her, she heard a bell jangle far below.

"Snag ahead and it's catching some driftwood," she called down to the tube. "Reverse engines, slow."

The boat jolted as Jamie and Charlie hastened to obey. The paddle wheel battled with the powerful current, causing the *Sprite* to remain nearly stationary while she assessed the situation.

There was room to pass to the inside, she noted. They could do it, but it would require caution, time and a good deal of luck.

"Stop engines," she ordered, seeing the leadsmen taking their positions on the bow. "And release steam. We don't want to blow any boilers."

Steam belching from the stack, the *Sprite* lurched as the paddle wheel was stilled. Then the boat crept forward on the current, the silence almost eerie.

Tossed against the side of their pen, the pigs squealed in fright and kicked against the flimsy slats surrounding them. Battering a hole in their cage, they darted out onto the main deck.

Hank sat outside the galley, watching the deckhands. They lined the *Sprite*'s rails the length of the boat, armed with poles to push away logs as the boat passed. Suddenly a small black-and-white blur passed him, racing forward. With a cry, he pursued the hog, trying to divert it from the bow where the attention required of the crewmen was especially critical.

Frowning, Nathan stepped around the forecastle to investigate the commotion. A solid little pink body slammed against his legs, nearly bowling him over, then doubled back toward the stern.

"Damnation," he swore, and followed the little sow into the engine room.

Up in the pilothouse, Serena struggled to concentrate as the boat coasted through a narrow gap in the debris. What the devil was going on below? The lap of the river against the hull was nearly drowned out by pounding footsteps, shouts and what sounded suspiciously like a pig's squeal.

Where was Nathan? He was the captain. He was supposed to keep order aboard, she fumed, scarcely aware that Will had climbed slowly, painstakingly to the wheelhouse.

"You're doin' just fine, Rena," the elderly pilot encouraged. "Watch your larboard. Atta girl. You're doin' fine."

Gritting her teeth, she forced her full attention on passing through the obstacle, which now extended on either side of the boat.

Down on the main deck, Hank's pig evaded him and charged up the stairs to the boiler deck. The boy followed, just in time to see a streak of black and white disappear into the salon. At Dory's startled shriek and the sound of breaking glass, he raced inside, a determined expression on his young face.

In the wheelhouse, Serena sagged in relief when the boat rounded the bend close to shore and safely made the crossover to midstream.

Clapping her on the back, Will cried exuberantly, "Jehoshaphat, gal! If you weren't a lightnin' pilot before, you are now. You brought the *Sprite* through that snag without a scratch."

"I did it," she breathed delightedly. Abruptly her look of dazed disbelief transformed into cold fury. "I did it," she grated, "in spite of everything.

"Do you feel well enough to take the wheel for a few minutes, Uncle Will?" she asked with an ominous gleam in her blue eyes. "I want to have a few words with Captain Trent."

"Take your time, sugar." Sober and efficient, Will took the wheel and ordered the firemen to build steam. But he grinned when Serena stormed out of the pilothouse.

Striding forward along the boiler deck in grim silence, she passed the salon just as Hank wrestled a black-and-white shoat out the door. He stared up at her apprehensively, but she did not even acknowledge his presence.

After the excitement, a pall of doom seemed to hang over the silent boat. Most of the crew stood near the forecastle, talking among themselves and shaking their heads. They eyed Serena speculatively when she paused at the bottom of the stairs and looked around for her nemesis. He was nowhere in sight.

Hearing a racket from the engine room that had nothing to do with pistons, she marched toward the door where Nathan, oily, mussed and almost unrecognizable, appeared. Framed by the doorway, he grappled with an uncooperative, squirming black form.

All at once, the grease-covered pig he gripped so tightly shot from his arms. With a strangled curse, the captain lunged after it, sprawling on deck.

The sow slammed into Serena's legs, knocking her off balance. Unhurt, it snorted and scampered away over Nathan's back, bolting directly into Charlie Flower's waiting arms.

The striker's pleased smile faded when he looked up and saw Serena teetering at the edge of the deck, her arms flailing as she attempted to grab anything that would keep her from falling. With a frustrated screech, she tumbled backward into the river, taking a section of the removable railing with her.

"Man overboard," Charlie hollered.

"My God, Serena!" Scrambling to his feet, Nathan dived in after her.

"Man overboard!" the cry went up all over the *River Sprite*.

When Nathan surfaced, he looked around desperately, spying Serena's head bobbing on the surface as she was carried by the current toward the bow of the boat. The second mate already poised anxiously at the rail.

Buffeted by the fierce current and dragged down by her voluminous skirt, she fought to stay afloat. Small bits of debris that had broken free of the jam upriver rushed past, dangerously close. Throwing back her head, she gulped in air and tried to paddle toward the outstretched pole, but kicking her encumbered legs seemed to take more energy than she had. She had to rest. Surrendering to the undertow, she was not even aware when the water closed above her head.

Nathan's heart pounded in alarm when Serena disappeared below the surface. He swam toward her, his arms chopping through the rapids as he dodged flotsam, his chest aching from exertion. Shouts of encouragement from the boat measured his painful progress, but he did not hear.

Reaching the tangle of auburn hair floating on the water, he grabbed a fistful of it and yanked Serena upward. She emerged from the water, sputtering and flailing blindly.

"Hold still," he choked, trying to gather her in his arms. When the girl continued to fight, he doubled his fist and hit her, hoping to jar her from her hysteria. With a whimper, she sank again below the surface.

Drawing her limp body toward him, he wedged her head in the crook of his arm and swam with a tenacious one-armed stroke toward the boat where Roger waited apprehensively at the rail, his hand outstretched. The weary captain heaved his burden up to him, then hauled himself, gasping, onto the deck.

His face anguished, Roger knelt beside the girl and pushed back her hair from her ashen face. "Are you all right, Rena?"

"Get a blanket," Nathan ordered, coughing up river water. While the clerk obeyed, he crawled to Serena's side and turned her onto her stomach, tilting her head to one side so that dirty brown water streamed from her slack mouth.

Rising to his knees above her, Nathan began to press on her back, forcing the water out of her lungs and the air in. When a convulsive cough racked her body and she began to breathe in deep, ragged gasps, he turned her onto her back again and bent over her. Oblivious to the activity around him, he chafed her limp hands and muttered feverishly, "Don't die. Please don't die, Serena."

Her lips moved, but no sound emerged.

"What is it?" Nathan leaned close. "Tell me, my love. Are you all right?"

Serena's eyelids fluttered and opened. She stared up at him, her blue eyes burning with wrath, and said hoarsely, "I am not your love, you calamitous, ruinous child of desolation... you—"

Sitting back on his heels, he glared at her in injured astonishment. "That's a fine way to talk after I jumped in the river after you."

"If it hadn't been for you and those damned pigs, I wouldn't have been *in* the river," she croaked, propping herself on her elbows.

"And if it hadn't been for you, I probably wouldn't have been *on* the river," he snapped, slogging away with as much dignity as he could muster, leaving her to stare after him, wide-eyed.

"Serena, are you all right?" Grace arrived with Roger. Together, they helped the girl to her feet and wrapped a blanket around her.

"I'm fine," she said firmly. "I just swallowed enough river water to uncover every sandbar and towhead between here and New Orleans."

"I take it that's a great deal," Grace said archly, relieved her daughter seemed none the worse for wear. "Where is Nathan?"

"I don't know," Serena answered tersely, "and I don't care."

Withholding comment, Grace commanded, "Let us get you to your cabin, dear. You need to rest."

"Mother—"

"She's right, Serena," Roger seconded. "You must rest."

"I'm wet, not sick," she objected, bringing on another bout of coughing.

"You've been through quite an ordeal," he insisted. "Let me carry you."

Despite her condition, Serena almost smiled at thought of the slight clerk struggling up the staircase under her waterlogged weight. "No, thank you. I'm perfectly capable of walking."

To prove it, she started for the stairs, but she swayed on her feet unsteadily. Without a word, Grace and Roger moved swiftly to her side, each taking an arm.

"I must say," her mother remarked as they climbed, "my heart stood still when Hank told me what happened."

"What exactly did happen, Serena?" Roger asked.

She rolled her eyes and sneezed in response. From below, came the sound of a hammer as a crewman repaired the damaged crate containing two pigs, exhausted after their escapade.

At the same time, Nathan slouched on the bench in the pilothouse, his wet clothes creating rivulets on the floor. Curled up near Will's feet, Catastrophe rose when the puddle crept too close and walked away with a disdainful look.

"I appreciate your concern, Nate," Will said, "but I reckon I can steer for a spell. Jamie's buildin' steam and we can make up some of the time we lost. I'll stop when I get tired. Why don't you go change, and stop drippin' all over the wheelhouse?"

"I figured I'd give Serena some time to get settled in her cabin first," the captain answered morosely.

Gauging the distance to the polished brass spittoon on the floor nearby, Will ejected a brown stream of tobacco juice neatly into it. "In that case," he said with a gusty sigh, "why don't you look in the stove."

"The stove?"

"That's where I keep my bottle during the warm months. It's a dern sight harder to hide from Serena in the winter, I can tell you," the old man grumbled.

Opening the door of the potbellied stove, Nathan thrust in his hand and withdrew a bottle of fine Tennessee whiskey.

"Take a nip," Will urged, "'fore you catch your death."

"Thanks." Nathan uncorked the bottle and tipped it to his lips briefly before passing it to the elderly pilot.

Will drank, then smacked his lips. "Jest a tetch remedies most of what ails a man."

"I don't know that anything will remedy this afternoon."

"You plannin' to make it up with Rena?" Will asked frankly.

"I'm going to try."

The pilot returned the bottle to him. "Have another drink. Under ordinary circumstances, a feller needs to fortify himself before he faces my niece. But she was hoppin' mad when she left here while ago and she wasn't even wet yet."

Glumly Nathan took another tiny sip. "It wasn't my fault the pigs got loose."

"Nope, and it wasn't your fault Rena fell in the river or that we had to get past a snag that coulda took the bottom out of the *Sprite*. It was all beyond our control and right poor timin', but she might take it nicely if you was to apologize."

He hoped she'd take it nicely, Nathan thought somberly as he hesitated outside her cabin door. For years, he had had his emotions under control. He had not been angry, had never had to apologize, had not been afraid as he had been when she went overboard. He had not cared about anything...or anyone.

When he knocked, Serena's testy voice answered from within, "If that's you with more of your vile cold cure, Mother, I don't want it."

"It's Nathan and I don't have any cold cure to my name. May I speak   u?"

He blinked in surprise when the door flew open and Serena stepped out on deck. He had expected to see her incapacitated and helpless. Instead she was slightly damp, fully dressed and very aggravated.

"Aren't you supposed to be in bed?" he asked, glancing through her open door at the bed where a white nightgown had been flung in an obvious statement of rebellion.

"I'm going up to relieve Uncle Will as soon as the coast is clear," she announced defiantly. Caught off guard when the engines started and the stern-wheeler lurched forward, she stumbled against Nathan.

"Are you sure you're all right?" he asked softly, his arms closing around her. "You look a little flushed to me."

"Of course, I am," Serena insisted shakily, stepping back within his embrace. "I'm sorry I lost my temper with you... again. I realize what happened was an accident. I shouldn't have said what I said."

"I'm sorry, too," Nathan apologized sincerely. "I should have made sure the pen was more secure. Maybe I shouldn't have taken the pigs aboard, at all."

"I would have done the same thing. And so would my father."

He smiled down at her, glad she did not seem to realize he still held her in a loose embrace. "I understand that getting through that snag was a close call! Will says he couldn't have done it better... without all the bedlam. You did a good job, Serena."

"Thank you." Her blue eyes glowed at his praise. "And thank you for going into the river after me."

"I had to," he murmured, his arms tightening involuntarily around her waist.

"Why?"

"Because," he chuckled, "even though you're an impossible female, life is interesting with you around."

Later Serena was not certain whether she had swayed against him. Nathan did not know for sure if he had leaned over her. But suddenly they were kissing, gently and so sweetly.

The sound of the paddle wheel faded away and all Serena could hear was the blood rushing in her head. The mist from the wheel wetted Nathan's already sodden clothes, but he did not notice.

When, at last, their lips parted, he held her for a moment and whispered, "Life with you is extremely interesting, Serena." But when he released her, his expression was troubled. "I...I shouldn't be here like this. I have a lot of work to do before we reach Helena."

He was halfway forward before he remembered he still wore wet clothes, but he could not go back. "Damnation," he muttered.

"Well, well, the whole family," Nathan greeted the Caswells when he climbed to the texas that evening. Surrounded by cargo, they sat with Roger near the captain's cabin and watched a small Fourth of July fireworks display from town. The evening breeze carried the scents of gunpowder from shore and roses from Grace's bushes beside the door.

"How are you feeling, Will?" Nathan asked the old man who drooped in a wicker rocker, Catastrophe curled in his lap.

"A bit tuckered," Will admitted. "I reckon I'm not as ready to pull a full watch as I thought I was."

"And how are you now, Serena?" he asked politely, noticing she seemed unwilling to meet his eyes after what had occurred between them that afternoon.

"As good as new, thank you," she replied quietly.

Dragging over a cotton bale, the captain sat down. "We'll have some passengers when we leave in the morning," he announced with satisfaction. "A Reverend Morris just made reservations for five people."

To his amazement, Serena moaned.

"You know Reverend Morris?"

"And his wife and his three marriageable daughters," Will affirmed tragically. "Those gals are lookin' hard for husbands and they ain't gettin' any younger. You fellers better make yourselves scarce when they come aboard," he advised Nathan and Roger. "You, too, Hank," he teased with a twinkle in his eye.

"Aw, Uncle Will." The boy rolled his eyes skyward.

"I'm not worried as long as I have the Caswell women to protect me," Nathan jested, winking at Dory. "You won't let them carry me off, will you?" he asked Serena drolly.

"After today, I think life would be a lot quieter on the *Sprite* if I did," she retorted, blushing.

"But not nearly as interesting," he drawled.

Thankful for the cover of darkness, she reddened all the more.

"Didn't your father bring Reverend Morris home to dinner some time ago?" Grace asked Serena, unaware of the undercurrent between the captain and her daughter. "Henry said he was one of the *River Sprite*'s most regular passengers."

"He's the one. The stuffiest, the most pompous..." She broke off at her mother's warning look. "It'll be noon again before we get out of here."

"Nope." Nathan smiled. "I told the reverend quite nicely that if they weren't here by seven o'clock, we'd leave without them."

"It sounds as if we must be up and about early, children," Grace said brightly. "So, everyone to bed."

Rising at once, Roger extended his hand imperiously. "I'll walk you to your cabin, Serena."

In spite of herself, she found herself glancing at Nathan. Seemingly engrossed in a discussion with Grace, he did not move from his seat or even look in her direction. Taking the hand Roger offered, she bade everyone a good-night and, together, they went to the dark deck below.

Excusing himself from his conversation after a few minutes, Nathan went down to make sure the night watch was in place. At the foot of the companionway, he halted, staring aft, listening for voices. When he saw and heard nothing, he forced himself to walk forward. If Serena and Roger were on the stern, they did not wish to be disturbed.

On the bow, Nathan stopped to look out at the dark river. He had realized this afternoon that he was beginning to care for Serena. Then, holding her in his arms, he had felt a jolt of scalding, undeniable desire. But that was not love, he told himself fiercely. It was madness.

What he was feeling could ruin everything. He and Serena had to work together, had to get along together. They could be friends ... business associates ... nothing more.

Serena had been in bed for nearly an hour when Nathan returned to his quarters, but she was not asleep. She heard him moving about the adjacent cabin. She even heard as he settled in his bunk. She was surprised, however, when he called softly through the wall, "Are you asleep, Rena?"

"No."

"I ... I want to know if you are still my friend ... after everything that happened today."

She stared into darkness, her throat aching with unexpected, unwelcome tears. She should be glad Nathan wanted to be her friend. They had to work together every day. They *should* be friends. What was wrong with her?

"Yes," she answered after a long silence, "I'm your friend."

"I'm glad. Good night, Serena."

Chapter Eight

The next morning, the entire Caswell clan was assembled near the gangplank to await their passengers. One, Mr. Dudley Frasier, had boarded just after dawn. Suspecting the young planter, who was obviously worse for wear, had come from a night of carousing, Nathan was relieved when he went directly to his cabin and stayed there.

"You sure the Morrises are comin'?" Will asked as they watched the empty road to the dock.

"They've still got five minutes," Nathan answered.

"Uh-huh," Will said dubiously.

"Here they come now." The captain's smile was smug as a coach careened around a curve in the road and rolled onto the dock.

Reverend Morris was the first to step down. Pulling his waistcoat down over an expansive belly, he offered an arm to his equally round wife. Together, they proceeded to the boat while their daughters alit, arguing over which enormous hatbox belonged to whom. All dispute ceased, however, when the girls glimpsed Nathan standing on the bow. Hurriedly they followed their parents up the gangplank.

"Mrs. Caswell," Reverend Morris boomed, "what an unexpected pleasure to find you traveling on your late husband's steamboat. This young man—" he indicated Nathan with a nod "—told us the sad news of his death when we booked passage last night. Our sympathy is with you, madam.

"Permit me to introduce my wife," he went on. "And these are my daughters, Hannah, Hallie and Hilda."

Ranged behind their mother, the girls curtsied in turn.

"It is a pleasure to meet all of you," Grace said. "We're delighted to have you as passengers on the *River Sprite.*"

The minister's eyebrows shot up questioningly. "Dear Widow Caswell, you cannot mean that you are involved in commerce."

With a slight frown for the title he bestowed upon her, Grace countered, "What I am involved in, Reverend, is the *Sprite.* She now belongs to me and my children . . . and to my partner, Captain Trent.

"I'm sure you remember my brother-in-law, William, and my elder daughter, Serena, from your other trips," she continued smoothly. "These are my other children, Pandora and Hank."

The man nodded to Will and directed a disapproving glance at Serena before turning his attention to the younger children. Except for the widow, not one member of the family was clad in full mourning, he thought, scandalized. "How long has it been since your husband passed on, Mrs. Caswell?" he asked delicately.

Grace met his reproving gaze with a level stare. "Nearly three months."

"Yes, well, er . . ." he stammered, shocked, "you seem to be going on with your life. How strong you must be, my dear woman."

"How strong we all must be," Grace amended quietly, "if we are to support ourselves."

"Reverend, Mrs. Morris, may I show you to your stateroom?" Nathan invited. "Mrs. Caswell has prepared Virginia for you. Hank, will you escort the young ladies to the Empire State?"

"Yes, sir," the lad answered importantly though he wanted as little to do with the Morris girls as possible. Gesturing for them to follow, he prepared to lead the way, but the sisters stood in a clump, staring at the captain with undisguised interest.

"Come, girls," Mrs. Morris summoned as she and her husband fell into step behind Nathan. Without even a glance over her shoulder, she repeated, "I said, come, girls."

As the band disappeared from view at the top of the staircase, Will wheezed with laughter. "Did you see those gals? Moonstruck, ever' one of 'em. Poor Nate ain't gonna have a minute's peace from here to Lake Providence."

"He doesn't know what he's in for," Serena agreed before asking thoughtfully, "Uncle Will, did you think Hannah looked prettier than she used to?"

"Didn't hurt my eyes none to look at her," he admitted, regarding his niece speculatively. "Some gals are just late bloomers."

Like me, she thought later. One hand on the *Sprite*'s wheel, she leaned back far enough to see her reflection in the mirror beside the pilothouse door. Will had hung it there, teasing that a rich widow woman might come aboard at any time. He never left the wheelhouse without checking his appearance in it and he never seemed displeased with his lean, wrinkled visage.

But what Serena saw was not encouraging. Making a face at her reflection, she steered the boat southward and looked out over the texas where the sun beat down, reflecting from the white baled cotton.

Through the morning, she had watched the activity from the pilothouse. Usually chaos ensued when the Morrises came aboard, but not this time. It seemed the new captain was particularly adept at dealing with passengers, especially female passengers.

Down on the boiler deck, Nathan was hailed by one of those passengers. "Captain Trent," Hannah Morris called flirtatiously, "you're just the gentleman I was looking for to accompany me on a promenade."

"I'd be delighted," he responded with appropriate gallantry, "though I warn you, I must be about my duties very soon."

"Surely you have time to escort me to the texas," she entreated, taking his arm. "I am about to perish from heat and I'm sure it must be cooler up there."

When they stood on the uppermost deck, Hannah turned her face to the breeze and sighed. "This is bliss, Nathan. You don't mind if I call you Nathan, do you?"

"No, ma'am." Leading her to the forward rail where the wind would cool them, he glanced up toward the pilothouse in spite of himself, hoping Serena was not watching.

All at once, a slender column of steam escaped from the stack with a hiss as the valves were opened slightly in the boiler room.

"What is that?" Hannah cried in feigned alarm and Nathan found his arm clutched tightly against her breasts.

"Nothing more than escaping steam."

"Oh, dear, you're going to think me foolish." She loosened her hold, but she did not release his arm.

"It's not foolish to be afraid of something you don't know or understand." Gingerly he reclaimed the limb again.

"Some people are simply afraid to live life. I'm not afraid," Hannah proclaimed daringly, "of steamboats—or life."

"Well, I'm afraid, Miss Morris," Nathan responded with a charming smile, "that if I do not return my attention to my duties, I will miss our next stop."

Above, Serena seethed as the couple descended the companionway. She was annoyed that Hannah Morris could not keep her hands off Nathan and incensed that he did not seem to mind. Most of all, she was disgusted with herself for caring.

When Serena went down to dinner she found Nathan surrounded by the sisters. Hank stood staunchly at his side while Grace, Roger and Dory chatted with the minister and his wife. The other passenger, young Mr. Frasier, who had appeared on deck for a wobbly moment during the afternoon, was nowhere to be seen.

"I vow there is not room for a person to turn around in our cabin," Hallie was complaining when Serena entered, "never mind that there are three of us."

"The Empire State is our largest stateroom, miss," Nathan replied, unperturbed.

"And the hottest. The sun shone in all afternoon."

"The sun couldn't shine in all afternoon," Hank argued. "The river twists and turns too much."

Hallie sniffed.

"Pay no attention, Captain. My sister likes to complain." Hannah smiled disarmingly. "You probably think we're terrible, that not one of us appreciates your efforts to accommodate us."

"On the contrary, Miss Morris, I think you are all delightful company, indeed." Suddenly Nathan's face lit with a smile. "Here's Serena."

The girl's heart hammered crazily at the glow in his eyes, but before she could take a step to meet him, Roger was at her side. When she looked back at Nathan, his expression was shuttered and the glow was gone. Deliberately he turned to Hannah Morris.

At dinner, the minister was seated to the captain's right. Hannah immediately claimed the chair to his left. Nathan could see Serena across the table. Roger hovered beside her like a faithful servant.

As soon as he had completed a lengthy blessing, Reverend Morris looked around and asked, "Why is it so dim in here? We can hardly see what we're being served."

"I'm sorry, but the pilots ordered the lights covered," Nathan replied.

"Why?" Hilda asked.

"During the dark of the moon, any unnecessary light interferes with the running of the boat. You'll notice the skylight is shrouded and, if you were to go below, you would discover that even the furnaces are covered with tarps."

"If I went below, would I also find a barrel of rotgut in the engine room?" Reverend Morris asked accusingly.

"I believe you'd find fine Scotch whiskey," Nathan answered frankly. "Our engineer is from Glasgow."

"Disgraceful," the minister muttered, spearing a steak. "Perhaps the temperance fight should not be waged for the wayward souls drinking in saloons, but for the dangerous, dissolute wretches drowsing in the engine rooms of steamboats."

"Jamie McPherson is neither dangerous nor dissolute," Serena erupted.

"He's not a wretch, either," Hank piped in.

"He's a fine engineer," she went on hotly, her cheek colored telltale pink. "Jamie doesn't allow wood chips to get into the doctor and cut off the water to the boilers. You're as safe in his hands as in your own mother's."

"I agree," Nathan and Grace said in unison, then regarded each other in surprise.

Outvoted, Reverend Morris turned his attention instead to Jamie's chief defender. "Do you still suffer under the misbegotten delusion that a woman can become a pilot, Miss Caswell?"

"I didn't hear you complaining this afternoon, sir, when I brought you past that hulk without misfortune," she answered with a bland smile.

"You were steering then?" Mrs. Morris was horrified.

Grace opened her mouth, but before the subject could be changed, Hilda gushed, "How exciting, a lady pilot!"

"Hilda!" Hannah cut her off derisively. "I've never heard of such a thing in my life."

"Fifty years ago, no one had heard of steamboats," Serena informed them, getting to her feet. "And now you're traveling on one. If you will excuse me, I must go and navigate this one."

Alone in the pilothouse, Serena heard voices coming from the texas.

"Don't be that way, honey," a man slurred. "I never knew a maid who argued yet if I could make it worth her while."

Peering out into the darkness, Serena almost did not recognize Dudley Frasier, the passenger who had spent most of his journey in his cabin. Drunk again, he had emerged. And it seemed he was looking for trouble, she thought grimly, throwing open the window.

"Leave me alone," a frightened, feminine voice protested.

"Dory!" Serena gasped. "Slow engines half," she shouted down the tube. With a quick glance at the river, she sprang for the shotgun. In an instant, she had trained it on the drunken man. "Leave her alone!" she yelled down at him.

"Who are you?" Gripping the weeping Dory's wrist, Frasier blinked up at Serena in surprise.

"The pilot of the *River Sprite*, you lecherous, mule-headed jackass. If you don't want to spend the night on a sandbar, let go of my sister and clear off the texas."

"You can't put me off," the young man countered in drunken indignation. "I'm a paying customer."

"You're lucky I don't throw you overboard," Nathan growled, climbing up the companionway behind him. Deliberately he pulled Dory from the man's grasp and sheltered her in the curve of his arm. "As it is, we'll just put you ashore at the next town."

"You can't treat passengers this way. I was just trying to have a good time. And did you hear what she called me?" the planter sputtered, pointing toward the pilothouse.

"You got off light if she called you names instead of shooting you. I would have done both. How far to the next town, Serena?"

"An hour or so," she answered, relieved when Frasier, much chastened, staggered down to the boiler deck to pack. Then, remembering the wheel was untended, she yanked her head inside and returned to her post.

Below, Nathan walked the trembling Dory to the captain's cabin.

Serena awoke to a rap on her door and Chanticleer's unreliable crow. She was surprised to see the sun was already up.

Stumbling to the door, she found Will lounged on her chair, Catastrophe wrapped around his legs. "I'd like to take the *Sprite* out this mornin', if you don't mind," he requested gruffly.

"If you're sure you feel up to it." She yawned.

"Druther be in the pilothouse than in the salon with that stuffed-shirt minister."

"It is Sunday, isn't it?"

"Yep, and it seems my scripture readin' ain't needed this Sabbath," the old man said flatly, scooping up the cat. "I might as well take the mornin' watch."

"Shame on you, William Caswell." Serena shook her head in mock exasperation. "Abandoning your own niece to one of Reverend Morris's two-hour sermons."

"I do regret that, sugar." As he limped away, his voice drifted back to the stern, "Jest not enough to take your place."

Donning one of her coolest frocks, Serena went to breakfast in the salon. Roger bounded to his feet the moment she entered. Nathan rose distractedly, his attention monopolized by the Morris girls. Dory sat at his side, looking subdued, as Grace listened politely to the minister.

When Serena joined the others at the table, Mrs. Morris scrutinized her. Her daughters were more fashionable, she noted with satisfaction, but glancing at them, she noticed trickles of perspiration rolling down their necks. Under her own elaborate coiffure, the woman's ruddy face was splotchy and her upper lip was beaded with sweat.

"My, it is hot. Summer is the only thing about Louisiana to which I cannot become accustomed. Just getting dressed in the morning is torture. How do you stay so cool, my dear?" she asked, eyeing the petite girl in her crisp muslin gown.

"I suppose I'm just used to it." Serena shrugged, deciding against telling the minister's wife to take off some of the layers of clothing she wore.

After breakfast, the *Sprite*'s company who were not on duty gathered in the salon for worship services. But before the first hymn was finished, the boat's great paddle wheel was stopped, reversed, stopped again, then started again with an ominous grinding sound from the stern.

At once, the officers and crew poured from the door. On deck, the captain and the pilot went in opposite directions: Nathan to the main deck; Serena to the wheelhouse, where she found Will cursing down the speaking tube while a matching blue streak rose to mingle with his.

"What is it?" she asked when the old man paused for a breath.

"Driftwood caught in the wheel. Saw nary a sign of it. Jest all the sudden, it's wedged against the hull. I could understand it durin' spring thaw, but durin' fallin' water . . ." He shook his head in disgust.

"It could happen to anyone, Uncle Will," Serena sympathized as he maneuvered the silent boat on the current.

"Seems it's a tree limb," he reported, "not big, but sturdy enough to keep the wheel from turnin'. We might crush it to Lucifer matches, but we could damage the paddle floats. Jamie and I figure the crew should be able to work it out if we can jimmy the wheel."

"Isn't that pretty dangerous? Someone could get hurt."

"That's why you need to put yourself right outside the engine room door. Jamie has his hands full with the engine while Charlie's mindin' the steam gauges and Nathan's overseein' the deck crew. You're gonna have to pass word back and forth between 'em."

For the next two hours, Serena watched, helpless to do more than to call instructions back and forth, as the deckhands strained to dislodge the tree limb, moving with difficulty among the tightly packed cotton bales.

Stripped to his shirtsleeves, Nathan oversaw the efforts, sometimes joining the crew on the lever they had devised. All the while, the firemen stood by vigilantly as Charlie monitored the gauges, opening valves to release steam when necessary. The atmosphere on the quiet boat was wary and watchful.

"Heave to, you lily-white ladies," Levi bellowed as the hands strained. "That branch will rot in the water before you work it free. Heave now!"

Suddenly there was a loud crack and Nathan's intent face broke into a triumphant smile. "Pull it in," he ordered, "and let the engine room have a shot at it."

"Stand by, Jamie," Serena called. When the lever was drawn aboard, she gave the command, "Ahead half."

The engine strained a moment and the great wheel remained stationary. She was about to order the engines cut when the limb gave with a resounding snap and the wheel began to turn, sweeping the debris under the surface of the churning water.

As the crew cheered, Nathan joined Serena. Her shoulders slumped wearily. Her lovely dress was limp and grease stained. Her hair had worked free of its pins and hung in damp ringlets around her face, but he thought she looked lovely.

"Fine work, Rena," he complimented her, his voice barely audible over the din.

"Fine work, Cap'n," she returned the compliment. Picking up his discarded jacket, vest and tie, she looped her arm in his gaily. "Let's go see how Uncle Will is doing."

They found the elderly pilot steering on the current, anxious for steam to build. "Shall I spell you, partner?" she asked.

"At noon, as scheduled," he answered sharply. Then his expression softened. "I'm fine. You and Nate look plumb wore out."

"I should go change clothes," Serena said without enthusiasm. Looking down, she realized for the first time that her dress was soiled. "Hell's bells," she muttered.

"You have time before your watch," Nathan murmured. Capturing her wrist loosely, he pulled her down to sit beside him. One arm draped on the back of the bench, he stretched his long legs in front of him. "Rest for a minute."

As they sat, Serena's head began to nod. Fatigued from the night and the morning's crisis, she fell asleep, her head dropping to rest on Nathan's shoulder. Smiling crookedly, he settled himself more comfortably and soon dozed himself. Will grinned at them over his shoulder as the *Sprite* continued downriver.

Voices awoke Nathan. He opened his eyes to find his cheek rested against the top of Serena's head and his arm had tightened around her while they slept. Her small body fit against his and he sat still for a moment, savoring the feel of it.

"What can I do for you, Reverend?" Will was asking.

Turning his head, Nathan saw Reverend Morris through the open doorway. Halfway up the ladder, he poised, a thick Bible under his arm, his shocked gaze fixed on the entwined couple. "I thought since none of you were able to attend services this morning—"

"That's mighty friendly of you," the old pilot cut in, "but I'm about to turn the wheel over to my niece."

Unmoving, the minister frowned toward the sleeping girl. "She hardly looks capable of steering a steamboat. Women were never meant for such work."

"Serena does just fine," Nathan maintained. Giving her a gentle shake, he coaxed, "Wake up, sleepyhead."

With a drowsy protest, she snuggled closer. One eye flew open when she realized the man held her in a cozy embrace. Sitting up, she smoothed her rumpled clothing. "I must have fallen asleep."

"I knew it when you started snoring," Nathan teased.

"I must say, you both show remarkably little remorse for such unseemly behavior," Reverend Morris interjected.

Serena's face flamed when she turned to see the black-clad minister, perched like a censorious crow on the ladder outside.

But before she could reply, Will stepped back from the wheel. "You ready to take over, Rena? It's noon and I'm in need of lunch. You comin', Nate?"

"You and the reverend go ahead. I'll be down in a minute."

He lingered after the other men had departed, watching Serena. Though she now stood efficiently at her post, her eyelids were still heavy and her temple was marked with a red spot where it had pressed against his shoulder.

"Don't worry about what the good reverend thinks, Rena," he said softly. "You did nothing worse than take a catnap."

"I know." She sighed. "He always makes me feel as if I've done something wrong. But I guess he makes everyone feel that way. He lectured Mother all through breakfast about the evils of bringing up children on a boat. And after what happened to Dory last night, she looked as if she believed him. It's bad enough when he preaches entire sermons at me because I'm a pilot. And last time he was aboard, he called me a heathen because I couldn't recite the names of the books of the Old Testament."

"What did you say to that?"

"I told him we have readings on the *Sprite* every Sunday and I know how to look those books up better than he knows how to read the river."

"And then?" Nathan prompted, grinning broadly.

"After he lectured me on the sin of false pride, I offered to let him steer."

He bellowed with laughter. "Serena, you're incorrigible."

His attention drawn by Nathan's booming laughter, Roger stared across the tops of the cotton bales on the texas, his fists clenched reflexively, until he saw the captain leave the pilot-house. Then, tearing his gaze from the ornate structure, the clerk stalked back to his office.

In a good mood, Nathan took the companionway two steps at a time, nearly colliding with a small form emerging from the linen locker on the boiler deck.

"Fetch this, fetch that," Dory muttered under her breath behind a tall stack of folded towels. "If Reverend Morris is so set against laboring on the Sabbath, why are his daughters trying to work me to death? If one more person tries to order me around..."

"Whoa, watch where you're going," a masculine voice commanded, and a big hand on her arm steadied her. "Who's behind there?

"Dory," Nathan answered his own question when he peered over the wobbling stack of towels she carried. "You nearly ran me down."

"I'm sorry." The girl looked stricken. "I didn't mean to."

"I didn't think you did." Taking the greater portion of her burden, he asked cheerfully, "Where are we taking these?"

"To the Morris girls' cabin," she nearly squeaked, thrilled by his attention.

He frowned in exaggerated wariness. "I'll walk you as far as their parents' cabin, but I don't think I'd be wise to go any closer.

"That's better," he said when she giggled. "I almost didn't recognize you before when you were wearing that big frown. Is everything all right today, Dory?"

"Everything's fine now." She beamed at him. "Thank you for rescuing me last night."

"You're more than welcome. I couldn't let anything happen to one of my favorite girls." Nathan stopped and replaced the towels he carried on Dory's stack. "This is close enough."

"I'll be glad when we get to Lake Providence and the Morrises get off the boat," the girl said with a gusty sigh.

"I know what you mean." Nathan also sighed. "But we've got to be as hospitable and as gracious as we can be. A good part of the *River Sprite's* business is hospitality."

"That's what Mother says," she replied glumly. "She says we'll dance in circles, if we must, to please our passengers."

"I agree." The captain's manner was solemn, but his eyes twinkled. "And when these particular passengers disembark, we'll dance in circles to celebrate." As he departed, he bent to whisper in Dory's ear, "Just don't tell anybody I said so."

The next day when Serena climbed up to relieve Will, he whistled softly.

"I just thought I'd try something different today." Self-consciously she smoothed the skirt of her blue-and-white dress over the cage crinoline she wore.

"Even without that contraption, I think you're purtiest gal on this boat," the old man snorted, "but I don't suppose you'll pay much mind to what your old uncle has to say. I'll jest go since there ain't room here for two pilots and your petticoats.

"By the way," he added, pausing on the ladder. "Devil's Elbow was stickin' up out of the water."

"Low water at Chute 92. Thanks, Uncle Will."

As Serena steered southward, she negotiated a difficult passage between island and riverbank, but once it was done, her mind turned to the night before.

Roger had appeared at her cabin door to escort her to dinner, taking her hand possessively and holding it even after they joined the others in the salon. Nathan had turned when they entered, but seeing the clerk at Serena's side, he had simply nodded and resumed his conversation with Hannah Morris.

For Serena, dinner had been interminable as she struggled with Roger's dogged attention and Nathan's apparent indifference. The captain had seemed to ignore her, but when she glanced in his direction, she discovered he was watching her. He had looked away quickly when their eyes met, but not before she glimpsed a flare of...

A flare of what? she asked herself realistically now. Of friendship? That's what they were after all...friends. But friendship was what she felt for Roger. Why had life become so complicated since Nathan came aboard the *River Sprite?*

"Sorry I'm late, Rena," Dory's voice cut into her brooding.

Over her shoulder, Serena saw her sister struggling up the ladder with a tray. "Careful," she called. "If you get your foot hung in your hoops, you'll tumble rump over rudder."

"Don't let Mother hear you say that," Dory advised, concentrating on her burden.

Glancing ahead, Serena ascertained it was plain sailing and stepped to Dory's aid, plucking a tottering pitcher from the tray.

"I can make it," the girl gasped. "Get back to the wheel."

Still holding the pitcher in one hand, Serena placed the other on the wheel to ease her sister's mind.

Setting Serena's lunch on the bench, Dory looked around in delight. "It's so lovely up here."

"You're welcome to visit whenever you like...as long as you don't get in the way."

"I'm not a child, Serena Elizabeth." Dory frowned, her manner an imitation of Grace's.

"I didn't say you were, Pandora Clarisse," Serena shot back.

Unconcernedly Dory stepped to the window and surveyed the texas where Nathan stood at the railing, the wind ruffling his hair as he doffed his hat to the Morris sisters. "Look at those three," she said bitterly. "They're such shameless flirts."

"So's Nathan."

"No, he's courtly and considerate. And he was so gallant when he rescued me from that terrible Mr. Frasier."

Serena bit her tongue to keep from reminding her that she and Grandfather's shotgun had been a part of that rescue, as well.

"I don't think you really know Nathan for the gentleman he is," the younger girl concluded airily.

"And you do?"

"I see the chivalrous side of him more than you do. I enjoy his company and I don't shout at him every time we're together for five minutes."

"Why, you little—"

"Please don't be common, Serena," Dory instructed haughtily. "Sometimes you're so childish."

Resisting the urge to let loose some common language, Serena eyed her sister with vexation. Then she turned a hard stare on the man who visited with the trio of females below.

When Nathan headed below, Dory hurried to the mirror. "I must tend to my other duties," she said, pinching her cheeks and biting her lips to bring color into them. "I'll send Simon up for the tray later." In an instant, she was gone.

Serena slapped her hand against the wheel. Dory was smitten with Nathan. It was one thing for him to carry on with Hannah Morris, but her sister was just a girl, a sensitive, impressionable girl.

Surveying the length of the boat, she saw Nathan walking far forward along the boiler deck. Suddenly he stopped and turned. Dory caught up with him and they walked together to the bow. Even at a distance, Serena imagined she could see his lazy smile and the bright expression on her sister's face. She must have a word with the *lady-killer,* she decided. The sooner the better.

When her watch was over, Serena found Nathan in the salon with Colonel Neal, a passenger who had boarded in Greenville, Mississippi. "May I speak with you, Captain . . . alone?"

"Of course." With a puzzled expression, he rose and gestured to his companion. "Have you met Colonel Neal?"

"I have." Her gaze barely flickered over the dapper man. She had met the colonel many times. She had always suspected he was a sure-thing player, but had not been able to prove it.

"I fear Miss Caswell does not approve of me." The gambler seemed to read her thoughts.

"She doesn't approve of me, either," Nathan joked, following Serena out on deck. "If I'm not back in ten minutes, you may assume she's pushed me overboard. Excuse us, sir."

Seeking a place where they could talk undisturbed, the girl led him to stand on the stern.

"What's the matter?" he asked, mystified by her gravity.

"It's about Dory."

"What about her?"

"I want you to stay away from her."

"What?" He goggled at her.

"Just stay away from my little sister, that's all." She started to walk away, but Nathan pulled her back.

"What are you accusing me of?" he growled.

"I'm not accusing you of anything yet. Dory has a crush on you and I don't want you to encourage her anymore."

"I never encouraged her in the first place. My God, Serena, Dory is young and sweet. I'd never—"

"You'd never what? What about the girl I saw you with in Baton Rouge that time? She looked pretty young and sweet."

"What girl?" The man's brow furrowed in confusion.

"The one with the carriage. I saw you embrace her. Right out on the dock."

"That was my sister," he exploded. "Damnation, Serena, what an accusation. You don't have to worry. I'm not trying to seduce your baby sister."

"No, you're too busy trying to seduce every other female on this boat," she charged, sorry the moment the words left her mouth.

"How would you know when you spend all your time leading on poor Blake?"

"I am not leading him on!"

"Then what do you call this?" He flicked the sleeve of her dress with his finger. "All dressed up to catch a husband."

"You must have me confused with Hannah Morris. She's so anxious to find a man, she'd even settle for you."

"And who would you settle for?" He towered over her furiously, but she refused to back an inch.

"I don't need a husband at all and, if I did, it certainly wouldn't be you!"

"Then you might wait until you're asked!" he bellowed.

"And I might push you overboard after all, you insufferable, strutting peacock—"

Without warning, Nathan's muscular arm wrapped around her, capturing her arms next to her body. His mouth came down on hers in a hard kiss, cutting off her tirade. Doubling her fists, she pounded on his back, but he was undeterred.

Gradually her struggling lessened and she moaned deep in her throat. Sensing her surrender, his lips gentled and he loosened his punishing embrace.

Instinctively Serena's arms slid around his waist and she clung to him, knowing she was drowning in the sweetness of his kiss. As the boat rounded a bend and the afternoon sun washed over them, she was aware of every detail . . . the warmth across her shoulders, the breeze that stirred her hair, Nathan's hands stroking her back.

Sinking onto the chair, he drew her onto his lap. She reveled in the feel of him, reaching up to trace the strong line of his jaw with a delicate touch. As desire raged through him, he pulled her nearer. Instinctively she molded her body to his, closer, until he thought he would explode with passion.

At the sound of jaunty whistling and approaching footsteps, Serena's sanity returned. Guiltily she shot up from Nathan's lap, just as Colonel Neal rounded the cabin section.

Taking in the couple's flustered appearance, he looked away in embarrassment. "Pardon me, I didn't know anyone was back here. I didn't mean to intrude."

"I was just leaving." Mortified and near tears, Serena fled. She was no better than the maid they had surprised with Fiske

Patterson that night, she castigated herself as she climbed blindly to the texas. She had behaved like a wanton and been caught. How could she face the colonel after what he had seen? How could she face Nathan after what she had done?

"Five'll get you ten, you marry that girl, Trent," Colonel Neal told Nathan thoughtfully.

"She was just explaining that she doesn't need a husband."

"I never saw a gal protest quite the way she was protesting."

"Doesn't matter. Even if I was the marrying kind...and I'm not," the captain said emphatically, "I wouldn't hook up with a feisty little firebrand like Serena Caswell."

"It's your call, son," the colonel opined, "but from what I just saw, you'd better marry her or get yourself off this boat."

"Right now, neither one is an option," Nathan said in disgust, stalking away. "But I'll bear it in mind."

Chapter Nine

No cloud marred the brilliant blue of the summer sky and the afternoon sun shone radiantly overhead, wilting the tender leaves of Grace's rosebushes and turning the cabins into ovens. Between cotton bales on the *Sprite*'s shady decks, the passengers lolled in chairs. Their faces turned to the scorching wind, they discussed the weather and waited for the cool of evening.

Between the two captains of the overburdened steamboat, tensions were high. If anyone aboard the *River Sprite* had been unaware of the attraction between Nathan and Serena, the strain now told it all. Scowling and short-tempered, they avoided each other while everyone else avoided them.

What had happened, Grace wondered when she took a shortcut through the deserted salon and saw Serena sitting alone. From the beginning, the attraction between the couple had been almost as powerful as the antagonism. But for the past two days, it seemed they could hardly bear to be on the same boat together. Frowning fretfully, the woman stepped through the open doorway and nearly collided with Nathan.

"Pardon me," he mumbled absently. When he caught sight of the girl in the dim salon, a determined look settled onto his face and he marched inside.

"What do you want?" Serena greeted him when he presented himself at her table.

"I want to talk to you."

"I don't want to talk to you."

"We have to get things worked out between us." Stubbornly he dropped into the chair across from her. "What happened the other day on the stern—"

"Shouldn't have happened."

"No, it shouldn't have," he agreed, "not if we're going to work together every day. We are friends, after all, and I am very fond of you, but I don't want . . . I mean, I'm not ready for—"

"Ready for what, Nathan?"

He met her icy gaze unflinchingly. "For love or for marriage."

"I wouldn't have you for either one," Serena informed him. "Furthermore, I can't believe your presumption."

"It wasn't my presumption I was worried about. I didn't want *you* to have the wrong idea."

"I haven't had a wrong idea about you since the day we met," she bristled. "I knew then you were a black-hearted son of—"

"Careful, Serena," he warned dangerously. "Colorful language is how you got into trouble on the stern."

"Nate! Rena!" Oblivious to the friction, Hank sped into the salon and placed himself between them. "Uncle Will wants you in the texas. He says the *Heron* is up ahead and it looks like she's stripped down, holding her steam and spoiling for a race."

"Blast that Wingate." Serena's ire found a new target.

"That's what Uncle Will says." The boy followed excitedly as she headed for the door. "He says the river doesn't need captains who don't pay any mind to safety."

"I've heard about this Wingate," Nathan said grimly, overtaking them on deck. "Isn't he the one who's famous for holding his steam and overstoking?"

"He the one," Serena confirmed. "He's going to get himself killed one of these days and take a lot of innocent passengers with him." As she clattered up the companionway behind Nathan, she ordered, "Hank, find Mother and Dory and stay with them."

"But—"

"That's an order, Hank," the captain threw over his shoulder. "They'll need you if there's trouble."

Sulkily he obeyed as Nathan and Serena climbed to the wheelhouse, where Will was keeping a wary watch on the boat they approached. On the decks below, passengers congregated at the railings. Even Serena felt the excitement of a possible race, though she knew the danger of Captain Wingate's actions.

As the *River Sprite* steamed toward the other boat, they could see that the *Heron* was indeed stripped and ready for racing. Though she carried a double crew for speed and efficiency, only a few passengers were on her decks, calling across the water.

Before the *River Sprite* could draw even with her, a distant rumble began. Suddenly the *Heron* lurched and bucked in the water as, with a mighty roar, the boilers exploded, spewing jets of white-hot steam.

In an instant, a column of flame and smoke erupted from below, cleaving the great boat in half, splintering the boiler deck and throwing debris and bodies fifty feet into the air.

The force of the explosion rocked the *Sprite* and threw Serena to the floor. Nathan lay atop her, shielding her with his big body as cinders and scraps of the *Heron* rained down on the hurricane deck.

Immediately he was on his feet, helping Will to rise from the floor where he, too, had fallen. Getting up shakily, Serena looked down from the pilothouse in horror. Shrieks reached her from the other boat as both halves tilted, throwing passengers and crew into the river. The wind fanned several smaller fires into one tremendous conflagration. People, their clothing aflame, jumped from the decks of the severed boat, joining the others in the murky water.

"Man overboard!" echoed aboard the *River Sprite*. On the main deck, Levi bawled orders to the crew rushing to their stations. Nathan vaulted out of the pilothouse with Serena following at breakneck speed.

"Roger," the captain bellowed as he sprinted across the texas, "gather the stewards and wet down every bale of cotton. If a spark or an ember ignites one, we'll go up like tinder."

"Reverse engines," Will's roar could be heard as he shouted down the speaking tube.

When Jamie reversed the paddle wheel to reduce their speed, the gears protested and the entire boat gave a tremendous creak and shudder. Pure white pressurized steam screamed from the gauge cocks and the great smokestacks vibrated and belched smoke into the sky.

In the companionway, Nathan bounced against the bulkhead, lurching down the steps like a drunken man. Regaining his balance, he glanced back at Serena and ordered, "Stay with Will. This is not going to be a pretty sight."

"Uncle Will doesn't need my help. Those people do." Gathering her skirt around her knees, she raced, on Nathan's heels, for the staircase at the bow.

Down on the main deck, a rescue was already underway as the *River Sprite* drifted on the current. Will was careful to keep the *Sprite* clear of the sinking boat, because the *Heron* was likely to blow apart.

Knowing the river was too treacherous for swimmers, Nathan ordered Levi to gather a small crew and set out in one of the *Sprite*'s sounding boats. While crew and passengers leaned over the railing of the main deck, extending poles and lifelines, the men in the boat plucked some victims out of the water.

Accustomed to being pressed into service as the boat's doctor, Gustave hurried forward from the galley, his medical kit under his arm, his white apron flapping around his legs.

"Mam'selle Serena, you can help me over here, *oui?*" He indicated a hastily cleared space with a nod of his head.

Kneeling over an injured man, they attempted to cleanse his wounds, only to have them contaminated again by the ash-laden wind. The smoke burned their eyes and left a coating of soot on their faces. Intent on her work, the girl was scarcely aware when her mother joined her.

"I have asked Dory and Hank to gather all the blankets they can find," the woman reported calmly. "What else can I do?"

"Where's Serena?" Nathan looked around as another casualty was hauled aboard. "I need some help over here."

"I'll go." Grace hurried to his side, her face blanching when she saw the blood gushing from the man's leg. But she bent over the wound with single-minded concentration, declaring at last, "I fear it needs to be sewn."

"There is a needle and thread in my kit," the cook called, "but the light, it is not good, no. Night is falling and soon none 'of us can see what we are doing."

"We'll use the forecastle as an infirmary. You'll find it easier to work in a shelter with some light," Nathan told Grace.

"You," he summoned a bewildered steerage passenger, "shove everything off the table in there and spread a blanket on it. Bill, Luke," he called two crewmen, "pick up this wounded man...gently now...and put him wherever Mrs. Caswell tells you."

Grace looked askance at Gustave.

"I trust, *madame,*" he said solemnly, his mustache drooping in the heat, "that your needle craft is finer than mine."

"Nathan," Serena called as she moved between the pallets, tending lesser wounds, "if the people are not badly injured when they're brought aboard, why not have them carried to the leeward side of the cotton bales, out of the wind until we can tend them?"

"Good. We'll set up a temporary morgue in there." He nodded toward the door of a spacious equipment locker nearby. "That will give us more room to work."

For a time, the couple worked side by side, their differences forgotten. Then Nathan returned to his post at the rail.

"Here are the blankets, Rena."

Serena turned to discover her sister and brother behind her, weighed down with blankets. "Thank you. Put them on the bench beside the forecastle. Then, Dory, see if you can help Gustave. No, wait . . . we'll soon need more water—"

"The Morris girls are getting it right now."

"What can I do?" Hank asked as Dory bustled to join Gustave.

"Go to the forecastle and hold the lantern for Mother while she sews."

"Sews?" The boy swallowed deeply.

"You can do it." She smiled when he hurried away to do her bidding. Surveying the activity on deck with weary satisfaction, she noted the yawl had returned to the *Sprite* with its burden. Nathan leaned precariously over the rail, helping to haul the survivors and the dead aboard. Already a dozen wounded, most of them men, lay on the deck while, at the railing, the rescue was still underway.

The female steerage passengers, who had at first huddled in a group, had recovered from their shock and were doing their best to make the wounded as comfortable as possible. The Morris girls walked forward, each bearing two buckets of water while their mother escorted the survivors who were unharmed to the salon. The minister circulated among the victims, stopping beside their pallets to offer encouragement or a brief prayer. When he saw Serena looking his direction, he beckoned her.

"Your cook says we have no way to tend the burn victims," he said without preamble. "In an account of a steamboat explosion I read, the victims were packed in flour to ease their suffering."

"I've heard of that. I'll have some flour brought from stores, but I fear that's the best we can do for them until we can get to the doctor in Lake Providence."

While Serena searched for an able-bodied man to fetch the flour, the last of the *Heron*'s boilers exploded, the impact rocking the *River Sprite*. The rescuers dived for cover and a cry rose from an unfortunate crewman who had not ducked fast enough. She raced to the railing to discover Fiske Patterson's arm had been cut by a bit of flying metal. When she saw the ugly gash in his skin, she forgot her dislike for him.

"Go inside, Serena," Nathan roared when he saw her in the open. "We'll bring him to you in the forecastle."

"There's not room," she shouted back, ripping the sleeve from around Fiske's wound.

Nathan moved to hover over her, sheltering her, though the *Heron* had completely disappeared below the surface. The other rescuers returned to their positions, straining their eyes to spot survivors in the twilight. As night fell, hope dwindled.

"I don't think it needs stitches," Serena announced after stanching the wound. "Let's move him alee so I can cleanse and bandage it."

"I can walk," Fiske said curtly. "It's my arm that's hurt, not my leg." Taking the cloth she held, he clamped it over the cut on his arm and lurched to his feet.

As the muscular deckhand wended his way toward the other side of the boat, Serena picked up a lantern, a small bottle and a basin of water. Remembering the flour, she sent two crewmen to stores.

Fiske waited for her on the other side of the cotton bales, pressing the wadded fabric against his wounded arm. She was aware of his unswerving gaze as she set her burden on the deck. Spreading out a blanket, she directed him to sit down.

When he complied, leaning his brawny back against one of the bales, she knelt to face him. Holding the lantern closer, she instructed briskly, "All right, let's have a look at that arm."

The blood-soaked fabric still held over the wound, he extended the injured limb.

"You'll need to move the cloth so I can see," she said, forced to meet his eyes.

He removed it, but his gaze did not move from her face as she inspected the wound.

"The bleeding is almost stopped. The cut is long, but it's not deep." She thrust the lantern toward him. "Hold this."

Sitting erect, he took the lamp and held it aloft with his good hand. His wounded arm extended across Serena's lap, the wrist propped against her hipbone as she scrutinized the gash on the inside of his powerful forearm. He maneuvered so his hand rested lightly at her waist, but, in her concentration, she did not notice.

"There don't seem to be any metal fragments in it."

"Good." Placing the lamp on the deck, he continued to sit erect, his head very close to hers as she washed out the cut. Feeling his breath on her cheek, she straightened, increasing the distance between them as much as her kneeling posture would allow, and glared at him. Then, picking up the small bottle of whiskey they were using for disinfectant, she doused the wound with it.

"Oww!" Fiske yelped, jerking back. When the stinging had ceased, he regained his composure and leaned toward her again. "This is not the way I would have chosen to get a lovely lady to pay attention to me."

She started when he bent his elbow, causing the blood to well up again in the cleansed gash, and ran his hand along the back of her arm. Her jaw set, she demanded, "Are you going to let me see to your arm or not?"

"I am." Allowing it to drop limply onto her lap, he sank back against the bale and smiled at her. "I'm weaker than I first thought. I may need a great deal of nursing."

"That can be arranged." Nathan stepped around the cotton bales and called over his shoulder, "Gustave, come and see to Patterson."

Fiske glared up at him, nettled by the interruption. Serena's eyes widened when she realized how their posture must look to Nathan. Fumbling with the roll of gauze, she began to bandage the man's wounded arm.

"Gustave will take care of that." Taking Serena's hand, Nathan drew her to her feet. "Come on, the worst is over."

"Miss Serena, I thank you for your tender—" Fiske's voice seemed to caress the word, deliberately goading the other man "—care. And thank you for yours, Cap'n." His smile did not reach his eyes as he watched the couple walk away.

"I knew you were tending the sick," Nathan muttered as they made their way to the stairs on the bow, "but I didn't know it included the lame, the halt and the useless."

Up in the wheelhouse, Nathan, Serena and Will discussed whether to proceed downriver or to turn back.

"Lake Providence is closer," Serena maintained stubbornly.

"But it's pitch-black out there," Nathan protested. "Didn't you tell me that going downriver is hazardous while the Mississippi is so low, especially since the boat is loaded down and drawing too much water?"

"It is dangerous," Will admitted, "but it's not impossible. If we stay with the current and keep two leadsmen on the bow, we can do it."

"We have to do it," Serena interjected, "even if we have to place a buoy every mile. The injured need medical attention as soon as possible."

"All right," Nathan yielded. "What do I do?"

"Tell Levi to stand by with the yawl and a sounding crew." Serena took the wheel from the exhausted Will. "And don't worry. We'll get through."

The boat moved slowly and silently through the night. As Nathan paced the main deck, the only sounds were the moans of the wounded and the voices of the leadsmen who measured the river's depth every few feet. Serena steered the *Sprite* past shallows and sandbars until she reached a shoal crossing she feared the stern-wheeler could not make.

Securing the *Sprite* at the riverbank, she watched anxiously from the pilothouse as the yawl set out toward the shoal. She strained her eyes to see them through the darkness. Nathan had gone along. What a damn fool idea for a man who didn't know the river.

Seeing Will climbing up the stairs at the bow, she suddenly knew why he had gone. Usually a pilot accompanied the sounding crew, but she had not thought her uncle would try to do so after his illness. How had Nathan managed to convince the old man to let him take his place?

At last, a light flickered out on the river and fought against the wind. After a moment, a buoy, constructed of a board and a paper lantern, was set afloat at the shallowest point and the men held their oars straight up in air.

Giving a blast of the whistle to let them know she had seen their signal, Serena took the *Sprite* out again. It crept on the current, maneuvering past the yawl and the buoy into safe water.

Once past the shoal, the *Sprite*'s wheel was reversed to hold the boat's position until the sounding crew could be taken aboard. When she heard a cheer below, she knew they had returned.

"Ready when you are, Madame Pilot," Nathan's voice drifted up the speaking tube from the engine room.

"Aye-aye, Cap'n," she answered, giddy with relief. "Give her all you've got, Jamie."

Almost the entire population of Lake Providence was roused from their beds near dawn that summer morning when the *River Sprite*'s whistle signaled an emergency. People poured out to the levee to lend assistance. The two local doctors came aboard and, after a hasty conference, decided to transfer the patients, more than a score of them, to a makeshift hospital in the hotel.

Nearly a dozen corpses were taken to the undertaker. Captain Wingate was not among the living or the dead and the *Sprite*'s crew had no idea how many others were missing. Nor would they ever know, the superstitious crewmen predicted, for the river never gave up its dead.

"Come on, gal." Shaking his stiff leg to ease it, Will climbed up into the wheelhouse, where he found Serena drooped against the wheel. "You did me proud last night, Rena. Now go along and get some rest."

"I will, if you will," she agreed with a wan smile.

"I will. We're gonna need our strength," he confided glumly as they walked to their cabins. "Your mother says we're goin' to a service this evenin' at Reverend Morris's church. He had it all figgered out before we got to Stack Island."

"Don't take it so hard, Uncle Will. The dead should be remembered and we certainly owe thanks to the good Lord for getting us through last night."

"Amen to that," Nathan said, ambling toward them.

Freed of the strain of the night, Serena could not keep a laugh inside when she saw him. It welled up, a sound of merriment and joy and pure relief. "Oh, Nathan, look at you."

Grinning, he led her to a window where they could see their reflections, wavering, distorted and definitely soot stained.

"When y'all finish laughin' like loons, mebbe you should go to bed," Will suggested. "That's where I'm goin'."

Shaking her head in mock exasperation, Serena teased, "Don't mind my uncle. He gets cross when he hasn't had enough sleep."

"And he gets downright cantankerous when he's been slickered," the old pilot added sourly. "Next time we cut cards, Nate, I'm furnishin' the deck."

"So that's how you convinced him to stay aboard during the sounding," Serena murmured as Nathan walked her to the stern.

"Cutting the cards seemed preferable to fisticuffs."

"Uncle Will thinks you cheated."

"There are a few things in life worth cheating for."

"And keeping Uncle Will out of the sounding boat is one of them," she granted with a grin. "Thank you. I know he can be stubborn."

"Stubbornness is a Caswell family trait," the captain said lightly. Stopping in front of her door, he turned to her seriously and asked, "Are you still mad at me, Serena . . . for what happened the other day?"

After a long moment's silence, she murmured, "I guess it was as much my fault as yours. After all, it takes two to kiss."

"That's what makes it so much fun," he teased, wishing he could see the flood of color in her cheeks, hidden by the layer of soot. Opening the door, he said gently, "Go on, get some sleep."

Chapter Ten

Nathan stood on the doorstep of the elegant house and debated. Though summer was the "sick" season as far north as Baton Rouge and most Creoles retired to their plantations to escape the threat of yellow jack, he had come to the town house in hopes of finding his family at home. But now that he was here, he was uncertain about his reception. He had been away for four years with very little communication.

Drawing a deep breath, he dropped the heavy brass knocker. Immediately the door was opened by an ancient black man who beamed in welcome.

"Lord-a-mercy, it's Mr. Nate!"

"Hello, Saul." Nathan smiled with genuine pleasure at the sight of the old servant. "How are you?"

"Tol'able." He stepped back to admit the young man. "Glad to see you, suh. Have you come home to stay?"

"No, just for the afternoon." Nathan paused to gaze around the familiar foyer.

"That's too bad. Your mama will be sad to have missed you."

"They're out at Le Jardin?"

"Yes, suh, till the end of August. You s'pose you'll be in Baton Rouge then?"

"I don't know."

"Come in and sit a spell," the butler insisted, leading him into the parlor. "Can I get you somethin' to eat?"

"No, thanks." Nathan stopped before the fireplace to stare at the painting above the carrera mantel. His father's face, so like his own, stared down at him from the portrait. Beside Micah Trent, sat Camille, his wife, her delicate Creole beauty still apparent despite the years and a softening of the chin. "They look well," he muttered.

"They've been well mostly. An' happy, 'cept for missin' you. They've been waitin' for the day you'd come home."

"Even Father?"

"'Specially your father."

"When I left here, I could not believe that he was right, that time would heal the hurt Addie had caused me. I wanted to go, to get away. He thought I was running from memories I should stay and face. He accused me being a coward, of wallowing in self-pity."

"Words spoken in anger," Saul replied gently.

"But they were true," Nathan said sadly.

"Mr. Micah knows you well, suh. The two of you are a good deal alike."

"You think he'll forgive me for four years of foolishness?"

Saul regarded him warmly. "The very same way you would forgive him, Mr. Nate."

Going to the window, Nathan looked out at the garden. When he turned to the butler again, his voice was hoarse with emotion, "I believe I'll leave a letter for my family. Then I'd better go."

Poised at the front door later, Nathan extended his hand. "Thank you, Saul. Thanks for everything. I'll see you soon."

"Yes, suh." With a pleased grin, Saul shook the hand the young man offered. Then he watched as he disappeared down the street toward the river.

At the busy dock, Nathan spied Serena stationed at the foot of the gangplank while a shipment for New Orleans was loaded into the boat's only remaining space. He sauntered toward her, the bouquet of flowers he carried already wilting in the heat.

"Where's Roger?" he called as he picked his way through crowds of passengers who waited until the last minute before boarding a nearby side-wheeler.

"Tallying kegs on the stern," she shouted over the din.

"For you." Reaching her side, Nathan presented the drooping flowers with a flourish.

Serena accepted them with a smile. "There was no reason for you to do that."

On the neighboring steamboat, a gong sounded and the voice of its head steward could be faintly heard, "All ashore that are going ashore!" A noisy party of well-wishers poured off the other boat and positioned themselves at the foot of its gangplank, laughing and calling to their friends among the passengers.

"There was no reason not to do it . . . since we're friends again," he countered softly, laying a gentle hand on her arm.

"Nathan Trent, is that you?" a throaty feminine voice called from behind him.

His fingers tightened involuntarily on Serena's arm before skimming down to claim her hand. Then, his face carefully neutral, he turned.

"It is you!" Detaching herself from the adjacent group, a black-clad woman glided toward him. Behind her, her friends watched curiously.

The woman was one of the most exquisite creatures Serena had ever seen. Framed by velvety brown curls, her face was fair and kittenish and, even at a distance, her eyes looked to be the most amazing shade of violet.

Serena's hand in his, Nathan greeted the newcomer blandly, "Hello, Addie."

"I can't believe it." The woman slanted a catlike smile up at him. "It's good to see you, Nathan, though I must say I'm surprised. Have you returned to Baton Rouge for good?"

"Just passing through."

Serena thought her fingers would break, but as she glanced up at the man's taut face, she knew he did not realize how tightly he gripped her hand. Turning a curious gaze on the woman, she wondered who this Addie was to have such an effect on the imperturbable captain.

"It's too bad you can't stay," the woman was saying, her husky voice somehow intimate. "You should, you know. You belong here."

"Not anymore. I've made a new life for myself." Drawing Serena forward, Nathan said evenly, "Mrs. Andrews, may I present Miss Serena Caswell? Serena, this is Adele Langley Andrews."

"How do you do, Mrs. Andrews?" Serena greeted the elegant woman awkwardly. Her eyes really were violet, she thought, inordinately saddened by the fact.

"How do you do, Miss..." Adele looked Serena over from her sturdy work shoes to the unadorned straw hat jammed over her auburn hair. Her eyes lingering on the pitiful bouquet Serena clutched, she asked haughtily, "Caswell, is it? Of the Virginia Caswells?"

"Of the Vicksburg Caswells." Serena bristled.

"I don't think I've ever heard of that branch of the family."

"How odd. We're known up and down the Mississippi."

"The Caswell family has owned the *River Sprite* for years," Nathan explained.

"River Sprite?" Adele turned a blank look upon him.

With wordless pride, he indicated the stern-wheeler moored behind them.

"Oh." Adele regarded the boat with distaste. "Are you traveling on it then? To New Orleans? Or beyond? I heard you had inherited your grandfather's plantation. Will you be going there?"

"I go wherever the *Sprite* goes."

"For as long as it goes," she said wryly. "Couldn't you have booked passage on a boat that was not quite so... old?"

Tired of Adele's attitude, Serena said artlessly, "Most steamboats are used so roughly, they don't last more than five or ten years, but the *Sprite* is fifteen. We take good care of her, don't we, Nate?"

"We?" Adele lifted a cynical brow.

"Serena is the pilot of the *River Sprite*."

"You mean she steers it?" the woman sputtered. Amused by her reaction, he smiled for the first time, despite himself.

"Nathan is the captain," Serena volunteered.

"Nathan, the captain of a steamboat?" Adele laughed aloud.

"What's so funny?" Serena scowled. "He's a partner in the *Sprite* and a good captain. He's only been on the river a short time and he's already one of the best."

"My dear," Adele purred with a sidelong glance at the man, "you have an admirer, so young and steadfast."

"Rena and I make a good team."

"I see you were not jesting when you said you had made a new life for yourself." The young widow drew herself up disdainfully. "What a strange life it must be with river people, away from your own kind."

Nathan glowered at her. "That comment was uncalled-for, Addie."

"It was," she acknowledged with an unrepentant smile. "I do beg your pardon, Miss Caswell." She leaned toward the man conspiratorially as if she had not spoken harsh words moments before. "I have missed you, Nathan. You're still the only one who will not let me get by with things like that.

"Will you walk me to my carriage? Most of my party seems to have gone to theirs."

"Of course," he agreed with reluctant politeness. "Excuse me, will you, Rena?"

"Doesn't this seem like old times?" Looping her arm through Nathan's, Adele shot a triumphant look at the girl. "I'm so pleased to have met you, Miss Caswell," she professed insincerely, "and to have had this . . . refreshing conversation. Perhaps I will have an opportunity to ride on your boat one day."

Watching the couple stroll toward Adele's waiting carriage, Serena wondered whether the woman's parting words had been a threat or a promise.

"I meant what I said. I've missed you," Adele was telling Nathan with a confidential smile. "Will you come to dinner tonight?"

"I cannot," he answered, his manner stiffly formal. "We leave within the hour. But, please, give your father my best."

Unaccustomed to rebuff, she said waspishly, "He'll be sorry to have missed you. He does regret that you and I did not marry, you know."

"Then he is the only one." Nathan's voice was cold.

Halting, Adele gazed up at him, her violet eyes brimming with tears. "How can you say such a thing? Don't you know I've never forgiven myself for what I did? If I had it to do again, I wouldn't have broken our engagement, I wouldn't have married George, I—"

"The past is past," he cut her off harshly.

"Then let us make a new start, darling," she urged with a tremulous smile. "Say you forgive me and I will do any-thing...*anything*...to make amends. You must know I've never stopped loving you, Nathan. I never will." A tear rolled down her cheek.

"Stop it, Addie," he commanded impatiently. "It won't work anymore. I know you can weep buckets at will."

"You've changed, Nathan," she accused, glaring at him, "and I can't say I like it."

"You're exactly as I remembered you."

"Then you remember I do not give up until I have what I want."

Silently Nathan guided the woman to the carriage and handed her in. Then he pivoted and walked back toward town.

Swatting the battered bouquet against her skirt in frustra-tion, Serena watched until he disappeared from view.

How dare Nathan treat her so...so casually! Adele fumed as her carriage rumbled along the dock toward the street. The way he had dismissed her and walked away without a look back, one would think it had not been four long years since he had seen her. He still felt something for her, she was certain. Otherwise he would not have introduced that plain little fe-male with red hair. He had held her between them like a shield.

As the carriage crossed the street that ran parallel to the river, she looked up and down it, but there was no sign of Nathan.

"Leo, stop here," she ordered the driver. Leaning forward, she handed him some money. "I nearly forgot. Father asked me to pick up some cigars for him. Run back to that tobacconist and buy a box. You know the kind he likes."

"Yes, ma'am." Leo descended, looking nervously up and down the street. The waterfront was no place to leave your mistress sitting in an open carriage, but he knew better than to argue with Adele Langley Andrews.

Opening her parasol, she sat, lost in thought, until a cocky masculine voice interrupted.

"Pardon me, miss, but didn't I just see you talking to Cap'n Trent of the *River Sprite?*"

"Yes." Adele looked down her nose at the good-looking man who spoke to her from the sidewalk.

"I thought so." Fiske Patterson smiled charmingly. "If you don't mind my saying so, ma'am, this street is no place for a lady alone."

"My driver is just in the tobacconist."

"Then I'll wait here with you until he gets back. The cap'n would expect no less of me."

"You work for Nathan Trent, Mr...."

"Patterson, Fiske Patterson," he said at once. "Yes, I do, ma'am."

"Then you must know Miss Caswell, too."

"Yes, ma'am."

Licking her lips, she asked, "Tell me, are she and the captain..."

"Friends?" Fiske asked, his voice heavy with irony.

Adele nodded delicately.

"I can't say exactly, miss...." He regarded her expectantly in his turn."

"Mrs.," she corrected. "Mrs. George Andrews."

"I can't say, Mrs. Andrews, but their cabins are next to one another."

"Is that so?" Adele purred. "Mr. Patterson, you are in a position to do me a great service."

"What might that be?"

"I would like regular reports on Nathan Trent's activities."

Fiske's brows lifted quizzically. "Why would a fine lady like you be interested?"

"Shall we say I'd hate to think the son of such a wealthy family might be involved with a fortune hunter?"

"Or shall we say, you'd like Trent for yourself?"

Irritation flashed in Adele's violet eyes, then she smiled. "The reason is really none of your business. I will pay you for your time. All you have to do is to make regular reports to me. You can write, can't you?"

"I can write. What is it you're wanting in these reports?"

"Nathan's schedule on and off the boat, his finances, his relationship with Miss Caswell...anything I might use to make him come back to Baton Rouge where he belongs."

"And what's that worth to you, Mrs. Andrews?"

Seeing her driver emerge from the shop, the woman said hurriedly, "We'll settle the details tonight. Come to Langley House at nine o'clock. Use the back door. My maid will let you in."

"I'll be there," Fiske promised, and swaggered down the street.

Frowning, Leo returned to the carriage. "That man bothering you, Miss Adele?"

"No, Leo," she answered serenely. "He simply asked the time of day."

"Any sign of Nathan?" Serena asked as she entered the wheelhouse.

"Not yet." Cradling Catastrophe in one arm, Will turned from the window where he looked out over the shadowy waterfront.

"Where could he be?" she asked irritably. "We should have taken off hours ago. Should we send someone to look for our intrepid captain?"

"Don't reckon he'd care much for that."

"We ought to cast off without him," Serena fumed, pacing the narrow room. "It would serve him right."

"Have a little patience, gal," her uncle advised mildly. "Boats don't up and leave without their captains...even when they have more than one."

After Will left the pilothouse, Serena remained at her post, but she saw no sign of Nathan.

Where was he? she fretted. What if he were lying somewhere, injured? What if he weren't coming back? Why had he taken off this afternoon, without so much as a by-your-leave?

Gradually the nearly empty street became deserted and Serena's worry gave way to temper. Who did Nathan Trent think he was, to hold up an entire steamboat? And all because of Adele Andrews?

She knew instinctively the beautiful young widow was the reason for his absence. What was she to him? Had he loved her? Did he love her still?

Her emotions in turmoil, Serena went down to the main deck to place a watch. Then slowly she went to join her family for dinner.

After how many drinks was it? the whiskey still burned the back of Nathan's throat. The din in the waterfront tavern was still deafening and the air was still smoky and stale, but he paid it no mind. More shaken by his unexpected encounter with Adele than he cared to be, he needed time to collect his thoughts, which were becoming more muddled by the moment.

It had been inevitable that he and Addie should meet again, he brooded. After all this time, he had thought himself ready. Then this afternoon, she had appeared, clad in mourning for her elderly husband, begging him for a chance to make things right between them.

Once he would have rejoiced to know she wanted him back. Now it seemed a lifetime ago that he had adored Adele, the beauty of three parishes. Through their adolescence, he, she . . . everyone . . . had assumed they would marry. But she had betrayed him.

Spoiled, duplicitous Addie—it had hurt him to lose her. But now he saw the worst wound had been to his pride. He was over Adele and it was time to get on with his life, he decided, rising unsteadily. He had to get back to the *Sprite*. Rash thoughtlessness had brought him here and he had lost all track of time. He had delayed their departure and Serena was probably furious.

"Damnation," he muttered. Tossing payment onto the bar as he passed, the captain lurched out into the night.

Serena woke with a start and sat up in bed, listening. The sliver of moon was hidden behind clouds and the night was black, but she knew it must be close to dawn. From the cabin next door came a muffled voice singing the lyrics of a bawdy song.

The bulkhead between the cabins vibrated suddenly when something heavy was tossed against it. She debated whether to get up and give Nathan a piece of her mind. Another loud thump as he removed his other boot decided her.

The nerve of the man to keep the entire boat waiting. Then to return in the middle of the night, making enough noise to wake the dead.... He was the rudest, most inconsiderate clod she had ever seen, she told herself fiercely.

Rising, she pulled a wrapper over her light nightgown and marched to the door, without even taking time to tie the ribbons ranged down the front.

As she stepped purposefully from her cabin, the deck felt cool under her bare feet and the breeze caused her robe to billow behind her. Outside Nathan's cabin, she faltered. The door was slightly ajar and inside she could hear movement, but no light burned.

At the sound of a crash and a muffled curse, she pushed the door open and said firmly, "I'd like a word with you, Nathan Trent." But she could see nothing in the murky interior until the man materialized out of the darkness in front of her.

The fresh air and the walk to the boat had done little to clear Nathan's head. Clad in only his trousers, he swayed slightly on his feet. His eyes narrowed when he saw the indistinct figure silhouetted against the predawn sky.

"So it's you," he growled. "Do you have to follow me to my very door? Why can't you leave me alone?"

"Because I have a thing or two to say," Serena snapped, refusing to be intimidated.

"Why should I listen to anything you have to say?" His arm shot out and slipped around her waist under her loose wrapper. Throwing her off balance, he yanked her against his bare chest. "The devil take you and your explanations."

"What are you talking about?" Serena gasped, horrified to find herself suspended above the floor, pressed against him, body to body with only a thin nightgown between them. Planting both hands flat against his shoulders, she pushed, arching in an attempt to free herself. Panicked by the hardness jutting against her through the thin material of her gown, she squirmed all the harder. "Let me go."

Aroused by her movements, Nathan groaned deep in his throat in answer. With one fluid move, he turned, holding her against him, and closed the door.

Disoriented in the dark cabin, Serena struggled in his grip and fought to hold on to her courage. "What do you think you're doing?"

"I might ask you the same thing."

She did not have to see his face to recognize the sneer in his voice.

"What brings you to my cabin, if not this?" The fingers of his free hand laced through her hair and cupped her head as he drew her even closer, trapping her hands between their bodies. "You told me you'd do anything to make amends, but I didn't believe you...until now."

"I didn't," she denied, trying in vain to turn her head, but his fingers, wrapped in her hair, held her inexorably.

"Liar," he rasped as his mouth descended to hers.

Demanding, consuming, his kiss held no tenderness, but it set her on fire. Serena had felt the heat of passion in his lips before, but she had felt more...gentleness, affection, perhaps even the beginnings of love. She had never known a kiss could convey both fury and desire...nor that she could respond in such a way. Shock gave way to desire and she returned his kiss passionately until she felt the very soul was drained from her.

With a strangled curse, Nathan lowered her to the bed, stretching out to lie beside her, their limbs intertwined. One of her arms was pinned beneath his solid body and one of his legs pressed between hers.

"I can't understand it." His voice was harsh, his words slurred. "I don't want to want you."

"Then let me go," she choked. Shaken, assailed by unfamiliar emotions, she was near tears.

"Be damned. Now that you're here, you're staying. I thought you wanted a chance to show me how much you love me."

"You're drunk."

"Of course," he confirmed, his breath hot and whiskey scented as he trailed a blazing path of kisses along her jaw toward her mouth. "How else could you feel so right when I know you're so very wrong?"

Braced on one elbow above her, he kissed her, his tongue claiming the treasures of her mouth as if they were rightfully his. His free hand roved the length of her body along her rumpled nightgown. Finding her bare thigh where the gown had ridden up, his palm skimmed the warm skin, moving upward.

"You miserable, misbegotten drunken lout!" she gasped, tearing her lips from his, "I'm telling you, let me go."

The man started at her words, shaking his head as if to clear it. "Serena?" he whispered wonderingly.

"Yes," she nearly sobbed in relief.

"Serena," he breathed, enraptured. His lips found hers again for a kiss that was prolonged and thorough and achingly tender. Unable to resist the fiery passion welling up inside her, she melted against him. When his mouth left hers to trail kisses along her jaw to her temple, he whispered against her hair, "My love."

She lay very still in his arms, her ragged breathing slowing. Without his kiss devastating her common sense, she began to realize what had nearly happened. Stiffening beneath him, she said coldly, "I've told you before, I'm not your love. Now let me go, Nathan, at once."

His dark silhouette rose above her in the dimness, but the lower half of her body was still ensnared by his legs as he fumbled to open louvers over the window at the head of the bed. The pale light seemed blinding after the darkness.

She glared up at him, disheveled and well kissed, her blue eyes conveying hurt and hatred. Rolling onto his side, he scooped her into his arms and held her gently. "I'm so sorry," he murmured. "I must have been drunker than I realized."

Pushing him away wordlessly, she sat up and prepared to swing her feet off the bed.

"Wait." He laid a hand on her arm to detain her. "I didn't know it was you. I swear it, Serena. I'm sorry."

Pointedly she looked down at his hand until he removed it. "Who did you think it was, the queen of the May?" she asked scornfully as she got to her feet.

"I don't understand." A perplexed frown on his face, he rose to stand beside her. "What are you doing here...in your nightclothes?"

"Are you saying I'm the one to blame?" she asked, rounding on him. "I was out on the deck and you hauled me inside. It's not my fault if you have no self-control."

"I have more than you know," he murmured as he gazed down at her. Her lips looked puffy from his kiss and a slice of creamy white breast could be seen where her robe gaped open.

Eyeing him warily, she retreated. "Don't you touch me, you lecher. Don't you ever touch me again or I'll shoot you as surely as you're standing there."

He blocked her way to the door. "Serena, you've got to believe me. I couldn't see you clearly. I thought you were someone else."

"You thought I was Adele Andrews, didn't you?" she asked in sudden, indignant comprehension.

"Let me explain," he implored, reaching out to touch her arm. He expelled a tortured sigh when she backed away, but he persisted, "Four years ago, I was engaged to marry Adele. She's the daughter of Senator Marshall Langley, one of our neighbors and my father's oldest friend. I loved her and, like a fool, I thought she loved me. But she loved money and power better."

"I don't want to hear this," Serena contended stiffly.

But Nathan would not be silenced. "When George Andrews, a wealthy man, came to Baton Rouge to buy political favors, he also bought my fiancée's affection. Three days before our wedding, she eloped with him, a man old enough to be her father."

"I told you," Serena protested hotly, "this is none of my business."

"It is your business . . . because of tonight. I want you to understand why it happened."

"And that will make everything just fine?" Her chin tilted haughtily.

"No. But you see, I hadn't seen Adele since she jilted me. When we saw her this afternoon, she swore she wanted to make amends. I told her she couldn't. She has always been very . . . single-minded. When you came to my cabin, I thought—"

"You thought I was your old love," she finished flatly, unwilling to make it easier for him. "Too bad I turned out to be the wrong woman."

Uncertain how to answer, he faltered. "It's over between Adele and me."

"That must be why you tried to bed her," Serena spat, her pride stung by the hesitation she found so revealing. "Because you wanted her to know how much you hate her."

"I don't blame you for being upset," he said with a sigh, raking his fingers through his hair. "I don't know why I did what I did and I don't know how to make it up to you. I swear, Serena, if I had taken advantage of you, I would do the right thing."

"You'd turn yourself in to the nearest sheriff?"

Flushing in the face of her scorn, he asserted, "I'd marry you."

"I don't want you to marry me. I don't want you at all and I don't want any more of your excuses. Now if you'll pardon me . . ."

In stark silence, he opened the door for her, remaining where he was long after she had gone into her own cabin and closed the door behind her.

The next morning, Serena barricaded herself in the pilot-house, disgusted and disturbed when she remembered the feel of Nathan's nearly nude body against hers. Why couldn't she forget his kisses, his touch? Last night he had left her shaking with passion and desire, then explained away his actions as a case of mistaken identity.

If it took every cent she saved from her wages, she would buy out his interest in the *River Sprite* and be free of him. Until then, she would manage to tolerate him when she could not avoid him. But she would not be his friend and she would not be satisfied until he was gone.

One booted foot resting on a coil of rope, the captain stood on the bow. His head pounded mercilessly and his stomach was queasy as the *Sprite* plowed through the widening river near New Orleans, past grand plantation houses and acres of purple-tasseled sugarcane.

But he did not see them. He, too, recalled the night…guiltily. He needed to speak with Serena, to rebuild the beginnings of trust so badly damaged last night, but she refused to talk to him, seeming to prefer the role of despoiled virgin. What had nearly happened was inexcusable, he thought. But, it was only nearly.

Her attitude this morning was particularly maddening, for though his memories of the night were hazy, Nathan recalled two things vividly: the feel of her body under his and her unrestrained responses to his kisses.

Perhaps Colonel Neal had been right, he reflected somberly, he needed to get off the boat and away from Serena. But for now, too many things remained unresolved between them.

Chapter Eleven

The *River Sprite*'s whistle blasted as the steamboat swung toward the teeming Canal Street dock. Beside Serena in the pilothouse, Will reckoned they might start unloading this afternoon. Despite the explosion, the rescue and that unscheduled layover in Baton Rouge, the *Sprite* had made good time. They were only a little behind schedule, but he did not relay the good news to his niece, who stood at the wheel, frowning forbiddingly.

"Do you feel like walking me over to the harbor master's, Uncle Will?" she asked, maneuvering the stern-wheeler into place. The boat gave a mighty shudder and released a billow of steam into the cloudless blue sky as the deckhands secured the lines.

"Be glad to, sugar," he answered, regarding her shrewdly.

As they descended moments later, they mixed with the passengers who crowded the stairs at the bow. Serena was not ready to face Nathan yet. Hoping to escape his detection, she led Will ashore with the others as soon as the plank was lowered.

"Serena, wait," a voice called as they walked toward the customhouse.

Glancing back at the big figure shouldering his way through the crowd on the pier, she announced unnecessarily, "It's Nathan."

"I know." Her uncle did not slow his stride. "Y'all can yammer all you want to, but I'm headin' for that shade tree yonder. Summer in Hades couldn't be hotter than July in New Orleans.

"Wait, Uncle Will." She had hoped the old man's presence would deter Nathan's pursuit.

"You might as well talk to him, gal," Will advised as he limped away. "You're gonna have to sooner or later. I think you've met your match for stubborn in that man."

Serena halted reluctantly and allowed the captain to catch up with her. Meeting his shadowed, bloodshot eyes, she realized he must have slept as little as she last night.

"Serena," he began hoarsely. "Things can't go on this way between us."

"Nothing is going on between us, Nathan."

"Too much has gone on," he contradicted her, "and most of it my fault. But surely you know I would never hurt you."

"You already have. You nearly took me to your bed last night . . . whether I wanted it or not. Then, when you realized your mistake, you apologized politely and offered what duty demanded. No, thank you," she concluded bitterly.

"Is that what you thought? I'm so sorry, Serena." Laying a gentle hand against her cheek, he bent over her earnestly. "Please, what will it take for you to forgive me?"

Tears clouded her eyes at his unexpected, undeniable remorse. "I don't know if I'll ever forgive you. I . . . I don't know," she choked. "Leave me alone, Nathan. I don't think clearly around you." Whirling, she hurried to where Will waited for her.

Standing on the dock, the big man watched her departure, then slowly, thoughtfully, he returned to the boat. He did not see his partner watching from the boiler deck. Grace shook her head, wondering when Nathan and Serena would realize they were falling in love . . . and when they would be willing to admit it.

While the captain was overseeing the unloading of the cargo, an elegant carriage rolled to a stop on the pier and Antoine La Branche stepped down.

"Welcome back to New Orleans, my boy," the Creole called.

"*Merci,* Uncle. It's good to see you. Come aboard," Nathan shouted from the boat. "I want to introduce you to my new partner."

The men found Grace on the boiler deck, her arms laden with fresh sheets for the cabins. A preoccupied expression on her face, she turned when Nathan called, her black skirt swirling gracefully. Her cheeks were slightly flushed from exertion and her pale hair, reacting to the steamy heat of the day, curled in wispy tendrils around her face. Antoine thought she was one of the most beautiful creatures he had ever seen.

"Grace Caswell, please allow me to introduce my uncle, Monsieur Antoine La Branche," Nathan said as they joined her.

"Your uncle? What a pleasure to meet you, *monsieur.*" The woman smiled over the stack of folded bed sheets.

"Your servant, *madame.*" Antoine bowed. "My belated condolences on your loss. I was saddened to receive Nathan's letter notifying me of your husband's death."

"Thank you."

"Please," he requested gallantly, taking the linens from her, "allow me to carry these for you."

Following along the deck, Nathan said, "My uncle was a friend of Henry's, Grace."

"*Oui,* he was a fine man," Antoine confirmed. "If there is anything I can do for his family, you have only to ask, Madame Caswell. I know how difficult these times can be. My own wife was taken by yellow jack some years ago."

"How sad," Grace murmured, tears springing to her eyes. Embarrassed by her emotion, she apologized, "I'm terribly sorry."

"You are very tenderhearted, *madame,* but do not be troubled for me," Antoine said kindly. "My grief is not as new as yours, therefore not as sharp. Your sadness will ease in time—

"*Mon Dieu,* what is this?" he exclaimed when a bundle of soiled linens flew through an open door and landed at his feet.

"Uh-oh," Hank spoke guiltily from the doorway. "I didn't know anyone was out there."

"No harm was done," Antoine soothed.

"No," Grace agreed, "but you must be more careful, Hank." Retrieving the folded sheets, she paused in the doorway to the cabin. "It is much too hot to work right now. Shall we all adjourn to the salon and cool off?"

"Hooray!" the boy cheered. "I'll go get Dory. Rena and Uncle Will went ashore."

"And tell Gustave to send up some lemonade," Grace bade with a smile.

When Will and Serena returned to the *Sprite*, Roger was overseeing the roustabouts and Jamie was settled on the bench outside the galley with a "wee tot" in his cuppa to sweeten it.

"Dinna come close to me, Serena Caswell," the engineer greeted her when she approached. "Ye'll spoil yer fine gown."

"I'm not worried about my dress," she answered, sitting down beside him, making room for Will on her other side.

As the three chatted, listening to the shouts of the mates and the songs of the stevedores, Jamie seemed distracted, a frown knitting his bushy brows. "I'm thinking ye should look oot for that one, Rena." He indicated Fiske Patterson with a nod of his sandy head.

"I ain't cared for him since he come aboard," Will added and squinted toward the crewman who dawdled a little way down the deck, looking frequently in their direction. "Fancies hisself a ladies' man."

"I dinna care for the way he watches ye," Jamie advised. "I think ye should dismiss him."

"Listen to you two," she protested. "Perhaps I made a mistake by hiring him, but I can't fire a man because he looks at me."

"I'm nae sure that's all he's aboot," Jamie countered.

"We're going to keep an eye on him," Will said emphatically.

"Aye," Jamie seconded. "And 'twould not be a bad idea, lass, for you to avoid him altogether."

"Are you saying I shouldn't come down here anymore?" A belligerent gleam shone in her blue eyes.

"What we're sayin'," Jamie explained patiently, "is that ye've grown to be a bonny woman and must learn to behave like one."

"But—"

"No buts, gal," Will cut her off. "Jamie's right."

"Ye ken I'm right."

"I ken ye both love me," she said with a sigh. Rising, she planted a kiss on Jamie's grease-stained brow, then on Will's. "I love you, too."

Will smiled with delight, but pleasure battled embarrassment on the Scotsman's ruddy face.

"Away wi' ye, now," he ordered gruffly, "before the crew thinks McPherson's gone soft. Will and I ha'e much to discuss . . . withoot the interference of a female."

Smiling broadly, she left the old men sitting in the sun and went in search of her family. She found them in the salon with Nathan and Antoine La Branche. Grace was laughing when Serena entered. She had not seen her mother look so carefree since her father died. For a moment, she resented the charming Creole.

Antoine smiled when he saw Serena. This was the Mademoiselle Caswell he remembered. Even in a work dress, she was pretty, not at all like the night she had come to his home.

"Serena, come and have some lemonade," Grace invited.

"I have to go up and fill in the logbook."

"Nonsense," her mother contended. "Even I know that duty will wait."

"Please join us." Rising, Nathan pulled out the chair beside him, his dark eyes challenging.

"*Oui, mam'selle,* please do," Antoine echoed the invitation and also got to his feet.

Hank shot out of his chair. "All us men think you should have some lemonade, Rena," he squeaked.

With a grudging smile for her little brother, Serena took the seat offered and wished it were anywhere but beside the captain. Her heart pounding traitorously, she felt trapped and short of breath. Even after their talk on the dock, she was not ready to be so near him.

"You'll never guess what we're doing this evening, my dear," Grace declared.

"What?"

"The *Sprite*'s owners and captains are going to celebrate the successful run to New Orleans by having dinner with Monsieur La Branche."

"A very quiet dinner," Antoine added, "at one of the finest restaurants in the Vieux Carré."

"This has to be Nathan's idea," the girl guessed at once. "He's the celebrating-est man I've ever known. He gave the entire crew permission to go ashore for the night.

"If you celebrate at the end of every run," she addressed the captain directly, "Caswell & Trent will go broke in six months."

"Less than that," he replied, unfazed. "Will you go?"

Despite the expectant faces around her, she shook her head stubbornly, "I really don't believe—"

"Ah, Serena," Nathan said with a sigh. "Am I going to have to convince you the same way I convinced your mother?"

"You played cards?" Serena stared at Grace in horror when he pulled a deck from his pocket.

"We cut," the woman answered with a shadow of a smile. "High card won. It seemed . . . sporting."

"Let's make the bet clear," Nathan said drolly as he shuffled. "If I win, I take you to dinner. If you win, you take me. Agreed?"

Frowning at Hank, who giggled aloud, she surrendered, "Put your cards away. If Mother said we would go, we will go. Although I've never known her to gamble, I don't think she would welsh on a bet."

"Très bien!" Antoine cried. "It's settled then."

The *Sprite*'s partners smiled, neither noticing the other's satisfaction.

"Why does Serena get to go and I have to stay home?" Dory sulked while her mother dressed for dinner.

"Because she is one of the captains of the *Sprite*," Grace explained patiently.

"Only because Nathan said so. She's no more captain than I am."

"Pandora," her mother said warningly.

"I just don't think it's fair she gets to dress up and go out with Nathan. She doesn't really want to go. She doesn't even care about looking nice."

"I think it might surprise you just how much she does care."

"Then why doesn't she ever try to look pretty?"

"I think Serena is pretty."

"She's all right, I suppose," Dory said grudgingly, "but she wears those old dresses and lets her hair hang down in a braid. And lately she looks absolutely terrible."

"Don't you mean haggard? Or exhausted?" Grace asked severely. "Shame on you, Dory. Without Serena's hard work as our pilot, we would still be in Vicksburg, trying to decide how to support ourselves. We have more important concerns right now than how we look. You would do well to remember that, my girl."

Storming down to the boiler deck, Dory fumed. It was always Serena. No one ever thought about Dory. Yet, as she stopped on the bow to look out at the river, she felt a twinge of guilt. It was true Serena worked hard to take care of the family and she had defended her against that drunken planter on the texas. But why did she have to be so stubborn and bossy all the time?

Her elbows propped on the rail, the teenage girl rested her chin on her hands, feeling mean and small. Sometimes she didn't know who she was. Sometimes nothing about her was right, nothing at all.

"What are you thinking about, little one?" Nathan joined her at the rail.

"I just got a lecture from my mother," she confessed, adding defiantly. "She treats me like a child."

"My father always lectured me," the man remarked. "It seemed at the time that he talked and talked and never listened."

"Did you wish he'd just be quiet?" Dory asked fiercely.

"Of course. I thought he was as dumb as a fence post and I was just naturally smart."

"I don't really think Mother is stupid."

"Then she's probably saying things you don't want to hear," he ventured. When she did not answer, he slipped an arm around her shoulders and squeezed sympathetically. "You know, the older I get, the more I think my father is one of the smartest men I know."

"Have you told him?"

"No." He shook his head ruefully. "No, but I plan to the very next time I see him."

"I guess I should go and make up with Mother before she leaves." Dory sighed. "I don't want to feel like this all night."

"That's my girl. Growing up is not easy," Nathan encouraged, "but you're turning into quite a young lady, Dory."

"Thank you." She tiptoed and kissed his cheek. As she walked away, her heart pounded. Nathan had noticed she was a young lady. Once out of his sight, she broke into a run and bounded up the companionway to the texas, taking the steps two at a time.

When Antoine arrived that evening in his carriage, his dark eyes, so like Nathan's, glowed with excitement. He gave his driver a crisp order in French and the carriage rolled through cobblestone streets to the St. Louis, the finest hotel in the Vieux Carré. Some said, the finest in the city.

At the graceful hotel, Nathan alit first and turned to hand down the ladies. Poised on the step, Serena faltered as he smiled warmly at her. Quickly she stepped down to the banquette and reclaimed the hand he held, wondering if she had made a mistake when she had agreed to come.

She had hoped to forgive...and forget...last night. But how could she forget when his every touch sent the blood coursing through her veins like liquid fire?

Watching Nathan assist Grace from the carriage, she felt reassured. Surely she would be safe with her mother along. Still, her expression was wary when the big man offered his arm.

As the four passed through the rotunda of the hotel, a merry party of Creoles was gathered at the foot of the curving staircase. Serena, clad in her best evening gown, felt drab and dowdy compared to the fashionable beauties who poised and flirted, wielding their fans with expertise. She did not realize that though her soft pink gown with its delicate lace trim was plain by New Orleans standards, it was elegant in its simplicity.

Unconsciously her chin rose and she walked proudly, looking neither right nor left. The pulse at the base of her throat was the only sign of her trepidation.

Nathan watched the petite girl beside him appreciatively. She did not need an elaborate coiffure or glittering jewels to look lovely. She was what his sisters enviously called a natural beauty.

While members of the closed Creole society watched curiously, Antoine La Branche and his roué nephew escorted two unknown and lovely ladies toward the music that seemed to beckon from above.

When they were settled at their table, Serena gazed around in awe at the magnificent room. Beneath a massive crystal chandelier, graceful couples spun around the dance floor; the women's gowns, vivid flashes of color against the men's dark evening attire.

Dinner was a sumptuous affair with excellent wines for each course. Both Nathan and his uncle proved to be chivalrous companions. Sensing Grace's uneasiness at being in public while in mourning, Antoine was solicitous and kind.

When a girl came to the table selling flowers, Nathan bought two, a small nosegay of yellow jasmine for Grace and a dainty corsage of one white rosebud and a single pink tied with a silvery ribbon for Serena.

Serena immediately pinned it to her décolletage where it rested against white skin. Pleased with the gift, her hand rose absently throughout the evening to caress the smooth petals, a gesture Nathan found both innocently appealing and provocative.

When they had finished eating, he leaned toward Serena to ask, "Shall we dance? Just once around the floor," he coaxed when she looked as if she would refuse. "Then if you're not having fun, we'll come back to the table."

Flushed with excitement or perhaps with wine, Serena accepted. But when Nathan took her into his arms, she experienced a moment of panic. His back warm and solid under her hand, the spicy scent of him, even the stir of his breath against her cheek seemed to chase away rational thought.

"You look beautiful," he whispered.

"You haven't always thought so." She reminded herself as much as him.

"Haven't I?" His arm tightened around her.

"Nathan..." She looked up, ready to protest, but finding his lips close to hers, ducked her head again.

"Relax," he commanded quietly, "and have a good time. You are having a good time, aren't you?"

"I'm having a lovely time."

His lips curved in a smile at the wonder in her voice. "I'm glad you decided to dance with me. I was afraid you wouldn't."

"Would it really have made a difference?" she asked, risking a look at him.

"My heart would have been broken," he assured her lightly, but the flare of passion in his dark eyes was unmistakable. Wordlessly he waltzed her around the floor, causing her skirt to billow gracefully around her and skim the toes of his boots. "You still haven't answered my question from this afternoon," he said at last. "Have you forgiven me, Serena?"

"I don't know what to think or to feel about you, Nathan," she answered slowly. "I can't believe you would hurt me intentionally. But every time I think I can trust you, you do something...unexpected."

"I was rather taken by surprise myself last night," he muttered regretfully. "I am truly sorry about what happened."

"It's not just last night. It seems when we're not fighting, we're kissing." She gazed up at him, her blue eyes candid.

"I don't find that so unexpected." He stared down at her lips, seemingly mesmerized. Suddenly he was grateful the music was ending. If he continued to hold her in his arms, he feared he would do the unexpected once more and kiss her soundly. And he did not know what she would do if he did. Releasing her, he led her back to the others.

"They make a handsome couple, do they not?" Antoine asked, as he and Grace watched from the table.

"When they are not arguing," she replied with a sigh.

To her surprise, the Creole laughed. "The Trent men are drawn to spirited women. My sister's *Américain* husband never seems to tire of her, no matter how often they disagree. In fact, they seem very happy together, indeed."

"Nathan never says much about his family."

"He and his father, both strong men, had a falling-out some years ago. Nathan left home and began to wander here and there, living a most dangerous life, having great adventures. I did not think he would ever settle down. Now I wonder."

As the younger couple approached, the older quickly changed the subject. "I confess I'm finding the Mississippi is not the most wholesome environment in which to bring up a family," Grace was saying when they took their seats.

"Listen to you two," Nathan chided playfully. "So serious when you should be enjoying yourselves."

"Actually I have been trying to convince Madame Caswell that we should all go on a picnic tomorrow," his uncle defended himself. "It's quite cool out at Lake Pontchartrain. It would be lovely."

"And I have been trying to explain to Monsieur La Branche that we all have work to do if the *River Sprite* is to leave on time," Grace countered.

"You have the morning," Nathan suggested. "I have to get a new cargo loaded and Serena insists she must bring the log up-to-date."

"Nathan's right," the girl agreed. "Even if there's not time for a picnic, you and Dory and Hank could still go out for a while."

"*Oui,* you and your children," Antoine invited. "I can show you the Vieux Carré as you have never seen it and have you back to the boat by three o'clock...in plenty of time before you must go."

"Go, Mother," Serena urged. "In all the years, I've been coming to New Orleans, I've never had a guided tour. It would be a shame for you to miss it."

"Well . . ." Grace wavered. "Very well, we shall be delighted."

"*Très bon,*" Antoine exclaimed. "And we will postpone our picnic until your next visit to New Orleans, *oui?*"

"Let us worry about the next time when it comes, Monsieur La Branche," the woman demurred with a pleased smile.

"But the evening is young," Antoine protested hours later when they stood at the foot of the *Sprite*'s gangplank. "Shall we have a nightcap before we say good-night?"

"Good morning would be more like it," Grace corrected. "If we are to be ready for tomorrow, we cannot keep New Orleans hours tonight."

"Then it's just you and me, Uncle," Nathan said. "I do need to talk to you, if you have the figures we discussed earlier."

"It is said pleasure sometimes pauses for business in New Orleans." Antoine sighed tragically as he escorted Grace aboard. "This seems to be one of those times."

At the door to the salon, the woman halted. "I must look in on the children before I retire. Serena and I will leave you to your business. Thank you, gentlemen, for a delightful evening."

"Yes, thank you very much," Serena echoed.

In front of the cabin Hank shared with Will, Grace turned to her daughter. "Do you know what business Nathan wished to discuss with Monsieur La Branche?"

"I suppose it has to do with one of Father's loans. Monsieur La Branche is the vice president of the Vieux Carré Bank."

"He is one of our creditors?" Grace frowned.

"Not for long. Nathan says the profit from the Trevarian shipment should just about pay it off." Fixing her mother with a level stare, Serena added, "Antoine La Branche did not invite you out for the morning because he is a business associate. He was a friend of Papa's and I think he wants to be your friend, too."

"I hope you're right," Grace responded. "He is nice and he seems a very proper gentleman. Good night, dear."

As she strolled to the stern, Serena's eyes were drawn to the raucous, dangerous area just beyond the waterfront called The Swamp. It was the chief reason New Orleans was called the "wickedest city in the world." Smoky torches burned in front of the many bars so the air was thick with smoke. Down one of the narrow streets, members of the *Sprite*'s crew staggered, out for a night of carousing.

She stopped to listen when surprisingly sweet music drifted across the water from a nearby tavern. Swaying to the rhythm, she reviewed the events of the evening, her hand rising to touch the corsage Nathan had given her.

It was gone and she hadn't even noticed! Retracing her steps, she found the corsage, luminous in the moonlight, at the top of the stairs. As she scooped it up and turned to go to her cabin, voices from below caught her attention. Looking over the railing, she saw Nathan and Antoine at the head of the gangplank.

"The bank will be glad to receive not only the payment which is past due, but this current installment, as well," the Creole commented, accepting a long black cigar from Nathan. Concentrating on lighting it, he added between puffs, "You've done well with the *River Sprite*, Nathan. I'm perfectly willing to pay off now."

The *Sprite*'s captain didn't answer while he lit his own cigar. "The wager," he said at last, exhaling a stream of smoke into the night air, "was that I would make the boat profitable within one year. Not that I'd pay off your bank."

"This is true." Antoine shrugged indifferently. "But already I can see you are going to win the bet."

Serena's hands tightened on the rail, her knuckles white, as Nathan's confident voice drifted up to her. "I intend to win."

With a low chuckle, Antoine crossed the gangplank to his carriage. "You will . . . with the help of Mademoiselle Caswell, *oui*? She is lovely, Nathan. As only love makes a woman."

"We are just partners, nothing more," Nathan said, mounting the stairs to the boiler deck.

"Perhaps you would care to make another bet?" Antoine called softly from the dock. "I wager you will win *la belle* Serena."

"No bet. She's quite a girl, but I'm not ready to settle down," Nathan answered, distracted when he saw a movement through the shadows in front of him. Serena. She must have been listening.

"*Bon soir,* Uncle." Tossing his cigar over the railing, he hurried after the girl.

Fleeing to the stern, Serena was unaware Nathan followed. Her eyes burned with tears and her chest ached as anger battled with betrayal and shame. She had actually come to believe Nathan had taken on the partnership because he felt something for her family.. for her.

But he had done it all on a wager. The gambler had given up poker to try a new game, playing with other peoples' lives. She should have known she couldn't trust him.

"Serena!" Nathan overtook her, catching her arm to swing her to face him.

In the dim glow of the deck lanterns, the girl's face was wrathful. "Don't you touch me, you contemptible, low-down gambling snake," she spat. "If the house was burning, you'd bet on when the roof was going to fall in."

"I don't deny I made a wager with my uncle," he acknowledged.

"You made more than one from what I heard." Her narrowed eyes glittered with animosity. "How far will you go to win *la belle* Serena, Nathan? Would you take her to dinner at a fine hotel? Would you dance with her and buy her a flower? Would you tell her she was beautiful?" she demanded, her voice catching in her throat.

"Serena, please—"

"You're a skillful gambler, Captain Trent," she concluded furiously. "You bet you'd make the *Sprite* a success and you're doing it. But that's where your skill and your luck give out. I can't be won...not on a bet." With that, she tore from his grip and went into her cabin.

His expression grim, Nathan pounded on her door. "Damn it, Serena, I'm not going to let you do this again. You're going to listen to me."

"Go away."

"I admit I made a wager with my uncle," he informed her through the door. "I bet I could make a success of the Sprite, but contrary to what you seem to think, I made no bets concerning you."

"I heard—"

"You heard Antoine propose a new wager, but you apparently did not hear my refusal. If you're going to eavesdrop, Serena, you might stay around for the whole conversation."

He poised on deck, listening, but there was no response from within. He had said what he had to say, but he felt no better. "I don't know why I even try to explain anything to you," he muttered. As he stalked away, he trod upon the delicate corsage Serena had thrown on deck, crushing it under his booted heel, but he did not even notice.

Chapter Twelve

The next morning, Serena went to her mother's cabin, where the door was open to admit the feeble breeze. Stepping inside, she heard voices from the bedroom as Grace and Dory dressed for their day on the town.

Dory emerged first, her petulant face framed by a simple bonnet. "What do you think of this hat, Rena?" she greeted her sister.

"It's very pretty."

"That's what Mother said. It's not too babyish?"

"It looks quite mature."

"I think I'll go ask Nathan his opinion."

Serena frowned. "Nathan has already gone to the Mercantile Exchange to find a cargo. Besides a man has other things to do than admire a girl's hat. And he is a man," she added pointedly.

"I know." With a dreamy smile, the younger girl stepped out on the deck.

"Good morning, dear." Fussing with the clasp of the brooch on her collar, Grace entered the parlor. "Help yourself to some coffee," she invited with a distracted nod at the tray on the desk. "It's not cold, is it?"

"Room temperature would be hot enough," Serena complained good-naturedly, pouring a cup for herself and one for her mother.

While they sipped their coffee, the girl mustered her courage. "Mother, did you kr w that Nathan agreed to your partnership on a wager?'' she blurted finally. ''He bet he could make the *Sprite* profitable in a year.''

''A year hardly seems fair to his challenger,'' Grace responded. ''He told me we could do it in six months.''

''His challenger was Monsieur La Branche,'' Serena revealed.

An amused glint in her blue eyes, Grace assured her daughter, ''It really doesn't matter, dear. Nathan has nearly accomplished what he set out to do. If he finishes early, perhaps he will leave early. In a short time, he could be—what is it you say?—out of your hair.''

''Yes, out of my hair,'' Serena mumbled.

''Mother,'' Hank shouted excitedly from outside, ''Mr. La Branche is here . . . with a matched team of bays!''

Down on the dock, Serena saw the party off. Then, relieved that Nathan was still nowhere to be seen, she got the log from the pilothouse and went in search of breakfast.

''What is that vile odor?'' she choked as she went into the galley.

Recovering from a night ashore, Gustave was in no mood for idle questions. His eyes were bloodshot and his mustache drooped as he stirred a pot simmering on the cast-iron stove. ''Me, I make a tisane that will cure the shaking of the hands and the throbbing of the head,'' he said curtly.

''If it does not stop the beating of the heart to drink it,'' Serena retorted, her nose wrinkled in distaste.

''Go to the salon, *s'il vous plaît, mam'selle,*'' he ordered with scant patience. ''I will bring you a tray, *hein.*''

With no argument, she fled to the deserted salon and found a spot in the cross draft. Sniffing cautiously to ascertain the breeze was not tisane scented, she sat down.

After eating the breakfast the cranky cook brought, the girl opened the log on the table and began to map a changing stretch of river. Engrossed, she did not hear the clatter of wagons on the dock or the creak of the capstan winch as the loading of a new cargo began. She did not even look up until a playful voice spoke from the doorway.

''I thought you might be here.''

"Roger, come in. I think I've found the coolest spot on the boat."

"I think you're right." Dropping onto the seat next to her, the young man lounged, his head against the back of the chair, his eyes closed as he savored the breeze. "This is wonderful."

"Mmm, wonderful," she murmured, following his suit.

Opening his eyes, he looked at her. "What's even more wonderful is having you to myself for a few minutes. I've missed you, Serena."

One eye opened and she lolled her head to the side to peer at him in amusement. "How can you miss me on a boat that's smaller than some sandbars?"

"Because you never seem to have time for me anymore."

Both eyes opened to regard him contritely. "Of course, I have time for you. You're my best friend."

"I could be more than that . . . if you'd let me."

She sat up in her seat uneasily. "Roger—"

"Don't say no, Rena." Rising, he placed his hands on the arms of her chair and bent over her. "Don't say anything at all." Leaning forward, he kissed her, his cool, dry lips covering hers momentarily.

Out on the sunny deck, Nathan clambered up the stairs at the bow. The last of the cargo was being loaded. Bolts of oiled canvas destined for the wagon makers at the head of the Oregon Trail filled the *Sprite*'s shallow hold and now crates of hemp cloth were being stowed in the storeroom just forward of the galley.

He was free for the moment and determined to find Serena. He had had enough of their wars of silence where nothing was resolved. Today, they were going to talk . . . if he had to sit on her to do it.

As he passed the shady salon, Nathan stopped short, seeing two shadowy figures inside. Unaware of his presence, Roger bent tenderly over Serena, who sat still and motionless in her chair, her face tilted up to his.

From the deck, he watched their intimate exchange, his face suddenly stark. Though he could not see whether she returned Roger's kiss, she did not seem to mind it, he thought bitterly.

Without making his presence known, he pivoted and went downstairs again to position himself at the foot of the gangplank. Around him, the stevedores, their work finished, prepared to leave.

He should be glad for what he had just seen, Nathan told himself fiercely. In the past few weeks he had found himself thinking silly, dangerous thoughts about Serena. He had convinced himself he cared for her and he might have told her today. Blake had just saved him from making a fool of himself.

Still, when Roger joined him on the dock, the captain frowned dourly and growled, "Where have you been?"

"Talking to Serena." Watching the stevedores' departure, Roger missed the other man's glower.

"Well, if you've finished your *tête-à-tête*," Nathan said curtly, shoving a paper into his hand, "you can take this bill of lading to the broker's office."

A perplexed frown in his face, the young clerk set out at once toward Canal Street.

Serena soon appeared on the stairs with the tray she was returning to the galley. Feeling Nathan's stony gaze upon her, she met his eyes briefly. Then recalling their hot words last night, she looked away and hurried around the corner of the deserted main deck.

At that moment, Fiske emerged from the forecastle and the girl barreled directly into his powerful chest. With a soft exclamation, his large hands closed on her waist, steadying her.

"What's your hurry, Miss Serena?" He smiled down at her, his face showing little ill effect from the previous night. Ready to go ashore, he was freshly shaved and wore a clean shirt.

"I'm sorry. I was on my way to the galley." She stepped nimbly from his grasp.

"Allow me. A lady should not have to haul such a heavy tray." Wresting it from her, he headed aft. "I'm glad I ran into you," he told her over his shoulder. "Would you see to my arm? I think it needs a woman's gentle touch. Gustave is a hamhanded Cajun quack."

Watching him carry the tray, Serena doubted the arm was troubling him at all, but courteously she agreed to look at it.

Uncomfortably aware of Nathan's hostile stare from the dock, she waited outside while Fiske went into the galley.

When the deckhand emerged, gagging at the stench within, she gestured toward the bench beside the door. Obediently he sat down and rolled up his sleeve, extending his arm for her examination.

"Wouldn't you like to go into town with me this afternoon, Miss Serena?" Fiske coaxed softly.

"No, thank you."

"New Orleans is a grand city, full of things to do and people to meet." He smiled expectantly, sure of his effect on women.

"I'm sure it is." She did not look up. "Be still, please."

"I'd show you a good time," he cajoled. "You can depend on it."

Straightening abruptly, she frowned down at him. "Your arm seems to be healing well, Mr. Patterson. Use Gustave's ointment and I doubt it will need any further attention at all."

With that diagnosis, she marched forward, painfully conscious of the two sets of eyes following her progress. Perhaps Will and Jamie had been right. Perhaps she should fire Fiske Patterson. How she would hate to broach the subject with Nathan while he was in his present mood. And how she would hate to admit to him she had been wrong to hire Fiske at all.

"Patterson, get ashore if you're going," Nathan barked as soon as Serena disappeared up the staircase. "Or perhaps you'd like me to find something to keep you busy."

A wolfish smile on his face, Fiske sauntered down the gangplank. "I can think of plenty of things to keep me busy, Cap'n, some more enjoyable than others."

With narrowed eyes, Nathan watched until the hand disappeared along the crowded street beyond the wharf. Then, stalking up to the boiler deck, he halted Serena, who was about to climb to the texas.

"A moment of your time, Miss Caswell," he ordered. Behind her, he saw her shoulders stiffen before she whirled to face him.

"If it's about last night, Captain," she said hotly, "I've already told you—"

"It's about today. I want you to leave my crew alone."

"Leave your crew alone?" she sputtered, taken off guard.

"Your place as pilot is the wheelhouse. And your place as a woman is almost anywhere but the main deck. In the future, please confine your flirtations—"

"My flirtations? You pompous, brass-buttoned fancy man—"

"Just steer clear, Serena," he cut her off rudely. "I don't want any more scenes like the one with Patterson . . . or with Blake," he warned, striding back toward the stern.

Her face flamed at the realization that he must have seen Roger kiss her, but she followed him doggedly around the corner. "You listen to me, Nathan Trent—"

"What's going on, Serena?" Roger called. His pleasant face was troubled as he hurried along the boiler deck toward her. "I heard you and Nathan arguing before I was halfway up the dock."

"There's nothing unusual in that." Glaring in cold disgust at the man who stood out of sight on the stern, she walked forward to meet Roger. "We argue as often as not."

"I don't like it when Trent makes you angry," the clerk objected vehemently. "What did he say to you?"

"Nothing of importance." Taking his arm, she tried to lead him toward the salon. "Come on, Roger, let's go."

"He really should learn he cannot get away with speaking to a lady so disrespectfully," the diminutive clerk insisted, balking.

"Would you like to teach me, Blake?" Nathan stepped into view around the cabin section, his face ominous.

"Perhaps." Roger gulped but refused to back down from the powerful captain.

"What did you have in mind? A duel?"

"Perhaps." Roger gulped again.

"Enough!" Serena's ire erupted in a screech. "I don't know what has gotten into you. If you want fight like a couple of mangy mongrels, go right ahead. But I refuse to be the bone you're fighting over.

"Men!" she shouted, clambering up the companionway, leaving Nathan and Roger on deck to stare after her in astonishment.

"Men!" Serena was still seething when Will tottered onto the *River Sprite*.

Nathan met the unsteady old man on the dock and helped him aboard. Most of what Will said was drowned out by a blast of the boat's whistle, but the captain heard the blistering conclusion as the boat paused midriver for a good ready.

"Coulda waited till I had both feet on it before pullin' in the gangplank," the elderly pilot hollered.

"Tell your niece," Nathan advised truculently, pointing the inebriate toward the stairs. "She's the one who was already backing the boat out of the slip."

Hauling himself into the pilothouse, Will demanded, "What're you in such an all-fired hurry for, Serena Elizabeth? I was s'posed to take out the *Sprite* this afternoon."

"You weren't here, were you? Where have you been? Mother, Dory and Hank have been back more than two hours."

"I had important business," the old man replied with dignity as he swayed in the doorway.

"I know what kind of business it was. You smell like a distillery." His niece sighed. "Sit down before you fall down."

"A man likes a little respect in his old age, youngster," Will grumbled, settling on the bench. "What's goin' on with you and Nate? You're both as tetchy as a couple of broody hens."

Deliberately ignoring the question, Serena asked, "Where have you been, Uncle Will?"

"Gettin' a couple of them Benevolent Association pilots ripsnortin' drunk," he answered with satisfaction. "Nice fellers, too, Rena, downright helpful."

"We don't need the help of the Benevolent Association."

"Pride goeth before a fall, gal," he quoted sadly. "Their news of the river is never more than half a day old. Jes' 'cause we ain't members, don't mean we can't use what they give us . . . even if I have to liquor 'em up to get it.''

"What did they say?" Serena asked with weary patience.

"That there's a towhead buildin' up in the east channel about ten miles below Donaldsonville."

She digested the information with a considering frown. "You think we'd better tie up?"

"I wouldn't want to approach it in the dark," Will sounded sober for the first time since his arrival. "Too much chance the *Sprite* would run aground."

"Then I'll take her to shore below town tonight. By the time we reach the spot in the morning, we should have light enough to see."

"That's what I'd do." Easing back, Will whistled low between his teeth. "Come here, Catastrophe. I'm ready for a nap after a hard day's work." The cat curled on his lap, he pulled his cap over his eyes and was asleep within moments.

"Jackson Square was so beautiful. The new statue is a marvel," Dory told her sister again as they sat in the parlor after dinner. "And the flowers were so beautiful and the people promenading around the park were so elegant."

"And the food was so-o-o good," Hank mimicked his sister. "I had a candy called a praline and it was so-o-o delicious."

Dory frowned at her brother in annoyance. "Mother, would you please make him stop that?"

"That's enough from both of you," Grace admonished. "You've been chattering away at Serena for an hour without pause."

"Where's Nathan tonight?" Will asked from the corner where he and Roger played checkers. The clerk watched the old man carefully, having played with him many times.

"I haven't seen him." Grace was intent on her mending.

"I wish he were here," Dory declared. "I wanted to tell him all about New Orleans."

"He would find it so-o-o fascinating," Hank goaded.

Before her siblings could resume their quarrel, Serena rose. "I have to get to bed if I'm going to take the *Sprite* out at dawn."

"I'm right behind you soon as Roger and me finish our game," Will muttered.

Mindful of the girl's ire of the afternoon, Roger suggested cautiously, "If you'll wait, I'll walk you to your cabin, Serena."

"No need," she answered lightly. "Good night, everyone."

As she rounded the corner to the stern, Serena half expected to find Nathan sitting in the darkness. She knew he had been there. The scent of his tobacco lingered in the still night air.

Unanticipated, unwelcome disappointment washed over her. What had she wanted? To find him waiting so that she could prove to herself that she could withstand his charm? To conclude their current argument as so many others had ended...in his arms?

Standing beside the railing, Serena stared blindly at the swarms of fireflies hovering over the riverbank. How could she care for Nathan when she could not even trust him? It seemed he deliberately kept her off balance. When he had spoken to her through the door last night, she had nearly swallowed her pride and opened it to him. She might have listened to him today, but he had unexpectedly taken the offensive and ordered her to keep away from the crew.

His eyes had been dark points of ice when he had looked at her this afternoon and his coldness had hurt more than she ever imagined. She must stay away from Nathan, she knew. She must forget his kisses and the effect he had on her. They were business associates and nothing more...no matter how many bets he made.

On the bow, Nathan gazed out at the same swarms of fireflies. The lap of the river against the bank usually brought a feeling of peacefulness to him, but not tonight.

What was he to do about Serena? he wondered. After hours of soul-searching, he had admitted to himself that he was beginning to care for her. But she did not care for him, did not trust him, and was probably in love with another man. What was there to do?

With a derisive smile for his useless deliberation, Nathan made a decision. He would do the honorable thing and step out of the picture. Over the next few weeks, a new clerk could be hired and Blake could be trained as captain. Until he left the *Sprite* and the partnership he had undertaken, he would avoid Serena completely.

I'll be free, Nathan assured himself, free of steamboats and auburn-haired vixens, free to go to California. Though if I had any compassion I would stay to protect Roger from Serena.

He lingered on the bow until he was thought Serena would be safely in bed. His resolve was still new. If ever he was to avoid her, a warm moonlit night like this one was the time.

At last, he climbed to the highest deck of the sleeping steamboat and made his way to Grace's cabin. Though the texas was deserted, a lamp still burned in her window.

His imperturbable partner looked surprised when he knocked on her door and invited her to take a walk. Slipping a shawl over her shoulders, Grace joined Nathan on deck. She said nothing as they strolled, waiting for him to speak.

At last, he drew a deep breath and began hoarsely, "Grace, I've decided I should leave the *Sprite* in St. Louis."

"What about our agreement that you would stay for six months?"

"You wouldn't hold me to it now, would you?" He hesitated, searching for the right words. "Things have changed.... My being here has not worked out as well as I had hoped."

"I thought it was working out very well indeed." Stopping, Grace peered up at the big man through the dimness. "We're managing to pay our bills and the *River Sprite* is beginning to show a profit, but I don't think we qualify as a full-fledged success quite yet, Nathan."

"You're on your way," he told her gently. About to resume their promenade, he was rooted to the deck by her next question.

"But what about your wager? Won't your uncle win if you go?"

"You know about the wager?"

Suppressing a smile at his guilty expression, the woman nodded.

"There are other considerations more important than a bet," Nathan floundered uncharacteristically. "I have to go. I was on my way to California, you know. Blake can take over my job if you'd like or we'll hire—"

"This isn't about the boat or the bet or even California, is it?" Grace interrupted.

"No." He shook his head. Rubbing the back of his neck, he flexed tense shoulders. "If you want the truth, partner, I've done a very foolish thing. I've done a hundred foolish things since I came aboard the *Sprite,* but the stupidest one by far was falling in love with your obstinate, infuriating daught..." He trailed off, blinking in surprise at the admission that had just poured from his mouth.

Grace showed no amazement. "Have you told Serena how you feel?"

"She knows I think she's obstinate and infuriating." He grinned in spite of himself. "She wouldn't believe me if I told her I love her. I'm not sure I believe it myself. Besides, she's in love with Blake."

"I do not think so."

Hope flickered in Nathan's eyes, but he protested, "So many things have gone wrong between Serena and me, I don't know if I can ever make them right."

"You certainly can't if you don't try," the woman said briskly. "If you love my daughter, you'll have to fight."

"We do nothing but fight," he countered, amused by her unexpected attitude. "I'm about ready for some peace in my life."

"You won't find it by running away."

"I'm not sure I'll find it by staying, either."

"Perhaps you won't," Grace said pleasantly, "but one thing you know with certainty, life with Serena will never be dull."

"A mixed blessing, if ever I heard one," Nathan snorted, directing their steps toward Grace's cabin.

"Will you at least consider staying with the *Sprite* for the full six months?" she requested as they halted before her door. "We still need your help and I think you and Serena need each other. Those sparks between you don't all come from anger."

"I'll think about it and give you my answer when we reach St. Louis." A smile lurking at the corner of his mouth, he asked, "Did you just give me permission to court your daughter, Mrs. Caswell?"

"I gave you permission to try."

Standing at the window, Grace watched the broad-shouldered captain stride away into the darkness. She hoped she had done right by trying to convince him to stay. She did not want to meddle, but she feared that if Nathan left the *Sprite* now, both he and Serena would be unhappy for a very long time.

Chapter Thirteen

"They're at it again," Will announced, consulting his watch, "and it ain't even nine o'clock."

"I don't know why I even bother to try to talk to an impossible bit of baggage like you," Nathan bellowed.

"I don't know why you bother with anything," Serena shot back, "if you're leaving the *Sprite* anyway."

"I told you, I haven't decided yet," the captain's voice thundered from the pilothouse.

"I wish I had never mentioned the possibility of Nathan's departure," Grace muttered, beside Will at the forward rail of the texas. "It has upset everyone, even Pandora and Hank."

"Sure made Serena tetchy."

"William," his sister-in-law said reprovingly. "*Tetchy* is not the word for Serena. How long do you suppose they'll quarrel before they make peace?"

"Or she shoots him."

"She wouldn't do that...would she?" Peering up at the wheelhouse, Grace sighed. "I suppose I should go and talk to her."

"I s'pose you should steer clear and let 'er cool down. Looky there." Will nodded toward the clerk who stood in the doorway to his office, staring up at the pilothouse. "Even Roger's got better sense than to go up there now."

"I'm glad. With both Roger and Nathan in love with Serena, it could be a most difficult situation."

"Try not to worry," the old pilot encouraged. "Rena'll fig-ure out she loves Nathan sooner or later."

"Do you think so?"

"She wouldn't be so riled at the thought of his leavin' if she wasn't."

"And if you came up here to yell at me," Serena yelled in the pilothouse, "you can just get out!"

"Gladly!" Nathan roared back.

Silently Grace and Will watched as the captain stalked across the texas to the companionway, unaware that, behind him, Roger hurried to join Serena in the pilothouse.

"I'll tell you this, Nathan Trent." Surrounded by her lug-gage on a landing just north of Donaldsonville, Tansy Shu-macher lectured the captain, "I'd wait for another steamboat if I didn't have to get to Baton Rouge right away, if my niece's baby did not have the colic—"

"If you didn't hate ferries with every ounce of your being," Nathan interjected teasingly. Then he frowned down at the short, round woman. "I'm afraid I don't understand, Miss Tansy. Do you object to me or the *River Sprite*?"

"Don't play the innocent with me, my boy." The spinster's pale eyes snapped. "I've known you your entire life. You've always been high-spirited, but this escapade, living on a river-boat with your—" her voice dropped "—your paramour is simply too much."

"My what?" he yelped.

"Nathan, please," she entreated with an uncomfortable glance at the deckhands awaiting orders nearby.

"Miss Tansy," he addressed the old woman patiently, "where did you hear such a thing?"

"From Leticia Morgan, who got it from Fanny Watson who received a letter from Adele Andrews . . . oh, dear." She trailed off when the man's face settled in stony lines.

"So my business is the subject of gossip up and down the river?"

"I'm sorry, Nathan." Tansy looked stricken. "Letty said Adele had actually seen you with this woman."

"She didn't waste any time letting the world know about it," he said bitterly. "We saw her just a week ago in Baton Rouge.

"Luke," he called, "bring the bags aboard. Levi, cast off."

Taking her arm, he escorted the old woman across the gangplank. "Come with me, Miss Tansy. I want you to meet this hussy."

"Oh, no," she objected.

"Oh, yes," he insisted, guiding her to the texas.

Climbing up to the wheelhouse, Nathan turned to assist the woman. "Here's someone to meet you, Serena. This is Miss Tansy Shumacher who has known me since I was in knee breeches."

"How do you do, Miss Shumacher." Though she was upset with Nathan, Serena could not be rude to their guest. Graciously she greeted the old lady who stepped uncertainly into the pilothouse.

Tansy blinked at her in surprise. This was not the painted harlot she had expected. Clear-eyed, with skin like porcelain and an angelic smile, the girl standing at the wheel was trim and petite and rather young.

"Serena is the daughter of my partner, Miss Tansy, and a lightning pilot," Nathan introduced her proudly.

"Sit down, won't you?" The girl gestured to the bench. "Just scoot Catastrophe over."

Accepting the invitation, Tansy set about getting to know her. A female pilot was rather unusual, she thought, but Serena Caswell seemed a simple, straightforward girl.

Lounging in the doorway, Nathan watched them, enjoying the beginning of a budding friendship. Soon Serena even put aside her anger of the morning and pulled him into the conversation, describing how his partnership in the *Sprite* had come to be. They all laughed at her account of their first tense days together.

As Serena prepared to dock the boat in Baton Rouge, Tansy rose and said warmly, "It's been a pleasure, dear. I hope we meet again soon. I must say Nathan is fortunate to have you."

"Thank you." Serena's eyes clouded as she remembered that Nathan was thinking of leaving. As he smiled down at her now, it was hard to imagine the *Sprite* without him.

"I am sorry, Nathan," Tansy apologized as he escorted her ashore. "I've misjudged you...and Serena. She's a lovely girl."

"You'll tell Mrs. Morgan and Mrs. Watson?"

"I will and I'll ask them to stop spreading such vile rumors."

"I am still upset with you though, Nathan," she announced in parting. "It's time you went home. Your family misses you."

"Yes, ma'am. I intend to visit as soon as they return from Le Jardin."

Standing on tiptoe, she kissed his cheek. "You always were a good boy, Nathan...high-spirited, but good."

As soon as he had placed the old lady in a cab and sent her to her niece, Nathan walked a short distance to Greaves Chandlery to pay on the *Sprite*'s outstanding account.

Jonathan Greaves greeted him pleasantly and their business was conducted in his cluttered office. As he wrote out a receipt, he remarked, "You know, Trent, a lawyer came to see me the other day and offered to buy your account, cash on the barrel head."

"Only ours?"

"Yep. I thought it odd and I thought you should know. I've done business with the Caswell & Company for a long time. Henry was always straight with me and I want to be straight with his family and with you."

"I appreciate that, Mr. Greaves. What's this attorney's name?"

"Murray."

"Titus Murray? Marshall Langley's clerk?"

"Used to be. He's hung out his own shingle now."

"Thank you for the information, sir." Nathan got to his feet. "I believe I'll pay a call on Titus Murray."

Nathan's visit to Murray's office was unsuccessful. The lawyer was out of town and his clerk knew nothing of his attempts to buy the debts of a steamboat company called Caswell & Trent. But Nathan knew without being told that Adele was behind the scheme.

The *River Sprite* was holding its steam when the captain dashed up the gangplank and ordered it pulled in behind him. Just as the boat was about to pull away from the dock, a wagon, crammed with nearly a dozen people, clattered along the wharf. A young man clad in a colorful jacket and waistcoat balanced precariously on the back and shouted through cupped hands, "Ahoy, wait for us."

The cart had scarcely stopped when he bounded to the ground and raced toward the boat. Behind him, the wagon's occupants scrambled down with their baggage. With a word to Levi, Nathan leapt to the dock to meet them.

"Good afternoon, Captain," the young man puffed. "I am Barrett Gallagher of the Edwards Traveling Dramatic Company. We seek transport to Natchez. Have you room for eleven more passengers?"

"If you're willing to double up. We only have a few cabins available."

"Marvelous." The actor smiled confidently at his waiting company. "We'll take them all."

"You do understand the fare is payable in advance, Mr. Gallagher?"

"In that case, we'll take a small one for the ladies. The men will make do in steerage."

"That sounds like a practical plan." Nathan signaled for the gangplank to be put into place again. "Come aboard."

At Barrett's summons, the company moved forward. One of them, a middle-aged man, looking as if he were somehow impaired, was supported by two men carrying musical instrument cases.

"This is Spencer Edwards, one of the world's finest actors and the head of our troupe." Barrett introduced him.

Contrary to first impressions, Edwards was not injured. Exhaling a fog of brandy fumes, he lifted his head and peered at Nathan blearily. "Hap' to make your 'quaintance, Cap'n," he managed before his head lolled back.

"We've just parted with the Ransome Touring Theater Company and struck out on our own. Spence has been celebrating," Barrett explained, unabashed.

"So kind of you to wait for us, Captain." A woman in a garish cerise dress greeted Nathan with a coy smile.

"Not now, Iva," Barrett cut her off. "What's keeping Olivia?" Frowning, he looked back toward the wagon where a shapely actress was talking with the man who had driven them to the dock.

"You know Livy," Iva answered. "She can't resist a conquest"

Rolling his eyes, Barrett summoned her, "Miss Pryor, come at once. We don't want to be late for our next engagement. The theater manager would have apoplexy and you don't want that on your conscience, do you?" He tapped his toe impatiently.

With a buss on the cheek for her would-be swain, the woman walked to the boat. Her skirt swirling around her, she seemed to glide. All activity on deck stopped as the men watched her approach, spellbound. Even Nathan looked dazed as he met her at the foot of the stageplank.

Regarding the handsome captain appraisingly, Olivia laid her gloved hand in his. "I apologize for keeping you waiting. I wouldn't have wasted so much precious time if I had known the trip upriver had such interesting ... possibilities."

"Livy..." Barrett began warningly.

"Shh, Barry," she murmured as she passed him, "you have an audience."

Turning, the actor discovered passengers and crew lining the railing. Sweeping his hat from his head, he bowed grandly. "That's everyone," he told Nathan. "Let's go."

In the pilothouse, Serena blew a long blast on the steam whistle and turned the *River Sprite* upriver.

Through the sunny afternoon, flamboyant women strolled the decks with parasols and flirtatious smiles. Debonair men bowed to every female and generally got in the way of the crew.

From the highest point on the boat, Serena watched glumly as the beautiful actress who had come aboard last claimed Nathan for a stroll around the boiler deck. Her mood was not improved when she overheard Dory and Hank talking below her window.

"It's not that Nathan flirts," Dory complained. "That Pryor woman is the one who is flirting. It's just that he seems to enjoy it."

"He's trying to be nice," Hank defended his hero. "He was even nice to dumb ol' Viola Howard."

"Viola Howard . . . the Morris girls," the girl fretted, "now an actress."

"She's only going as far as Natchez," Hank reminded her.

"I know," his sister said sadly as she departed. "It's just that Natchez seems so far away."

"Good Lord, a vision descends," a voice gasped when Serena stepped to the boiler deck after her watch.

She turned to find herself eye to smiling eye with the young actor who had hailed the *Sprite* in Baton Rouge.

"Permit me to introduce myself." He bowed extravagantly. "I am Barrett Gallagher."

"And I am Oliver Norman." The man at his side also bowed.

"How do you do, gentlemen." She could not resist a smile at their theatrical mannerisms. "I'm Serena Caswell."

"Of Caswell & Trent? Did you hear that, Ollie? She's wealthy as well as beautiful." Barrett wagged his brows playfully.

She laughed aloud. "Believe me, Mr. Gallagher, no one who owns half a steamboat is wealthy."

"Then I'll settle for just beautiful. Shall we promenade, Miss Cas—"

"Pardon me, fellows." Nathan elbowed his way into their midst and placed a proprietary hand at Serena's waist. "My partner and I have business to discuss that will not wait."

"What do you want, Nathan?" she asked as he guided her away with a hand at the small of her back.

"To rescue you from those slavering wolves."

"Why do you assume I needed to be rescued?" she asked indignantly.

"You did," he insisted, mildly exasperated, "whether you realized it or not."

"Both gentlemen seemed perfectly charming to me."

"They may have been charming, but they weren't gentle-men. You would have found that out if you went off with one of them alone."

"Who says I would have gone—"

"You did seem to be enjoying yourself," he cut in.

"Are you accusing me of flirting, Nathan?"

Realizing the conversation was escalating into another quarrel, he shook his head. "I'm not accusing you of flirting, Serena. I don't think you know how. You do have an amazing vocabulary and a pugnacious charm I find very appealing." He grinned, his smile fading when Serena's temper flared.

"I do know how to flirt," she informed him with a wither-ing stare, "and I can do it as well as the next female. In case you haven't noticed, I am a female."

"I've noticed now and again," he answered, the infuriating grin returning, "but you didn't seem to like it."

"Serena!" Roger hailed her before she could reply.

"Hello, Roger." She smiled brightly as he approached. "Shall we have that promenade this afternoon?"

The clerk's step slowed and he looked surprised. Then he beamed at the girl. "Of course."

"If you'll excuse me, Captain . . ." She turned away, miss-ing the cantankerous gleam in Nathan's eyes.

So Nathan didn't think she knew how to flirt. Linking arms with Roger, she fought the urge to look over her shoulder to see if the captain was watching.

Roger hoped he was.

Petite and well matched, the couple strolled in the gathering twilight. Surrounded by other promenaders, Roger made no advances to Serena's relief. As they chatted, she realized how much she enjoyed his company. They had years of friendship in common.

"When will you tie up tonight?" he asked when they re-turned to the companionway. Around them, a stream of pas-sengers returned to their cabins to dress for dinner.

"In a couple of hours. We won't try to pass the Graveyard tonight. The river is low and there are too many hulks."

"I'll be waiting for you."

"You don't have to do that."

"I want to," he assured her, giving her arm an affectionate squeeze as they parted. "I'll see you later."

As she ascended to the texas, the girl made out Nathan's broad-shouldered figure in the dusk, slouched against the ladder to the pilothouse. "Shouldn't you be at dinner, Captain," she greeted him, "entertaining the passengers?"

"They won't miss me for a few minutes," he replied lazily.

"Oh, I'm certain someone will. Olivia Pryor seems downright fond of you."

"I can't help it if the ladies find me irresistible."

"Indeed?" She eyed him coldly. "Well, we all have our crosses to bear."

"It's not so difficult," he retorted. "Besides, keeping the passengers happy is part of my job."

"And piloting the *Sprite* is mine." Drawing herself up, she nodded in dismissal. "If you don't mind..."

As immovable as a boulder, Nathan asked sarcastically, "I take it then that your duties include promenading with the clerk?"

"Whether I promenade and with whom is none of your business. You've already warned me away from the main deck. What's next, the boiler deck? Or are you going to lock me in my cabin when I'm not on watch?"

"Damnation, Serena, you certainly make it hard for a man to talk to you."

"Roger just talked to me for nearly an hour with no difficulty at all," she baited him. "I don't really think you came to talk. I think you came to pick another fight."

"Right now I don't want to do either one," Nathan grated, pushing himself off the ladder and striding to the companionway.

"In the future," Serena called after him, stopping him in his tracks, "I'd appreciate if you would keep your hands off our passengers...no matter how irresistible they seem to find you."

His back to her, Nathan smiled slowly. Serena was jealous.

* * *

The next day, Serena stared out moodily from the wheelhouse without really seeing mile after mile of dense wilderness lining the shore.

Nathan had been promenading with Olivia Pryor all morning, from bow to stern, from texas to main deck. They had probably been together last night, as well, the girl brooded, for she had fallen asleep listening for his return to the cabin next door. Why should she care what he did? He was going to be leaving the *Sprite* soon anyway. To her dismay, the thought depressed her.

Up ahead, she spied a log cabin, smoke curling from its rock chimney. As the *Sprite* drew even with the small farm, she saw a calico-clad woman, scattering feed from her faded apron to the chickens that pecked in the hard-packed dirt at her feet.

A boy raced along the bank, vaulting tree stumps, whooping exuberantly, until his exertions were rewarded with a piercing blast of the whistle. Then he slowed his pace, stopping at the end of the cleared field to wave farewell as the boat rounded a bend.

Oddly cheered by the lad's exhilaration, Serena began to hum as she steered. They were making good time and would arrive in Natchez before dark. Edwards Traveling Dramatic Company and Olivia Pryor would not spend one more night on the *River Sprite.*

She was still in a good mood that afternoon as she guided the *Sprite* toward a dock jutting out into the Mississippi, passing close to Natchez-under-the-Hill. Atop the bluff that seemed to curl over the disreputable waterfront district, was the town of Natchez, fifty feet above and a world away from the ramshackle buildings below.

Clustered at the foot of the bluff, Natchez-under-the-Hill was known up and down the river as one of the most dangerous places in the country, harboring thieves and cutthroats, gamblers and young bucks hungry for adventure. But, as the *River Sprite* glided past, Natchez-under-the-Hill did not look dangerous, only shabby. Along narrow, rutted Silver Street, the seedy buildings seemed to lean against one another, their paint blistering in the sun.

When the steamboat was docked, Nathan took his place at the foot of the stageplank to assist the disembarking passengers. On the texas, Serena watched as the theater troupe clattered ashore with a great deal of commotion. She smiled when Barrett Gallagher caught her eye and bowed gallantly.

She did not smile when Olivia Pryor descended the gangplank and claimed Nathan's arm. Walking the actress to a waiting cab, he kissed her hand, opened the door and helped her inside.

As the carriage rolled away, Olivia looked back, her elegant face long with disappointment. The *Sprite*'s captain had been a pleasant, if distracted, companion, but she could not count him among her conquests.

At least Nathan had done no more than to kiss her hand in farewell, Serena was thinking with satisfaction when another carriage bounced along the pier toward the boat. Uttering a glad cry, Grace hurried down to meet Dean and Theola Everett, two of her oldest friends, who invited her and the entire Caswell family to spend the night at their home in Natchez-on-the-Bluff.

That evening Grace, Will, Dory and Hank went to the Everetts' home. Most of the crew went ashore for the wild times only Natchez-under-the-Hill could offer. Night had fallen and the *Sprite* was quiet when Serena ambled along the boiler deck, occupied with her thoughts. For a reason she did not understand or would not admit to herself, she had stayed aboard. She wanted to talk to Nathan reasonably, to find out what he planned. And she didn't know what she feared most: that he would go or that he would stay.

"Good evening, Miss Serena." Fiske Patterson stepped from the shadows near the companionway to intercept her.

"Good evening, Mr. Patterson." She halted, frowning up at him, uncomfortable in his towering presence but unwilling to retreat.

"Isn't it a grand evening?" His smile shone white in the dimness. "Though it's not as beautiful as you."

"Thank you." She nodded coolly. "If you'll excuse me, I was just on my way—"

"Surely you're not working this evening?" he asked, blocking her way. "Don't you ever play or pick flowers or walk out with a beau, Miss Serena? If you'd come with me, I know where there's a field of wildflowers and soft green grass to lie in through the night."

Though shocked by his audacity, she tried not to let it show. "Let me pass, Mr. Patterson."

"As you wish, miss." With a deep sigh, the crewman allowed her to proceed. As she disappeared onto the texas, he shrugged and muttered to himself, "Perhaps another time."

"I don't think so," the captain said behind him. "Pack your gear, Patterson. You're fired."

"If you're thinking of firing me because of Serena, Captain, I can tell you nothing has happened between us," Fiske defended himself.

"It's not going to, either," Nathan assured him. "You've been panting around her ever since you came aboard. Enough is enough."

"Aren't you the greedy one?" the big deckhand fairly snarled at the captain. "You want to parade around the boat all day with the ladies hanging on your arm and still have Serena to warm your bed at night."

"What?" Nathan exploded.

"Don't try to deny it." Fiske smiled cockily. "I saw her coming out of your cabin one night—or should I say, one morning—when I was on watch."

"Pick up your wages in the clerk's office," Nathan spat, his temper barely in check, "and be off the *Sprite* in five minutes or I'll throw you off."

In the familiar surroundings of the pilothouse where she had sought refuge, Serena tried to control the shaking of her hands. Just remembering Fiske Patterson's hot gaze on her caused her skin to crawl. Sinking down onto the bench, she vowed to speak to Nathan about what had happened as soon as she calmed down. Her pride had gotten in the way long enough. The arrogant deckhand had to go.

"So this is where you're hiding."

Startled, she stared with wide eyes at the huge figure looming in the doorway. "What do you want?"

"A moment of your time." Fiske's voice was light and casual, but his eyes were intense as he stepped inside. "We are old friends, after all, since you tended my arm."

"What I did for you, Mr. Patterson, I would have done for any member of the crew," she answered, rising.

"I don't think so," he crooned. "Because it's me you want."

"What?" She glared at him in disbelief. "What are you talking about?"

"I know you want me. And I want you . . . enough that the captain just fired me. It's all your fault, you know," he added, almost teasingly.

"My fault? I never—"

"You didn't have to," he cut her off. "I know women and you're all woman, Serena Caswell . . . even when you wear those britches." Certain of his success, he leaned forward to kiss her.

"And you are a vexatious, black-hearted child of perdition!" Planting her hands against his chest, she shoved with all her might.

As the brawny deckhand lurched backward, hitting his head against the doorjamb, she yanked down the shotgun hanging beside the door. "If you ever touch me again, Fiske Patterson, I'll send you straight to Hades with a hole in your middle and a bushel of buckshot in your rump."

Slowly straightening, the deckhand found himself staring down twin barrels. "Why are you afraid of me, Serena?" he asked mildly, the look in his eye belying his tone.

"I'm not afraid of you. I should think that's very clear."

"Then put down the gun," he coaxed, edging toward her. "Once you've had a real man, you'll forget Trent. He'll go back where he belongs and you and I will get along just fine."

"I want you off the *River Sprite* now." Serena pulled back the hammers for both barrels. "Get off and don't come back."

She squeezed one trigger when Fiske lunged at her, deliberately shooting to the left of him. The entire row of windows beside his head exploded, showering him with glass shards, nicking him in a dozen places.

"You little fool," he snarled. "You might've blown my head off."

"And I will if you don't get out. The second barrel is for more than a warning."

For an instant, they faced each other, movement and time frozen. When shouts reached them from below, the man glanced out the shattered windows to see Nathan and Roger racing from the clerk's office. His plans for Serena forgotten, he gave a strangled curse and vaulted from the pilothouse door. Racing to the railing, he dived into the river.

"Serena, are you all right?" Nathan and Roger nearly tumbled over each other as they scaled the ladder to the wheelhouse. "What happened?"

"I ran off Fiske Patterson," she answered shakily.

"I'll kill him." His face grim, Nathan crossed the narrow room in two strides to stand at Serena's side.

"I would, too," Roger echoed the sentiment, "but he's gone."

"And I don't think he'll be back," she muttered.

"Send someone for the sheriff, Roger," Nathan ordered, taking the gun from her and expertly uncocking it.

"Damn right," the clerk choked in agreement, clattering down the ladder.

When he had removed the remaining cartridge from the shotgun, Nathan propped the weapon in a corner and turned to the girl. Placing one hand on her shoulder, he nudged her chin gently with the other so she was forced to look him in the eye. "Did that bastard hurt you?" he demanded hoarsely.

"No...but I thought he was going to." An unwanted tear rolled down her cheek.

"My poor little love," he whispered, drawing her into his arms.

Cradled against his broad chest, Serena's reserve crumbled and she began to cry, her shoulders heaving with wrenching sobs.

"It's all right now, Rena. I'm here," he reassured her, one big hand stroking her tumbled hair tenderly.

Locked in a comforting and comfortable embrace, the couple did not know that Roger had returned, until he spoke.

"Bill went for the sheriff. Are you all right, Serena?"

"I'm fine," she answered, reluctantly stepping out of the warm circle of Nathan's arms. "I just wish you hadn't sent for the sheriff. My blood still boils from the last time we did business. He'll probably say what happened was my fault for working on a steamboat."

"Probably," Roger concurred, his expression still disturbed, "and he'll tell you again that the river is no place for a woman."

"After tonight, I would agree," Nathan said somberly.

"And I," Roger added.

"I can take care of myself." Serena glared mutinously at them.

"So far." Nathan surveyed the wrecked room ruefully. "But you shouldn't have to take care of yourself...not like this. I'm going to make sure what happened tonight never happens again."

"We'll look out for you, Rena," Roger assured her. "We'll stay right here with you when the sheriff comes."

"I'm not some helpless female," Serena protested. "I don't need you to protect me from that self-righteous, potbellied, slack-jawed—"

"Then we'll stay to protect the sheriff from you," Nathan insisted.

The sheriff came and went. He poked around the *River Sprite,* surveyed the damaged windows with little interest and, in general, reacted just as Serena had expected he would.

And she reacted just as Nathan expected. "I'm not the one who did something wrong," she shouted before endowing the astonished lawman with no less than fifteen imaginative epithets, most of them disparaging his ancestry. Then she stormed from the wheelhouse, followed by Roger.

"River people," the offended man complained as Nathan walked him to the dock. "If you're new, I reckon you don't know yet how much trouble they can be, Cap'n Trent. But I'll tell you what I'll do. I'll be on the lookout for this Patterson fella, though it ain't likely we'll find him. Too easy to disappear into Natchez-under-the-Hill or to take a berth on a boat. Then, too, there's the Trace. But I'll sure keep an eye open for him." Mounting his horse, he rode away.

From the dock, Nathan glimpsed Roger heading toward his office. Serena must be safe in her cabin, he decided, because the clerk would not have left her otherwise.

Going to the stern, the captain quietly tried her latch. Satisfied to find it locked, he pulled the chair in front of her door and settled for the night. Harmonica music drifted up from below as a mountain man who had signed on for wooding up in New Orleans played for the steerage passengers who had not gone ashore. The melody was sweet and haunting, but it did little to soothe Nathan's jangled nerves. He sat, awake, his arms crossed on his chest, for a long time until, at last, he dozed fitfully.

He awoke near dawn, his clothes damp with dew, and moved to stand stiffly beside the railing. It was a peaceful time aboard a riverboat and Nathan was grateful for a moment to admire the rosy sunrise.

The aromas of coffee, ham and boiling grits wafted to him on the breeze, and the faint clattering of pans came from the galley. Roused by the sounds, Chanticleer gave a halfhearted crow, then fell silent. Somewhere in the distance along the riverbank, another cock greeted the sun. Crowing lustily in response, the *Sprite*'s rooster heralded the new day, proclaiming an end to the long night.

Chapter Fourteen

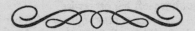

"Grace, wait, I need to talk to you." Nathan strode across the texas toward the woman. "Have you considered my proposition?"

"I have considered it," she replied, "and the answer is still no. I do appreciate your concern for my family's safety, but you and I began this endeavor as partners and we will end as partners."

"You're as stubborn as your daughter." Rubbing his neck wearily, the captain watched a glazier replacing the windows in the wheelhouse while Will supervised, delighted to have a new audience for his yarns. "Be reasonable. I'll give you a good price for your half of the *Sprite*. You can live ashore in comfort... and out of danger."

"You are generous, Nathan, but I don't believe we are in danger." Grace's sweet tone was at odds with the defiant rise of her chin. "I talked to Serena this morning and she assured me that after Mr. Patterson's hasty departure, the remaining crew are old hands who are faithful to Caswell & Trent. We are as safe here as we would be at River's Rest. There's nothing for you to worry about."

"I worry about your hotheaded daughter most of the time," he retorted. "I just wish I could talk some sense into her."

"Presently I would not advise you to try. She is upset that both you and Roger have urged her to leave the *Sprite*."

"For her own good."

"Indeed. However, she did chase the cad away and she is quite well today after her ordeal. Better than you are," she added with a smile. "Levi told me you slept in a chair on deck all night."

"I needed to know she was all right," he explained lamely. "I promised myself I wouldn't allow anything bad to happen to her again. I'll keep her safe, if I have to tie her to me to do it."

As the man departed, Grace exulted quietly, "You must have a very long rope, Nathan Trent, or you must stay aboard the *Sprite* after St. Louis."

Unable to sleep that night, Nathan prowled the main deck, remembering the feel of Serena in his arms, feeling anger again at what had happened the night before. He could have killed Patterson if he had gotten his hands on him.

His savage thoughts were interrupted when the big boat swung starboard. Stepping to the bow, he discerned a snag ahead in the darkness. Up in the wheelhouse, Will had already seen it.

Calling for the leadsmen, the captain was not concerned. An able and experienced pilot, Will was already making for a chute, a narrow opening behind one of the islands along the falling river.

The paddle wheel slowed as the *River Sprite* nosed into the pass. The chute was gently curved and the water was placid and calm, making it impossible to estimate the depth. The leadsmen threw out their chains, calling the measurements to word passers stationed on all three decks. Great caution was necessary for, once in the chute, there was no backing out. Suddenly the engines were reversed and the paddle wheel kicked up foaming white water.

"Tree down across the pass, sir," Luke called as the boat, carried forward by momentum, lodged against the fallen giant, the prow nudging it with every lap of water. The obstacle was already causing a bar of silt to build. It had to be removed quickly.

"Levi," Nathan hollered, "take some men down to chop up that tree while I alert the passengers."

What followed was a familiar exercise for steamboat travelers. They filed ashore while the first mate bellowed orders and the crew set about removing the obstacle in the gathering night. Oil-soaked wood in cressets provided illumination. A fire was also lit ashore, more for light than to allay any chill.

Aware of the difference the weight of even one person could make in clearing the bar, Serena wished Will luck and went ashore with the others. As Roger tended the fire, the adults congregated around it. Hank and several other children found a spot close enough to see the fallen log but far enough to be out of the way of the crew.

At the river's edge, Nathan paced, his attention alternately claimed by his passengers and the work proceeding in the chute. Unable to assist the men, Serena stood near the fire, calculating how long it would take to build steam again.

All at once, a massive form blocked out the firelight, casting a huge shadow over her. She looked up...and up...at an enormous mountain man. In the dimness, she could barely make out his homely whiskered face lit with a gap-toothed smile.

"Yer a purty little thang...even purtier than I thought." His wondering voice rumbled in his vast chest. "I seen ya once, comin' outta the galley. Where ya bin keepin' yerself?"

"Mostly on the texas and the boiler deck," Serena answered politely, backing away to increase the distance between them.

"C'mere." Taking her arm in his big paw, he tried to pull her into the fire's glow.

"Let go of me," she insisted, planting her feet stubbornly.

His face clouded when she tried to pry his fingers from around her wrist. "Ol' Jed ain't gonna hurt ya," he said reasonably. "I'm jes' lookin' for a wife and I wanna git a look at ya."

"Well, I'm not looking for a husband, you big lummox."

"No reason to git riled, though I do like a woman with gumption," he remarked admiringly as he hauled her into the light.

"Let me go!" Serena punctuated her words with three blows against his chest, then followed them with one more. "Now!"

"Stand still," he ordered. "I done tol' ya, I ain't gonna hurt ya."

"The lady wishes to be left alone," a voice warned quietly from behind them.

"This is between me and the gal." Jed wheeled belligerently on the intruder, swinging Serena off her feet. As they spun, she glimpsed Roger across the open flames. His arms full of kindling, he watched wide-eyed, seemingly transfixed by her predicament. Grace and Dory stood beside him, their faces pale and horrified. As Jed set Serena on her feet with a thud, Nathan materialized from the darkness.

"No," he contradicted the mountain man, "this is between you and me."

Jed's bushy brows knit in a frown and he looked Nathan over. They would be evenly matched in a fair fight. The captain was big and he looked to be spoiling for a tussle.

"Well?" Nathan asked severely.

Though he enjoyed a good scrap, Jed deliberated. If he won the fight, he might lose his transport, but he would have the woman. If he lost, he wouldn't have either one and he didn't like the idea of walking to St. Louis. Seeking to preserve his pride, he nodded at Serena and asked gruffly, "This your woman?"

"Yes," Nathan answered at once.

"I am not."

"Is she or ain't she?" Jed demanded.

"She's mine." The captain took hold of her other arm.

Bending over Serena, the mountain man said earnestly, "I got a fine cabin in good trappin' country an' I'm willin' to fight for ya. You don't hafta go with him if you don't wanna."

"I want to," she managed to say.

"Ya best be good to her," Jed warned the other man, "'cause I'll be watchin'." Abruptly he released his hold and Serena lurched against Nathan. He drew her to his side, holding her in the curve of his protective arm.

"I din't mean no harm," the mountaineer announced unhappily, watching the couple with a disgruntled expression. "Don' want another man's woman. I jes' wanted a look at them purty blue eyes."

"Don't move, Serena," Nathan ordered quietly, continuing to hold her at his side, "and, for once, don't argue."

Aware the danger was not yet over, she nodded and allowed him to lead her to stand beside her stunned mother.

"Stay here, darling," he suggested loudly for Jed's benefit, "till we're clear of this chute. I'll come back for you as soon as I can."

His hands circling her waist, he kissed her. Tender and fleeting, it was over before she knew what was happening. Resting his cheek against hers, he whispered in her ear, "Smile, Rena, or Jed's going to think you're not happy with me."

Serena's heart pounded and her breath had deserted her, but she smiled tremulously and looped her arms around his neck.

"That's better," he murmured just before his lips claimed hers again sweetly. For a moment, they shared the same thought, the same breath, the same heartbeat. Then, releasing her, Nathan said softly, "I hope he understands now that you're my woman."

Their brief kiss had been more than a display for the mountain man, Serena realized as Nathan returned to his toiling crew. His gentleness had affected her as greatly as his passion that dark night in Baton Rouge. Her emotions confounded her, but she could not deny the feelings he roused in her. And he was not immune to her touch. His kiss had told her.

Lost in wonder, she touched her lips with gentle fingers, unaware of the restrained reactions to the scene that had just been played out in the flickering firelight. Jed sulked. Concern gave way to speculation on Grace's face. Dory fought back tears while Roger stared despairingly, but did not approach.

Hurriedly donning her robe, Grace answered a quiet rap on her door. Nathan stood on deck, his bulk dark against the moonlit sky.

"Is something wrong?" she whispered when she saw him.

"I'm sorry to disturb you," he apologized softly. "Were you sleeping?"

"No." She stepped back so he could enter. "But Dory is, so do be quiet." Lighting a lamp, she turned to look at him. Rumpled, with a shadowy growth of beard on his jaw, he obviously had not slept yet. "What brings you here at this hour, Nathan?"

"I wanted to tell you I've decided to stay aboard the *Sprite*."

Fixing him with reproving stare, she said, "And what, may I ask, brings you to this decision?"

"Actually my mind was made up when I kissed Serena at the chute."

"There are less flamboyant ways to reach a decision. Everyone there was horrified. No one knew quite what to do."

"Serena did." Nathan grinned at his partner without remorse. "She kissed me back."

Grace pursed her lips, hoping to convey utmost disapproval, but somehow she found herself smiling, too. In the bedroom, Dory buried her head in her pillow, hot tears scalding her eyes.

Adele sat at the writing desk in her room at Langley House and stared off into space. Her plans to force Nathan home were getting nowhere. And worse, Fiske Patterson, forced to flee the *River Sprite*, had tried his hand at petty blackmail until she referred him to her cousin, the parish sheriff. Then he had bothered her no more.

She didn't need the bumbling deckhand anyway, she mused, now that she had Titus Murray. But even he was not meeting with much success. The lawyer had done well enough, investigating Caswell & Trent's debts, but he had found only a handful of creditors willing to do business with him. She could hardly pressure Nathan to leave the river in return for the cancellation of the company's debts, if she held so few.

What was the good of the fortune George had left her, she thought crossly, if Nathan was immune to the power it gave her? Perhaps he would prefer it if she appeared weak and contrite, begging his forgiveness. She would do what she must.

Sighing, she picked up a pen and began to write a letter to her lost love.

In St. Louis, the bustling wharf was stacked high with bundles of pelts. A middle-aged man, his smile framed by a drooping mustache, strode toward the docking steamboat. With a whoop, Nathan leapt the dwindling space between pier and boat before the *River Sprite* was even moored, and landed beside him, pumping his hand enthusiastically in greeting.

From the pilothouse, Serena watched as he introduced the stranger to Will and Grace. As the last of the passengers poured down the gangplank, Jed threw a reproachful look at the boat over his brawny shoulder. Serena had kept to the upper decks since their meeting and he had never seen her again.

Roger's manner toward her had been nearly as affronted as Jed's after the incident at the chute, Serena thought, watching the mountain man depart. Still her mood was light when she descended from the wheelhouse. She was pleased to feel no longer a prisoner on her own boat.

"Hey, Rena," Hank greeted his sister around a mouthful of pecan cookie. "Mother wants you to come to tea in her cabin."

"Don't you know not to talk with your mouth full?" she chided.

Unconcerned, he swallowed the cookie and asked, "Know what, Rena? Nathan's friend, Amos, is a real Indian scout."

"The man who met the boat?"

"Yep. And he's staying for dinner, 'cause he really wants to meet you."

"Me?"

The boy nodded, bounding away a few steps before he explained, "Amos says he's powerful interested to meet a half-pint gal who can do a man's job. 'Specially if you're as pretty as Nate said."

Feeling pleasantly flushed, Serena went to the captain's cabin.

"Oolong or pekoe, dear?" Grace greeted her, looking up from the tea caddy.

"Oolong, please." Serena took the chair opposite her mother.

"Isn't this exciting?" the woman asked, measuring out the tea. "St. Louis doesn't seem nearly as primitive as I had imagined. Though I must say Nathan's friend, Mr. Vance, is rather rustic."

"Is that Amos? I just heard about him from Hank."

"Yes. He and Nathan were to join a wagon train. Mr. Vance waited, even though Nathan sent word to him months ago. He says he did not want to 'light out' without giving him a chance to change his mind about going to 'Californy.'"

"What did Nathan say?"

Discerning a great deal from the anxiety in Serena's voice, Grace answered casually, "He said he can't leave the *Sprite* just now. Personally, I'm glad Nathan is in no hurry to rush off. I would miss him. He reminds me of Henry."

"Papa wasn't a gambler."

"Neither is Nathan . . . anymore," her mother countered. "But do not tell me Henry wasn't a gambler, my dear. I was married to him for nearly twenty-five years. He carried around a pocketful of IOUs from people who had nothing to recommend them except honest faces. He knew when the boat's engine was about to give out and he would bet it could last just a little longer."

"Well, he certainly wasn't a ladies' man like Nathan."

"I think Nathan is charming and not libertine in the least."

"I think he's charmed everyone on this boat," Serena muttered.

"Except you?"

"Except me."

"You don't want to like him, do you?" Grace asked accusingly.

"I do like him . . . sometimes." Setting her cup aside, Serena rose to pace the cramped parlor. "But he confuses me. Sometimes he makes me feel wonderful. Other times he makes me nervous and uncertain . . . and furious. I can't get away from him . . . or what I feel. This boat just isn't big enough."

"The entire world isn't big enough," Grace told her gently. "Why don't you face it, Serena? You're in love with Nathan."

Stopping midstride, the girl stared at her in disbelief. "I am not in love. And if I were, it wouldn't be with Nathan Trent."

As she went down to the deck below, Serena mumbled under her breath, "I am not in love with Nathan." Dressing for dinner, she muttered, "I am not in love."

But when she poised on the dark deck outside the salon and saw the elegant, assured captain inside, the words turned to dust in her mouth.

She was in love with Nathan, she admitted to herself miserably. But whom did he love...if anyone? Plain, practical Serena? Beautiful Adele from his past? Or one of the many women who had tried to snare him since he came aboard the *Sprite*?

Love was a game to him. Though he had kissed her sweetly at the chute, she was not his woman nor was she likely to be, Serena brooded. And despite what she had allowed herself to think at the time, it had been a performance acted out for the buckskin-clad stranger. Glumly she went in to be introduced to Amos Vance.

After a delicious, sociable dinner, the trapper settled back in his chair in the mood to spin a few yarns. Charmed by the petite redhead, he smiled at Serena and launched into a story, a tall tale to match any of Will's. While he talked, not a sound could be heard but the lap of the river against the still boat.

After several anecdotes, each more unbelievable than the last, Grace excused herself and the children. Sitting beside an appreciative Will, Serena stayed while the men sipped brandy and a new round of storytelling began.

Amos spoke of the war in Mexico and scouting in Texas for the army, of the frontier and life among the Sioux, and, too frequently for the captain's liking, of Nathan's knack with the ladies.

Nathan's past seemed to fascinate Roger, who asked many questions while the big man's jaw worked in exasperation. Oblivious to his discomfiture, Nathan's friend embellished each account with minute detail, blending truth with fiction, and his lies became more and more fantastic as the night wore on.

"The winter Nate and me spent in Galveston," he reminisced, "he met this—"

"I don't think what we did in Galveston two years ago would interest anyone," Nathan cut in.

"This is one of my best yarns," Amos complained.

"I've enjoyed Mr. Vance's stories so far," Roger interjected. "Let him tell it."

"He jest don't wanna hear it because he's modest," the trapper assured the young clerk.

"Amos," Nathan said warningly.

Collecting his thoughts, Amos stared off into space, missing the admonition. "Lemme see now, where was I?"

"In Galveston," Roger prompted.

"Oh, yeah." A slow smile lit his face. "That was when Nate met up with this opry singer, Mademoiselle Fifi."

"Madame Fiona," the captain growled.

"Who was real hoity-toity," Amos went on, ignoring the interruption, "from Paris, France. But she took a shine to our boy Nathan right off.

"As you may have gathered, he was havin' uncommon good luck with the ladies from the Rio Grande to the Black Hills. So me and Lem Saunders, another of Gen'ral Taylor's boys, made a bet. I said inside a week Nate would be spendin' the night at Fifi's little house down along the shore. Lem didn't disagree, but he said it had to be all night or it wouldn't count for nothin'.

"So, unbeknownst to Nate, we found us a sand dune that very night and settled down to watch. Had a bottle to keep us warm, but pretty soon it commenced to rainin' and blowin'. I tell you the wind comin' in off the gulf is cold." He shivered at the memory. "We like to froze to death.

"Anyhow Lem wanted to call off the bet, but I was too close to winnin'. He was carryin' on 'bout sufferin' three kinds of chilblains and losin' the feelin' in his toes when Nate come outta the house and ol' Lem perked right up.

"Nate came to where we was hunkered down, pitched a blanket at Lem and told him to quit his caterwaulin'. He was keepin' the lady awake. Then he went back in the house. He was still there when we left at dawn and, as I recall, we didn't see him again for three days." The trapper dissolved into gales of laughter. "Easiest money I ever made. I don't reckon I ever thanked you proper for that, Nate."

"No thanks are needed," the man grated, glancing at Serena.

The report of Nathan's long-ago love affair had brought bright spots of color to her cheeks, but her manner was composed as she rose from the table. "Good evening, gentlemen. Mr. Vance, it was a pleasure to meet you."

"The pleasure was mine, gal." The frontiersman sprung to his feet and bowed stiffly. "If Nate don't treat you right, you let me know," he added with a meaningful look at the captain, "though I reckon he's met his match in you."

Blushing, the girl turned toward the door.

"I'll walk you to your cabin, Rena," Roger volunteered hopefully.

"No, thank you," her answer drifted back.

Nathan watched her departure. Then, with a distracted frown, he forced himself to turn his attention to the conversation. Roger, too, seemed preoccupied and the party broke up an hour later.

In her cabin, Serena lay on the narrow bunk, unable to sleep. Her thoughts roiled, matching churning emotions when she remembered Nathan's last tender kiss. She had hoped against hope that it had meant something. And it had, she told herself fiercely. It had meant Nathan thought he had made another conquest.

Mentally rehearsing what she would say to him the next time they were alone, she nearly missed his footsteps on the stern. The man walked as quietly as the Indians Amos said he had lived with. She saw his shadow and smelled the fragrance of his tobacco as he lingered on deck.

Outside Serena's door, Nathan debated. He realized Amos's talk had stirred her jealousy, but he had to see her. Drawing a deep breath, he tapped on her door.

"What is it?" she responded promptly from within.

"I'd like to talk to you."

"I've already retired, Nathan. Can't it wait until morning?"

"No."

The door opened and Serena stood warily before him, wearing a robe that buttoned up to her neck. "What's so important that you must speak to me tonight?"

"I...I wanted to apologize...for Amos," he answered, feeling suddenly tongue-tied.

"There's no need. I thought he was a nice man."

"The salt of the earth, but a little rough. And some of his stories—"

"Border on the truth, I'm sure." She waved a hand breezily. "I've always known you're a ladies' man, Nathan."

"You accused me of that from the very first."

"And you denied it, but I'd already heard you broke hearts in New Orleans," she continued airily. "A lot of them."

"Serena, don't," he commanded quietly.

Her speech begun, she could not be deterred. "And now I learn you blazed a trail through the Western Territories, as well...." Her air of sophistication deserting her, she looked rather forlorn.

Gently Nathan's big hand cupped her chin, his thumb stroking her cheek. "I wouldn't break a heart on the Mississippi," he murmured. "I wouldn't break yours, Serena."

"No." She stared up at him for a moment, her eyes dark with emotion, before she pulled away. "Because you're never going to get the chance. Good night."

"*Bonjour,* Sisters," Nathan's voice reached Serena from the dock. As she went to relay Will's order to build steam, she saw the captain, positioned in the long morning shadows at the foot of the gangplank, greeting a pair of black-habited nuns.

When she finished in the engine room, she discovered the nuns, milling around the boiler deck uncertainly. "Good morning, Sisters," she greeted them. "I'm Serena Caswell. May I help you find your cabin?"

"Non, merci," the taller of the two answered. "We seek *le capitaine.*"

Glancing over the railing, the girl said, "In a few minutes, he'll give the order to take in the plank, then he'll come up."

"Merci." The tall nun nodded.

"T'ank you," the smaller twittered.

"If you'd like to wait in the salon, I'm sure you would be cooler," Serena suggested, leading them to a table framed by the open door.

"Oui," the short nun murmured, eyeing Serena's cool yellow dress with something akin to envy.

As they chatted, the girl learned they were members of a French order, teachers at the local convent school, on their way to New Orleans. The tall, thin one with a Roman nose was Soeur Thérèse. The other, short and round, was Soeur Berthe who smiled and nodded for she understood little English.

Ready to draw in the stageplank, Nathan winced when a shrill, familiar voice rang out over the idling engines, "Yoo-hoo, Nathan, wait for us."

Turning, he greeted Viola Howard and her long-suffering aunt. "Ladies, how nice to see you. What are you doing in St. Louis?"

"We came up with my sister last week. Now we're goin' back to Memphis. Is there room for us on the *River Sprite,* Captain?" Viola asked flirtatiously from the dock.

"There's always room for you, Miss Howard, Miss Duffy," he responded gallantly.

Standing at the railing, Serena watched as Viola, clad in a fashionable periwinkle gown, came aboard. Claiming the captain's arm at once, she gaily demanded to be shown to her stateroom. The smile Nathan turned on her was entirely too warm, Serena decided.

As Nathan mounted the stairs to the boiler deck, he caught a glimpse of skirt as Serena swept into the salon and nearly groaned aloud.

"Hank!" Disengaging himself from Viola's grip, he summoned the hapless lad, "Please see the ladies to the Pennsylvania Suite."

"But Nathan, I thought you were going to escort us all the way to our door," Viola objected.

"I cannot neglect my other passengers." He smiled charmingly. "And Hank will take care of you. Won't you, Hank?"

"Yes, sir," the reluctant boy mumbled. "If you'll come with me...."

Equally reluctant, Viola followed with her aunt in tow, as Nathan sauntered into the shady salon.

"*Bonjour* again, Sisters. Good morning, Rena," he greeted them amiably. "I see you've met. Are you settled in, Soeur Thérèse?"

"We did not unpack until you answer for us a question, *Capitaine*. The cabin, it is so much more commodious than we expected. Perhaps there has been a mistake?"

"No, ma'am." He shook his head. "Empire State is yours. We just hope you enjoy it."

With a flurry of thanks, the nuns returned to the luxurious stateroom Grace had given them.

"Hadn't you better go see about Viola?" Serena asked sourly when Nathan did not leave. "A charming girl," she mimicked, "and so feminine."

He grimaced at his own long-forgotten gibe, back to haunt him. "I only said that to get under your skin, you know."

"Didn't work," she lied jauntily. "Welcome aboard," she greeted Viola on her way out of the salon.

"'Lo, Serena," the other girl answered absently before her face lit with a smile. "There you are, Nathan."

He had vowed to keep Serena safe, Nathan thought wryly as he was joined by the eager Viola. He wondered if she would do the same for him.

The sun was setting three days later when the captain returned to the *River Sprite* from Trevarian's office. He was pleased to think the *Sprite* would steam downriver from Memphis tomorrow, laden with hides and Trevarian cotton. And he was elated that they would not be carrying Viola Howard.

Nathan did not know when he had met a more determined young woman in search of a husband. Viola had dogged his steps from morning until night. At first, he had been mildly amused by her persistence but, as the run from St. Louis to Memphis neared its end, his patience had dwindled.

So, apparently, had Serena's. One of the only moments he had found to be alone with her, she had commented icily that his reputation as lady-killer seemed well deserved.

A little jealousy wasn't a bad thing, he had mused as she walked away. It had been her unwitting signal that she was beginning to care for him. He had started after her, intending to tell her how he felt, to vanquish the hurt she seemed to feel. But before he reached her, Viola had stepped into his path.

While the blond girl chattered at him, Roger had hailed Serena. Over Viola's shoulder, Nathan had observed as the diminutive couple strolled forward arm in arm.

That was the way it had been since St. Louis. If Viola did not get in the way, Roger did. But tonight, the captain thought, boarding the boat and heading for the stern, he would manage to be alone with Serena and he would tell her that he loved her.

But Nathan's step checked and his smile dimmed when he rounded the cabins. Unaware of his presence, Serena and Roger stood at the opposite railing, silhouetted against the river. Nathan stepped back into the shadows, hating himself for eavesdropping but unwilling to leave.

"I do love you, Roger," Serena assured the clerk softly.

"No, you don't. Not really."

"Don't be difficult." Though he could not see her clearly, Nathan was comforted by the reproving tone in her voice, but his heart skipped a beat at her next words, "You know I've always loved you, Roger Blake. You're my best friend."

"I don't want to be your friend. I want to be your husband." The young man braced both hands against the rail. "Why won't you marry me?"

"Because I don't love you that way," she answered gently.

"Love could grow after we're married. It happens all the time . . . unless you're in love with someone else?"

"I—I'm not in love with anyone." Caught off guard, she was unwilling to share her feelings about Nathan with anyone, least of all a disappointed suitor.

"Then marry me," Roger persisted.

"I can't. I'm sorry," she whispered.

Still unseen by the couple, Nathan opened his cabin door noiselessly and slipped inside.

"Can't things go on as they always have?" he heard Serena blurt. "Can't we just be friends?"

"No," the clerk answered thickly, "it's not enough anymore."

As Roger's footsteps faded away along the deck, Nathan sank down onto his bunk. He could not very well reveal his presence after what he had just witnessed. Serena would resent his eavesdropping and she needed a moment of privacy. Though he had come to the stern to tell her that he loved her, she would hardly want to hear it at the moment, he thought bleakly. Besides, she had just denied that she loved him ... or anyone.

"Damnation," he muttered, lying back on the bed, when her door quietly opened and closed.

Several hours later, Nathan awoke to the sound of voices. He must have dozed off. He lay, fully dressed, atop his bunk. Going out on deck, he discovered Serena leaning over the railing. Roger stood on the gangplank below, looking up at her. His expression was surly and out of place on his pleasant face.

"Wait," she called to him. "I want to talk to you."

"Nothin' to talk 'bout. 'M goin' ashore to get a drink." He lurched toward the dock.

"What's going on?" Nathan asked, joining her at the rail.

"It's Roger," she replied breathlessly. "Someone has to look out for him and I can't very well follow him into a tavern. Will you bring him back ... please?"

Glancing down, the captain swore under his breath. Roger was reeling determinedly across the dock toward a seedy bar. Obviously drunk and out to get drunker, he was sure prey for the miscreants who frequented there. "I'll bring him back as soon as I can.

"A fine thing," he fumed to himself as he strode ashore. "She's not in love with either of us, but we're both dancing to her tune like monkeys on a string. You can bet Miss Caswell and I will have a word together before I perform another jig.''

When he entered the shabby, smoky bar, Nathan spied Roger perched on a high stool at the counter. The young man downed his whiskey in one gulp and demanded another. Easing onto the stool at his side, the captain ordered coffee and sat quietly, unperturbed that Roger ignored him.

After another drink, the clerk turned to him. ''What're you doing here? I thought you'd be with S'rena. She's faithless, y'know, utterly faithless.''

''I can see how you'd feel that way,'' Nathan answered, refusing to be drawn into a quarrel. ''How about some dinner?''

''I c-can' eat,'' Roger hiccuped, swaying on his stool. ''C-can' sleep. Can' do an'thin'. Rena doesn't love me.''

''Starving yourself won't change that. You'll feel better when you've got some food in your stomach to soak up the whiskey.'' Summoning the barkeeper, Nathan ordered two dinners.

''Guess you're right.'' Roger slumped beside him. ''She loves me or she doesn't.'' Then, recalling his last conversation with Serena, he straightened and added almost lucidly, ''She did say she loves me . . . but not tha' way.''

Seemingly heartened by the memory, he attacked his dinner, an unappetizing-looking stew, with gusto and did not speak again until he had finished.

''Whiskey,'' he called. Spinning on his stool, he faced Nathan. ''I prob'ly shouldn' tell you, Trent, but S'rena's in love wi' you.''

''Not me,'' Nathan murmured, staring out at the river beyond the open door.

Roger drew himself to his full height. ''Wanna bet, gamblin' man?'' Tottering, he steadied himself with a hand on the bar, knocking his drink into Nathan's lap. ''Sorry,'' he mumbled, and awkwardly tried to pull himself back up onto the high stool.

"It's all right." Nathan hauled him back onto the seat. Mopping up the liquor, he asked, "You really think Rena loves me?"

"I know it. I'm her best friend," Roger declared arrogantly. "She loves you and I'm not happy 'bout it. No offense 'tended."

"None taken."

"So I mus' t-tender my res-resignation, Cap'n. I mus' leave the *Sprite*."

"I hate to see that," Nathan said though he knew it was best. "You're a nice fellow, Blake."

"You, too." The clerk hoisted a wobbling glass. "Le's drink to frien'ship."

"To friendship," the captain agreed, lifting his cup, "then I'm taking you back to the boat."

Serena strolled along the boiler deck, her face turned toward shore. Dinner was long finished, the passengers had retired, but of Nathan and Roger, there had been no sign. With a sigh, she decided to go to bed, but as she reached the stern, she heard a crash from the dock, a splash and laughter.

Nathan wasn't sure what happened. One minute he was holding the inebriated clerk erect. The next, Roger's knees buckled and their legs tangled together. They sprawled on the dock, watching a cask of wine roll into the river. Limp with laughter, Roger slapped the tarred planking in his mirth.

Getting to his feet, Nathan located his hat and reset it untidily on his head. Then he hoisted the clerk up, throwing his arm around his waist and looping the other man's arm over his shoulders. Together they staggered toward the boat.

"That you, Cap'n?" The night watch's voice was soft enough not to disturb the passengers who might still be sleeping.

"It is. Could you give me a hand here, Bill?"

In seconds, the deckhand had slung the protesting Roger over his shoulder. Poised to carry him aboard, he recommended, "You better wait here, Cap'n. I'll come back for you."

"I'm not drunk," Nathan corrected Bill's misapprehension. "Blake spilled a drink on me."

"Uh-huh," the crewman said, unconvinced. "Smells like it was a whole whiskey barrel."

"Let him cross," Serena ordered, descending to the main deck. "He might make it. If he falls in, it'll sober him up and give the passengers a good laugh."

Glancing up at the shadowy figures who had come on deck to investigate the disturbance, Bill agreed reluctantly, "Yes'm."

Paying their impromptu audience no heed, Serena greeted the captain, "Nathan Trent, you're a sodden, staggering, cock-eyed fool. You smell like a distillery and look a sight."

"You're a sight, too, Rena." From the ramp, he smiled at her wickedly but did not argue.

"A vision of loveliness," Roger confirmed. Draped over the deckhand's shoulder, he peered at her upside down.

"I cannot believe I asked you to take care of him and you both come back drunk," Serena accused Nathan hotly.

"I am not drunk. Roger is drunk. And while Bill is putting him to bed, I want to speak to you, Serena."

"Speak then."

His gaze rising to the onlookers, the man suggested delicately, "Couldn't we talk in privacy?"

"Why?" she snapped. "The entire boat knows our business."

"All right, then..." Deliberately Nathan raised his voice so the spectators could hear his pronouncement. "I love you, Serena Caswell. And I know you love me." Capturing her wrist, he drew her onto the gangplank and kissed her soundly to cheers from the upper decks.

She emerged from his embrace, red faced and mortified. "How could you...in front of..." she sputtered. "How I ever fell in love with such a...such a..."

Grinning when she faltered, he stepped back and spread his arms in a wide, theatrical manner. "You see," he called up to the observers, "she loves me."

"Oooh," was all Serena could say as she whirled and marched aboard.

Chapter Fifteen

One eye on the faded, cloudless sky, Serena walked from the galley after breakfast. The day was young and already promised to be scorchingly hot. Hoping for a breeze on the boiler deck, she skimmed up the stairs. Her pace slowed at the sight of Roger, obviously ailing after the night, preparing to descend with his bags.

"Where are you going?" she asked, her expression bewildered.

Shading his eyes with a hand, he gazed down at her apprehensively. "I'm leaving the *Sprite.*"

"Because of me?" she whispered.

"No, no," he denied too quickly. "The last time I saw Captain Leathers, he offered me a position on the *Natchez.* I might as well wait for him here as in Vicksburg."

"But—"

"It's time I moved on, Serena." Stepping down beside her, he cut off her protest with unexpected firmness.

"Well, I'm sure it will be a good job. I hear Captain Leathers pays well," she said awkwardly.

Roger looked away and did not answer. For a moment, the two old friends were silent. "Will you walk me down?" he asked after a moment.

"Of course," she responded, trying to swallow the lump in her throat.

They said nothing until they reached the dock. Halting abruptly, Roger blurted, "May I kiss you goodbye, Serena?"

When she nodded, he placed his hands on her waist, closed his eyes and pressed his lips against hers . . . tentatively at first. Then he wrapped his arms around her and kissed her ardently, taking her breath away. Smiling sadly as he released her, he advised, "When you explain that to Nathan—and you are going to have to explain—you might try telling him freely and honestly that you love him. Goodbye, Serena."

"Goodbye . . . and good luck," she choked, fighting back tears. "I hope you'll be happy."

"So long, Nate," Roger shouted, and waved at the captain, who could be seen glaring down from the boiler deck.

Nathan slapped the rail in frustration. Last night Serena had admitted, in spite of herself, that she loved him. This morning she was kissing Blake on the dock. They were due for a long talk.

But before he could take a step, the Trevarian wagons turned the corner. Rolling past the carriage that bore Roger, they lumbered down the pier toward the *Sprite*.

The talk with Serena would have to wait until the cargo was loaded, the captain concluded grimly as he headed down to the dock. Passing the weeping girl on the stairs, he wordlessly shoved a handkerchief into her hand and marched on.

Serena paused to watch his progress, but he did not look back. She had not seen him since last night's public profession of love and just now he had not even spoken to her. If Roger's departure disturbed her, Nathan's aloof gesture filled her with dread.

Trudging toward the stern, she discovered her sister on a bench overlooking the river. The girl's slender shoulders quaked with sobs, and tears streamed down her face.

"Dory, what's wrong?" Serena bent over her anxiously.

"Go away," Dory sobbed. "You ruin everything."

"I do?" Serena stood bolt upright, stung by the accusation.

"You chased Roger away, didn't you? And you took Nathan—"

"I didn't 'take' Nathan."

"He's in love with you," Dory snapped. "He told the entire boat last night."

"He was drunk," Serena said dryly.

"He wasn't drunk ten minutes later when he came up to ask Mother for your hand in marriage."

"He what?" Serena jumped to her feet.

The younger girl rose, too, and faced her sister, her small fists clenched. "He wants to marry you, though I don't know why. You don't deserve him." Dory blinked in surprise when Serena whirled and stormed down to the dock.

Balancing a large notebook, Nathan stood on the dock and tallied the cotton bales being carried onto the boat. He glanced up when Serena, her face set, halted in front of him. "I'd like a word with you, Nathan Trent."

"And I with you." Setting the notebook on a nearby barrel, he waited for her to begin.

"Am I to understand you asked my mother's permission to marry me last night?"

"A few minutes after you so unwillingly admitted you loved me," he confessed.

"Of all the—"

"Don't start, Serena," he interrupted, unwilling to suffer one of her tirades. "Just tell me if you meant what you said. Do you love me?"

Her color rose. "What's that got to do with—"

Stepping back among stacks of cotton bales, Nathan pulled her with him, out of sight of the workman. "Tell me," he persisted, clasping his hands behind her back to form a loose restraint.

Straining in his embrace, she countered accusingly, "You might have asked me first, Nathan."

"I will ask you, but I have to know if you meant what you said." His voice was hoarse with longing as he murmured, "Because I love you, Serena, very much."

Her movement stilled. "You love me?" she repeated incredulously, the dawning of hope and elation on her face. "You meant it? You really love me?"

"I do," he murmured, his arms tightening around her. "That's why I want to marry you."

"And I love you, Nathan."

"Really?" His smiling lips were close to hers.

"Real—" she whispered, the rest of her answer lost when his mouth covered hers.

He gloried in her response to his touch. For the moment, as they stood wrapped in each other's arms, the heat, the sun, the song of the stevedores faded into nothingness. Their world was a cramped, airless space surrounded by cotton bales where they could be alone.

The kiss they shared was tender and rife with promise, but when their lips parted, Serena's expression was troubled. "I do love you, Nathan," she said quietly, "but I can't marry you."

"Why not?" Though he did not release her, he drew back to regard her with a perplexed frown. "It's what usually happens when two people love each other."

"Yes . . ." Staring at his crisp white shirtfront, she did not meet his eyes. "It's just that I'm not really free to marry."

"Don't tell me you've been hiding a husband in the hold all this time," he teased with a playfulness he did not feel.

"It's not that. I promised the cap'n I would take care of the family and that's what I must do. They're my responsibility."

"When I'm your husband, they'll be my responsibility . . . one I'll see to gladly." Cradling her against his chest, he murmured, "You've been taking care of everyone, my love. Now let me take care of you. I don't want you to worry about anything anymore."

Serena's wind left her in a puff. She had no doubt that she loved Nathan and she believed he loved her, but she did not want to be his responsibility any more than she wanted her family to be his obligation. And if Nathan began taking care of her, how long before he started telling her what to do? How long before he told her to leave the river?

"I'm sorry, Nathan," she said unhappily, "I'm not ready to talk about marriage.

"Do you know when you're likely to be ready?" His face stony, he released her and stepped back. "I've loved you almost since the day I met you and you've loved me, too, even though we both tried to deny it. I have waited patiently—"

"Patiently?" she cried, disturbed by his coldness. "You've snarled and bellowed at me from the upper river to New Orleans."

"Only because I've never known such an impossible female in my life," he roared.

Her eyes narrowed, Serena spun to leave and nearly collided with a hemp-wrapped bale behind her.

"I'm sorry, Rena." While she still sought the exit of their hideaway, Nathan caught her arm and pulled her back to him gently. "We both fought it so long, I guess we need to get used to the idea of loving each other. If we take it one step at a time, things will work out, you'll see."

"I'm sorry, too, Nathan." Relaxing in his grip, she sighed. "I shouldn't have lost my temper . . . not right after I told you I love you."

"Do you think people in love never lose their tempers?" he chuckled. "It happens all the time."

"It was our first fight," she declared unsteadily as he led her out into the fresh air on the dock.

Throwing back his head, he bellowed with laughter, causing the hands to look around with good-humored surprise. "We have done nothing but fight since we met," he contradicted wryly.

"I mean, it was our first quarrel since we fell in love."

The big captain grinned but did not try to argue with that absurdity as he walked her up the ramp to the boat.

At the foot of the stairs, Serena turned to him curiously. "What did my mother say when you asked for my hand?"

"Before or after she swooned in delight?" he joked, then added seriously, "She said you would make up your own mind in time. I'll try to be patient, love. I just hope it's sooner than later."

On the dock in Vicksburg, Orren Ralston waited. Stout and red faced from the heat, he stood with his hands clasped behind his back while the *River Sprite* docked. He smiled and waved when his niece favored him with a blast on the whistle.

Though stacked cotton bales had crowded the boat and blocked the feeble breeze on every deck, the trip downriver had been pleasant for Nathan and Serena. During the dog days of August and the sultry summer nights, they had spent companionable hours together, becoming better acquainted. As they discovered each other's virtues, faults and foibles, their friendship and their love had deepened. The only difference that remained between them, unspoken and unresolved, was the question of marriage.

After the *Sprite*'s hawsers had been secured, the appropriate cargo unloaded, and Will had made the obligatory visit to the harbor master, Nathan met Serena, clad in her apricot gown, descending as he mounted the stairs at the bow.

"There you are." He stopped a couple of steps below her, so the difference in their heights was lessened. "Your family has been looking for you. They're ready to go."

"I'm coming," she called down to where the rest of the Caswell clan waited in Orren's big phaeton. "You're not dressed yet," she said to Nathan. "Aren't you joining us?"

"I'll be there before dinner," he promised. "I've been busy, talking to Mr. Hart."

"I didn't see him."

"We talked on the dock. He wouldn't come aboard. You can hardly blame him after his last visit," Nathan needled with a grin.

Blushing at the reminder of her skirmish with the creditor, she asked, "How long did he put off foreclosure this time... Out-of-the-goodness-of-his-heart?"

"The goodness of his heart had nothing to do with it." The captain pulled a paper from his breast pocket with a flourish. "The lien has been paid in full."

"We don't owe him anything anymore? We really are going to make a success of the *Sprite,* aren't we, Nathan?"

"We're doing it," he confirmed, warmed by her sparkling eyes. "You'd better go. I'll see you at Orren and Bonnie's." Bending to kiss her on the forehead, he was delighted when she lifted her lips to his. Planting a quick kiss on her mouth, he ordered, "Go now ... before you make us all very late to dinner."

Nathan watched from the boiler deck until the carriage rolled out of sight, then he ambled toward the stern. As he patted his pocket in search of a cheroot, he found the letter the harbor master had been holding for him. Pulling it out, he frowned when he recognized Adele's handwriting on the envelope. Then, deliberately, he stuffed it, unopened, into his pocket again and went to dress for dinner.

"You make Nathan sound like a fish and I'm the worm," Serena complained.

"And I think you're just the kind of bait he likes," Bonnie answered through a mouthful of hairpins. Under her high, up-swept coiffure, her brow was knit in concentration as she attempted to arrange her niece's hair in a similar, sophisticated style. "I've seen how he looks at you, and Orren told me that he kissed you this afternoon ... right out in plain sight."

When Serena said nothing, she went on, "You are not getting any younger, Serena Elizabeth. How old will you be on your next birthday?"

"Twenty-one," the girl gritted as a pin poked her scalp.

"On your way to becoming a spinster. The captain would be quite a catch. He's tall and good-looking and eligible—"

"The most important trait for a husband," Serena cut in sarcastically, "if I were looking for one."

"I'm serious," her aunt scolded. "Think about what I've said. Nathan Trent is charming and handsome and—"

"Eligible. I know." Serena sighed in exasperation.

"And he's downstairs waiting for you." Greatly pleased with her handiwork, Bonnie twirled the stool so the girl could look in the mirror. "Aren't you pretty?"

Staring at the mirror, Serena scarcely saw her reflection. Nearly an old maid, she brooded, suddenly disturbed by the notion. An old maid both by circumstance and by choice...for Nathan had proposed and she could not, would not accept.

Downstairs in the parlor, Grace clapped her hands and bounced in her seat with uncharacteristic exuberance when

Nathan told her their debt to Mr. Hart had been paid. Spirits were light and the dinner party quickly turned into a celebration.

The only one who did not seem affected by the mood of the company was Dory. Next to Serena at the long table, the girl was quiet, smiling wanly when addressed. Most of the time, she watched her sister and the captain with resentment smoldering in her blue eyes.

Seated across from Nathan in his elegant gambler's attire, Serena thought he looked as handsome as he had the day they met. Observing her pink-stained face, he wondered what she was thinking to bring that blush to her cheeks. Despite the unfamiliar, elaborate coiffure she wore, she had never looked more beautiful, he decided. Love brought a glow to her entire appearance.

With a private smile, he caught her eye and lifted his glass in a wordless toast. Serena beamed at him in return while, beside her, Dory tried not to watch.

The moon was high and the evening had grown surprisingly cool when Nathan and Serena walked, hand in hand, along the *Sprite*'s deck. Contentedly she rubbed her cheek against the collar of the jacket he had draped over her shoulders. It held his warmth and smelled of tobacco, bay rum and him.

"There are two things I've wanted to do all night," he told her quietly when they reached the darkness of the stern.

"What?" Serena's voice floated from the shadows at his side.

"This." Turning her to face him, he plucked the combs from her hair and let it tumble heavily to her shoulders. Lacing his fingers through it, he tilted her head to look at him. "And this," he whispered, his mouth slanting across hers.

Serena stood very still, her eyes closed as she savored now-familiar and volatile feelings his kiss awakened. A flicker of desire stirred at the center of her being, fanned into full flame by his caresses. Her heart thundered, silencing reason, as his lips, so sweet, teased and tormented and claimed hers.

With a soft welcoming sigh, Serena molded her body to his and wrapped her arms around his waist. Her lips parted beneath his and invited him within. He entered and took possession, losing himself in the taste, the scent, the very feel of her. Her body arched against him, her firm breasts pressed against his shirtfront as she kissed him with unforeseen passion. He felt as if he were drowning in her sweetness, but he did not care to save himself.

His fingers still laced in her hair, he traced her jawline with his thumbs and murmured thickly, "I love you, Serena."

"I love you, too." Instinctively her lips sought his. He growled deep in his throat when she mimicked his earlier actions, her tongue circling his.

"My God, Serena." Nathan drew a shuddering breath, aroused by her unexpected spontaneity, her unashamed sensuality, her kisses of honey and heat. Shaken, he gazed down at her rapt, upturned face in the moonlight. Her blue eyes, heavy lidded and dark with desire, opened to look at him.

With a wondering smile, she took his face into her hands and drew him toward her, kissing first one eyelid, then the other with infinite tenderness before moving down to his lips again lovingly.

His mouth never leaving hers, he sank down onto the chair, taking her with him.

Serena was afire as Nathan held her on his lap, ensnared by his strong arms. Feeling his touch through the bodice of her gown, she felt as though her breast were throbbing, swelling to fill his hand. When his mouth left hers to trail kisses down her throat to the mound of her breast above her décolletage, she swayed toward him. Reveling in his touch and the consuming heat it brought, she moaned softly.

The sound seemed to bring the man back to himself and he pulled away. "This can't be, sweetheart."

Sitting up, Serena stared at him in dazed confusion.

"I want you," he told her, his voice rough with desire, "but when we make love, I want everything to be right. I want you as my wife."

"Wife?" she repeated, still stunned by the passion he had aroused in her.

"Yes, wife. I want no regrets, no recriminations between us, only love."

She shook her head. "Nathan, I—"

"We'll talk about this tomorrow." Rising with her in his arms, he set her on her feet in front of the door to her cabin. Then he opened it without another word.

Silently Serena went inside and closed the door behind her.

Going into his own cabin, Nathan lay awake until the crimson dawn, aching with desire but comforted by the conviction that he had done the right thing.

What kind of girl must Nathan think she was? Serena wondered bleakly while she dressed. She had thrown herself at him last night. If he had not had self-control, she would be a fallen woman this morning.

Stepping out on deck, she discovered the day was overcast and almost unbearably muggy. Her starched cotton dress seemed to wilt as quickly as her confidence when she saw Nathan on the dock, ready to greet new passengers.

When he spied her with her collar and cuff buttons neatly fastened and her hair pulled back in a tidy bun, he smiled, knowing the reason for her demure mien. "Good morning, Serena."

"Good morning," she responded without stopping. Unwilling to face him, she hurried off to breakfast.

Jamie found her in the galley. Dropping onto the chair across from her, the engineer related a problem that had to be rectified before the *River Sprite* could depart. "Charlie has already gone for the part," he reported, "but if we're to leave today, we maun start tearing doon the engine now."

"Just let me change my clothes," Serena volunteered, glad for something to do. With luck, she could hide in the engine room until departure time.

An hour later, Nathan passed the open door of the engine room and glimpsed Serena inside. Her bun had slid askew and strands slipped from their pins. Her baggy shirt was tied at the waist and grease streaked the snug trousers she wore. Sweat dripped down her face, making runnels in the oil that smudged her cheek.

"Good morning, my love," he said quietly, stepping into the grease spattered compartment.

"Good morning." She retreated a step.

"How did you sleep last night?" He advanced one.

"Very well, thank you." She stepped back once more, determined to maintain the distance between them.

"I see Jamie's keeping you busy." Indicating the disassembled motor, he edged closer.

"He needed help with the p-pump." The last word was punctuated by a clang as her heels met the machinery behind her. There was no place else to go.

Standing very near, Nathan asked, "What's wrong, Serena?"

"N-nothing."

"Why are you sidling away from me like a nervous schoolgirl?"

"I just wish last night hadn't happened." She stared out the door and would not meet his eyes.

"Which part of last night?" With an intimate smile, he pulled her into his arms. "The hugging part?"

Gently he nudged her chin up so she looked into his eyes. "The touching part?" he asked.

"Or the kissing part?" As she had, he brushed each eyelid tenderly with his lips. "I enjoyed all of it."

"Oh, Nathan." With a relieved sigh, Serena slipped her arms around his neck, forgetting the oil-stained clothes she wore. "I do love you."

"Then everything is as it should be," he murmured against her hair. "I love you and you love me . . . and I still want to marry you."

"Nathan—"

"Don't worry. I'm not going to press you, Serena." His expression disgruntled, he loosened his grip but did not release her. "A man wants to know a woman wants him in return."

"I do want you."

"I got that idea last night." Though Nathan tried to keep the tone light, his voice was husky with desire. He brought his mouth down over hers in achingly sweet possession.

Serena's hands moved up his shoulders, the fingers exploring the strong column of his neck. Her fingertips traced the line of his jaw, lighting delicately on his cheekbones so his face was cupped in her hands.

At last he stirred. "I suppose I should go or people will talk, since you're just about the prettiest striker I've ever seen."

"Just about?" She grinned mischievously.

"Well, I think Flowers is tolerable to look at."

"Don't let him hear you say that or we'll lose him the next time we're in swimming distance of the Arkansas shore."

Chuckling, Nathan stepped out on deck where Levi was working. "What are you looking at?" he asked when the first mate's round face split with a broad grin.

"You got a little grease on you, suh."

"Damnation." The captain looked down. His shirtfront was no longer white.

"Ain't jest your shirt." His eyes dancing, Levi offered him a relatively clean rag.

When he had wiped the smudges from his face where Serena's hands had rested, Nathan returned the rag and strode forward, nearly colliding with Grace as she came out of the galley.

Her blue eyes widened. "Nathan, whatever happened to you?"

"I must have gotten too close to something with oil on it."

"Or it got too close to you." Headed forward, she called over her shoulder, "You've oil on your neck, too."

"Damnation," Nathan muttered, and pulled out his handkerchief. Unnoticed, an envelope fluttered to the deck. Scrubbing at the grease stains, he strode toward the bow.

Serena stepped out onto the deck and lounged against the bulkhead a moment to relish the fresh air. It was sweltering in the engine room. As her eyes idly swept the length of the boat, they fell upon a white paper laying on the shady deck. Curiously she picked it up, her expression frozen as she turned it over in her hand. It was a letter from Adele Andrews and it was addressed to Nathan.

"Luke," she summoned the crewman, "take this to the captain. And tell him he really should be more careful with his personal correspondence." Dully she returned to the engine room.

As she steered the *River Sprite* downriver that afternoon, Serena performed unthinkingly, her mind on Nathan. She still did not know where she stood with him. He said he loved her, that he wanted to marry her. But how could she believe him? He had told her that there was nothing left between him and Adele Andrews, but today she had discovered a letter that convinced her there was.

She was in love with him, Serena thought sadly, but she didn't trust him not to betray her or to tire of her or to try to run her life. Ensnared in love, trapped by suspicion, she did not know which way to go.

She spent the torrid afternoon alone in the wheelhouse while Nathan went back and forth between the boat and shore. The *Sprite* made nearly a dozen stops along the levee, barely starting when they were hailed again.

When her watch was over, Serena went wearily to the stern, where she dropped onto her chair to rest.

Finding her there, Nathan bent to kiss her. "Hello, my love."

"Hello," she replied coolly.

With a knowing glint in his eye, he perched against the railing and crossed his arms across his chest. "I think we need to talk, Serena."

"What about?"

"About when you're going to start trusting me." Pulling the letter from his pocket, he asked, "Why didn't you come and ask me about this when you found it?"

"What was I supposed to ask you? It's a letter to you from Adele Andrews."

"And I told you it was over between Adele and me."

"Then why are you still corresponding?"

"She wrote to me, not the other way around." Kneeling beside her chair, he said earnestly, "Serena, it's you I love. It's you I want to marry. I just want you to love me in return."

"I do love you," she cried, stung.

"Then why don't you trust me? You never even gave me a chance to explain. I've told you we can work out anything if we talk about it."

"I'm sorry, Nathan." She looked genuinely distressed. "I'm so confused. I'll talk to you when I know what I'm thinking."

"I'll be waiting." Rising, he kissed the top of her head and walked away.

Her head aching, Serena leaned against the bulkhead and closed her eyes. She had never known love could hurt so much in every way. It hurt to be jealous. It hurt to think she might be hurting Nathan. If this was love, she was not sure she wanted any part of it, after all.

That evening in Natchez, Lucky Underhill, a gambler Nathan knew slightly from the gaming tables of New Orleans, came aboard.

"Trent," he called, mounting the stairs to the boiler deck where Nathan stood. "I heard you'd forsaken high-stakes poker for the drudgery of a riverboat, but I didn't believe it."

"There's not much drudgery involved if you can manage to be the captain," Nathan retorted mildly, shaking hands with the newcomer. "How are you, Underhill?"

Lucky did not answer. Transfixed, he stared over the captain's shoulder as a beautiful red-haired woman stepped from the companionway and made her way to the stern, her skirt swaying as she walked. "Who is that?" he asked.

Glancing back, Nathan frowned and searched for the proper words to convey not just her identity, but her relationship to him. Finally he said, "That's Serena Caswell, one of the *Sprite*'s pilots."

Lucky's eyebrows lifted. "A lady pilot, eh? She sounds like a woman I need to know."

"Not necessarily."

"Oh-ho, that's how it is." The gambler smiled knowingly. "Well, if the lady shares your feelings, you don't have to worry about a little honest competition, do you, Nate? We're all square dealers here."

Summoning a cabin boy, the big captain strode away, scowling and muttering under his breath about sure-thing players.

Lucky was unable to approach Serena until the boat stopped the next evening to wood up at a clearing on the riverbank. Even then, he could do no more than introduce himself before Nathan loomed by her side. Since their conversation yesterday, Serena was relieved that the captain had returned to his usual bantering self, though she knew much remained unspoken between them.

After the work was completed and dinner had been served around a bonfire, several passengers and crewmen brought out instruments and an impromptu dance began. With a reckless glance at the other man, Lucky stepped forward to claim Serena for the first waltz.

"I'm sorry," Nathan drawled insincerely. "The first dance is the captain's prerogative."

"And the second belongs to her uncle," Will threw in.

Knowing he was beaten for the moment, Lucky acquiesced with a shrug and watched as Nathan drew Serena onto the dance floor sketched in the dirt near the fire.

"I think," Nathan murmured, smiling down at her, "that the captain should have the first dance, the last dance and all the dances in between."

"Uncle Will would have something to say if you took all of them," she answered, returning his smile.

"Knowing Will, he'd talk me to death. Maybe I'll just settle for most of the dances in between."

In Nathan's arms, Serena felt as if she were floating over the uneven ground. They made a graceful pair, the tall dark man and the petite auburn beauty sweeping around the forest-edged clearing.

As soon as their dance ended, Will claimed his niece for a polka. No sooner had the music died again than Jamie was at her side to request the honor of a dance.

"None of yer newfangled music," the engineer called to the musicians. "Play something wi' a bit o' life to it, lads.

"Ah, that's more to me taste" he declared, throwing himself into the lively reel with such abandon that Nathan and Dory, who danced nearby, fled laughing. Unfazed, the old Scotsman sallied toward Serena, pausing midstride to perform a Highland fling.

Breathless when the reel was finished, Serena was surrounded by passengers and crewmen eager to lead her out onto the floor. Blushing Charlie Flowers was followed by a debonair planter from St. Martinville.

After a painful turn with Hank, she insisted, to the boy's relief, that she needed a moment to catch her breath. Leading her to the fireside, he hurried back to the frog hunting that had occupied him earlier.

Seizing his opportunity, Lucky headed toward Serena. She saw the good-looking stranger as he picked his way through the dancers. Suddenly his eyes flickered to a spot over her shoulder and his smile faded. He stopped, narrowly avoiding being run down by the circling dancers. Hastily he swooped in a stiff bow and fled.

Serena glanced over her shoulder to see what had stopped him. Nathan strolled toward her, his hard stare still fixed on the retreating man's back.

She did not know whether to be exasperated or amused. "What are you doing?"

"Claiming the woman I love," he professed innocently. Taking her arm, he led her to stand on the riverbank near the *Sprite's* stern where they looked out at the water. "I need to propose to her again."

"Nathan—"

"I'm going to make an honest woman of you yet, my love."

"Of all the—"

"Careful, Rena." With a grin, he glanced up to where a stout figure could be seen at the railing above. Soeur Berthe was enjoying the sight of the dancing ashore. "Don't let your temper get the best of you. You might offend the good sister."

"She hardly speaks English," Serena countered lightly, "but if she did, I'm sure she'd understand if I called you a cock-eyed, cocksure, bowlegged, swaybacked son of a ragpicker's horse.''

"Does that mean you won't marry me tonight?"

"Not tonight."

Offering his arm to Serena, Nathan teased, "I can bear the disappointment if you'll speak to me in the language of love, my own. Tell me you find me irresistible."

"You are an accursed trial and a tribulation to those who know you, Nathan Trent," she said, laughing as they walked back toward the fire, "a plague of locusts and a pestilence upon unsuspecting strangers who don't know enough to get out of your way."

Smiling, Soeur Berthe commented to her companion who stood in the shadows, "Capitaine Trent and *la belle* Mademoiselle Caswell are such a lovely couple. And they seem so much in love."

"Only if you do not understand what they are saying," Soeur Thérèse muttered disapprovingly in English.

Chapter Sixteen

"You told me you were interested in the steamboats, you brass-buttoned fancy man. Get out of my wheelhouse," Serena shouted.

On the texas, Nathan and Dory turned to see Lucky Underhill catapult himself through the pilothouse door and land in a heap on deck. Serena could be seen above, replacing the shotgun to its customary place. Without even bothering to glance down, she yelled, "And don't come back."

Before the gambler could pick himself up, Nathan ambled over. "I'd appreciate it if you'd take Serena's advice, Underhill. The last time she had that shotgun down, I had to have half the windows in the pilothouse replaced."

"She does have a temper," Lucky granted breezily, dusting himself off. "I made her mad, but she'll get over it."

"I won't and you're not likely to, either."

Casting an appraising look at the captain, he shrugged. "What harm in becoming better acquainted with the fair Serena?"

"More than you know."

"I hurt enough, Nate." He grimaced good-naturedly. "I think I twisted my ankle. You may consider our competition for the lady at an end."

"Good." Nathan watched the other man limp away before he turned again to Dory. She stood behind him, her shoulders slumped, her face tragic. "What's the matter, little one?"

"Nothing," she muttered.

"Something's wrong." He put a hand on her shoulder and squeezed affectionately.

Squirming from his light grip, she glared at him. "Why should you care?"

"Same reason as always," he said mildly. "I'm fond of you."

"But you're in love with Serena."

"I am, but I still care about you. Just because I love your sister doesn't mean I don't realize what a special young lady you are, Dory...pretty and pleasant and smart. One of these days, you're going to make the right fellow very happy."

"Like Serena makes you happy?" she asked grudgingly.

"I'd recommend you be a little more cooperative than Rena is," the man chuckled. "You'd be more likely to catch a husband."

"Is that why you can't get married ... because she's stubborn?"

"Don't you worry. She'll come around," Nathan promised, bending to peck her on the cheek. "And when she does, you'll be my favorite sister-in-law."

"I'll be your only sister-in-law," she retorted as the captain crossed the texas to scale the ladder to the pilothouse.

My heart should be broken, the girl mused, but it's not. Through the open windows, she saw Serena look back from the wheel to greet Nathan, love shining in her eyes. Positioning himself beside her, he threw an arm around her shoulders and they stood in dreamy silence.

Feeling as though she had a wonderful secret, Dory went about her work. Perhaps Serena was not going to be an old maid after all.

The next morning, as she stood beside the captain on the bow, Serena felt a stir of excitement. Though she had arrived in New Orleans many times, she had never felt such anticipation. She felt alive and happy and in love. And today love did not hurt.

At the foot of the gangplank, she and Nathan bade the passengers farewell. In honor of their arrival in New Orleans, Serena had donned wore a seldom-worn lavender walking cos-

tume. Carrying a lacy white parasol, she felt elegant and sophisticated, but beneath the brim of her stylish bonnet, her blue
eyes danced with artless excitement.

Soeurs Thérèse and Berthe, the first to disembark, were met
by a compact, efficient Mother Superior who led them away
briskly on foot.

"So long, Nate." Lucky stopped to slap the captain on the
back. Taking Serena's hand, he brushed a kiss across her fingers. "Farewell, Miss Caswell, a pleasure to meet you."

"Goodbye, Mr. Underhill."

"Listen, Nate," Lucky addressed him confidentially, "about
that...er...item..."

"The riffle deck I took from you last night?" Nathan asked
baldly. "I've got it right here." He patted the pocket of his
frock coat. "You never know when it might come in handy.
Besides, I plan to keep it as a reminder, in case you ever decide
to travel aboard the *Sprite* again."

"It won't be soon," Lucky grumbled as he departed, "if you
don't even trust me not to cheat at cards."

All the passengers had gone and Nathan and Serena were
climbing up to the boiler deck when Antoine drove his carriage along the pier toward the boat. Reining in his team in
front of the *River Sprite*, he jumped down and bounded onto
the boat.

To their surprise, Nathan and Serena were nearly bowled
over as Grace swept down the stairs past them.

At the bottom, Antoine caught Grace's hands in his. "Welcome back to New Orleans, Madame Caswell."

"Thank you, Monsieur La Branche." The woman's eyes
sparkled. "How are you?"

"Bon, très bon." He still held her hands and neither of them
seemed aware of the other couple poised only a few steps away.
"I am glad you have arrived early in the day," he exclaimed. "I
wish to take you and Dory and Hank to the lake as I promised. I have already a lunch for us in the carriage. You will
come, *oui?"*

"Yes...no...I mean, I don't know...." Uncharacteristically flustered, Grace finally glanced up at the pair on the stairs.

"Go and have a good time," Nathan encouraged.

"Perhaps when we finish our work," the blond woman wavered.

"Bill can tally."

"But the cabins . . ."

"If I help you, the work will go faster," Antoine declared unexpectedly. "You will be surprised at how good I can be placing the towels on the washstands, *hein?*"

When the work was finished and the merry band of picnickers was preparing to depart for Lake Pontchartrain, Antoine invited Nathan and all the Caswells to his home for a dinner party that night. "I fear we must mix business with pleasure," he told them, "but I assure you pleasure will be the greater portion."

At midafternoon, when Serena and Will returned from their obligatory trip to the customhouse, the old man halted on the levee. "Go on back to the boat, Rena," he instructed. "I'm goin' to Banks Arcade for the latest news."

"Gossip, you mean," she teased.

"If I'da known you were gonna get so sassy in your old age," he chided, frowning with mock severity, "I woulda barred you from the pilothouse when you were still green."

"I'm glad you didn't," she said, kissing him on the cheek.

She watched him limp away, muttering under his breath for effect, then she turned to take in the sights and sounds of the bustling riverfront. Steamboats lined the wharves stacked high with cotton. Throngs of people swirled around her, speaking dozens of languages.

"Haven't I told you a young lady should not go out without an escort," a familiar voice asked, "especially not in New Orleans and especially not looking like that?"

"I had an escort," she replied before she even turned. "And what's wrong with the way I look?"

"Nothing." Nathan grinned appreciatively. "In fact, I don't think I've ever seen you look so pretty . . . outside of the engine room."

"Where are we going?" Serena asked as he led her to a cab parked on Canal Street.

"Jackson Square, please," the captain requested when they were settled in the carriage.

As the carriage jolted toward the Vieux Carré, he draped his arm over the back of the seat and said companionably, "I'm not quite a native, but I've visited New Orleans often enough to make a passable guide. Would you like a tour after all these years?"

"Very much." Serena smiled with pleasure. Then, glancing toward the driver, she whispered, "Will you promise me one thing, Nathan . . . just for today?"

"What's that?" he whispered in response.

"That you won't propose all day?"

"If you promise to behave like a lady and keep your hands to yourself," he agreed in a loud whisper.

She blushed predictably, her face reddening even more when she noticed the driver's shoulders shaking with mirth.

As the carriage turned onto Decatur, the thoroughfare that bordered the French Market, they bounced along narrow cobblestone streets in the shade of galleries, or balconies, overhead. Rolling past wrought iron gates, the girl glimpsed courtyards, cool and private and mysterious.

"This is not the best time to see the city," Nathan told her. "Most Creoles go to the country during the summer to escape the danger of sickness. Only four years ago, ten thousand people died in New Orleans during one of the worst yellow jack epidemics ever."

"I remember," she murmured. "We were not allowed to enter the port. And those who were already here were quarantined."

"Jackson Square, *m'sieur et mam'selle,*" the driver intoned.

Pigeons took to the air in noisy clouds as the couple alit at the beautiful parklike square that fronted the newly refurbished St. Louis Cathedral. On either side of the square, the new apartment buildings built by the Baroness Pontalba loomed. Nathan and Serena strolled in front of them, looking in shop windows, before crossing to the market where vendors hawked their wares.

"La fleur à vous épouse." A vendeuse wearing a colorful tignon sold Nathan a gardenia from her basket.

"What did she say?"

"'A flower for your wife,'" he replied, giving it to her with a smile. "You see, even strangers think we belong together."

"You said you wouldn't mention marriage," she reminded him.

"I said I wouldn't propose," he corrected, taking her arm.

They strolled past nuns and sailors, past blanket-wrapped Indians and Creole gentlemen shopping for their families. A fruit merchant and his customer argued loudly amid hanging stalks of bananas. Nearby, a vendor broke an egg in the gutter to prove its freshness. Troughs of water, containing crabs and crawfish, lined the banquette in front of crates of squawking chickens.

After a time, the couple retraced their steps, stopping to sample a cala, a rice cake, and a cup of café au lait. Then Nathan hailed another cab, driven by a dusky man with a Creole accent.

He drove them along graceful Esplanade past grand homes that belonged to wealthy Creoles. On Rampart Street, they passed a church and a cemetery, its whitewashed tombs resembling a city of the dead.

After turning onto Canal Street, they followed it to St. Charles Avenue, the broad boulevard which led into the Garden District. Quiet and peaceful, the street was intersected by islands of green along which mules drew streetcars past homes as grand as any on Esplanade.

Dusk was falling when Nathan and Serena returned to the boat to dress for dinner. Though Antoine's carriage was parked on the dock, he was nowhere to be seen. One of New Orleans's ever-present street urchins, hired to guard the Creole's property, leaned importantly against the front wheel of the rig.

"*Bonsoir*, young people," Nathan's uncle called down from the *Sprite*'s boiler deck. He and Grace stood beside each other at the railing and smiled down at the younger couple.

"We were about to give up on you," Grace teased as they joined them. "Everyone is dressing for dinner. Everyone but us. We were waiting for you," she added hastily, abashed to be caught lingering in the twilight with Antoine.

"*Oui,*" the Creole said. "I am about to go home and dress myself. I will send a carriage for you at eight-thirty."

Following Serena aft, Grace said, "I want to show you something, Serena. Excuse us, gentlemen."

As the women hurried away, Antoine said sotto voce, "The last time you were in New Orleans, I wanted to bet that you would win *la belle* Serena, nephew, but you would not. You should have been more sporting and accepted my wager."

"Perhaps, Uncle," Nathan conceded quietly. "After all, I have won . . . something more important than your money."

"Still you might have given me the opportunity to win some of it back," Antoine grumbled.

As she walked toward the stern, the girl smiled.

Opening Serena's cabin door with a flourish, Grace gestured for her daughter to enter. Spread on the bunk was an exquisite blue gown trimmed with black lace. "Do you like it?" she asked anxiously.

"I've never seen such a beautiful gown." The girl fingered the rich fabric lovingly. "Is it really for me?"

"I made it for your birthday," Grace answered, "but since tonight is a special occasion, I decided you should have it now. I know you will look lovely in it.

"Oh, dear," she muttered, consulting the watch she wore pinned to her bodice, "it's nearly eight o'clock and I have not even begun my toilette. I will see you in the salon," her voice drifted back as she departed, her heels tapping briskly on the deck.

When Serena entered the salon that night, her family stared at her in amazement, seemingly rendered mute by her transformation.

Her elegant gown matched the color of her eyes exactly. Its fitted bodice came to point at her waist and flared into a graceful full skirt. Cut low and off the shoulders, its black lace bertha collar hung in soft folds almost to her elbows. Black lace gloves, silk fan and satin slippers completed the ensemble.

Her hair was drawn back simply in a crown of auburn ringlets and held with ebony combs. Three long, spiraling curls draped over her bare shoulder. A touch of rouge, judiciously applied, heightened her coloring.

"Holy Moses." Hank broke the silence at last. "You look just like a princess from a story, Rena."

"You do," Dory breathed, jealousy and differences forgotten.

"You look beautiful." Stepping to Serena's side, Nathan offered his arm. "May I have the honor, Miss Caswell?" His caressing voice brought a shiver to her spine.

"This is so exciting," Dory announced as she settled herself in the carriage. "It's not every night we get to have dinner with the governor."

"The governor?" Nathan repeated, his brow creasing in a frown.

"Governor Wicklisse and several of his party are to be Ant...Monsieur La Branche's other guests," Grace explained.

"Do you know who will be there?" he asked, his voice tight.

"The governor and his wife. The governor's secretary, a Mr. Keller, I believe. Senator Boudreaux and his wife. A couple named Guidry from the other side of the river. A Mr. and Mrs. Thomas and Mrs. Thomas's aunt."

He nodded woodenly. He had known all of Antoine's guests for years and he liked them. Why, then did he feel such foreboding?

Nathan's trepidation seemed absurd when they arrived at his uncle's town house. Looking dapper by the light of the citronella candles that dotted the courtyard, Antoine met them, smiling in welcome. They were seated, sipping sherry, when the front bell rang. Rising to meet the newcomers, they heard voices from the passage to the street and the governor's party trooped into the dim light.

"Antoine, so nice of you to have us." Governor Wicklisse pumped the Creole's hand. "I hope you don't mind a change of plans, but the Guidrys were prevented from coming across for the evening. So I brought along a couple of other old friends."

"Hello, Antoine, forgive a couple of tagalongs." Senator Marshall Langley stepped forward, his daughter on his arm. Lovely and self-assured, Adele was clad in the lavender that indicated her mourning was nearly at an end.

"Please do forgive us." She smiled charmingly at her host. "But wild horses couldn't have kept us away when we heard Nathan would be here."

"*Mais non.* Welcome to my home," Antoine answered, kissing her hand. In a city that prided itself on its hospitality, there was nothing he could say, particularly to the American governor who cared little for ceremony. Such alterations to guest lists occurred all the time in New Orleans, but how the Creole wished it were not tonight. Unhappily he glanced at his nephew, who approached stiffly.

Over the young man's shoulder, Antoine glimpsed Serena's face, white and strained, as she watched the governor's party gather around Nathan, all talking excitedly. The distinguished men greeted him familiarly with handshakes and slaps on the back, as if he were a long-lost relative. He was, after all, the son of one of their oldest friends.

A round figure detached herself from the governor's entourage and went to Serena's side. "Hello, my dear. When my niece convinced me to come tonight, I hoped I would see you again."

"Miss Tansy!" Serena could not keep the relief from her voice at seeing a friendly face in the group.

On the other side of the courtyard, Adele moved through the crowd with dainty determination to stand at the captain's side. "Hello, Nathan."

"Hello, Addie." His tone was as flat as his stare.

Pretending not to notice his aloofness, she claimed his arm possessively and whispered, "It's good to see you again, dear one."

Her intimate manner turned his blood to ice. Disregarding the flicker of annoyance in her violet eyes, he politely disengaged himself and suggested, "Perhaps you would allow me to make the introductions, Antoine?"

"*S'il vous plaît,*" the Creole concurred with a nervous glance at Serena. Fortunately, she was engaged in quiet conversation with Madame Thomas's aunt. He fervently hoped she would not lose her famous temper tonight.

Nathan began the introductions, presenting a handful of the most powerful men in the state. With the exception of Tansy, the women stood in a tight knot facing the Caswells, displaying a solid, unified front of disapproval.

With a disturbed frown, Nathan turned his attention to his own party. "May I present, first, my partner, Mrs. Caswell."

"Ah, yes, the lovely widow from Vicksburg." Governor Wicklisse bowed gallantly. "I feel I know you already, madam. Antoine has spoken of you often in the past few months."

"How kind of you, sir." Her cheeks blazing with a blush to rival any of Serena's, Grace would not meet Antoine's dark eyes. Graciously she greeted each new guest with all the tranquility she could muster in the face of the governor's revelation and the women's mysterious condemnation.

Drawing Serena to stand beside him, Nathan placed her hand in the crook of his arm and covered it with his own. "This is Mrs. Caswell's elder daughter, Serena."

"Oh, yes, the river pilot," Adele tossed in before Serena had even completed her curtsy. A bright smile masking her malice, she watched the newcomers' reactions as they murmured among themselves and stared at Serena, agog.

"She's a lightning pilot. Isn't that what you said, Nathan?" Tansy interjected, receiving a grateful look from Will.

"A pilot . . . how fascinating," Mrs. Wicklisse blurted. Serena Caswell was not at all what she had expected from Adele's description. Uncomfortable with the tension around her, the woman smiled at the young blond girl. "And who might this be?"

"This lovely young lady is Pandora Caswell," Nathan resumed the introductions smoothly.

The ice broken, James Keller, the governor's secretary, joked, "You haven't changed, Nathan. You still surround yourself with lovely ladies."

"Whenever possible." The captain chuckled. "But this pair, though not so lovely, are two of Caswell & Trent's best men . . . William Caswell, the *Sprite*'s other pilot, and Henry Caswell, Jr., who is turning out to be quite a cabin boy."

Hank beamed, his skinny little chest swelling proudly, as the conversation among the adults swirled over his disinterested head.

The large gathering quickly broke into smaller groups. Antoine stood beside Grace's chair, talking to Mrs. Wicklisse, Mrs. Thomas and Madame Boudreaux as the butler served sherry to the ladies and coquetiers to the gentlemen. The Caswell siblings clustered around Tansy and Will, who were engaged in a spirited conversation on steamboat racing. The men of the governor's party monopolized Nathan, but Adele stayed stubbornly at his side.

When the call to dinner came, she looked at the man expectantly, but he did not even notice. Going directly to Serena, he offered his arm.

While Antoine and Grace led the others into the dining room, he leaned close to whisper encouragingly in Serena's ear, "Don't let Addie make you feel bad."

"She certainly is trying," she murmured. "Nathan, do you know what she told those ladies about me? She told them I'm your . . . your . . ."

"Paramour."

"You've been talking to Miss Tansy."

"After she met you, Miss Tansy didn't believe Adele's lies. These other women won't, either, if you'll just be your usual sweet self this evening."

Rolling her eyes, she smiled mischievously. "Then I suppose I shouldn't call Adele Andrews a lying, low-down, despicable child of a snake."

"No," Nathan bellowed with laughter, "though it would be interesting to see what would happen if you did."

Frowning to see Nathan's dark head so close to Serena's bright one, Adele accepted James Keller's arm and stalked inside.

Locating the seat originally intended for Madame Guidry, the young man seated her. Then he switched his name card with Monsieur Guidry's and took the chair beside her.

Adele responded distractedly to James's attempts at conversation. Critically she inspected Serena, who sat across the table. The girl was not as plain as she had thought, Adele thought grudgingly; in fact, she was actually pretty. At least Nathan seemed to think so. He hardly took his eyes off her.

At the head of the table, Antoine rang for the first course.

The moment she tasted the turtle soup, Adele gushed, "Isn't this delicious? Doesn't this remind you of the soup Trudy used to make, Nathan?

"Trudy is my father's cook," she explained to Serena without waiting for his response. "I vow, half the time I didn't know whether Nathan was coming to Meadow Wood for Trudy's soup or for me."

"If it was as good as this, he probably came for the soup," James teased.

"Jimmy Keller, you've always been incorrigible...even when we were children. Remember what a brat he was, Nathan?"

"I remember he always had the best horseflesh in the parish," Nathan said coolly. Looking across at James, he asked, "Do you still have that chestnut gelding?"

"I wouldn't part with such a jumper," James answered.

"Is that the horse that won the steeplechase over near Livingston five years ago?" Adele demanded, looking back and forth between the men.

"That's the one," Jim confirmed proudly.

"What a wonderful season that was...the balls, the house parties and the hunts." As if she had just remembered Serena's presence, Adele leaned toward her and said in contrived apology, "You must think we're terrible going on like this, Miss Caswell, but we've known each other most of our lives. We grew up knowing all the same people and going to all the same places.

"Of course, there must be plenty of social events in Vicksburg, Miss Caswell," she cajoled, making great show of including the other girl in the conversation.

"I'm sure there are," Serena replied uncomfortably, "but I was never around for them. I've spent most of my time on the *Sprite* for the past six years."

"You poor dear. And you haven't taken her to any of the balls at Le Jardin or at your family's house in Baton Rouge, Nathan?"

"We've been busy the last few months."

"Nathan's mother always held the most gracious dinners and garden parties. And the harvest balls after the cane was in, weren't they grand?" Adele looked to the men for agreement.

Nathan nodded brusquely. He recognized the signals. Once Adele had gotten hold of something, she wouldn't let it go. She was obviously determined to make Serena feel like an outsider, and from Serena's closed expression, she was succeeding.

Determined to steer the conversation from the past, he called down the long table, "What is the news of the proposed railroad, Governor?"

For better than a quarter hour, the politician held forth on the possibilities for the state and the benefits of western expansion to the nation.

"*Pardon*, M'sieur Nathan." Antoine's butler appeared at the captain's elbow apologetically. "One of your crewmen is at the gate."

Levi was waiting nervously when Nathan stepped out onto the banquette. "I'm sorry, Cap'n," he blurted, "but Gustave is in jail."

"In jail? What happened?"

"Well, suh, we were in this tavern and this fella from Kentucky was drunk and complainin' 'bout the food in New Orleans. Said there wasn't a decent cook in the entire state of Louisiana. When Gustave allowed as to how he was a decent cook, the fella said that no decent cook would boil crawfish and only a Cajun would eat 'em, but then Cajuns eat anything. And that's when Gustave hit him. It wasn't his fault, suh."

"I can see that," Nathan said wryly. "How much is his bail?"

"Ten dollars."

"Here." He handed the money to the first mate. "Get him out and take him back to the boat...straight back."

"Yes, suh." Saluting smartly, Levi marched down the street in the direction of the jail.

"Nathan," a voice called softly as he walked back toward the dining room.

Stopping, he made out a figure in the shadows beneath the magnolia tree. "What are you doing out here, Adele?"

"Waiting for you," she said breathlessly, stepping into the dim light.

"Isn't it rather improper for a proper widow to pursue a man into a dark courtyard?"

"I don't care." Positioning herself in front of him, she laid her hand on his chest. "I had to talk to you alone."

"Give up, Addie." Purposefully he lifted her hand and, just as purposefully, he dropped it so it hung at her side.

Tears welling in her violet eyes, she looked up at him sadly. "I can't give up, Nathan, I love you. I told you before, I'll do anything to get you back."

"Including spreading lies about Serena and trying to ruin me in business by buying up Caswell & Trent's debts?"

Slanting an appraising look at him, she changed her tack, shrugging carelessly. "I couldn't ruin you, Nathan. You have too much money. Besides I was going to cancel the debts."

"And ask for what in exchange?"

"I just wanted you to go home where you belong and forget that shabby old steamboat."

"That shabby old steamboat is named the *River Sprite* and I'm rather fond of her."

"The boat or that hoyden Caswell girl?" Adele asked waspishly.

"Both. In fact, I intend to marry Serena, if I can ever convince her to be my wife."

"You can't be serious. The capitol is just crying for a man as talented as you, Nathan," she argued. "You could have everything you ever wanted...power, prestige. I can help you. I have influence now, not just in Baton Rouge, but in Washington. And I have money.''

"George Andrew's money.''

"I deserved something from that marriage,'' she declared with a toss of her head. "My life with George was wretchedly unhappy. I suppose he knew I never stopped loving you. I still love you.''

"And I love Serena,'' he said coldly.

"You...love her?'' she repeated pathetically.

"More than anything. More than power or prestige or money.''

"I don't believe it,'' the woman whispered, her face blanching. "I can't believe it.''

"Believe it.''

"But why that little nobody when you could have me?''

"You've said enough, Addie. And you've caused enough trouble. There's nothing more to say...or do.'' Turning on his heel, he strode back to the house.

Nathan's face was set in anger when he entered the dining room, but he smiled reassuringly when he saw Serena looking at him. With a murmured apology for taking so long, he slid into the chair beside her.

"You know, Nathan and I were just talking out in the courtyard and he had the most marvelous idea,'' Adele announced, sailing into the room behind him. A brittle smile was the only evidence of her consternation. "Since we all must get back to Baton Rouge, why don't we sail on the *River Sprite* tomorrow afternoon?''

"What a wonderful idea,'' Marshall Langley boomed enthusiastically from his end of the table.

"Yes,'' Nathan muttered, glaring at Adele. "But you must remember the *Sprite* is not large or luxurious.''

"All the better. If we chartered the entire boat, we could have her all to ourselves,'' the governor said. "I'd like some private leisure before we discuss that infernal budget again.''

"We do have one reservation,'' Grace interjected, "but other than that the *River Sprite* is at your disposal.''

"Won't this be fun," Mrs. Wicklisse cried.

"Yes, won't it?" Adele purred, her malevolent amethyst gaze on Serena.

Nathan said very little for the rest of the evening until he and Serena stood on the deck outside their cabins.

Pulling her into his arms, he whispered, "I'm sorry about tonight."

"It wasn't your fault Adele did her best to make me feel out of place." Serena's arms wrapped naturally around his waist and she rested her cheek against the rough texture of his jacket.

"She was very rude to you."

"Yes, but I'm afraid she's right, Nathan," she murmured. 'No matter how I try, I'll never fit into your world."

His chin resting on top of her head, the man smiled. Though she might not realize it, Serena had just told him for the first time that she wanted to be a part of his life.

"You fit with me," he whispered, kissing her briefly, "and that's all that counts."

A crooked smile on his face, he watched as she went into her cabin.

Chapter Seventeen

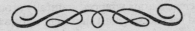

Still fuming about Adele's behavior last night, Nathan super
vised the loading of a chandelier for a hotel in Memphis th
next morning. He was distracted, however, when Reveren
Morris alit from a cab on the dock and made his way towar
the boat. There was something odd about the man, he muse
before realizing the minister was alone. He had never seen hi
without the females of his family.

"Good day, Reverend." Nathan went to meet him.

"Good day, Captain."

"Are you headed back to Lake Providence?" Nathan cas
ally relieved him of the burden of his bag.

"I am, and not a moment too soon," the portly minist
puffed. "What the denomination could have been thinking
hold a meeting in New Orleans during the 'sick' season, I w
never know."

"Simon, take Reverend Morris up to Michigan, will you?
Nathan instructed the cabin boy. "I hope it suits you, sir. It
one of our most comfortable staterooms. We cannot give yo
your usual quarters because a large party will be coming aboa
quite soon. You'll be traveling in good company, however. O
other passengers are Governor Wicklisse and his party."

"Indeed." The clergyman looked gratified. He did not c
ten get a chance to have a word with the governor. He w
feeling expansive when Serena appeared on the deck abov
wearing a fashionable gown, her hair neatly arranged. Sm
ing, she waved at them and disappeared into the salon.

"Though I did not believe so at first," Reverend Morris said jovially, "I must say, you have been a calming influence on Miss Caswell, Captain."

"No more than she has been on me. She's got me thinking of marriage."

"And when is the happy day to be?"

"As soon as I talk her into it, Reverend, as soon as I talk her into it."

"Here they come!" Hank's shout from the texas brought crew and family out on deck as five carriages rolled to a stop on the pier. Watching Adele step down from one of them, Serena remembered her words the first time they met. Adele had gotten her way. She was traveling on the *River Sprite*.

"So this is your boat." Governor Wicklisse strode across the gangplank.

"Half of her is mine anyway. Welcome aboard."

Halting to look around the main deck, the governor pronounced, "Well, she's a fine-looking vessel, son."

"Thank you, sir."

"I'm glad Addie suggested we travel with you," Marshall boomed as the passengers trooped aboard.

"My goodness, Miss Caswell," James exclaimed over the hubbub, "you look prettier every time I see you."

Turning, Nathan saw Serena descending the stairs to join them. "I forgot to warn you." He smiled up at her. "Jim Keller is painfully shy. It sometimes takes him weeks to say what he really thinks. Ah, there's Grace."

Poised on the stairs, the woman called down to the party crowding on the bow, "Welcome. Please come up and let us see you to your staterooms."

The passengers were settled and the time for departure had nearly arrived when Serena shed her petticoats and climbed to the pilothouse.

From the boiler deck, Adele watched her. "You, boy," she hailed the first cabin boy she spied, "I want to see the pilothouse. Do you think Miss Caswell would mind if you took me up?"

"No, ma'am, I don't think she'd mind. Pilots get lots of visitors. I do think you're going to have a hard time fitting through the door, though." Hank nodded tactlessly toward the hoop skirt she wore.

"I'll manage, thank you."

At the ladder to the wheelhouse, Hank went first. "You have a visitor, Rena," he announced, assisting Adele inside.

The woman's skirt hung on the door frame, breaking free with a bounce that set it swaying. Serena shifted to one side, for the skirts seemed to occupy most of the small space.

"Thank you, young man." Taking a coin from her reticule, Adele dismissed Hank.

The boy stared at the coin with unconcealed delight. "Thank you, ma'am. Call me if you need help getting out again."

She frowned as he scampered down the ladder, then she looked around with feigned interest. "So this is the pilothouse. Why, it's as I suspected, Miss Caswell. That wheel is bigger than you." Gesturing toward the bench, she asked, "Do you mind if I sit down?"

"If you'd like . . . until I have to take the *Sprite* out." Serena shrugged indifferently.

Sitting down, Adele regarded her with mild interest. "You don't like me, do you?"

"I don't have any reason to like you. You've spread lies about me up and down the river."

"I think it's more than that." Adele did not bother to deny the accusation. "I think you're jealous because I was Nathan's first love."

"I might be jealous if I thought he still loved you."

"But he does. Oh, he's upset because I married George, but my husband is dead now."

"And your love for Nathan lives on?"

Adele ignored the sarcasm. "You're smarter than I originally thought, Miss Caswell. Surely you're smart enough to realize you're not the kind of wife Nathan needs. He needs a woman of wealth and breeding, not a steamboat pilot. You don't even have the background to manage his household."

"I've never thrown a garden party or a harvest ball, either."

"If you are still not convinced of what a mistake it would be to marry him, let's talk about when Nathan tires of floating around and decides to return to the life he knows. He can be an important man someday. Are you going to stand in his way? If you love him, you will break it off now and let him make a suitable match."

"Like you?" Serena asked, her temper barely in check.

"Like me." The other woman smiled serenely.

"I think it's time you leave the wheelhouse, Mrs. Andrews, before I throw you out on your wealthy and well-bred ear."

"I'm going." She rose without haste. "I've said what I have to say. All that remains is to get what I want. And I shall . . . by the time we reach Baton Rouge. Good afternoon, Miss Caswell."

The afternoon was overcast and dreary, matching Serena's mood. When Will came to relieve her near sunset, she slumped on the tall chair by the wheel and stared moodily at the mottled sky.

"Ain't you gonna change for dinner?" her uncle asked after a while.

"I don't think I'm going to dinner."

"What's wrong with you, gal? I'll stand double watch for you, but I won't let you leave Nate to that black widow's mercies. She's been after him all afternoon. 'Oh, Nathan this, oh, Nathan, that,'" he mimicked in falsetto. "'Oh, Nathan, remember when.'"

"I know. Every time I looked out the window, she was with him."

"If you looked close, you'da seen he wasn't 'xactly overjoyed about it though he's too much of a gentleman to show it much. I don't think this is easy for him."

"She says she's going to get him back," Serena said moodily.

Will frowned at his niece. "What she says ain't worth a spit in the river."

"She says I'm not a proper match for him."

"Said as much last night, too, and it didn't bother you then." He snorted in disgust. "What a sight you are, Serena Elizabeth, feelin' sorry for yourself. If you love Nathan, get down to the salon and show him. He'll decide who's a proper match and who ain't."

"You're right, Uncle Will." With an abashed smile, the girl jumped to her feet and kissed his whiskery cheek. The next moment, she was gone.

Serena dressed with special care for dinner, choosing her pink gown. Though it would not equal anything Adele might wear, she remembered the gleam of admiration in Nathan's eyes the night she had worn it to the St. Louis Hotel.

Arriving at the salon, she discovered the meal was a buffet. Mrs. Wicklisse had prevailed upon Grace to serve an informal repast, insisting she could hardly bear the prospect of the heavy formal dinners that awaited her at the capitol.

Most of the passengers were already dining at the small tables that dotted the room when Serena entered. Nathan lounged near the door, waiting for her, engaged in conversation with James Keller and the ever-present Adele.

They filled their plates with tempting morsels Gustave had prepared. Nathan led Serena to a small table and pulled out a chair for her. Adele immediately took the seat opposite. Seated between the two women, Nathan looked glum. On the other side of the table, James smiled in contentment and dug into his dinner.

The meal seemed interminable to Serena. She said little and Adele treated her with scant civility, addressing her directly only when dessert was served.

"I must say, Miss Caswell, last night I had second thoughts about encouraging the governor and all these people to travel aboard the *River Sprite*. First I remembered a description of steamboats I read somewhere, that they're just floating volcanoes. One does hear of explosions and accidents. Then I recalled that your boat is rather...old. Well, I hardly slept a wink."

"You had no reason to lose sleep over the *Sprite*, Mrs. Andrews," Serena replied evenly. "I assure you, she's safe."

"I'm sure. Otherwise Nathan would buy a new boat. In all the years I've known him, he's never been one to make do with second best." Adele smiled meaningfully.

Putting his napkin on the table, Nathan rose. "These idlers can do as they please." He indicated their dinner partners with a pleasant nod of his head as he helped Serena from her chair. "But we have work to do. We must see to our other passengers, if you'll excuse us."

Serena got up gratefully. For a time, the couple moved from table to table, spending a few minutes with each passenger. She was painfully aware of Adele's violet gaze following them through the room. Several times, the woman whispered to James behind her fan. From the uncomfortable frown on his face, Serena knew she had been a victim of Adele's stinging tongue.

When the wind began to rise, billowing the tablecloths in the salon and putting out the candles under the chafing dishes on the buffet, the stewards closed the big doors on either side of the long room, leaving the windows open in the muggy heat.

"There's a storm blowing up," Serena told Nathan. "I must relieve Uncle Will, but you don't need to leave the party," she insisted when it looked as if he would accompany her.

As she slipped out onto the dark deck, the freshening breeze, cool after the closeness of the lantern-lit salon, swept over her. From behind her came the sound of laughter. The heat and the impending storm seemed to have no effect on the passengers' enjoyment. But Serena was glad to escape.

The moon, a scant crescent, offered little light as she climbed up the ladder to the wheelhouse. Her light cotton dress billowed around her and a gust tore at her hair, pulling it from its pins so it flowed behind her.

"Looks like we're in for a bad squall before the night is over, partner," Will greeted her. The wind streamed through the open windows, constant and hot, bearing on it the promise of rain.

Beside him at the wheel, she absently plaited her hair to keep it from whipping into tangles. Her eyes were on the roiling thunderheads and the lightning that flashed in the distance to the south. "We might outdistance it."

"Might for a spell," Will answered as he climbed stiffly down the ladder, "but it's gonna catch up with us sooner or later."

The storm still had not overtaken the *Sprite* after midnight when Nathan waited for Serena on the boiler deck, his jacket removed in the oppressive mugginess. The passengers had finally retired and the big boat was quiet. All that could be heard were the rush of the wind and the slap of the paddle wheel against the current. The moon was obscured by clouds and, against the velvety blackness of night, foam-covered whitecaps chased across the water toward the shadowy wooded shore.

A soft shuffle sounded on the deck behind him. "What are you doin' out here, Nate?" Will asked softly.

"Waiting for your niece. I didn't want to bother her in the wheelhouse when it looks like the storm is going to be upon us most any minute."

Joining him at the rail, Will turned a weather eye to the sky. "I reckon we'll spend a coupla hours nosed in to shore before mornin'."

In her stateroom, Adele paced. She had prepared for bed, she had even lain on the narrow bunk, but she had not been able to sleep. What was wrong with Nathan? At one time, he had been putty in her hands. But now, nothing she said or did seemed to have any effect on him. She had tried to appeal to him practically and emotionally, but neither approach had worked. Perhaps he would respond physically. If she could get him to kiss her just once, she was certain the old attraction would return.

But there wasn't much time for seduction. Tomorrow they would arrive in Baton Rouge and the *River Sprite* would continue upriver, taking Nathan with it. If only she could convince him to stay for a visit. She just needed a short time to renew her claim on him.

The woman was distracted from her scheming by soft voices coming from the deck. Parting the lace curtains slightly, she peered out to see Nathan and Serena's uncle engaged in quiet conversation at the railing. After a moment, the old man limped up the companionway. Nathan, his shoulder braced against a tall post, showed no inclination to leave.

Perfect, Adele thought. Unwilling to light a lantern and alert the man to her wakefulness, she fumbled in the darkness for her hairbrush. As she dragged it through her hair, she peeped out to see that he still lounged on deck. At the door, she paused to draw a deep breath, collecting herself for their encounter.

Suddenly a bang and a scrape came from the bow and the *River Sprite* rocked. Out on deck, the captain leaned over the railing to look forward. A strange quietude fell over the boat and he realized the paddle wheel had been halted.

In a matter of seconds, another rasp sounded amidship as the current carried the boat. From the main deck, Nathan heard Levi's calm voice as the men poured from the forecastle.

"It's a sawyer, but it ain't a big one. Stand by aft, in case it fouls the wheel."

Even as the first mate gave the command, a loud grating noise came from the stern as the *Sprite* passed over the hazard. The moment the boat broke free of the floating branches, Jamie started the wheel and the boat lurched forward.

In the same moment, Nathan heard a sharp bang as a door behind him was thrown open and bounced against the bulkhead. Clad in only a diaphanous nightgown, Adele burst from her stateroom and flung herself in his arms.

"It is true! Steamboats are floating volcanoes." Apparently near hysterics, she wrapped her arms tightly around his neck. "Are we going to sink, Nathan?"

"No." Awkwardly he tried to step back, but Adele held fast, undeterred when other passengers in various stages of undress poured out of their cabins, drawn by the commotion. His arms full of unwanted female, the captain reassured them, "It's all right, folks. We just passed a sawyer and we're in no danger."

"Are you sure?" Adele whimpered, melting against him. "The boilers are not going to explode?"

"No." Nathan tried again to extricate himself, feeling as if her clinging arms would choke him.

Serena emerged from the companionway, slowing when she saw the crowd gathered on the boiler deck. Nathan stood in its midst, the scantily clad Adele in his arms. His face fell when he saw her descend from the texas.

Adele saw her, too. Flashing a triumphant glance in Serena's direction, she crooned, "You've always taken such good care of me, Nathan. I don't know what I would have done if you hadn't been here with me tonight."

Without a word, Serena turned on her heel and went back up to the texas.

"Damnation," Nathan swore under his breath. Deliberately he peeled Adele's arms from around his neck and thrust her toward her chagrined father. "Here's your daughter, Marshall, safe and sound, if not quite presentable. I'd appreciate it if you'd see her to her cabin."

Without a look back, the captain worked his way through the crowd, stopping briefly here and there to offer a reassuring word to a worried passenger. When he reached the companionway, he found his way blocked by Will, who was descending.

"I'd wait to go up there if I was you," the old pilot advised. "Serena took the wheel and she's making for shore till the storm passes. I don't think she's in the mood for talk."

"She'd better get in the mood," Nathan answered, impatient for the other man to pass.

In no hurry, Will halted. "I don't know what you do to get her so riled, son, but I figure you'd better marry her before you two hurt each other."

"I'm trying," Nathan growled, brushing past him.

Nosed up to the bank, the boat rolled with the white-crested waves. Steam belched from the stacks, creating fleeting white apparitions against the murky sky. His eyes on the domed wheelhouse where Serena could be dimly seen, Nathan crossed the texas.

As he mounted the ladder, the light in the pilothouse wavered, then died, blown out by the draft. Hoisting himself inside, he searched for and found Serena's trim figure in the darkness. "I want to talk to you."

"All right." Her voice was calm. "But first help me close the windows."

When the pilothouse was snug and secure, Nathan caught her hand and pulled her to sit beside him on the bench. Willingly she nestled into the crook of his arm. They sat in silence, the first fat drops of rain drumming against the windows the only sound.

"Will said you were upset," he murmured after a moment.

"I was," she confessed. "I just needed a few minutes to get over seeing Adele Andrews in your arms."

"I know how it must have looked, but—"

"Never mind, Nathan. I trust you."

Nearly giddy with relief, he planted a kiss against the top of her head. She smelled of roses and fresh air.

Her voice drifted to him on the low rumble of thunder. "I know you've been waiting for me to talk to you about marriage and I'm sorry I've taken so long. But I've been afraid."

"Afraid of what, love?" He turned her to face him. In the sudden glare of lightning, his expression was perplexed.

"I was afraid you would betray me."

"I haven't betrayed you, not even when Addie launched herself at me, half-naked."

"Or tire of me."

"What if you tire of me?" he countered reasonably.

"Why should I tire of you? I love you. I enjoy your company."

"I love you and enjoy your company, too," he told her, tucking her back against his side.

"But there's my family, Nathan," she went on, determined to continue now that she had begun. "I think your willingness to take care of them...and me...is noble. But you don't need a wife with a mother, a brother, a sister and an uncle."

"Nobility has nothing to do with it. I love you and your family. And just what kind of wife do you think I need?"

"A pretty little wife who will let you take care of her, even make up her mind for her. Someone who will have babies and garden parties and harvest balls. I don't know anything about those things. And I don't know anything about plantations or—"

"I've told you that we can work out anything as long as we talk," he cut in firmly. "You just covered a lot of ground, so now I'd like to say a few words.

"First about my wanting to take care of you...I do, because I love you. But I never thought you would be a complacent wife who would allow me to make decisions for you. I don't even think you'll be a very conventional wife, but I don't care because I fell in love with an unconventional girl. I wouldn't change you for the world, Rena."

"You told me from the very first that if I were your wife, I'd need to be more a woman and less a pilot," she reminded him.

"That was before I knew you. I have no complaints on either count."

"But how long before you ask me to leave the river, Nathan? The *Sprite* is my home. I haven't lived ashore for more than a month at a time since I was fifteen."

"I don't want you to give up your home any more than I want to give up mine. Marriage is made of compromise. There's no reason we couldn't live on the boat part of the time and at my plantation the other part. Our home is with each other. We'll be happy as long as we're together. Marry me, Serena."

Her eyes filling with tears, she regarded him with wonder. He had said all the things she had needed so much to hear. His reassurances had given her a stronger certainty of his love...and hers. "Oh, Nathan," she said unsteadily.

Mistaking her diffidence for reluctance, the man's jaw set and he pulled a deck of cards from his pocket. "If you're still having trouble making up your mind, let's cut to decide it once and for all."

Taking the deck from him, she brushed her thumb over the edge. "Lucky's riffle deck," she accused, her eyes sparkling.

"There are a few things worth cheating for," he owned sheepishly.

Laughing and shaking her head, she threw her arms around his neck. "I can see I'm going to have to make an honest man of you, Nathan Trent."

"You have a lifetime to try." Smiling in delighted comprehension, he lowered his mouth to hers.

After a time, Serena withdrew, listening. "The rain has let up. We'd better go down to our cabins...unless we want to spend the night here."

"Sounds fine to me," he murmured contentedly.

"But it will make it hard for Uncle Will to navigate in the morning."

Leaving the pilothouse to Catastrophe, the couple went out into a gentle rain. Hand in hand, they walked across the texas to the companionway.

As they stepped onto the boiler deck, there was a crash of thunder and the heavens opened up. Together, they raced for the stern. Sheets of rain slanted beneath the overhang, drenching them as they dashed into the nearest cabin, Nathan's tiny stateroom.

Rain dripping down his face, Nathan pressed his shoulder against the door and pushed it closed against the wind. Behind him, Serena tugged at the skirt plastered to her legs. Lighting the lamp on the table beside the bed, he picked up a towel from the washstand. "Look here," he ordered gently.

Water beaded in her eyelashes and trickled from her chin as she lifted her face cooperatively. Smoothing back her hair, which hung in sodden ropes, he dabbed at her forehead. Their eyes met and they smiled at each other, oblivious to their wet clothes dripping puddles on floor.

"You look like a drowned rat," she teased.

"So do you. But you're beautiful."

"Beautiful? Plain, practical Serena?"

"My Serena," he murmured.

They kissed lingeringly, unhurriedly and the kiss deepened to match their feelings. The desire between them had smoldered too long. It ignited, blocking out all but their hunger for each other.

Nathan shuddered when Serena wrapped her arms around his waist, molding her body to his, her hands tracing delicate patterns along his spine. He had known she would be a sensual lover, but her instinctive, unrestrained passion set him ablaze.

She moaned for the loss when his lips left hers, the moan turning into a sigh of bliss when he nuzzled at her neck, nipping and licking. Through her wet, clinging bodice, the shape of her breast could be clearly seen. Nathan bent to take the jutting point of it in his mouth. His breath warm against the wet fabric kindled unexpected fires in Serena and she arched, straining back in his arms.

He groaned at the feel of her body pressed against his. Cupping her buttocks through damp layers of petticoat, he pressed her closer, his hardness telling her of his need.

His usually skillful hands were clumsy with longing as he unfastened the buttons running down the front of her dress. Untying the ribbon that held her camisole in place, he freed her breasts. She gasped and drew a shuddering gasp as bare flesh was touched by cool air. When his hand followed, cupping one of the pliant mounds, teasing the peak with his thumb, she nearly sobbed at the exquisite, torturous pleasure of it.

"This has gone too far," Nathan murmured, his voice rough with desire as he looked down at his sun-bronzed hand resting on her white breast. The eyes he lifted to hers were heavy lidded with passion, hooding the stark yearning there. "I am tempted to the limit of my endurance," he said hoarsely, battling with himself. "I must take you to your cabin."

"Not this time," she answered huskily. "I want to stay with you."

"I've told you before I don't want to have any regrets between us."

"Only love," she quoted softly. "That's why I'm giving myself to you, Nathan. I love you and I'm going to marry you."

He knew she wanted him as much as he wanted her and, now he knew he would have her for his wife. He took what she offered, humbled by the magnificence.

Stripping off his cravat, he removed his shirt, the studs sprinkling on the floor, unnoticed. Serena stared at him, fascinated as the angles of his muscular torso were gilded by flickering lamplight. He stood very still as she reached out, almost fearfully, to touch his chest, yanking back when the skin twitched beneath her gentle fingers.

"Don't be afraid," he whispered, peeling her drenched dress over her head and tossing it onto the floor.

"I'm not," she replied, though she seemed shy, standing before him in her undergarments.

Nathan untied the tape that held her petticoat in place and allowed the garment to fall to the floor around her feet. Then, offering his hand, he helped her step out of it. Her camisole and pantaloons quickly joined the soggy pile of clothing.

When she stood before him, naked but for her slippers and stockings, he picked her up and laid her on the bed. Sitting beside her, he took off her shoes, rubbing her wet feet gently. Then slowly, tantalizingly, he removed first one garter, then the other and rolled her stockings down, running his palms along the length of her legs.

Rising, he looked at her lying on the bed. Now that her initial shyness had passed, she did not seem shamed by his gaze, nor did she seem embarrassed to watch him undress.

Stepping to his bootjack, he removed his boots, then his socks. In a moment, his damp trousers joined her wet clothes on the floor.

Naked, he joined her on the bed, stretching out on his side beside her, propped up on one elbow. He kissed her, his hand gently kneading her breast, his thumb teasing the peak. Poised above her, his hand skimming her flat stomach, he asked softly, "Are you sure, Serena? It's not too late to change your mind."

"I'm sure." Then her eyes widened. "Aren't you?"

Chuckling softly, he rolled on top of her so they lay together, center to center. "I'm sure."

Skimming her mouth lightly, his lips began an exploration of soft, warm, willing flesh. His mouth, his hands roamed where they would, igniting a hundred fires within her. Her hands grazed his lean sides and moved to stroke the muscles of his back as she writhed under his relentless touch.

When Nathan entered her welcoming warmth, he felt as if he would explode. Gently he thrust forward until he met with the resistance he had known he would find.

"It will only hurt for a moment," he whispered, "then it will be good."

She cried out softly, then began to move with him, rhythmically, slowly at first, then faster as they merged in the timeless dance of man and woman. Serena's body rose to meet his primal, searing thrusts, her hands clutching his broad shoulders, drawing him nearer, though he could be no closer than he was.

Their cries mingled, obliterated by a clap of thunder, as they reached the peak together. Then they lay together, their limbs intertwined.

Nathan had not intended to sleep, but Chanticleer's crow woke him near dawn. It was probably the only time, he thought drowsily, that the rooster had been on time since he had been on the boat.

Feeling Serena stir in his arms, he shook her gently. "Wake up, sleepyhead. We have to get you back to your cabin or our wedding will have to be even sooner than we planned."

He felt her stiffen, then she shot from the bed. Locating her damp, wrinkled dress in the dimness, she hurriedly pulled it over her head.

"We're not in that much of a hurry." He watched as she looked desperately for her other shoe.

"I don't want everyone to know what happened last night,"

"They won't, if you don't wake the entire boat." He reached for her, but she was already on her way out the door.

When Nathan emerged from his cabin a little while later, he found Serena, dressed, on deck, looking eastward. A bright crescent of crimson sun gingerly revealed itself above massive river oaks while wispy remnants of night fog still played around their bases. Ghostly morning light illuminated the silvery Spanish moss draped over their huge limbs, swaying slightly in the breeze.

"Isn't it glorious?" She looked out at the scene, refusing to look at him as he stood beside her.

"Glorious."

Reluctantly she met his dark eyes, as if fearing what she would see.

His gaze holding hers, he slipped his arm around her and drew her small body back against his. Relaxing, she smiled contentedly and leaned against him, her arms crossed over his at her waist.

"I'll grant you we should have waited," he murmured against her hair, "but what happened between us was not wrong. I love you and you're going to be my wife."

"It seemed right last night." She sighed. "But this morning . . ."

"Nothing has changed this morning. You promised you'd marry me before we made love and you're not getting out of it. In fact, I'm thinking about going to get Reverend Morris to perform the marriage ceremony right now."

"Before breakfast?" Serena teased. "Let the reverend sleep. Vicksburg is soon enough for a wedding."

Chapter Eighteen

"Don't the two of you look cheerful this morning?" Governor Wicklisse greeted Nathan and Serena when they appeared in the salon for breakfast.

"Cheerful is not the word for it." Nathan grinned. "I'm ecstatic. I just convinced Serena to become my wife." He paused to enjoy her blush before adding, "If she's cheerful, it's because she doesn't know what she's getting into yet."

"You're getting married?" Adele demanded in disbelief.

"Congratulations, Nathan." James slapped the captain on the back. "When will you tie the knot?"

"When we get back to Vicksburg. Serena and Grace already have the wedding planned, I think," Nathan responded with a chuckle.

"All we've decided is that it's going to be at River's Rest and that Serena is going to be a beautiful bride," Grace said.

"What wonderful news," Tansy exclaimed.

"It's absolutely delightful!" Mrs. Wicklisse cried.

"Woulda been more delightful if they didn't wake a body up at the crack of dawn to tell him," Will grumbled good-naturedly.

"Then how come you wanted to wake the whole boat to tell 'em, Uncle Will?" Hank asked innocently.

"You don't have to tell everything you know, boy," the old pilot exhorted as everyone trooped around the newly engaged couple to offer their felicitations.

Surrounded by smiling faces, Serena felt Adele's eyes resting on her and resolutely tried to ignore the animosity in their violet depths. Her arm tucked through Nathan's, she smiled up at him lovingly, reveling in the knowledge that she was loved in return.

Will moored the *River Sprite* in Baton Rouge just before noon. The chatter of the passengers gathering on the main deck outstripped the din on the dock as casks and crates were unloaded.

On the bow, Serena, Nathan and Grace were bidding the governor's party farewell when James and Adele appeared on the stairs.

"It's good to be back in Baton Rouge," Adele announced. "It's always exciting to be where things happen."

"Spoken like a politician's daughter," her father teased as she joined him.

"But it's true. There are so many things going on here. Why, I'll scarcely have my trunks unpacked in time for the governor's ball this evening."

Turning to Nathan, she urged, "You really ought to stay for the ball and bring your fiancée. Your parents will probably be there. Don't you think they should meet her before she becomes a member of the family?"

Then she stopped, seemingly chagrined, and stared at the governor. "Oh, I'm terribly sorry. How presumptuous of me to make such an invitation. After all, it is your ball, Governor Wicklisse."

"Yes, for my friends and supporters," he answered graciously. "Nate and I have been friends for years and I would like to think Miss Caswell will become one. Please come. You, as well, Mrs. Caswell."

"Oh, yes, please do," his wife seconded. "Instead of another wearisome political affair, we can celebrate Nathan and Serena's engagement."

Adele's kittenish face was smug as the others entreated them to attend.

"It is very kind of you to invite me," Grace managed to get a word in, "but I am still in mourning. Certainly the young people should go, if they wish."

"But we lost time last night because of the storm," Serena objected.

"Will one more day truly make a difference in your schedule?" Governor Wicklisse persisted.

Reading doubt on her face, Nathan began, "I don't think—"

"Be careful with that crate," the governor bellowed suddenly at the stevedores on the dock. "You're about to drop a case of very expensive French champagne."

Nathan followed him down the gangplank, relieved to see his crew was not at fault.

There was only one way to be sure Nathan stayed in Baton Rouge, Adele decided. While the rest of the group disembarked, she laid a hand on Serena's arm. "I'm sorry, Miss Caswell," she murmured so no one else could hear. "I don't know what I could have been thinking to have made such a preposterous suggestion.

"Of course you would not want to attend the governor's ball. You may not even know how to dance and you probably don't have a suitable ball gown ... living on the river. But there's no reason to be embarrassed. I'm sure if Nathan explains to Governor Wicklisse, he'll understand."

With a cold stare for Adele's insincere smile, Serena walked down the gangplank. "I hope you haven't refused the governor's kind invitation, Nathan," she said, looping her arm through his as he looked at her in surprise. "I've never been to a ball at the governor's mansion and I would love to go."

"That settles it then," Governor Wicklisse decreed. "I'll send a servant with a proper invitation this very afternoon and we'll look forward to having you as our guests."

Watching as the passengers were settled in their carriages, Nathan noted Adele's satisfied smile and knew without a doubt that she was up to mischief.

"Damnation," he muttered with a preoccupied frown as Serena and Grace went to select a gown for the ball. As soon as the unloading was completed, he went to the stern.

"I'm glad I went ahead and gave you the blue gown. I think it's the best choice for a ball," he heard Grace muse as he stood outside Serena's open door. "And you look lovely in it."

"I should never have let Adele goad me into going," the girl said gloomily. "The governor's mansion is no place for a river pilot."

"A river pilot who happens to be a lovely young lady," her mother maintained. "You and Nathan will have a wonderful time. You said you wanted to go, after all."

"Only because of my all-fired temper."

"Your language, dear," Grace reproved absently, looking up when the man stepped into the doorway, blocking the light.

"Put on your bonnet, my love," he told Serena lightly. "We're going ashore."

"What for?"

"If we're to celebrate our engagement tonight, my fiancée should have a ring to wear," he answered, his heart standing still when she beamed up at him, love shining forth in her eyes.

"Please don't dawdle," Grace requested. "Serena will need time to dress for the ball."

"Yes, ma'am, Madame Partner." Saluting smartly, he offered Serena his arm.

"Nathan," she ventured as they rolled along streets flanked by gracious homes and abundant gardens, "I don't know Baton Rouge very well, but I don't think we'll find a jewelry store this far from the business district."

"The ring I want for you doesn't come from a jewelry store."

"Where does it come from?"

"Right here," he said as the cab stopped before an elegant town house.

She stared at him with realization dawning in her eyes. "This . . . this is your parents' home, isn't it?"

He nodded.

"You might have told me," she protested.

"I might have, but knowing you already regret accepting the governor's invitation, I was afraid you'd refuse to come. I want for you to meet my family and for them to meet you."

"But Nathan, what if..." she whispered.

"What if they don't like you?" he asked gently, leading her to the shaded porch. "You're about to find out that they'll love you...almost as much as I do."

In response to their knock, the door was opened by a black butler. "Mr. Nate, come in this house."

"Nathan!" A coltish adolescent girl tore from an adjacent room, her voice ringing in the foyer. "*Maman,* Nathan is home!"

"Hello, Diane," Nathan greeted his sister with an affectionate hug. "How are you, *ma petite?*"

"*Mon fils,*" a hoarse whisper came from the doorway to the parlor. Camille La Branche Trent stared at her son, her plump, aristocratic face alight with joy.

"*Maman.*" Nathan's voice was thick with emotion. Almost as if in supplication, he opened his arms. His mother flew to them.

Forgotten for the moment, Serena watched the homecoming with a lump in her throat. She was the first to see the tall old man at the head of the stairs. He paused for a moment, then descended to a landing about halfway down the staircase. Though he depended heavily on a cane, he walked erectly as he struggled to hold his dignity while observing the scene below.

Spying him, Diane called, "Look, Father, Nathan's come home."

"I should have known you'd be the cause of such a ruckus," Micah Trent said gruffly. "You always made as much noise as all four of your sisters put together."

"Hello, Father." One arm around his mother, Nathan met the keen gaze of the older man. "Am I welcome after the way I walked out of here four years ago?"

Descending to stand before his son, Micah said simply, "You were always welcome here." Crooking an arm around Nathan's neck, he drew him near for a quick, awkward hug.

"I'm sorry, Father," Nathan's voice was muffled against his shoulder.

"Oh, but look. Who have we here?" Camille asked, turning dark, smiling eyes so like her son's on Serena.

Free of his father's embrace, Nathan drew his fiancée to his side. "This is Serena Caswell, who has promised to become Serena Trent."

Though she returned Camille's smile, Serena watched the faces of Nathan's family warily, and she was amazed and touched to see nothing but curiosity and acceptance reflected on them.

"We have heard about you, *chérie*." Camille beamed at her.

Serena threw a despairing glance at Nathan before his mother continued, "Both my brother, Antoine, and our friend, Tansy Shumacher, think very highly of you. We wondered when Nathan would bring you home."

"May I call you Serena?" Diane asked, seizing one of her hands. "When you marry Nate, you'll be my sister and I'm glad. I could use a new one. I'm tired of all the old ones."

"So you've found a bride at last." Micah looked Serena over approvingly. Bending toward her, he confided sorrowfully, "We despaired Nathan ever finding a wife to put up with him, Miss Caswell. He's such a terrible tease."

"He is." Her tragic sigh matched his. "It has always seemed he could not help but plague me, Mr. Trent, but I didn't realize until a moment ago that teasing is a hereditary condition."

Micah bellowed with laughter. "It's early to say, Nate, but I think you have met your match. Come into the parlor, children."

"Saul, please bring coffee," Camille directed. "I will join you in a moment," she told the family as she mounted to the second floor.

When she joined them in the parlor a few moments later, Micah grinned. "Camille, Serena is a river pilot. What do you think of that?"

"A river pilot?" the Creole woman repeated, taken aback.

"Yes, ma'am," Serena confirmed, her blue eyes apprehensive.

"I think it is most...unusual," Camille said cautiously. Suddenly she realized the girl was almost holding her breath, waiting to see what she would say. Even after many years, Camille remembered what it was to be shunned as she had been after marrying her strong, handsome *Américain*. "I think being a river pilot must be very interesting. Come, walk with me, Serena. I will show you the garden and the *pigeonnier* and we will become acquainted, *oui?*"

"Some things never change." Nathan chuckled. "No one escapes without admiring *Maman*'s doves, Serena. Tell her they're the most wonderful birds in the world and she'll be in your debt forever."

"If she admires them, it will be because she is a woman of refined taste," Camille retorted.

"I agree. She has chosen me for a husband, after all."

Rolling her eyes expressively, his mother held out a hand to Serena. "Come, *chérie*. We have much to talk about and I may have some good advice for you when you marry my son."

As they strolled through the formal garden, Nathan's mother asked few questions. They talked about families and steamboats and Nathan. Laughing at a story of Nathan as a small boy, Serena felt as if she had known the other woman for years.

They halted beside the *pigeonnier*, a small octagonal cage in the rear of the garden where nearly a score of cooing doves perched.

"They're beautiful," Serena breathed in genuine appreciation. "I've never seen any like them."

Camille fairly glowed with pride. "These are bleeding heart doves. My family has kept them for years. The legend says that a dove brushed against our Savior's wounds as he hung on the cross. Since that time, all bleeding heart doves have patches of red on their chests over their hearts."

"What a lovely story."

"I believe I'm going to like you very much, *chérie*," Camille said as they returned to the house, "and not just because you admire my doves."

When they returned to the parlor, the women found Nathan holding Micah, Diane, even Saul spellbound with descriptions of life aboard the *River Sprite*.

Going to her son's side, Camille handed him a small velvet box and murmured, "With my blessing, *mon fils*. I feared you would never find someone to love, Nathan, someone to love you in return. I thank *le bon Dieu* that you have."

"*Merci, Maman.*" With a joyful expression, Nathan accepted the small box and pocketed it.

"*Maman,*" Diane clamored excitedly. "Guess what! Nathan and Serena are going to Governor Wicklisse's ball this evening."

"Will you be attending the ball?" Serena asked.

"Not this time. Micah is troubled with the gout, you see. Tonight we stay at home, but tomorrow I hope he will feel up to visiting the steamboat. We must meet your mother and talk about the wedding, *oui?* Do you have a gown already?"

"I believe I'm going to wear my Grandmother Dearborn's wedding dress."

"Do you have a veil?" Diane asked. "Because if you do not, you simply must wear *Maman*'s veil. It's beautiful and miles of lace. All of my sisters wore it and I'm going to wear it one day."

Camille frowned at her irrepressible daughter. "She may not want to wear it, Diane. It's very old-fashioned. But you would look lovely in it, *chère*," she mused. "Perhaps you would like to try it on?"

"I would love to try it," Serena agreed, and was immediately whisked upstairs by the Trent females. In a matter of minutes, her hair had been taken down, put back up, arranged and rearranged, and the exquisite lace veil placed on her head. Nervously she stood in the shadows at the top of the stairs as Camille and Diane stationed themselves in the foyer.

"Nathan," Camille called, "come and see your fiancée now."

He emerged from the parlor, followed by his father, looking up when his mother gestured upward.

Serena stepped into view. Washed in the light from the window on the landing, the gold-shot lace seemed to glow. Beneath the ivory veil, her hair was down, framing her face. Rich auburn locks rested on her shoulders.

"Does she meet your approval?" Camille asked softly as Nathan stared wordlessly at the vision on landing.

"More than you know," he murmured huskily, climbing up to her. "You will be a beautiful bride, Rena."

Feeling suddenly shy, she whispered, "Thank you, Nathan."

Lifting her chin with a bent finger, he planted a light kiss on her lips. Serena blushed but met his dark admiring eyes. Absorbed in each other, their faces were bright with love. They did not hear Diane's rapturous sigh or notice when Camille discreetly herded her family into the parlor, leaving them alone.

"I want you to have this," Nathan said, pulling the small box from his pocket. "It was my grandmother's engagement ring."

Opening it, Serena gasped aloud at the blaze of sapphires and diamonds.

He took the ring from its velvet setting and slipped it onto her finger where it settled into place as if it had belonged there all along. "My mother kept it for me until I found the right girl," he told her with a smile. "She likes you, you know."

"And I like her . . . and your father and your sister."

"Good." He kissed her again lightly. "Because you're going to be stuck with all of us for a very long time."

The couple departed the Trent house a short time later amid fond farewells and promises to see one another the next day.

The ballroom of the governor's mansion was immense, tasteful and luxurious. Lit with hundreds of candles and packed with people, it was also sweltering on this late August night.

"Don't be nervous." Nathan smiled reassuringly at Serena as they joined the stream of people flowing past the receiving line.

"Nate, Serena, there you are," Governor Wicklisse boomed when he saw them. "So glad you could join us."

"Serena, you look absolutely stunning." Mrs. Wicklisse smiled in welcome. "You're going to be the envy of every woman here tonight." Without thinking, her eyes flickered to-

ward the lavender-clad Adele Andrews. Surrounded by a half-
dozen admirers, the young widow was oblivious to their attention as she watched Nathan and Serena with a perplexed frown.

"I'm almost finished with all this hand-shaking folderol,"
the governor told Serena conspiratorially. "I'd appreciate it if
you'd save a dance for me."

"And one for me," James Keller threw in, joining them,
"after the receiving line breaks up."

"I'm glad you both have things to occupy you for now,"
Nathan informed them good-naturedly, "because Serena's first
dance belongs to me."

"You lucky devil," James said, only partly in jest.

"Luckier than I've ever been before," Nathan agreed,
drawing her toward the circling dancers. But before they could
join them, they were halted by a gravelly, trumpeting voice.

"Nathan Trent! I haven't seen you in a coon's age."

"Hello, Eustace," he said before they had even turned to face
the source of the voice, a stout, smiling, middle-aged man.
Adele Andrews glided at his side, her violet eyes resting on
Serena coldly. "Hello, Addie."

"When you didn't come back to Louisiana after so long, I
figured you'd been scalped by wild Injuns. How are you, boy?"
The older man pumped Nathan's hand enthusiastically.

"I'm well, thank you. Eustace Grant, may I present my fiancée, Miss Serena Caswell?"

"A pleasure, ma'am." He bobbed in a polite bow.

"Eustace owns the place just downriver from Le Jardin, my
family's plantation," Nathan explained.

"I heard you'd gone and gotten yourself engaged, Nate,"
Eustace blurted, "but I sure wasn't expecting such a beauty.
That is...I mean..."

"You're very kind, Mr. Grant," Serena said smoothly, noting that Adele had the grace to blush at Eustace's revelation.

Relieved that Serena had not taken offense, Eustace added
gallantly, "That's a mighty pretty dress you have on. Don't you
think so, Miss Addie?"

"It is pretty," Adele cooed. "I liked it when you wore it in
New Orleans, too." Turning to Nathan, she said gaily, "So

many of your old friends are here. I was hoping you'd come with me to see Mr. Tonti over there in the corner. He's so decrepit now, he can hardly walk. But I know he would love to see you."

"I'd love to see him, too," Nathan answered with a charming smile, "but first I'm going to dance with my intended."

As he drew Serena onto the floor, the big captain murmured, "I think I should have at least the first dance."

"And the last dance and all the dances in between," she teased.

With an exultant grin, he spun her around the floor in a swirl of black and royal blue.

At the end of their second dance together, Governor Wicklisse appeared at their side. "Serena promised me a dance, Nathan, and I'd like to claim it before old Madame Duhon claims me."

As she spun away in the governor's arms, Serena looked back to see Adele standing in a circle of people, beckoning Nathan. Slowly, reluctantly, he joined them.

By the time, Serena's dance with the governor was finished, Nathan was beset by old friends and acquaintances. He scowled over their shoulders at the pack of young dandies who surrounded her, clamoring for a dance with the auburn-haired beauty.

His scowl deepened and he was ready to excuse himself to retrieve his fiancée when Governor Wicklisse led her toward him. Her admirers retreated immediately at the sight of the glowering captain.

For Serena, the evening passed with a blur of names and faces. Nathan introduced her proudly to the society he had known since childhood. All were curious, some were disapproving, but most were welcoming. Only Adele's face stood out in constant, resentful contrast.

"So, there you are," James Keller chided as he joined them quite late in the evening. "You promised me a dance, Serena, and I still haven't gotten it."

"And I haven't seen you since the receiving line," she defended herself.

"The price of popularity... and a budding political career," the young man admitted blithely. "May I have that dance now?"

With a quick smile for Nathan, she allowed James to lead her onto the dance floor.

"You haven't danced with me once this evening." An accusing voice interrupted Nathan as he watched them. Adele stood at his side, away from the crowd. "I can understand if you think you're in love with that girl, but I don't understand why you are trying to humiliate me. Are you punishing me for my foolishness four years ago?" She raised a suffering face toward him. "Don't you think I've been tortured enough?"

Nathan did not try to conceal his amusement. "I'm not punishing you, Addie. I don't even care about what happened four years ago."

"Then dance with me," she challenged, her color high. "Unless you're afraid of what you might feel."

"What do I have to do to convince you it's over between us, Addie?" he asked harshly.

"Dance this waltz with me... just like old times. Then look me in the eye and tell me you don't love me."

"I can tell you that here and now," he said coldly.

"You're afraid to dance with me," she charged, her voice rising.

"Damnation," he swore, and led her out on the floor.

Waltzing with James, Serena saw Nathan and Adele join the dancers. It was little comfort that the captain's face was grim as he held Adele at a stiffly decorous distance. They were a handsome couple, she thought with a pang. Resolutely she put away her jealousy. She had no reason to distrust Nathan.

Before their dance was finished, James was summoned by a page to handle a minor emergency.

"I'm sorry, Serena," he apologized, leading her to the edge of the dance floor near the entrance, "but duty calls."

"Another price of a budding political career."

"Our young friend here will stay with you. I wouldn't want to face your big fiancé if I left you alone."

"I suspect pages also have other duties. I'll be fine here until Nathan returns."

"If you're sure, ma'am...." The boy seemed eager to be on his way.

"Just go, both of you," she shooed them away.

In a matter of moments, Serena wondered if she had done the right thing. Three young dandies approached from three different directions. Prudently she retreated to the ladies' salon nearby.

Poised just inside the door, she overheard the conversation taking place in the room.

"I don't see how he could be in love with anyone else," one woman said. "Remember how mad he was for her?"

"Now it seems she is mad for him. She's determined to have him back," another said.

"And she will," a third predicted. "She's got the same stubborn gleam in those purple eyes that she had when she pushed George Andrews into running for senate."

"I hear Nathan Trent is getting married."

"Not if Addie has anything to say about it."

"That poor little redhead hasn't a chance."

Trying desperately to hold on to Nathan's reassurances from the night before, Serena fought back a wave of jealousy and stepped into the light. The three occupants of the room immediately fell silent and hastily excused themselves.

Alone in the salon, the girl was reluctant to return to the ballroom alone. Unwilling to face would-be swains and curious stares while Nathan danced with Adele, she let herself out of a side door onto the terrace.

She relished the cool air, pausing for a moment to allow her eyes to adjust to the darkness. A sudden exclamation from the shadows caught her attention and she saw Adele, her arms looped around Nathan's neck, as they kissed.

She whirled without realizing she had gasped aloud until Nathan tore his mouth from the woman's lips to call, "Serena, wait!" But she had already set out for the front driveway at a run.

"Let her go, Nathan," Adele insisted, clinging to him. "She may be hurt now, but it's better this way...faster. She would have heard that you came out here with me anyway."

"You would have made sure she heard," Nathan grated, yanking her arms from around his neck. "I wouldn't have come out here if you hadn't been faint from the heat, Addie. I suppose you faint as easily as you cry. This is a cheap trick, even for you."

"You're just angry." Desperately she grabbed his arm. "You can't really want her when you can have me."

Nathan wheeled on her. "Look me in the eye, Addie. This is the way you wanted it. I tell you now, I do not love you. I do not want you. It is over between us." With that, he turned and raced through the night after the woman he loved.

"Take me to the dock," Serena was ordering a cabbie when he reached the driveway.

"Wait," he yelled as the cab galloped toward the gate.

"Go suck eggs, you lying, fickle baboon," he heard before her raw voice was drowned out by the sound of the horse's hooves.

When she reached the *River Sprite,* Serena raced up the gangplank and pounded on the forecastle door. "Everyone up and out," she yelled, heading for the stairs. "We're leaving Baton Rouge tonight. Now! Jamie!" She pounded on the engineer's door as she passed. "Build steam."

Following her sleepily on deck, Jamie asked, "What's the hurry, lass? Where's the captain?"

"I don't know and I don't care." She shouted, climbing the companionway to the texas. "I don't care if I ever see him again."

Awakened by the ruckus, Serena's family poured out on deck. Gathering on the deck, they watched, aghast, as Serena, still clad in her ball gown, climbed up to the pilothouse.

"What on earth could have happened?" Grace muttered.

"Dunno," Will answered, rubbing his whiskered jaw, "but it's as fine a display of temper as I've seen in a blue moon."

"I believe I shall have a word with her," Grace said firmly. Holding her robe tightly closed, she started toward the ladder.

Above her, a window flew open and Serena shouted, "Don't come up here, Mother. We'll talk when we've left Baton Rouge and Nathan Trent behind.

"That man has been more trouble to me than all the plagues of Egypt," she added grimly as a carriage careened toward the *Sprite* at a full gallop. "Uncle Will, tell the crew to cast off."

"There's not enough steam to pull away from the dock yet," Will objected, though he ambled toward the companionway, trailed by Grace and Dory.

Down on the pier, Nathan bailed out of the carriage and, with a dire look toward the wheelhouse, marched toward the boat.

"Tell the crew to pull in the gangplank and stand by," she yelled frantically.

"I'll sure do that," Will called back. Limping along the boiler deck below, he called down casually to the bow, "Levi, tell the crew to pull in the plank."

But before the ramp could be pulled aboard, Serena saw Nathan stride up it and disappear from view on the main deck.

She locked the wheelhouse door and returned to the windows to watch, but there was no sign of him. Inexplicably Will disembarked and strolled across the dock to the carriage Nathan had vacated.

"Will Caswell, where in blue blazes are you going?" Serena yelled down at him.

"I have some business in town and I'll be back directly."

"At this hour? Get back on board or I'll leave without you."

"I don't reckon you will," he called back, unperturbed.

Suddenly the gauge cocks screamed, startling her as the steam was released from the boilers. Rushing to the speaking tube, Serena demanded, "Jamie, what do you think you're doing down there?"

Nathan's voice drifted up from the boiler room. "We're settling in for what looks like another stormy night."

"You have no right to countermand my orders."

"You are not the *Sprite*'s only captain," he reminded her quietly.

"Mutiny," she muttered as the crew made the lines fast again.

After a moment of silence from the boiler room, Nathan said, "I know you're angry, Serena. You're not even calling me names. But we must talk."

"I don't want to talk."

He sighed, the rush of his breath crackling noisily in tube. "I've told you that when we have a problem, we can work it out if we talk."

"Nathan, please, the entire boat can hear you."

"I don't care. You are not leaving me, my love, without giving me a chance to explain."

"What is there to explain? I saw you kissing Adele Andrews in the garden. I knew I should have put her off on a sandbar."

"You saw her kissing me—"

"You're not going to use that lame old excuse again."

"I told her that you're the one I love," he went on, undaunted, "you're the one I'm going to marry."

"I'm not going to marry you . . . ever."

"Calm down, Serena. That's your fine red-haired temper talking."

"I am calm. It would take a shotgun to get me to the altar."

"Damnation," he gritted through the speaking tube. "I'm coming up."

"Don't bother. I won't see you and the door is locked."

"I'm coming up," he repeated dangerously. "And if I have to, I'll kick the door in."

Returning to her post beside the windows, Serena saw Nathan mount the stairs at the bow, slowly and deliberately. Then he stalked along the boiler deck and out of sight.

She knew he must be climbing the companionway to the texas. In a matter of moments, he would ascend to the pilothouse and find the door locked. Nervously she waited, but he did not appear. He was nowhere to be seen.

Perhaps he had changed his mind and would not come, she brooded. She had told him to stay away. Now she did not know if she was relieved or hurt that he had listened.

Curse her pride. It had gotten in the way again. Now that her ire was cooling, she realized that what happened on the terrace at the governor's mansion was just like Addie.

Sinking down onto the bench, she wondered what to do next. Should she go and talk to him? Should she return his ring?

Suddenly Nathan was there, climbing the ladder to the wheelhouse, scowling at her through the glass panes of the door when he discovered the door was indeed locked.

Steadying himself on the ladder, he planted one booted foot against the flimsy door and kicked. With a splintering of wood, it gave and bounced off the bulkhead behind it.

"I told you I want to talk to you, Serena." Fury glittered in his dark eyes as she hurried to place the wheel between them.

He stepped calmly into the wheelhouse. Then, without a word, his hand snaked out across the narrow space and seized her wrist. As he dragged her toward the door, he grabbed the shotgun hanging on the wall in his free hand. Still holding her wrist in a steel grip, he hauled the protesting Serena down to the salon where her family and the hastily dressed Reverend Morris waited.

"What do you think you're doing?" Furious all over again at being manhandled, she pried at his fingers with her free hand.

"You said it would take a shotgun to get you to the altar. This—" he brandished the weapon "—is a shotgun. That is the minister." He indicated Reverend Morris. "And those—" he nodded toward Grace, Dory and Hank "—are our wedding guests. Or at least part of them. Will has gone for my family. They should be here any minute."

"I'm not marrying you."

"Yes, you are . . . tonight." Unmindful of the witnesses, he whirled her around so she lurched against his chest, and kissed her hard. Pulling back, he demanded, "Do you or do you not love me?"

"I—I do."

He kissed her again lingeringly and asked, "Don't you know that I love you?"

"I do." Her lips began to curve in a smile.

"Haven't I told you that you're just the kind of wife I want?"

"You have." Her arms slid up to encircle his neck.

"And didn't you say you wanted to marry me?"

"I did." She beamed up at him.

"Then why does it take a shotgun and a riffle deck to make you marry me?" he demanded with a smile.

"It doesn't," she whispered. "I'm yours, fair and square." Standing on tiptoe, she joyously met his kiss.

* * * * *

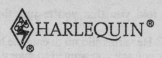

Harlequin Books requests the pleasure of your company this June in Eternity, Massachusetts, for WEDDINGS, INC.

For generations, couples have been coming to Eternity, Massachusetts, to exchange wedding vows. Legend has it that those married in Eternity's chapel are destined for a lifetime of happiness. And the residents are more than willing to give the legend a hand.

Beginning in June, you can experience the legend of Eternity. Watch for one title per month, across all of the Harlequin series.

HARLEQUIN BOOKS... NOT THE SAME OLD STORY!

MILLION DOLLAR SWEEPSTAKES (III)

**Harlequin®
Historical**

Looking for more of a good thing?

Why not try a bigger book from Harlequin Historicals?

SUSPICION by Judith McWilliams, April 1994—A story of intrigue and deceit set during the Regency era.

ROYAL HARLOT by Lucy Gordon, May 1994—The adventuresome romance of a prince and the woman spy assigned to protect him.

UNICORN BRIDE by Claire Delacroix, June 1994—The first of a trilogy set in thirteenth-century France.

MARIAH'S PRIZE by Miranda Jarrett, July 1994—Another tale of the seafaring Sparhawks of Rhode Island.

Longer stories by some of your favorite authors.
Watch for them this spring, wherever
Harlequin Historicals are sold.

HHB1G2

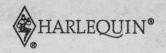

Harlequin proudly presents four stories about
convenient but not *conventional* reasons for marriage:

- ◆ To save your godchildren from a
  "wicked stepmother"

- ◆ To help out your eccentric aunt—and her sexy
  business partner

- ◆ To bring an old man happiness by making him
  a grandfather

- ◆ To escape from a ghostly existence and become a
  real woman

Marriage By Design—four brand-new stories by four
of Harlequin's most popular authors:

CATHY GILLEN THACKER
JASMINE CRESSWELL
GLENDA SANDERS
MARGARET CHITTENDEN

Don't miss this exciting collection of stories about
marriages of convenience. Available in April, wherever
Harlequin books are sold.

MBD94

This June, Harlequin invites
you to a wedding of

Promised Brides

Celebrate the joy and romance of weddings past with
PROMISED BRIDES—a collection of original historical short
stories, written by three best-selling historical authors:

> *The Wedding of the Century*—MARY JO PUTNEY
> *Jesse's Wife*—KRISTIN JAMES
> *The Handfast*—JULIE TETEL

Three unforgettable heroines, three award-winning authors!
PROMISED BRIDES is available in June wherever Harlequin
Books are sold.

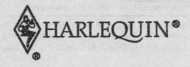

HARLEQUIN®

HARLEQUIN®

Don't miss these Harlequin favorites by some of our most distinguished authors!
And now, you can receive a discount by ordering two or more titles!

HT #25551	THE OTHER WOMAN by Candace Schuler	$2.99	☐
HT #25539	FOOLS RUSH IN by Vicki Lewis Thompson	$2.99	☐
HP #11550	THE GOLDEN GREEK by Sally Wentworth	$2.89	☐
HP #11603	PAST ALL REASON by Kay Thorpe	$2.99	☐
HR #03228	MEANT FOR EACH OTHER by Rebecca Winters	$2.89	☐
HR #03268	THE BAD PENNY by Susan Fox	$2.99	☐
HS #70532	TOUCH THE DAWN by Karen Young	$3.39	☐
HS #70540	FOR THE LOVE OF IVY by Barbara Kaye	$3.39	☐
HI #22177	MINDGAME by Laura Pender	$2.79	☐
HI #22214	TO DIE FOR by M.J. Rodgers	$2.89	☐
HAR #16421	HAPPY NEW YEAR, DARLING by Margaret St. George	$3.29	☐
HAR #16507	THE UNEXPECTED GROOM by Muriel Jensen	$3.50	☐
HH #28774	SPINDRIFT by Miranda Jarrett	$3.99	☐
HH #28782	SWEET SENSATIONS by Julie Tetel	$3.99	☐

Harlequin Promotional Titles

#83259	UNTAMED MAVERICK HEARTS (Short-story collection featuring Heather Graham Pozzessere, Patricia Potter, Joan Johnston)	$4.99	☐

(limited quantities available on certain titles)

DEDUCT:	AMOUNT	$
	10% DISCOUNT FOR 2+ BOOKS	$
	POSTAGE & HANDLING	$
	($1.00 for one book, 50¢ for each additional)	
	APPLICABLE TAXES*	$ _____
	TOTAL PAYABLE	$ _____
	(check or money order—please do not send cash)	

To order, complete this form and send it, along with a check or money order for the total above, payable to Harlequin Books, to: **In the U.S.:** 3010 Walden Avenue, P.O. Box 9047, Buffalo, NY 14269-9047; **In Canada:** P.O. Box 613, Fort Erie, Ontario, L2A 5X3.

Name: _____

Address: _____ City: _____

State/Prov.: _____ Zip/Postal Code: _____

*New York residents remit applicable sales taxes.
 Canadian residents remit applicable GST and provincial taxes.